SCARLETT HART
MONSTER HUNTER

Marcus Sedgwick   Thomas Taylor

SCARLETT HART
MONSTER HUNTER

:01
First Second
New York

For MG
−M.S.

For Max and Benjy
−T.T.

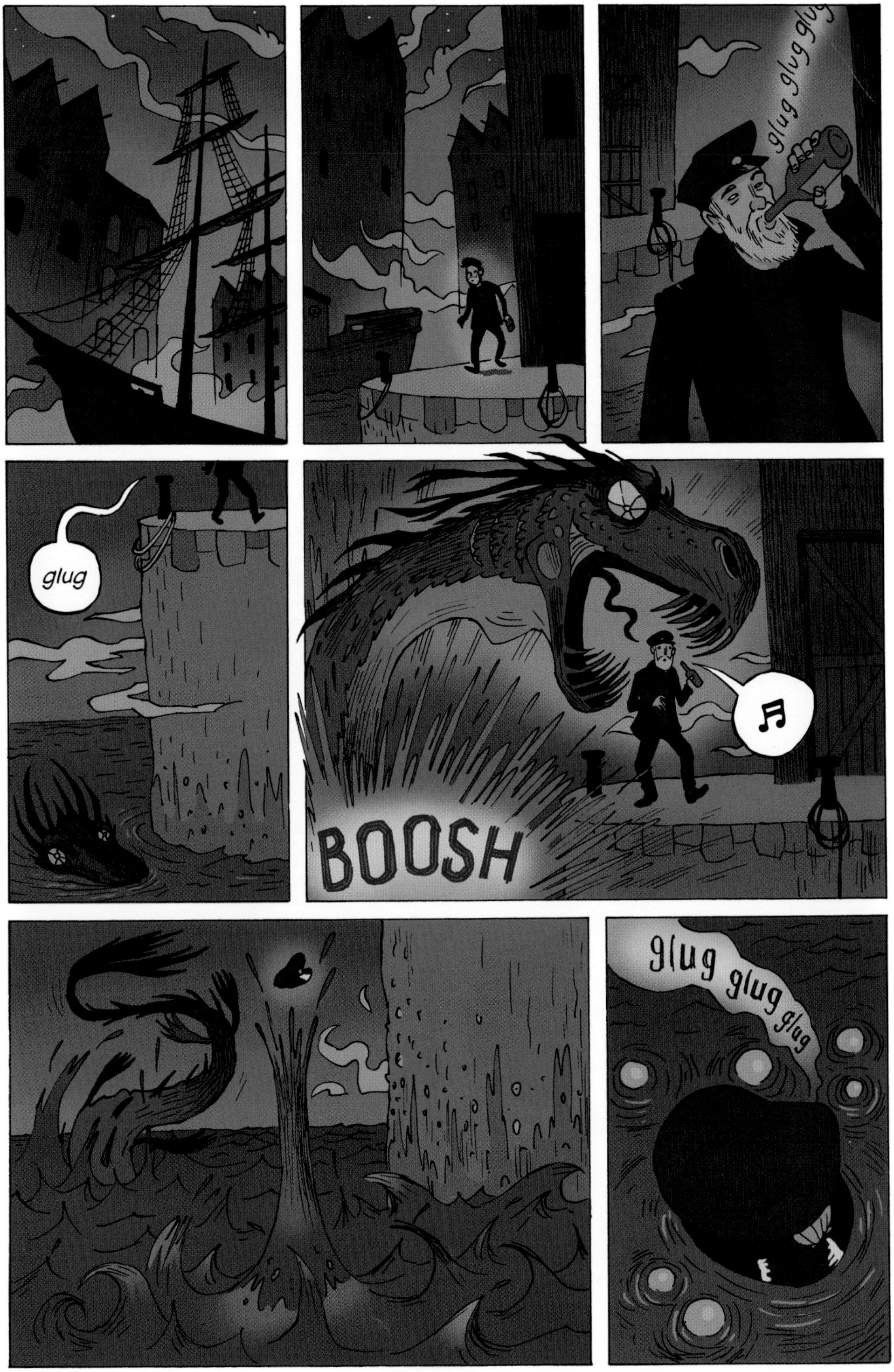
glug glug glug
glug
♬
BOOSH
glug glug glug

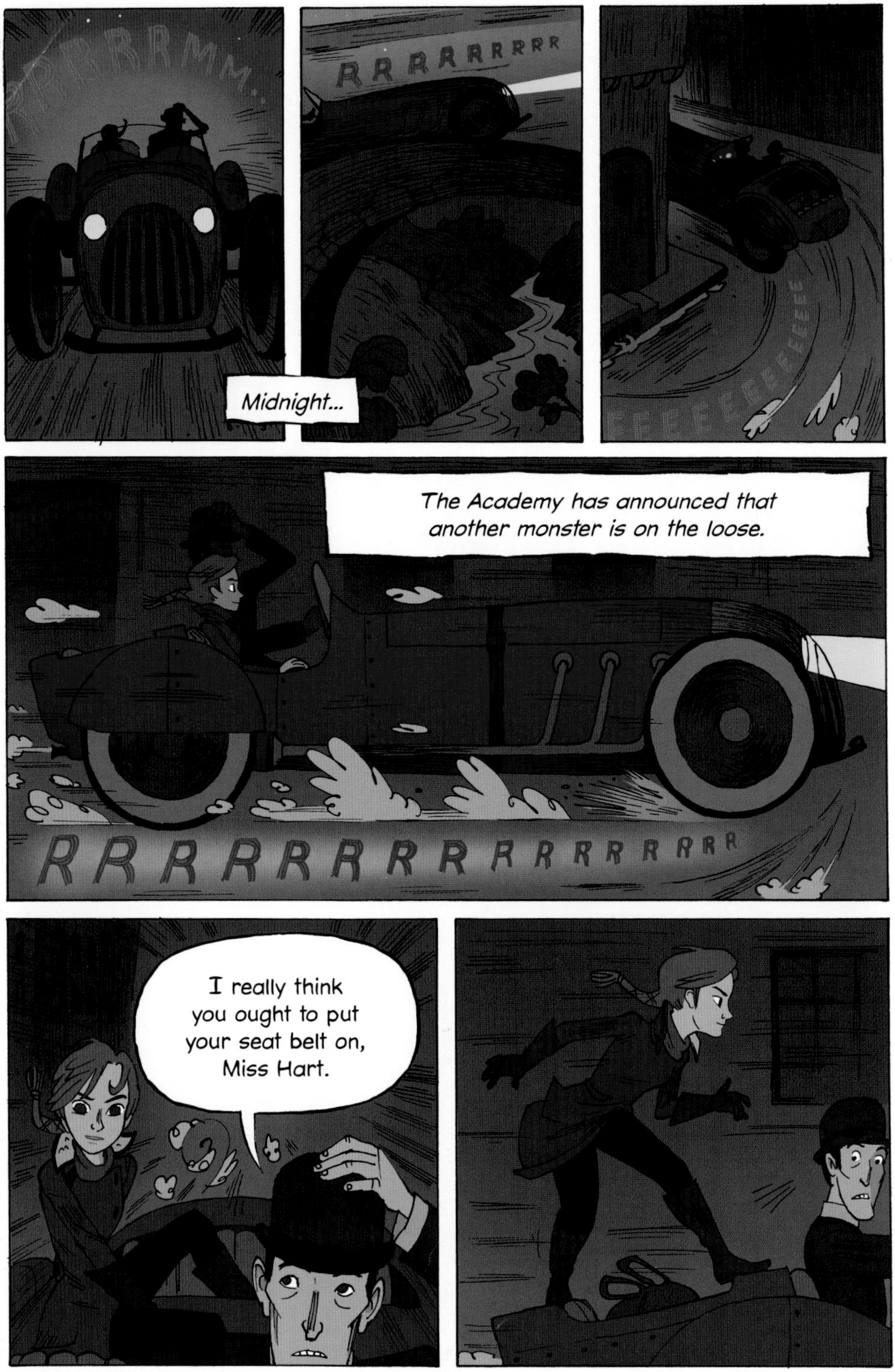
RRRRRMM...
RRRRRRRRR
EEEEEEEEEEEE
Midnight...
The Academy has announced that another monster is on the loose.
RRRRRRRRRRRRRRR
I really think you ought to put your seat belt on, Miss Hart.

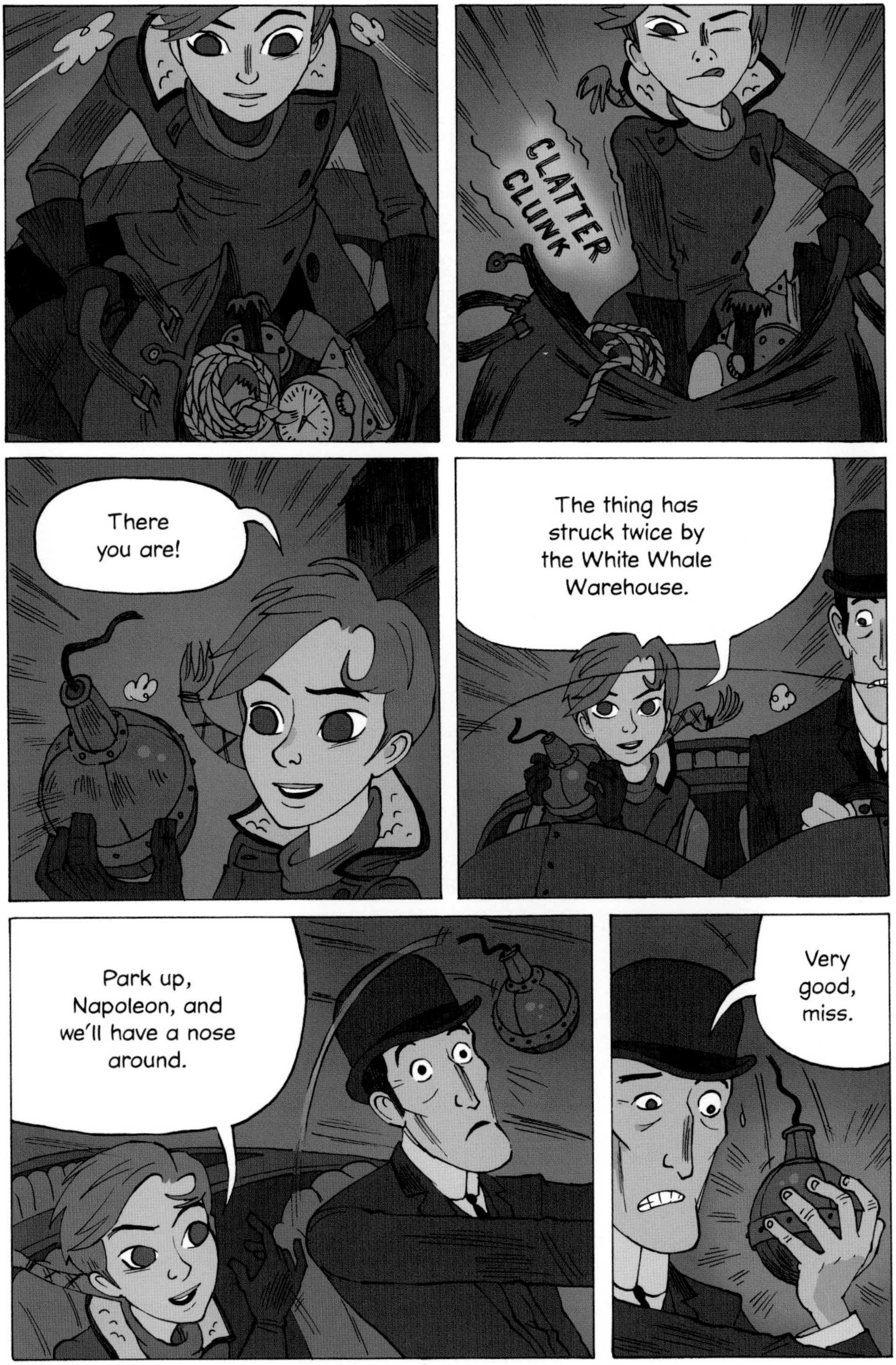
CLATTER
CLUNK
There you are!
The thing has struck twice by the White Whale Warehouse.
Park up, Napoleon, and we'll have a nose around.
Very good, miss.

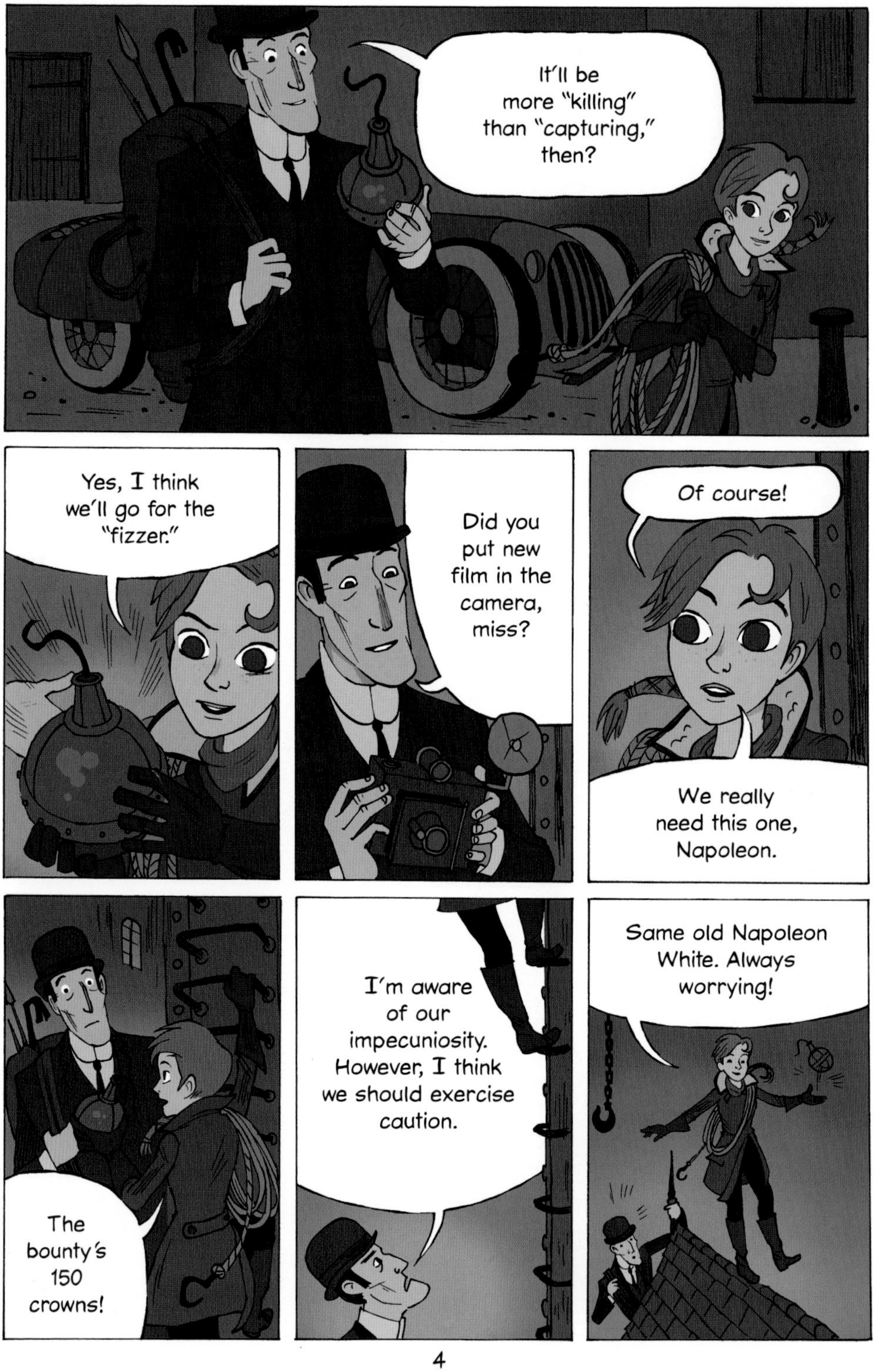
It'll be more "killing" than "capturing," then?
Yes, I think we'll go for the "fizzer."
Did you put new film in the camera, miss?
Of course!
We really need this one, Napoleon.
The bounty's 150 crowns!
I'm aware of our impecuniosity. However, I think we should exercise caution.
Same old Napoleon White. Always worrying!

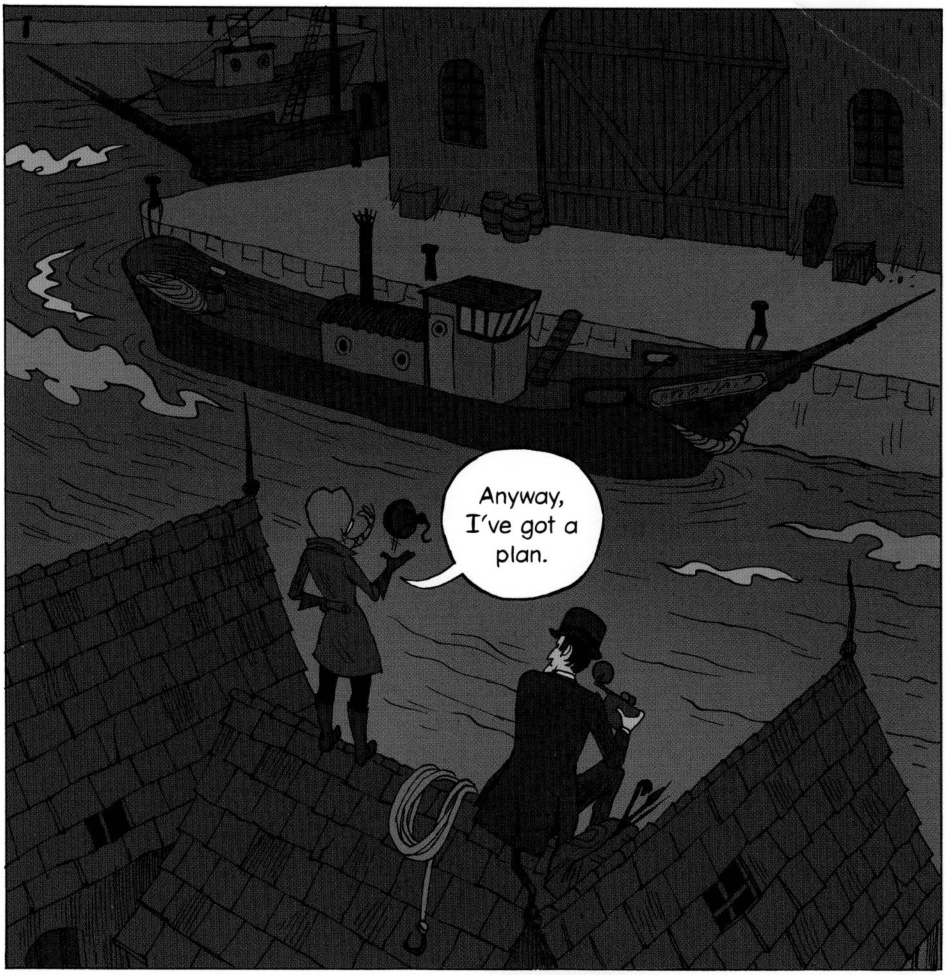
Anyway, I've got a plan.

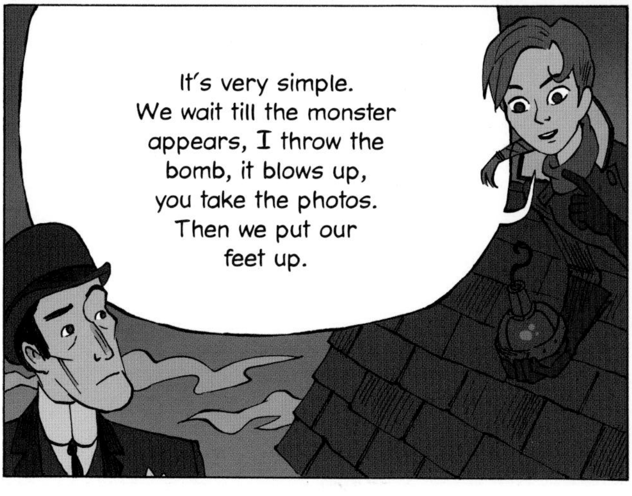
It's very simple. We wait till the monster appears, I throw the bomb, it blows up, you take the photos. Then we put our feet up.

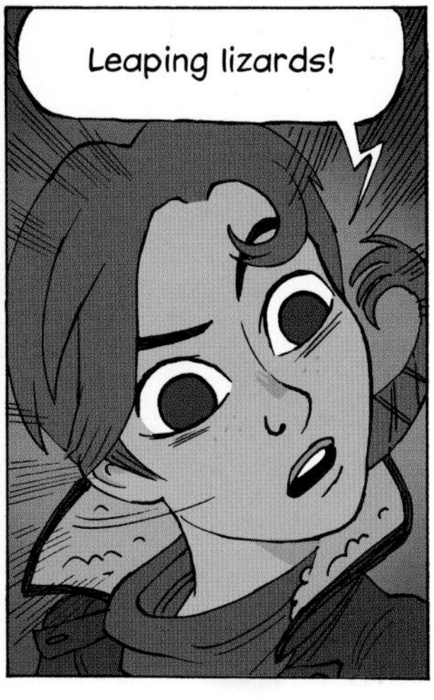
Leaping lizards!

The monster, miss?

No!
Look!

The
Count!

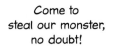

Come to
steal our monster,
no doubt!

Er, miss.

I think
you should
see this.

A-ha!

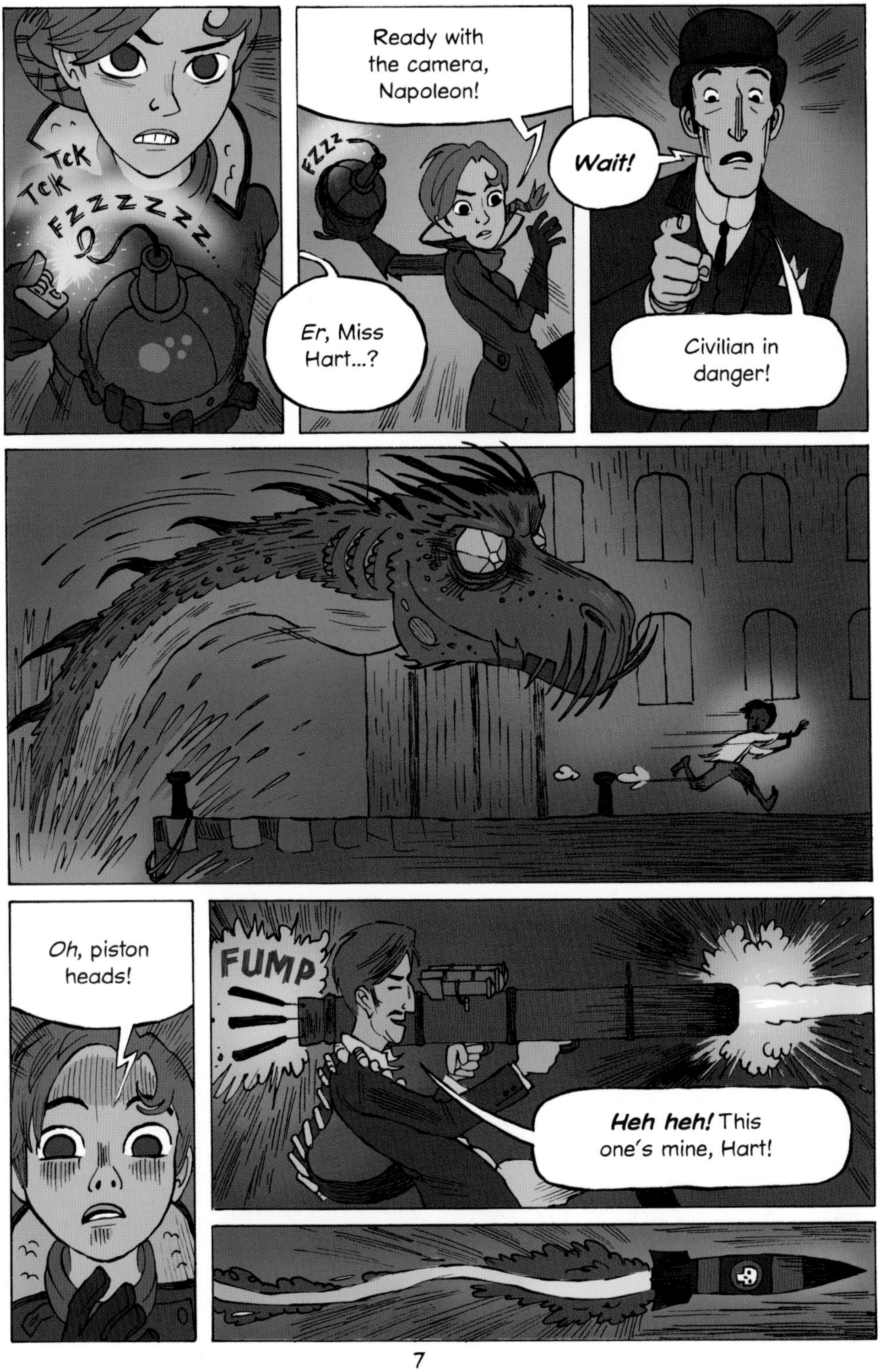
TCK
TCK
FZZZZZZZ...
Ready with the camera, Napoleon!
FZZZ
Er, Miss Hart...?
Wait!
Civilian in danger!
Oh, piston heads!
FUMP
Heh heh! This one's mine, Hart!

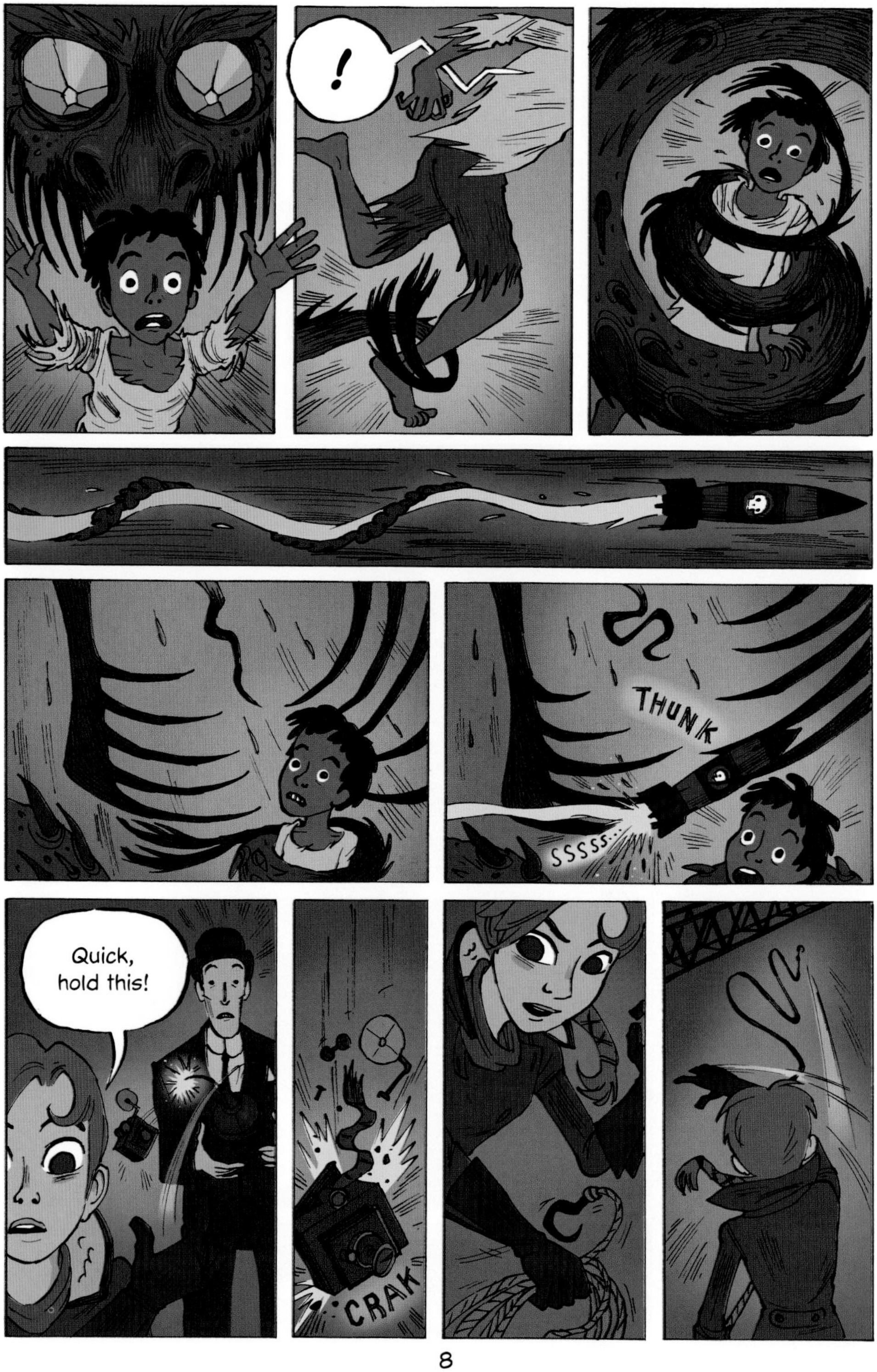
!
THUNK
SSSSS...
Quick, hold this!
CRAK

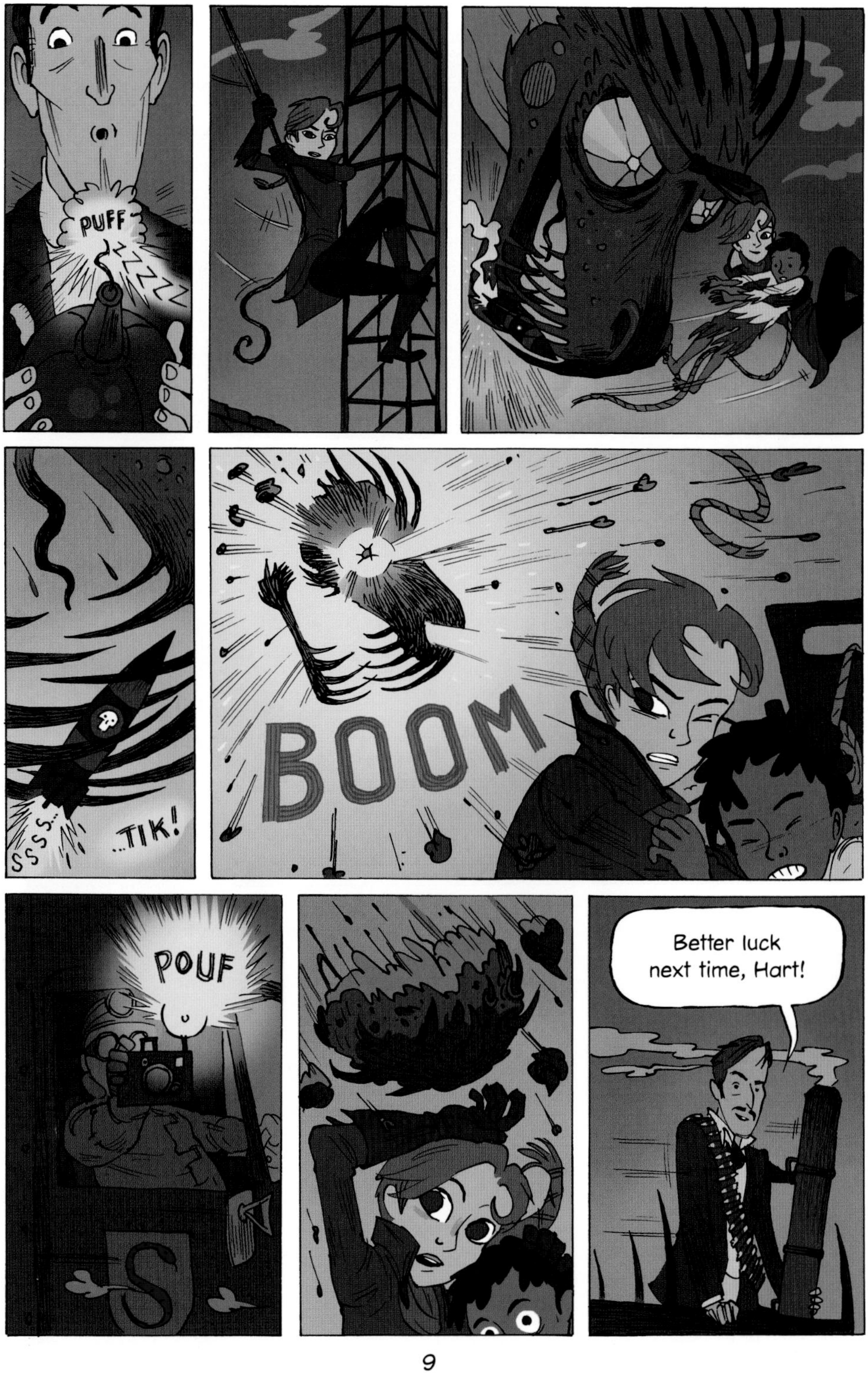
PUFF
ZZZZZ
SSSS...
...TIK!
BOOM
POUF
Better luck next time, Hart!

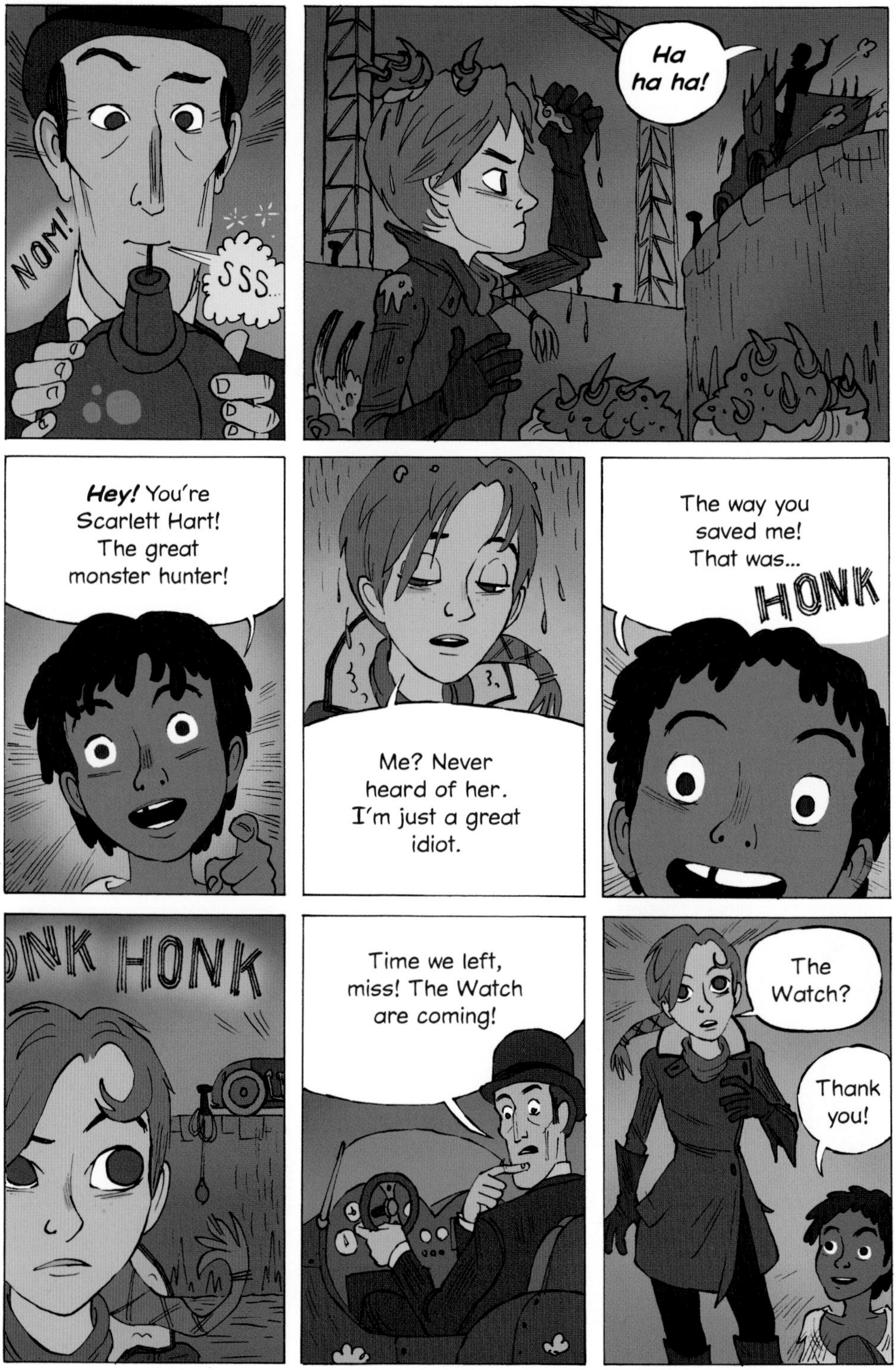
NOM!
SSS...
Ha ha ha!
Hey! You're Scarlett Hart! The great monster hunter!
Me? Never heard of her. I'm just a great idiot.
The way you saved me! That was...
HONK
ONK HONK
Time we left, miss! The Watch are coming!
The Watch?
Thank you!

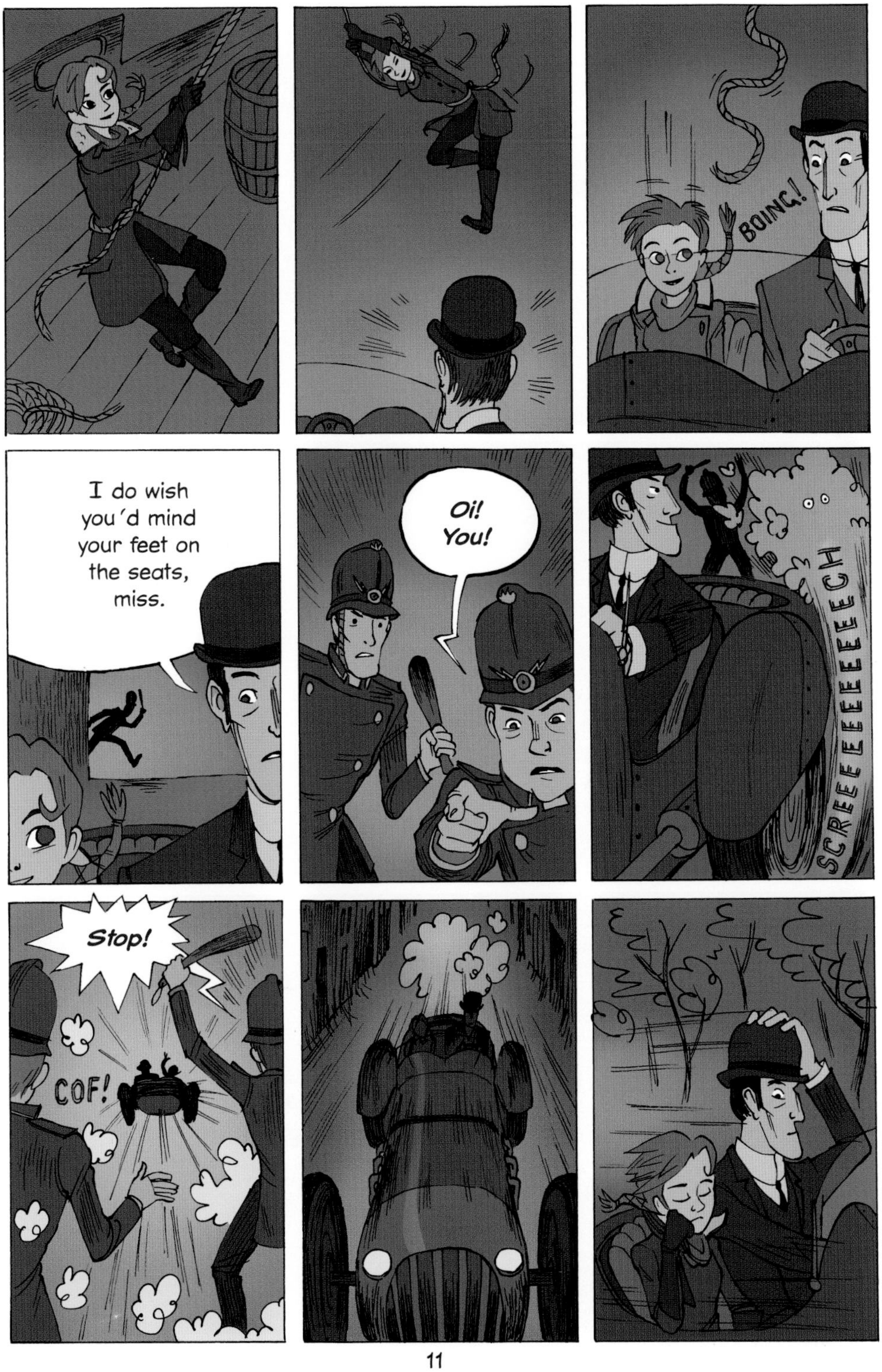
BOING!
I do wish you'd mind your feet on the seats, miss.
Oi! You!
SCREEEEEEEEEEEEEECH
Stop!
COF!

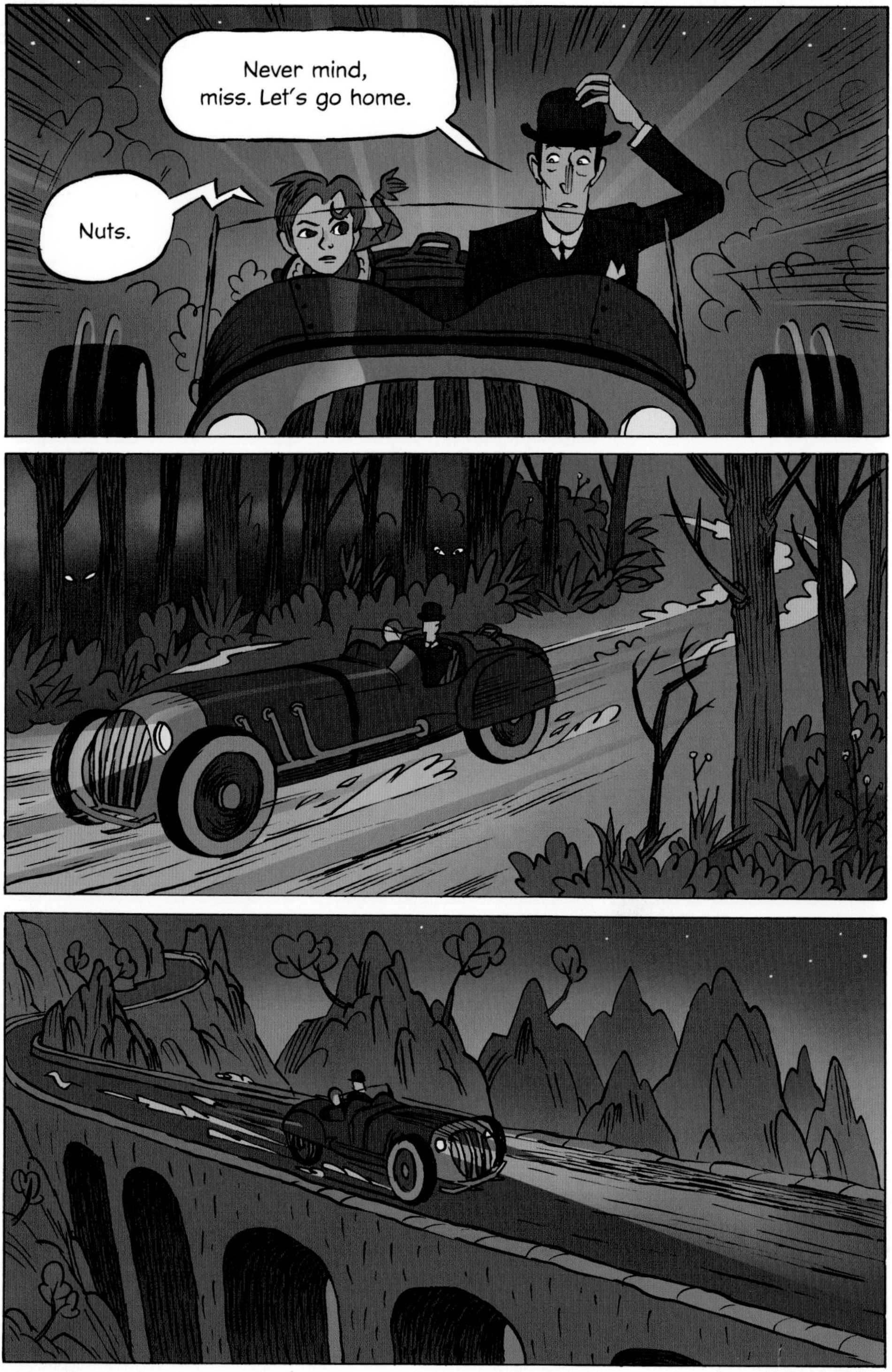
Never mind, miss. Let's go home.
Nuts.

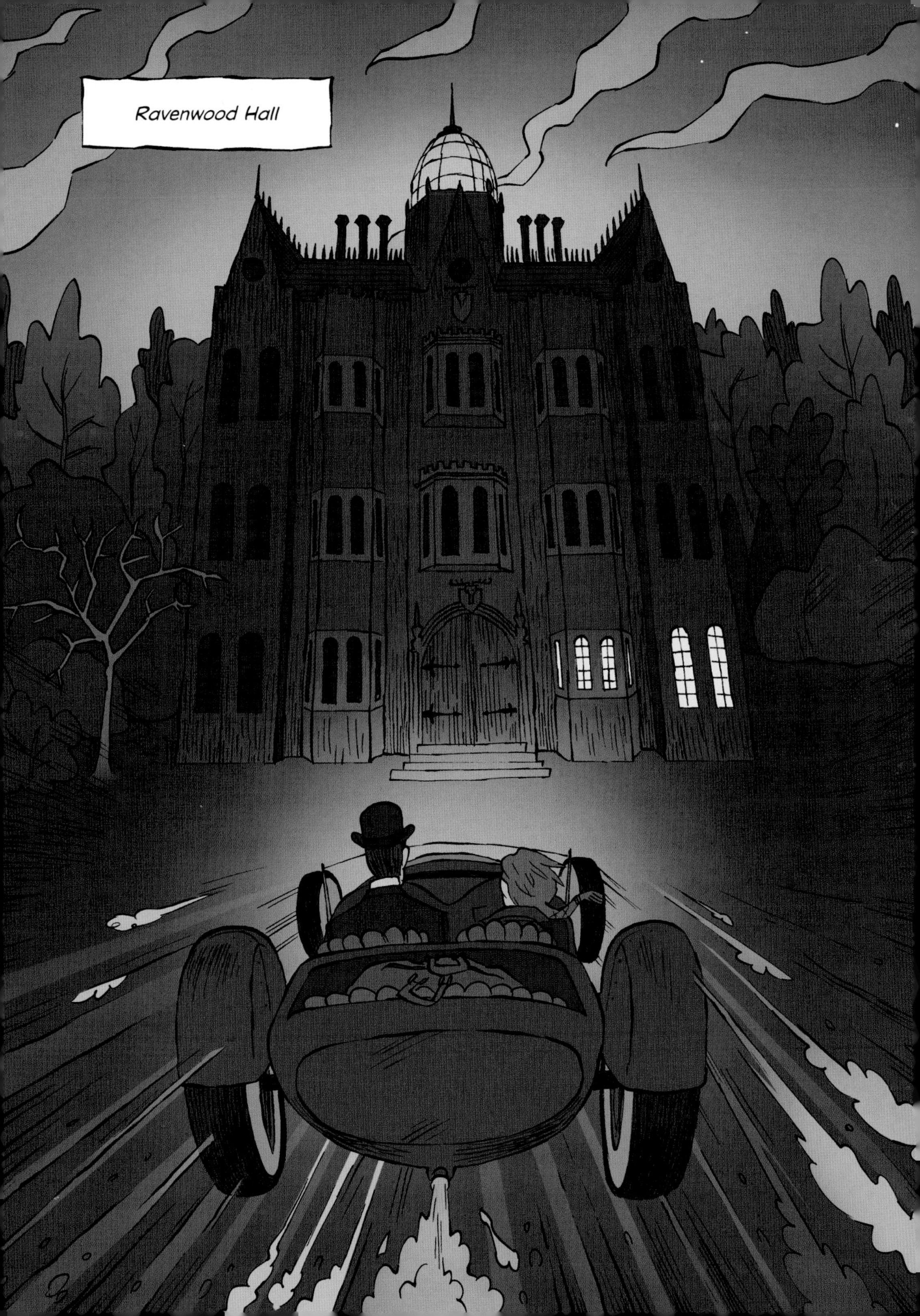
Ravenwood Hall

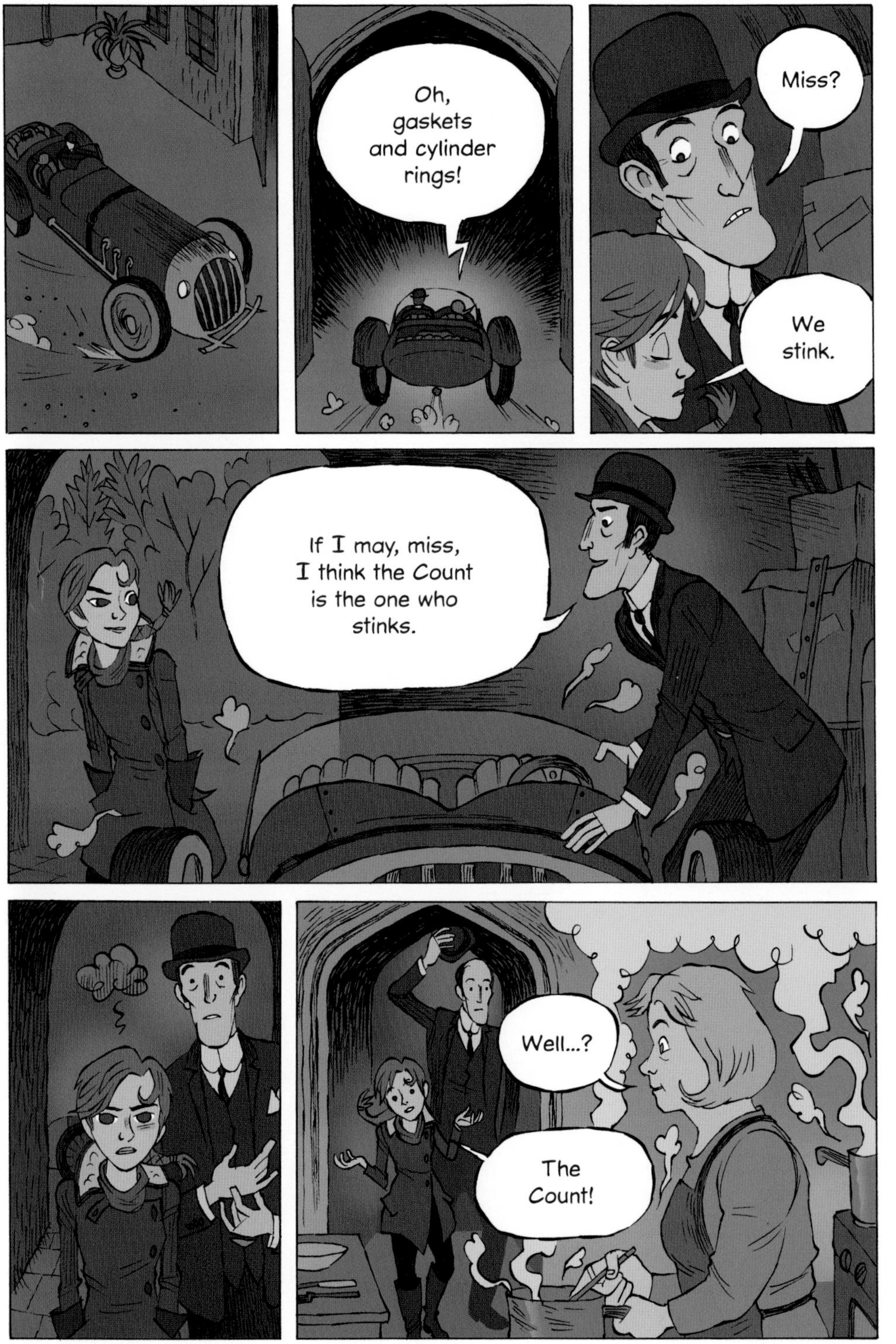
Oh, gaskets and cylinder rings!
Miss?
We stink.
If I may, miss, I think the Count is the one who stinks.
Well...?
The Count!

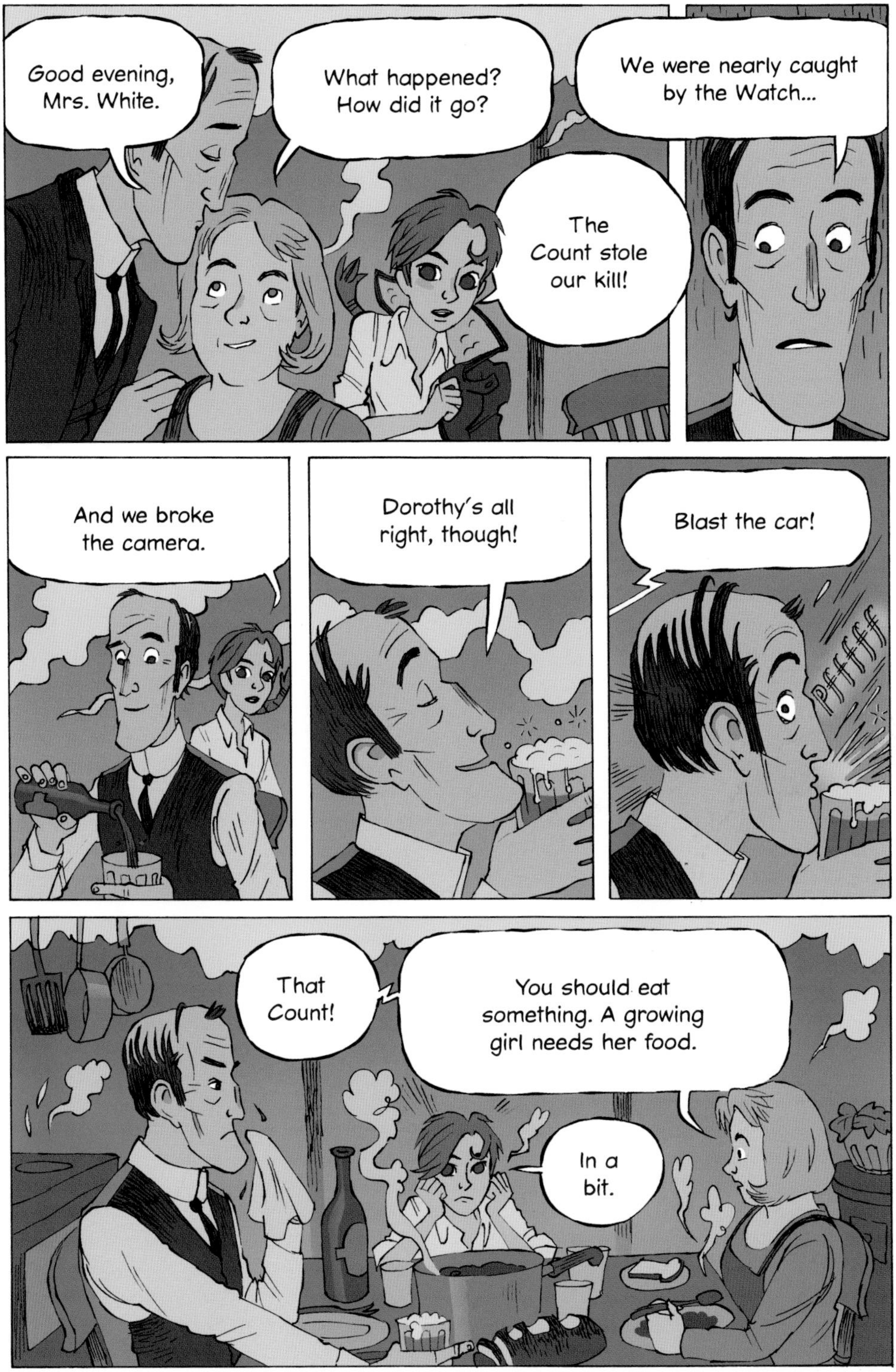
Good evening, Mrs. White.
What happened? How did it go?
The Count stole our kill!
We were nearly caught by the Watch...
And we broke the camera.
Dorothy's all right, though!
Blast the car!
Pffffff
That Count!
You should eat something. A growing girl needs her food.
In a bit.

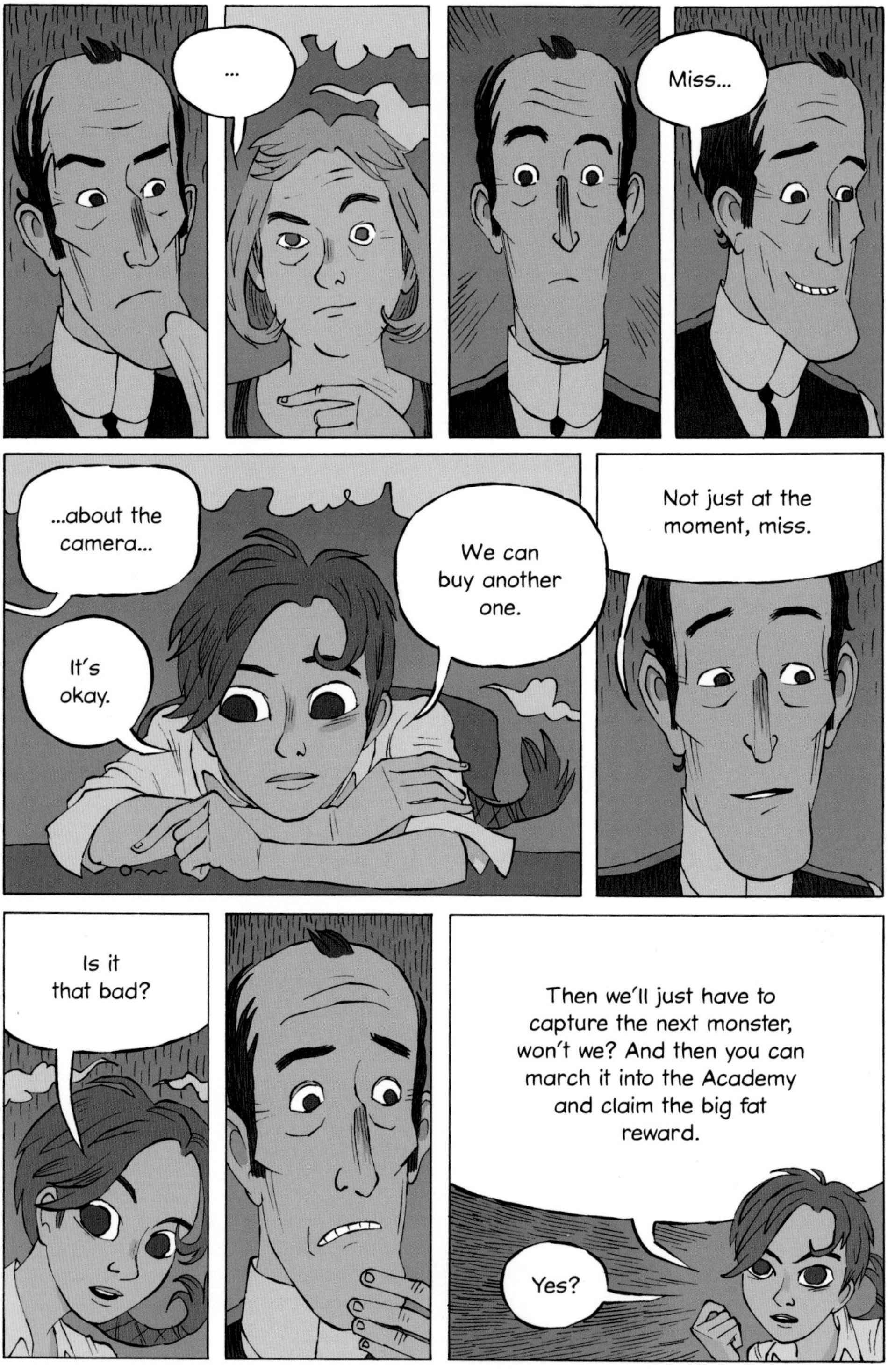
...
Miss...
...about the camera...
It's okay.
We can buy another one.
Not just at the moment, miss.
Is it that bad?
Then we'll just have to capture the next monster, won't we? And then you can march it into the Academy and claim the big fat reward.
Yes?

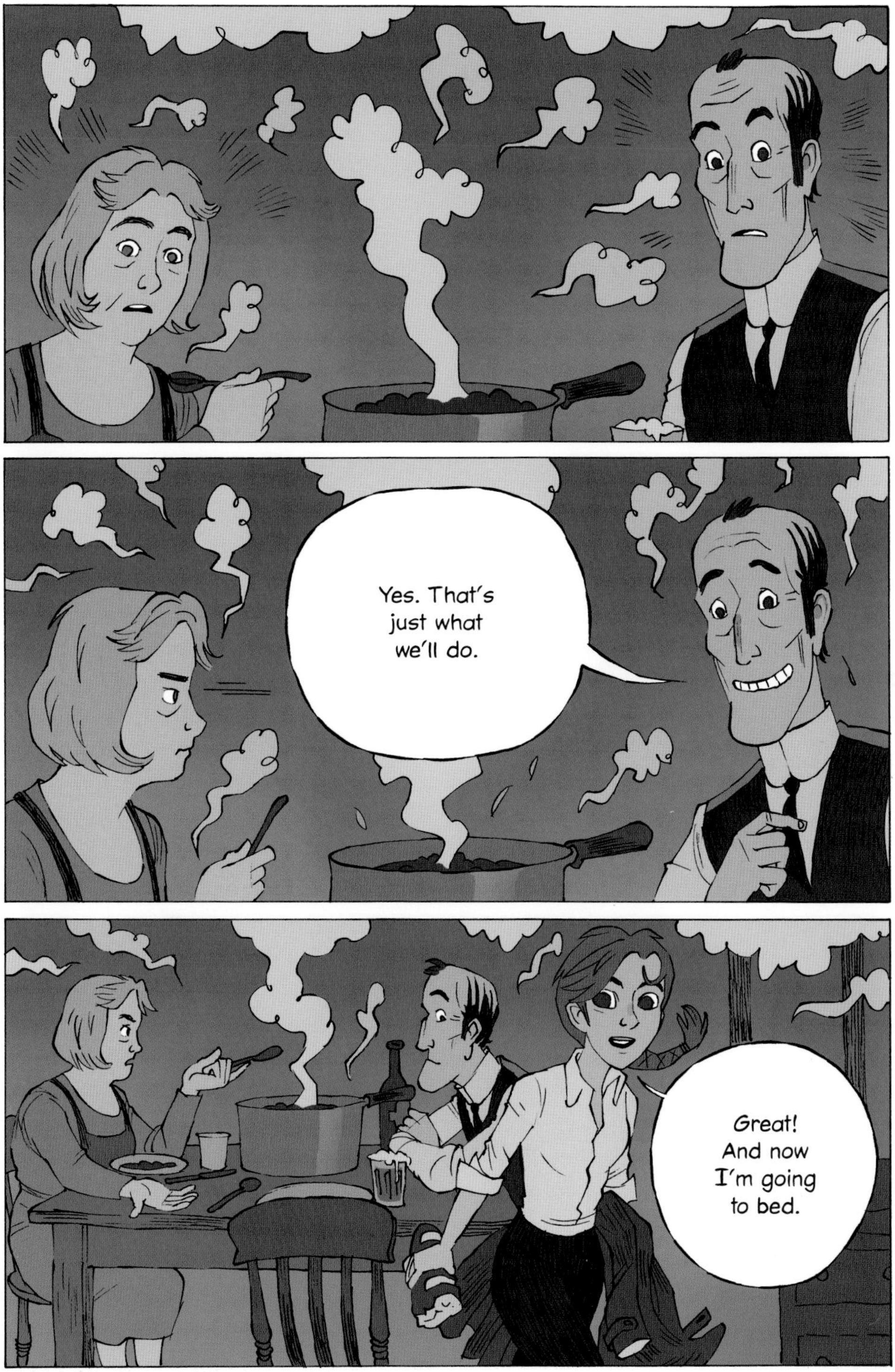
Yes. That's just what we'll do.
Great! And now I'm going to bed.

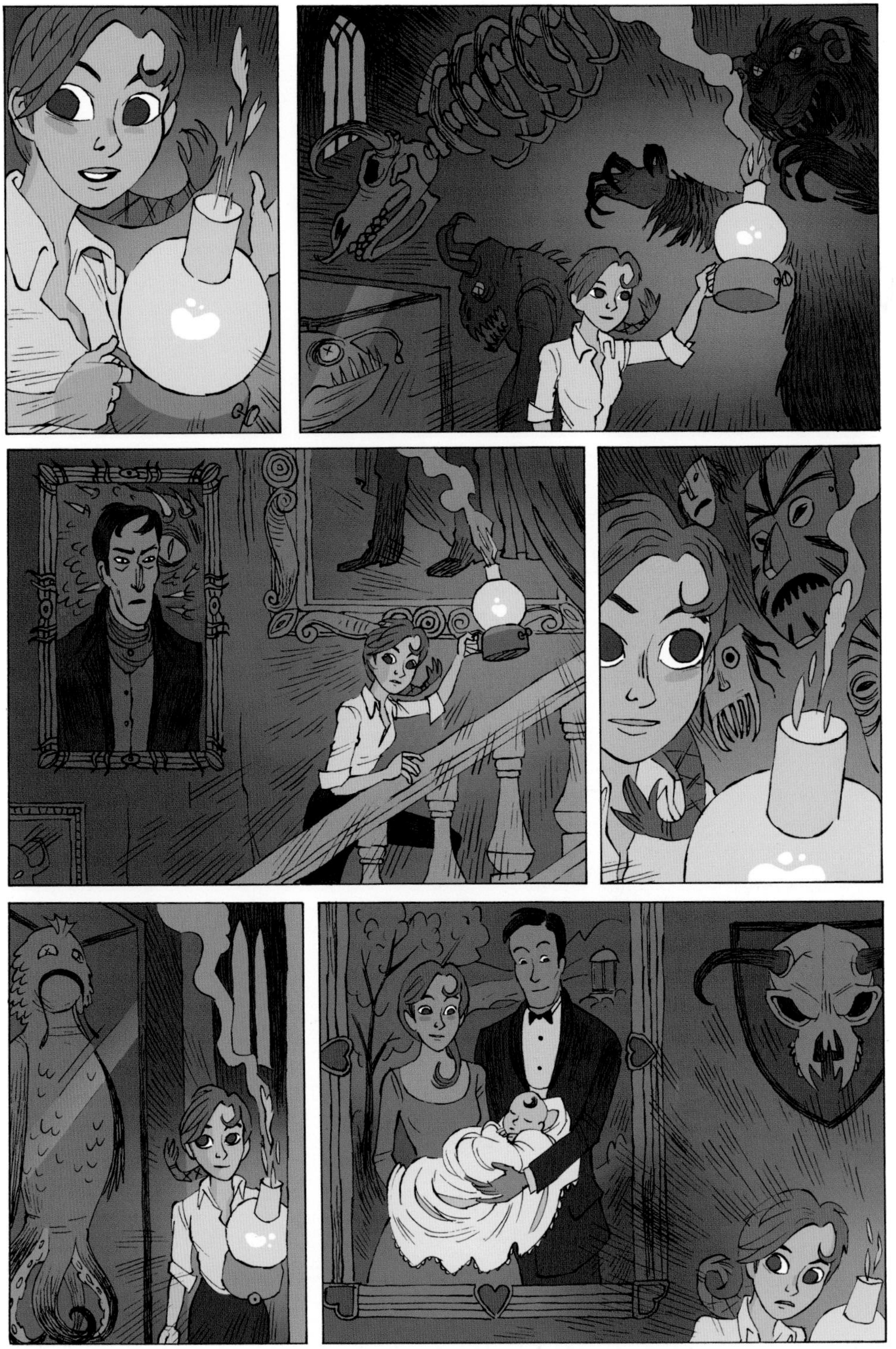

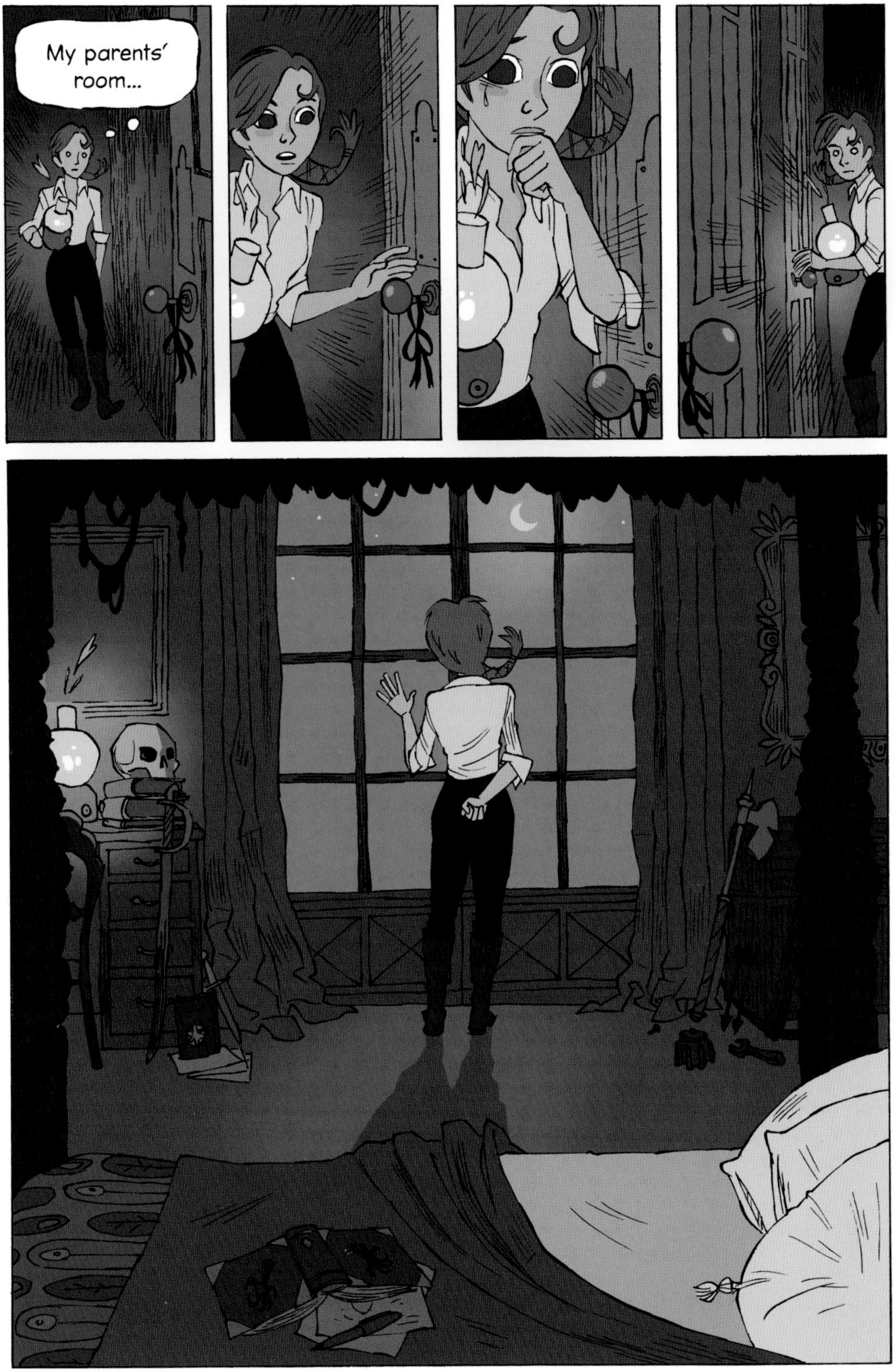
My parents' room...

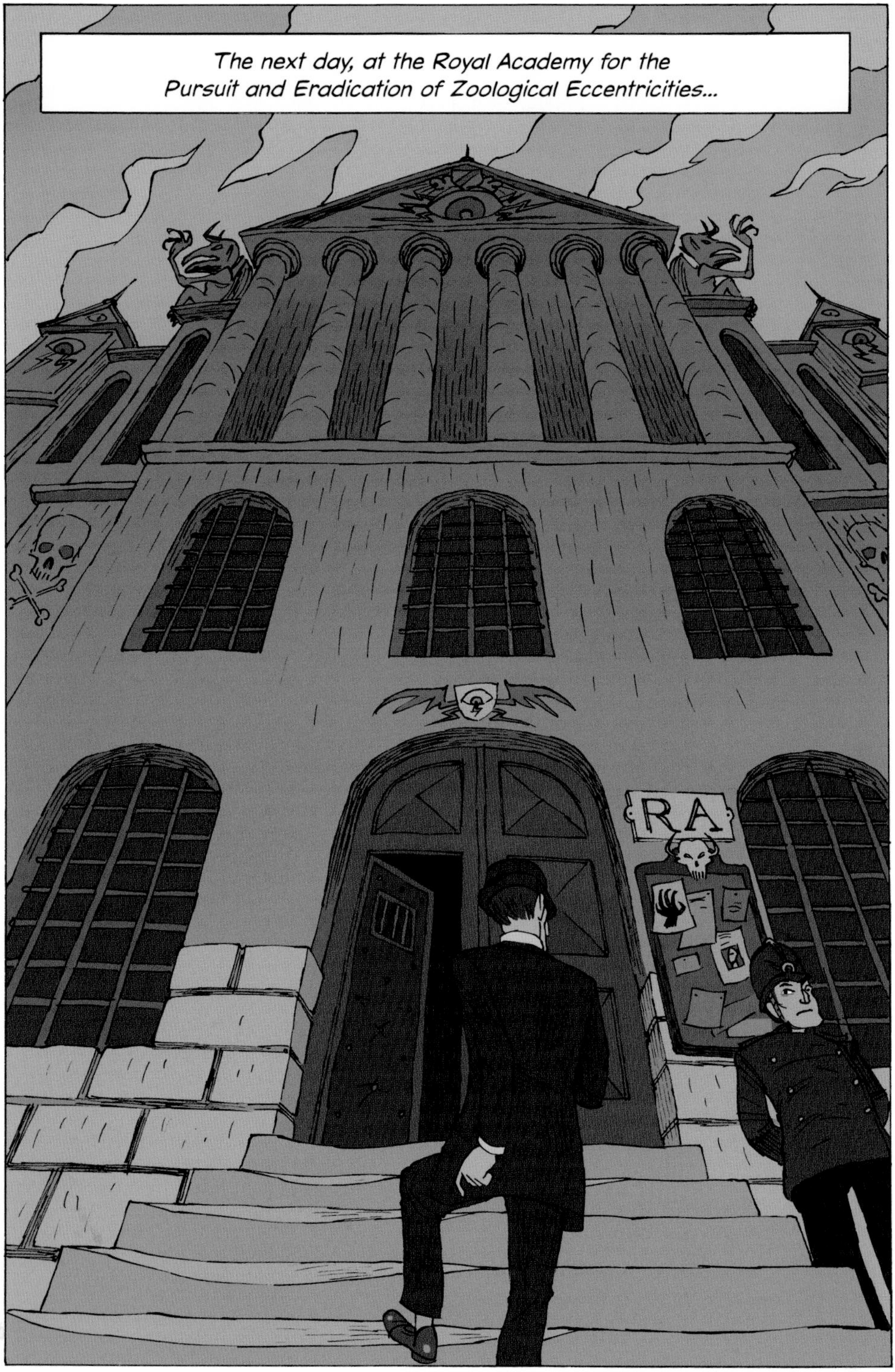
The next day, at the Royal Academy for the
Pursuit and Eradication of Zoological Eccentricities...
RA

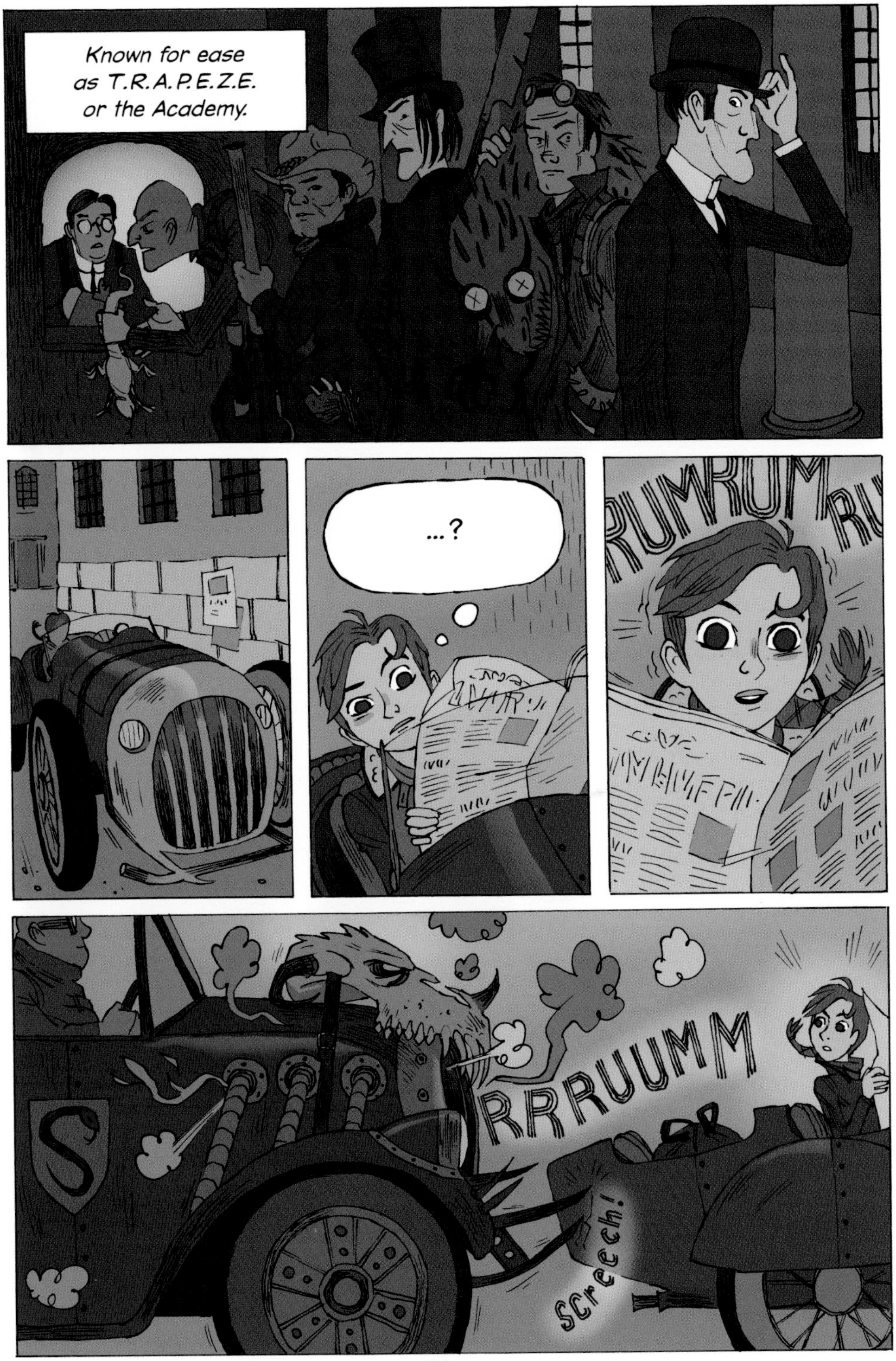
Known for ease as T.R.A.P.E.Z.E. or the Academy.
...?
RUMRUM RU
RRRUUMM
screeech!

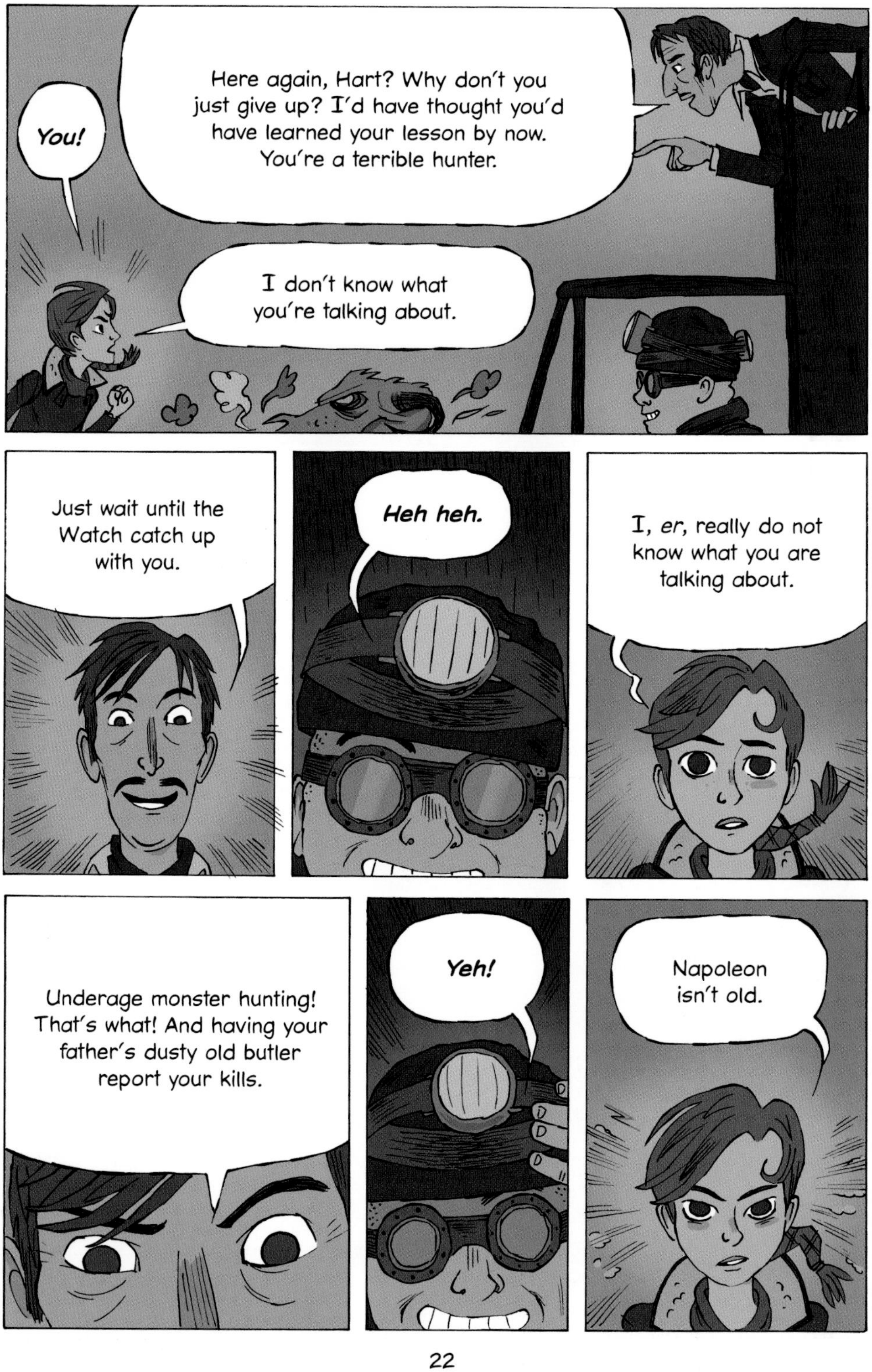
You!
Here again, Hart? Why don't you just give up? I'd have thought you'd have learned your lesson by now. You're a terrible hunter.
I don't know what you're talking about.
Just wait until the Watch catch up with you.
Heh heh.
I, *er*, really do not know what you are talking about.
Underage monster hunting! That's what! And having your father's dusty old butler report your kills.
Yeh!
Napoleon isn't old.

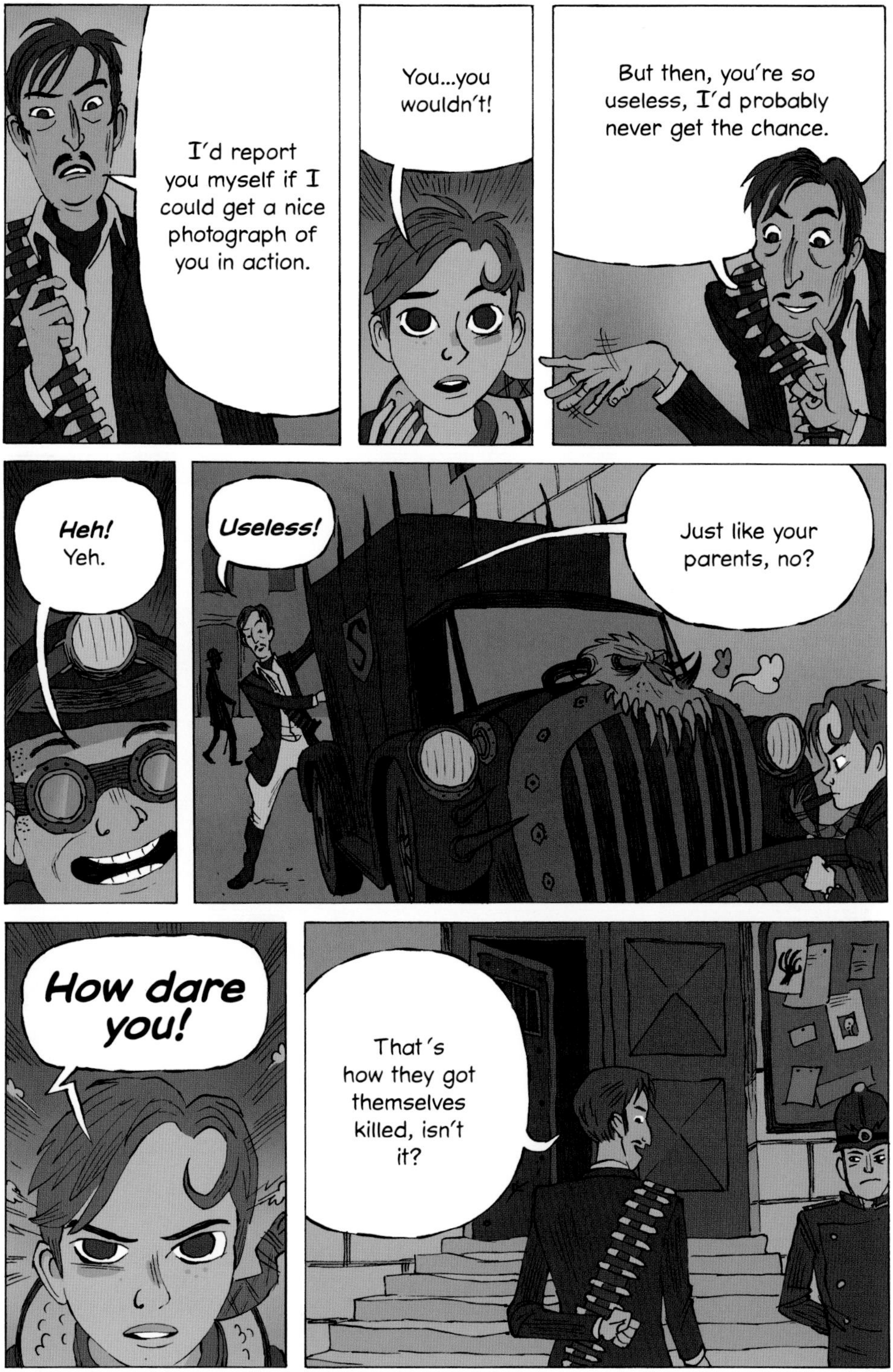
I'd report you myself if I could get a nice photograph of you in action.
You...you wouldn't!
But then, you're so useless, I'd probably never get the chance.
Heh! Yeh.
Useless!
Just like your parents, no?
How dare you!
That's how they got themselves killed, isn't it?

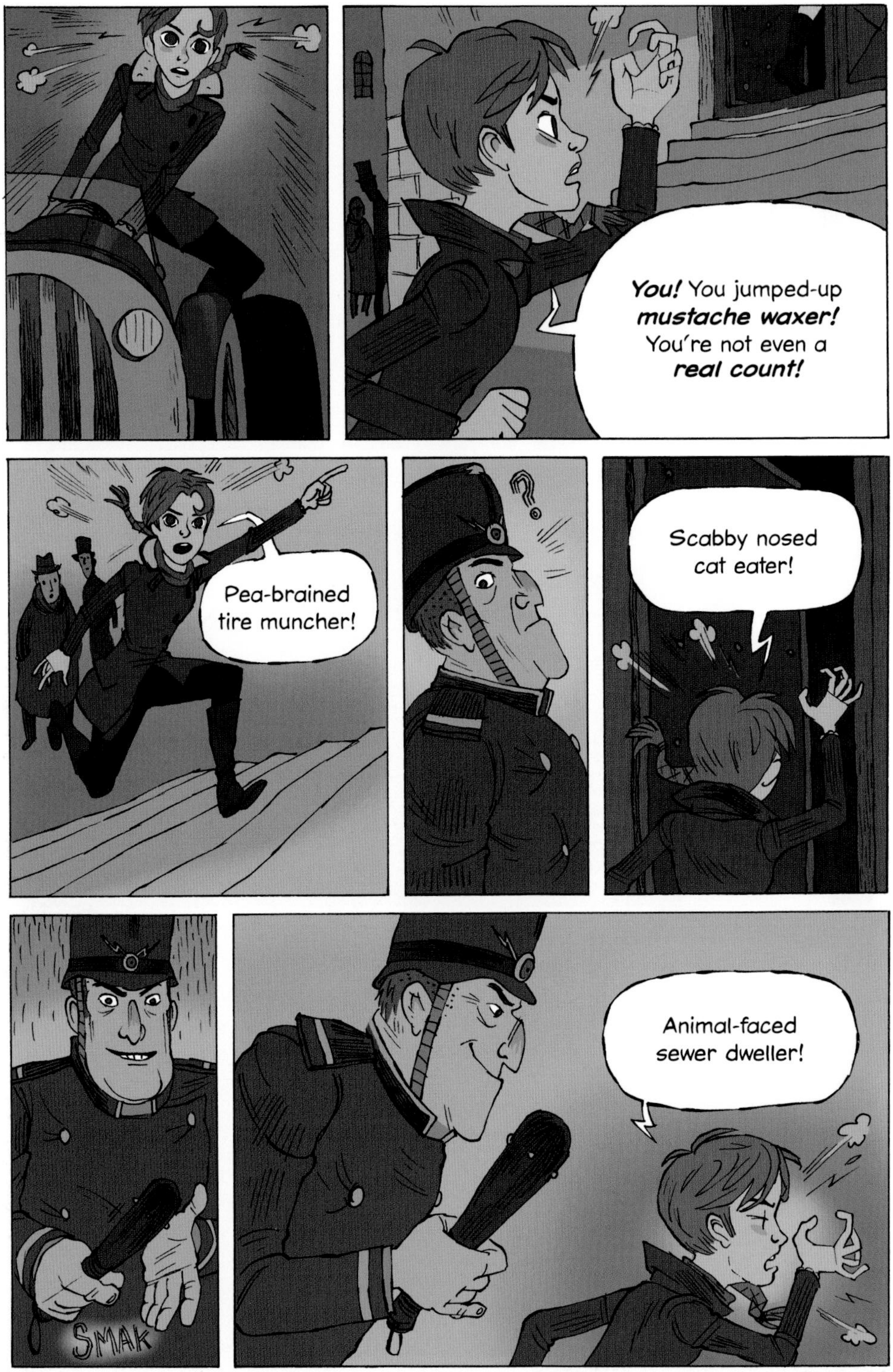
You! You jumped-up mustache waxer! You're not even a real count!
Pea-brained tire muncher!
Scabby nosed cat eater!
SMAK
Animal-faced sewer dweller!

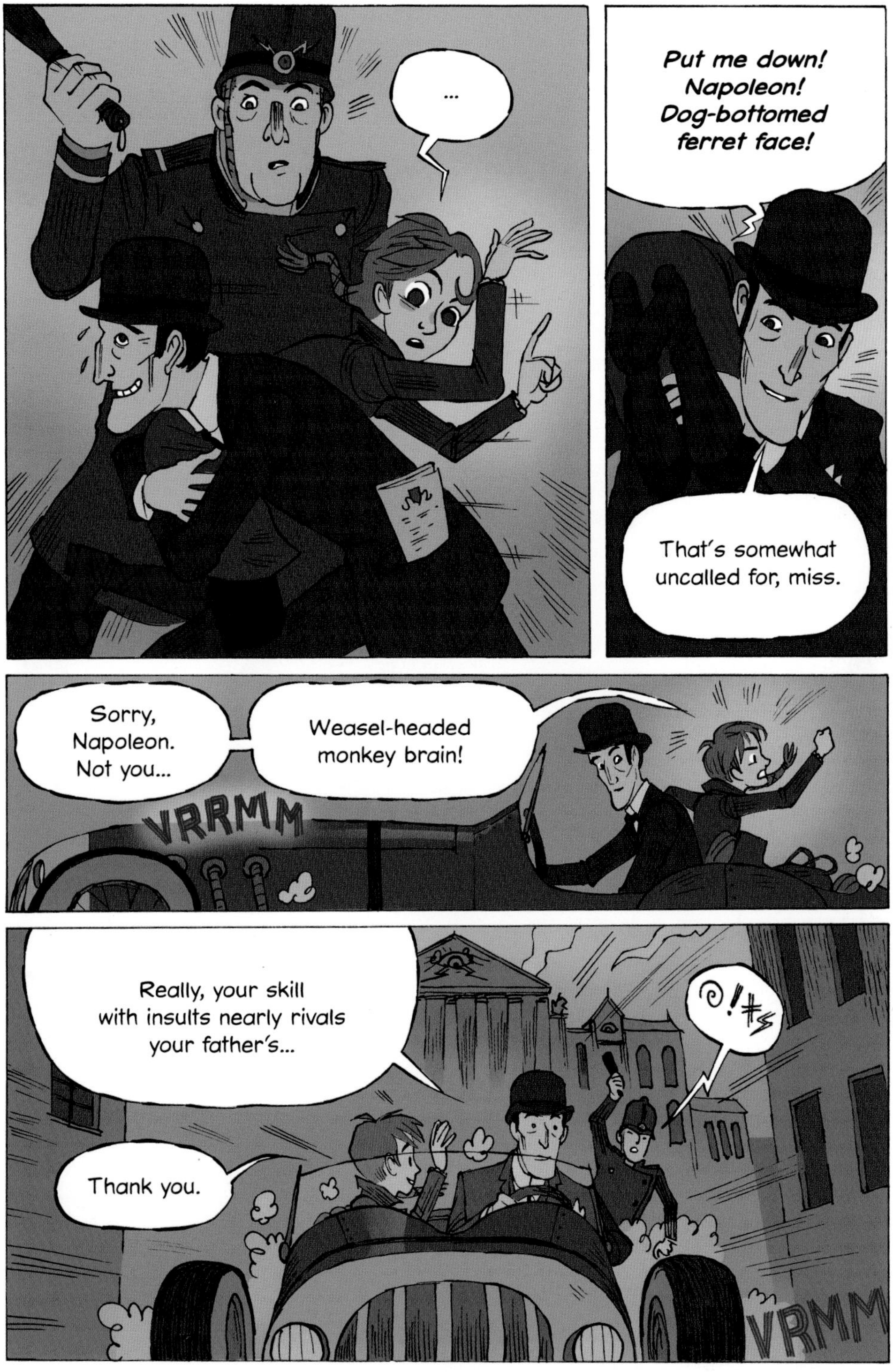
...
Put me down! Napoleon! Dog-bottomed ferret face!
That's somewhat uncalled for, miss.
Sorry, Napoleon. Not you...
Weasel-headed monkey brain!
VRRMM
Really, your skill with insults nearly rivals your father's...
@!#$
Thank you.
VRMM

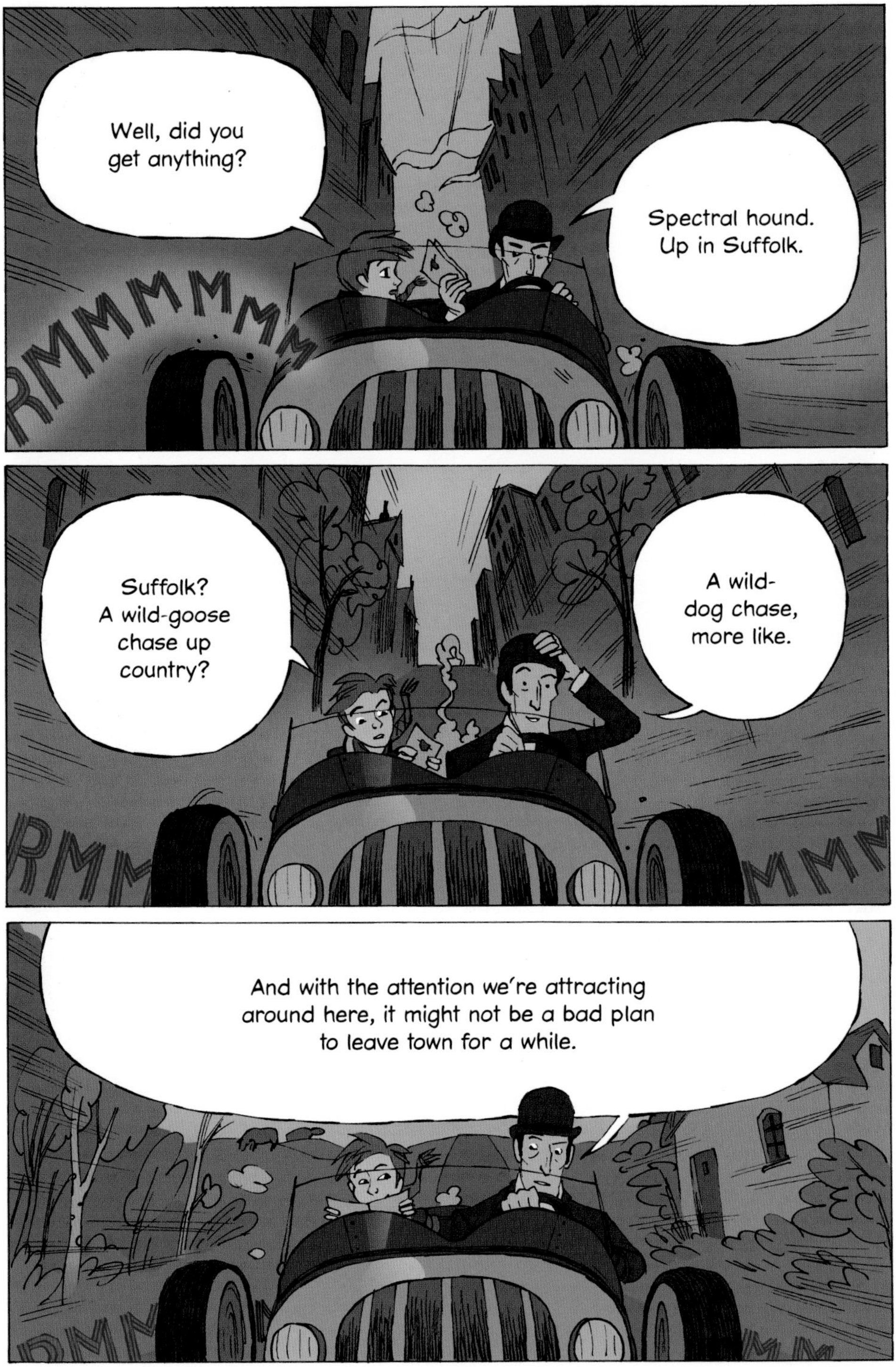
Well, did you get anything?
Spectral hound. Up in Suffolk.
RMMMMMM
Suffolk? A wild-goose chase up country?
A wild-dog chase, more like.
RMM
MMM
And with the attention we're attracting around here, it might not be a bad plan to leave town for a while.

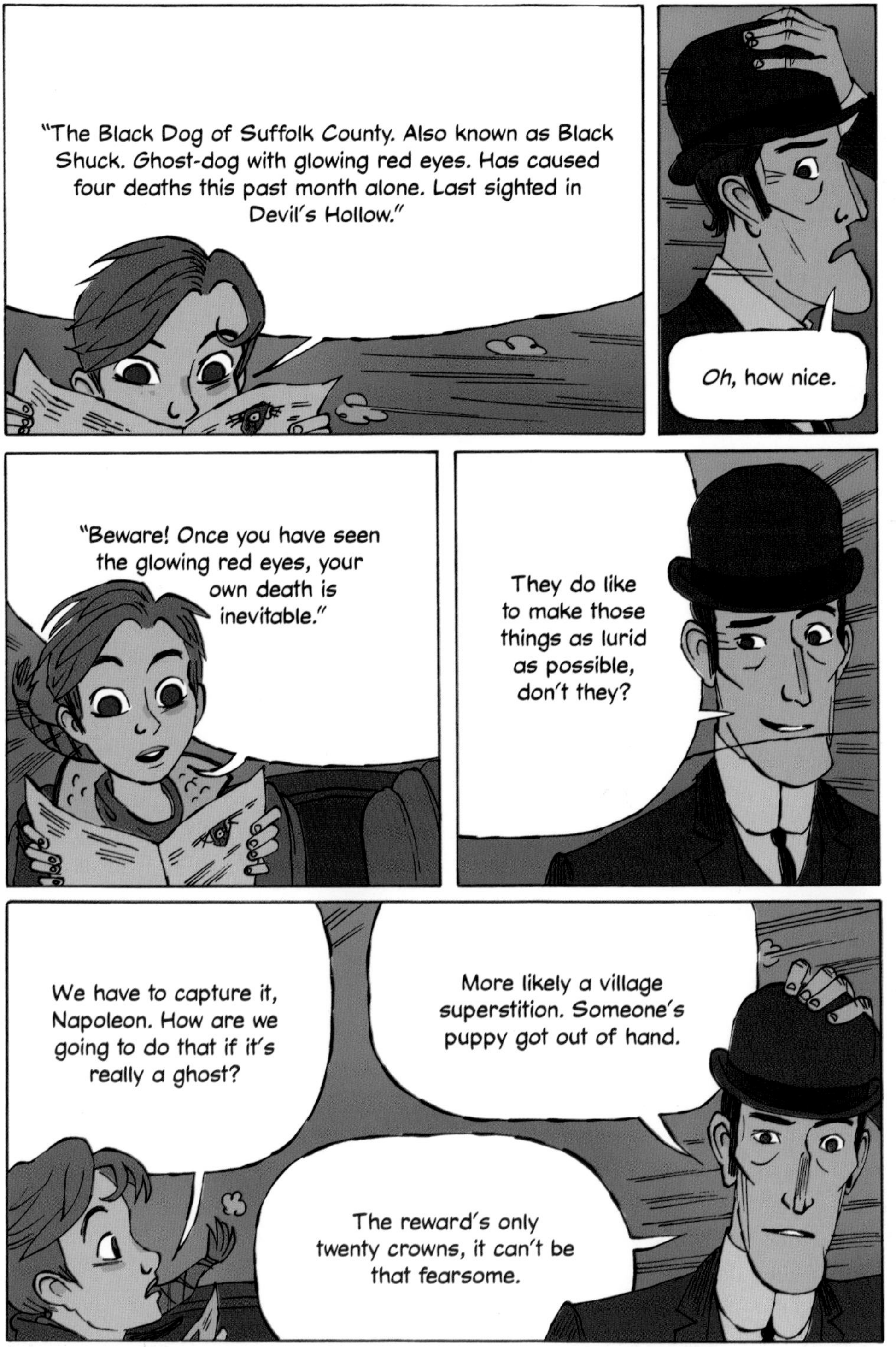
"The Black Dog of Suffolk County. Also known as Black Shuck. Ghost-dog with glowing red eyes. Has caused four deaths this past month alone. Last sighted in Devil's Hollow."
Oh, how nice.
"Beware! Once you have seen the glowing red eyes, your own death is inevitable."
They do like to make those things as lurid as possible, don't they?
We have to capture it, Napoleon. How are we going to do that if it's really a ghost?
More likely a village superstition. Someone's puppy got out of hand.
The reward's only twenty crowns, it can't be that fearsome.

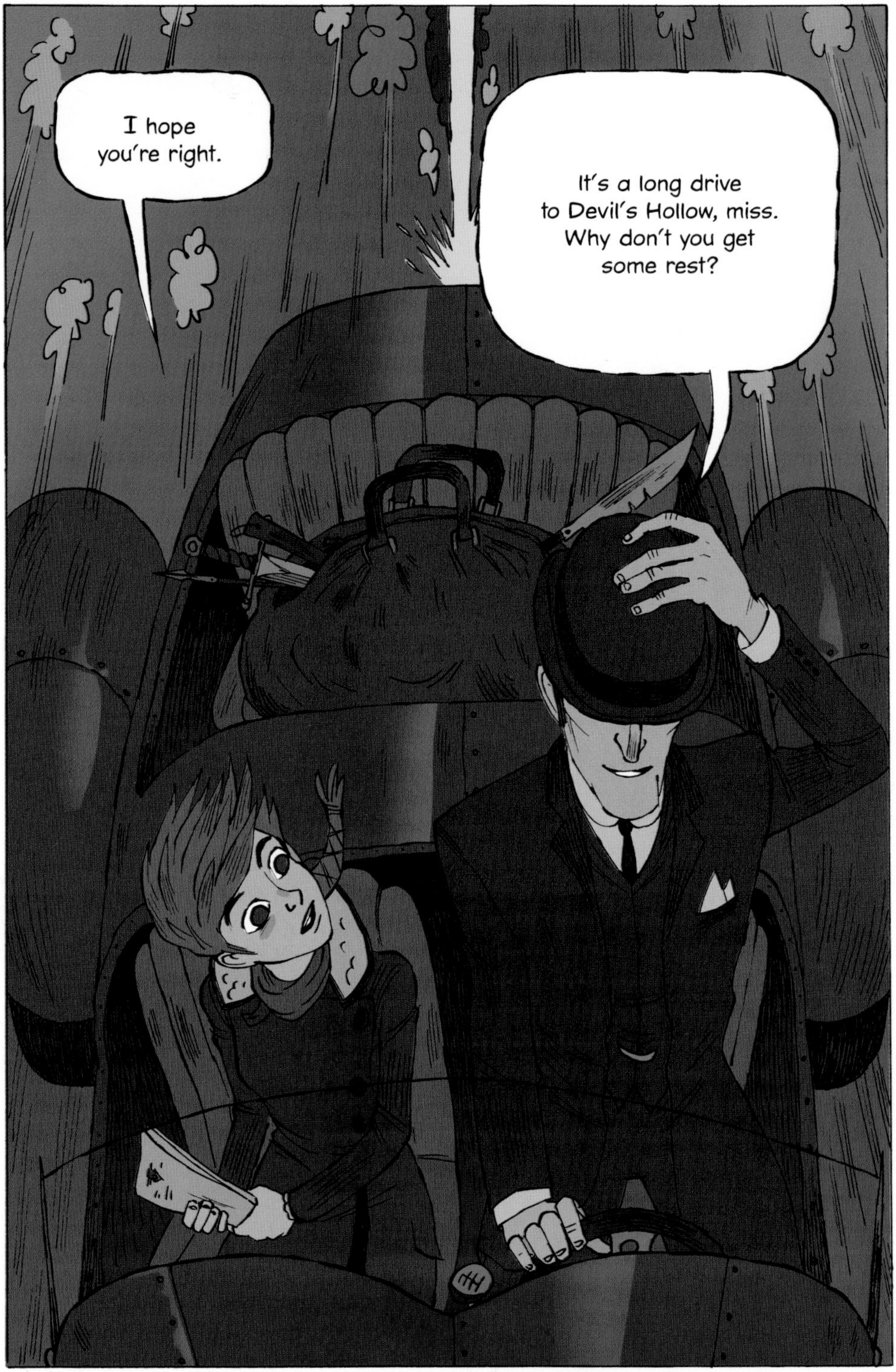
I hope you're right.
It's a long drive to Devil's Hollow, miss. Why don't you get some rest?

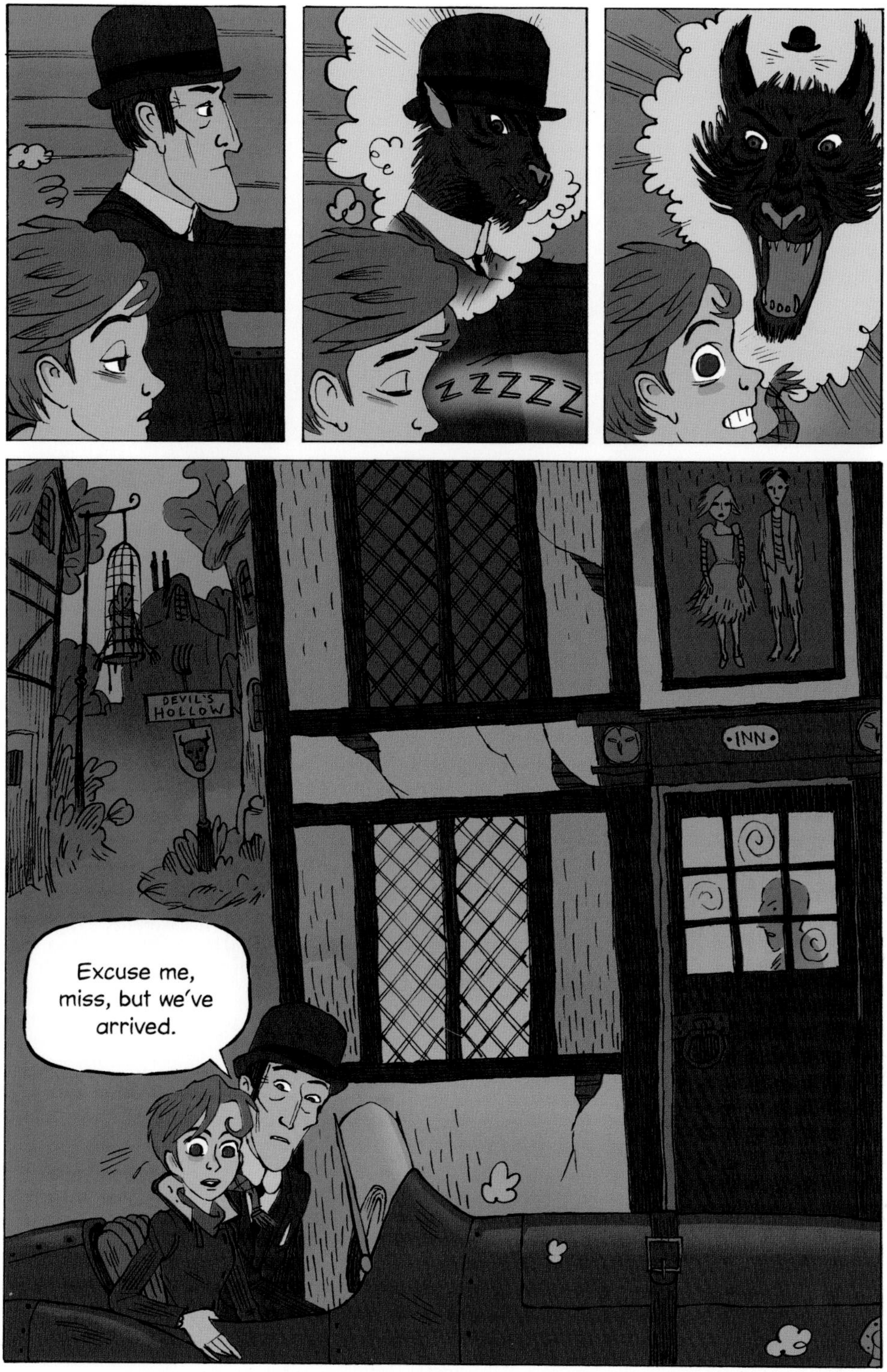

ZZZZZ
DEVIL'S HOLLOW
INN
Excuse me, miss, but we've arrived.

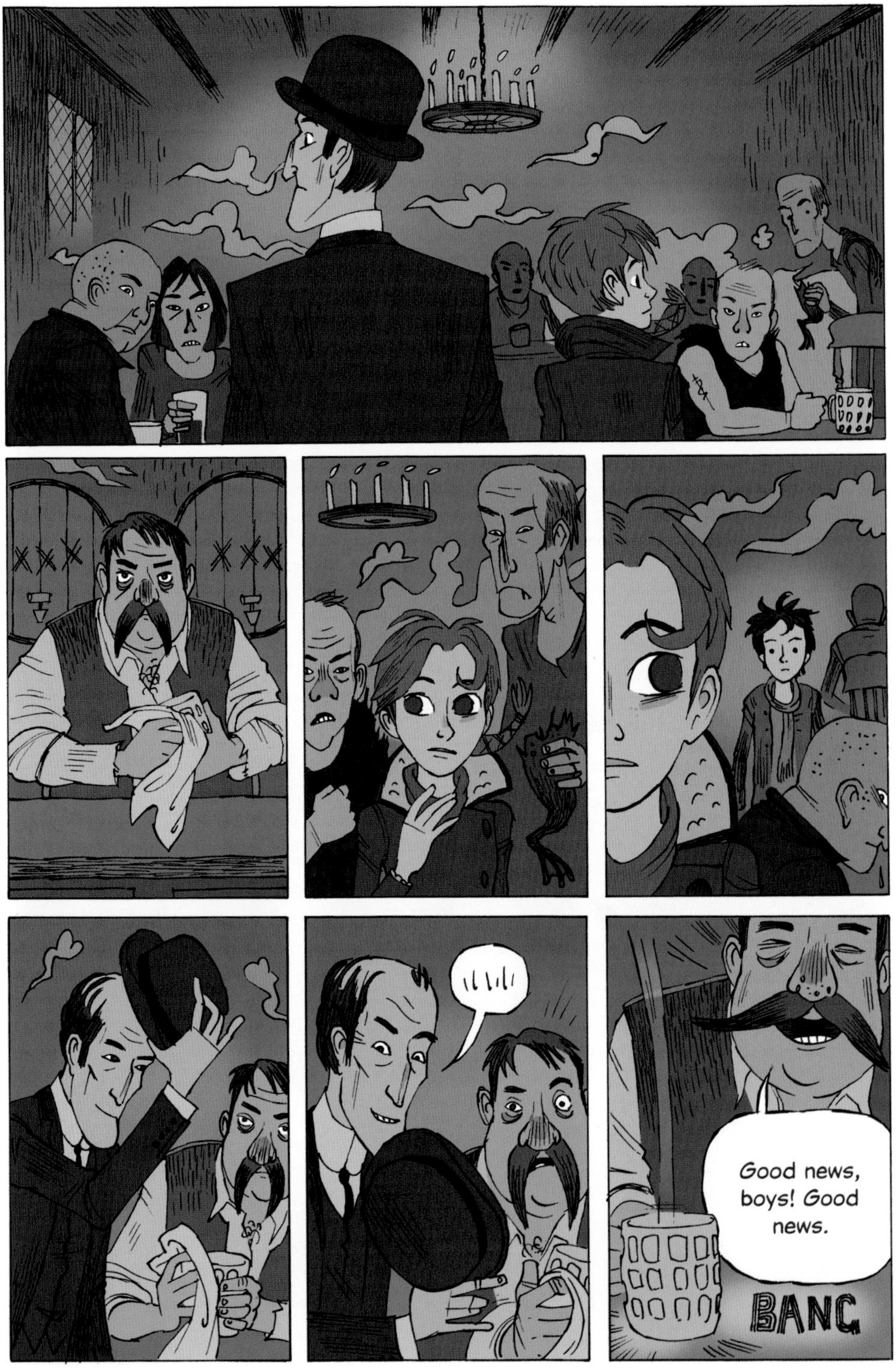
Good news, boys! Good news.
BANG

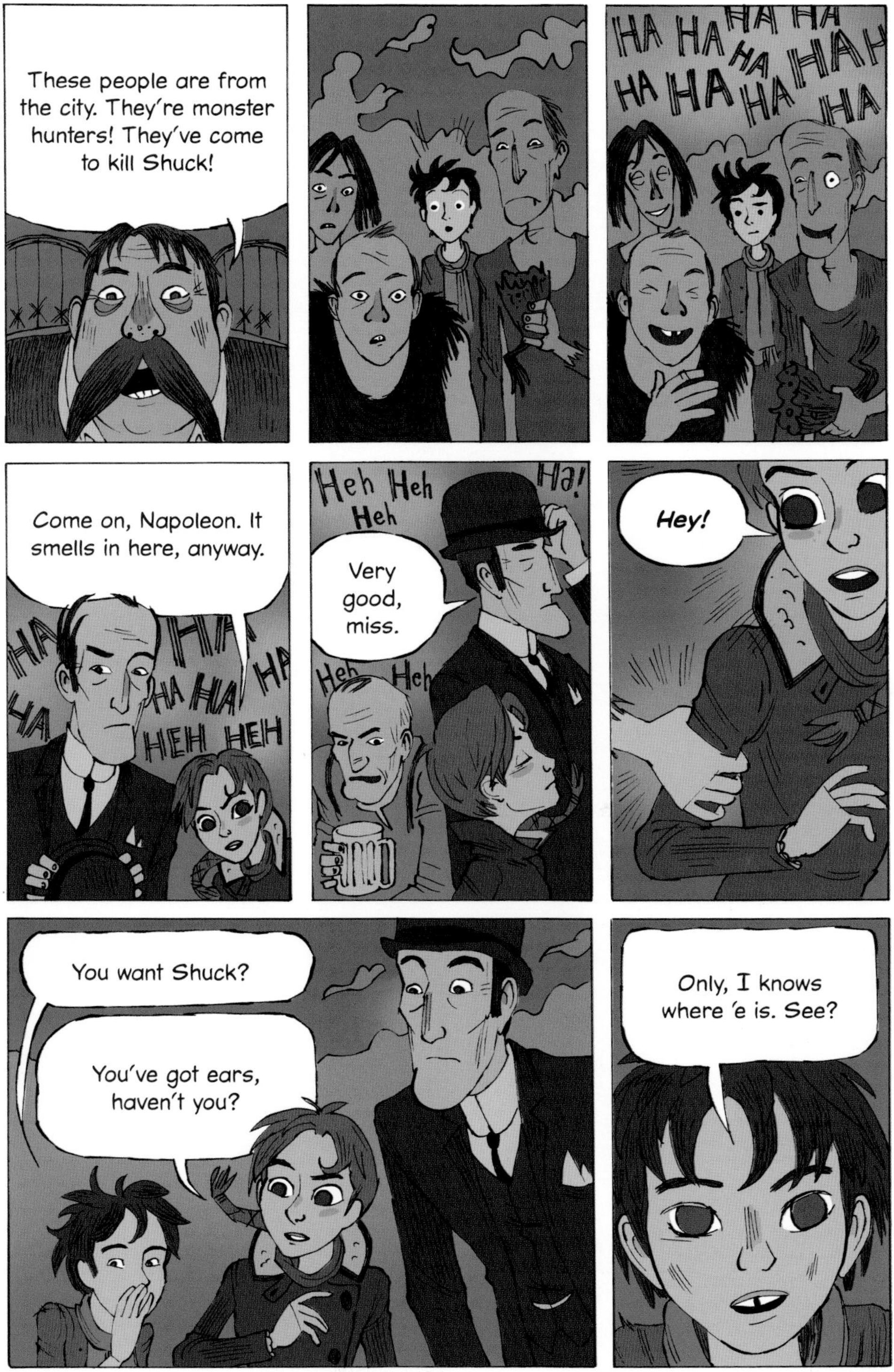
These people are from the city. They're monster hunters! They've come to kill Shuck!
HA HA HA HA HA HA HAH HA HA HA HA HA
Come on, Napoleon. It smells in here, anyway.
HA HA HA HA HA HA HEH HEH
Heh Heh Heh Ha!
Very good, miss.
Heh Heh
Hey!
You want Shuck?
You've got ears, haven't you?
Only, I knows where 'e is. See?

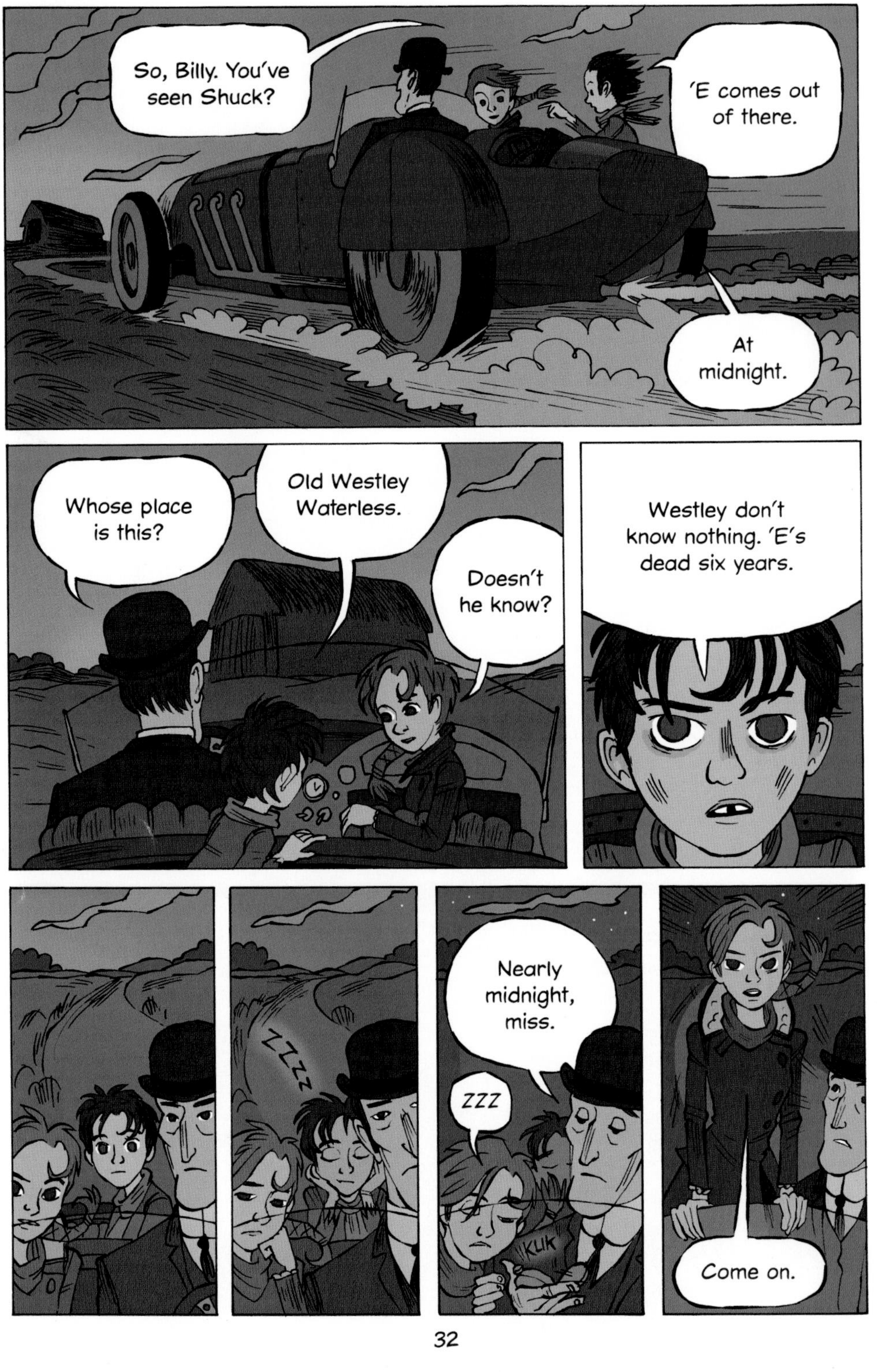
So, Billy. You've seen Shuck?
'E comes out of there.
At midnight.
Whose place is this?
Old Westley Waterless.
Doesn't he know?
Westley don't know nothing. 'E's dead six years.
ZZZZ
Nearly midnight, miss.
ZZZ
KLIK
Come on.

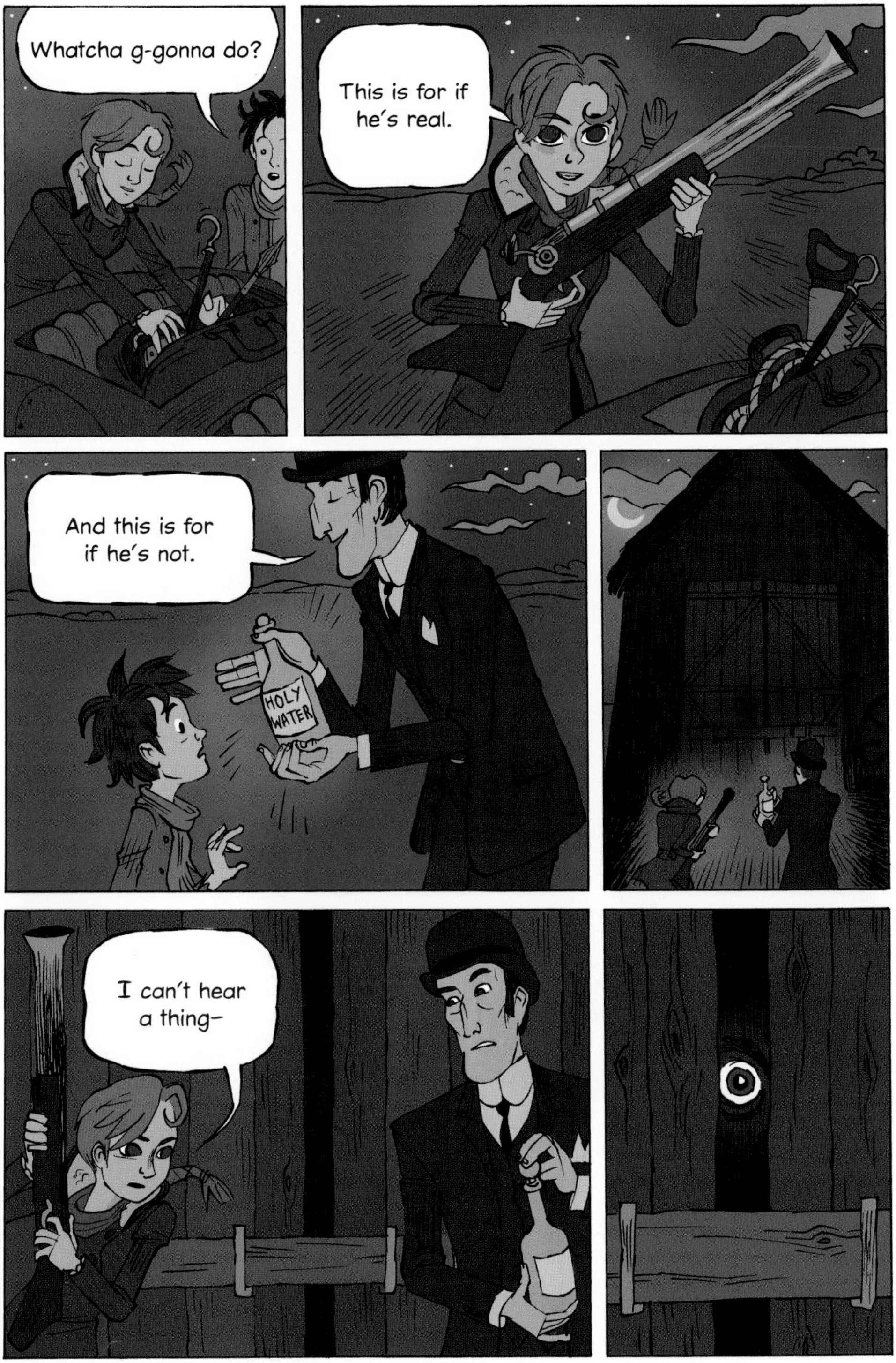
Whatcha g-gonna do?
This is for if he's real.
And this is for if he's not.
HOLY WATER
I can't hear a thing-

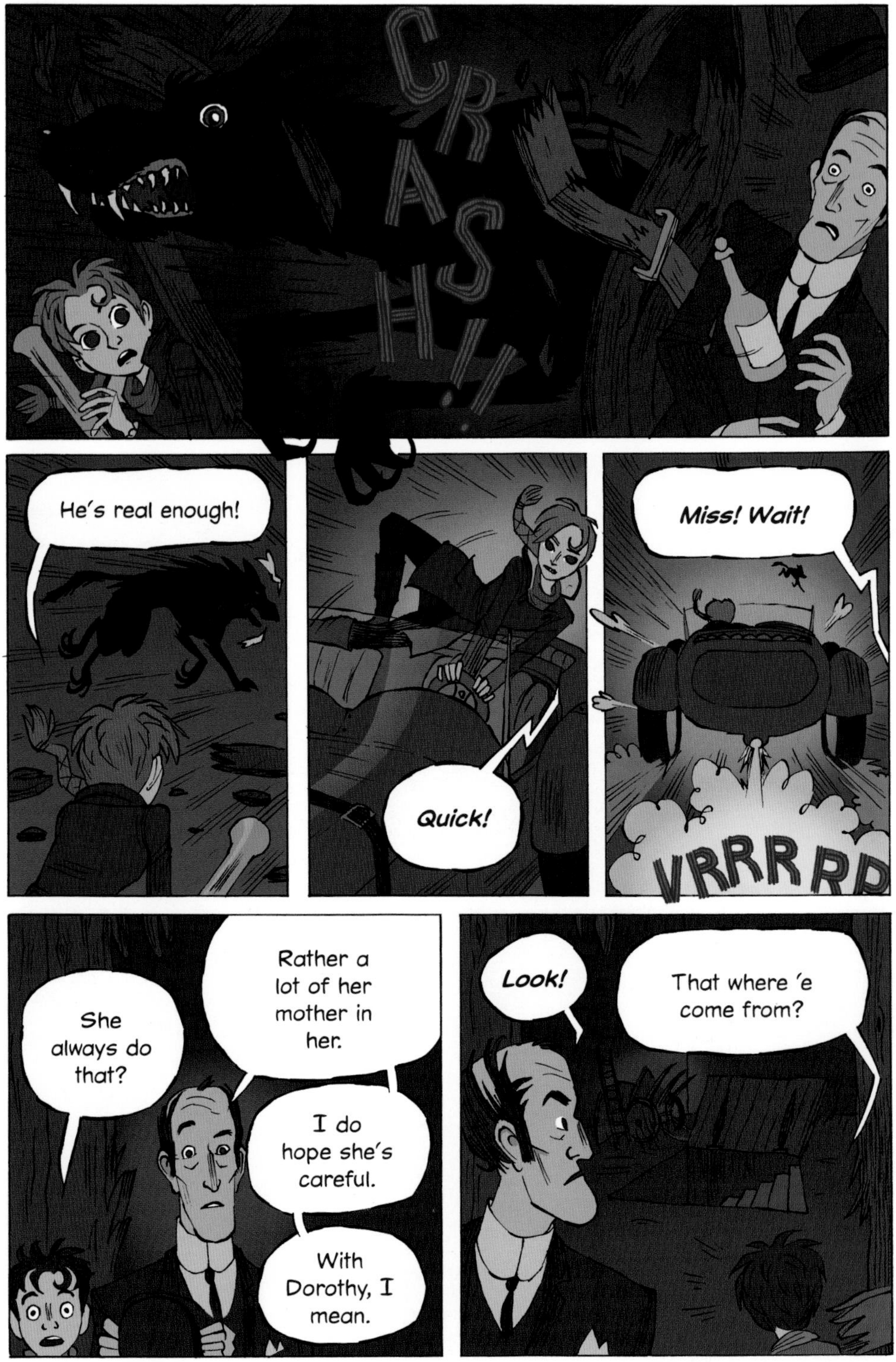
CRASH!!
He's real enough!
Quick!
Miss! Wait!
VRRRRP
She always do that?
Rather a lot of her mother in her.
I do hope she's careful.
With Dorothy, I mean.
Look!
That where 'e come from?

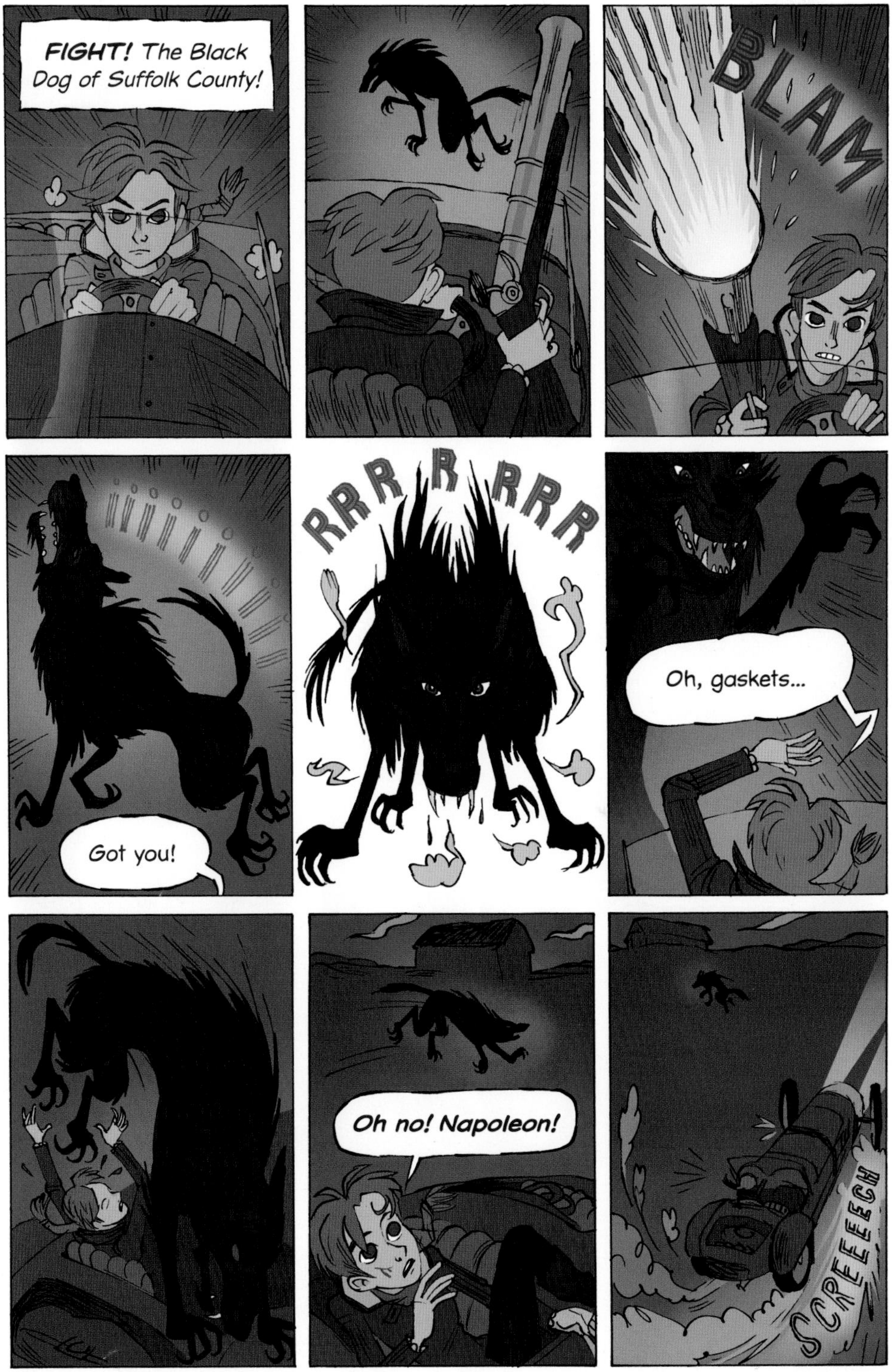
FIGHT! The Black Dog of Suffolk County!
BLAM
Got you!
RRRRRRRR
Oh, gaskets...
Oh no! Napoleon!
SCREEEECH

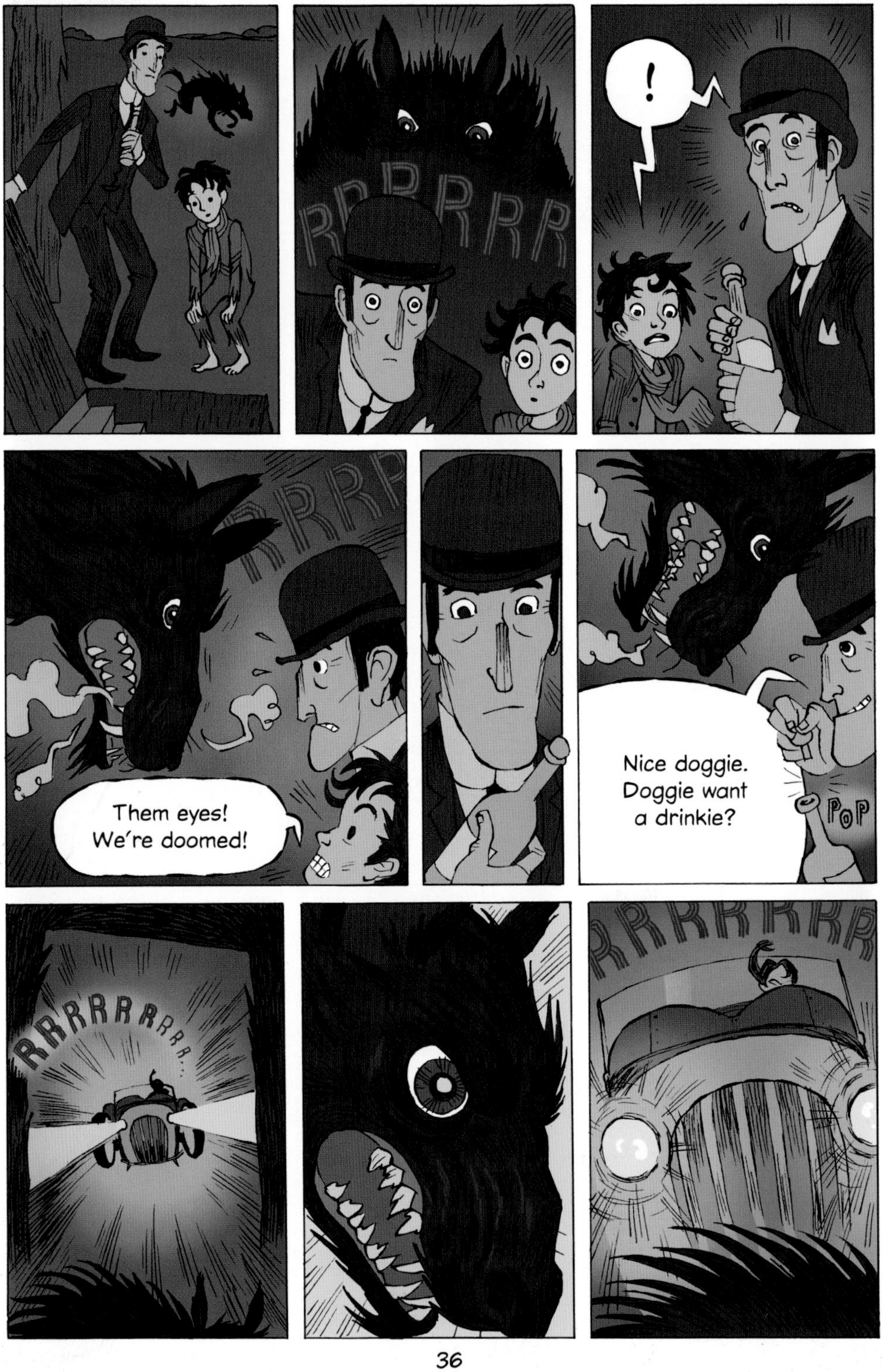

!
RRRRRRR
RRRR
Them eyes!
We're doomed!
Nice doggie.
Doggie want
a drinkie?
POP
RRRRRRRRRRR...
RRRRRRRRR

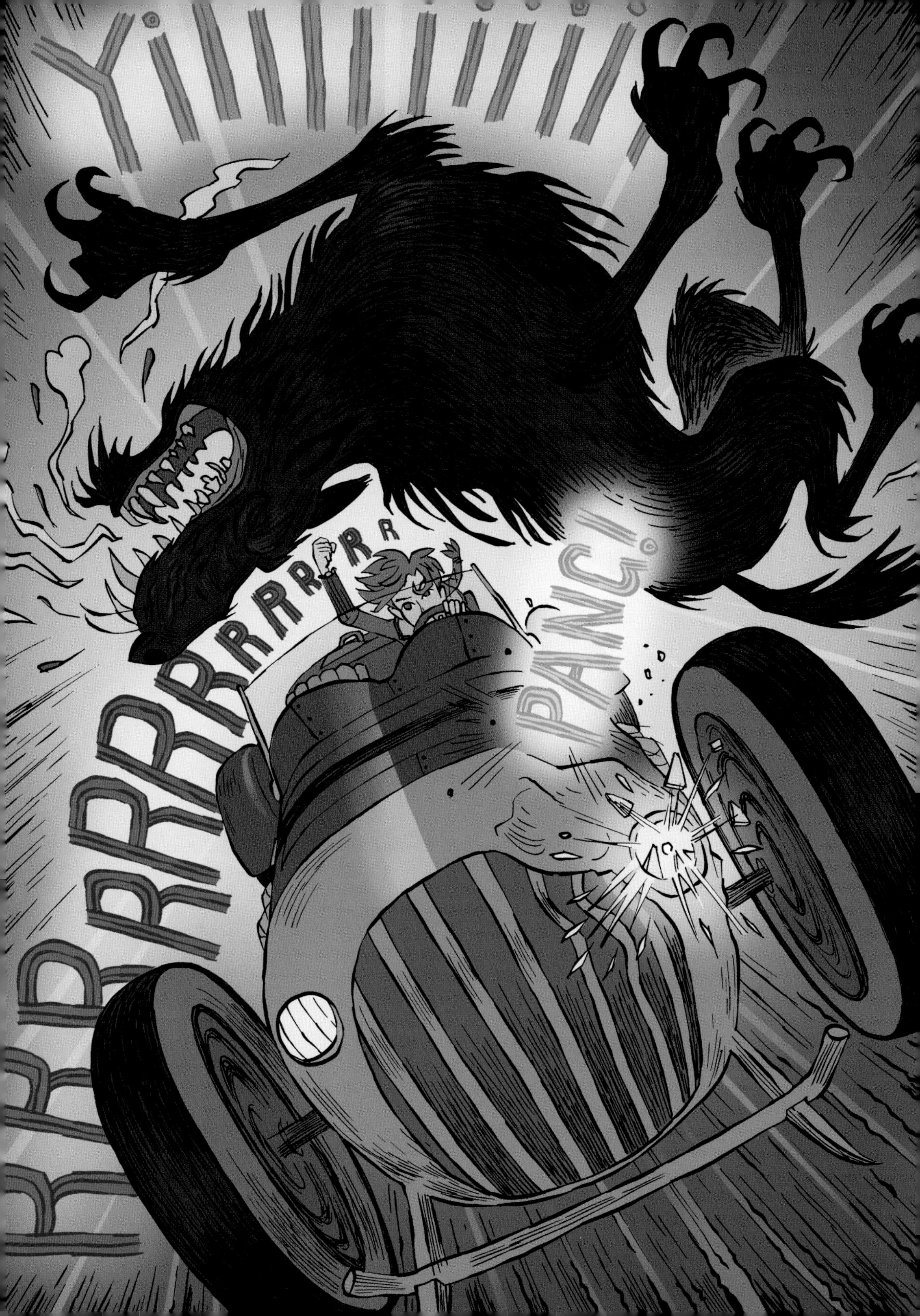

YIIIIIIIIIIII
RRRRRRRRRRRR
PANG!

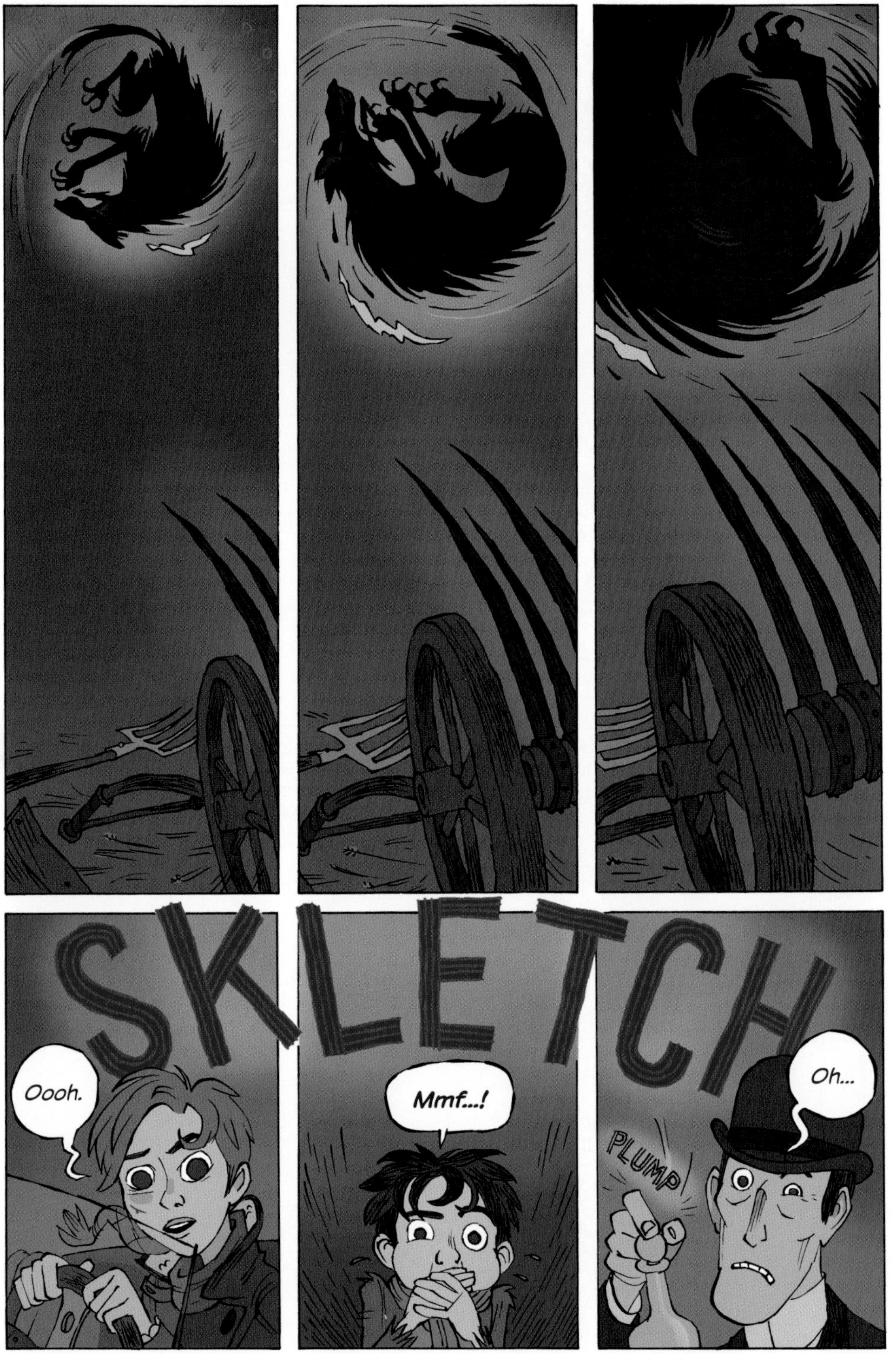
SKLETCH
Oooh.
Mmf...!
PLUMP
Oh...

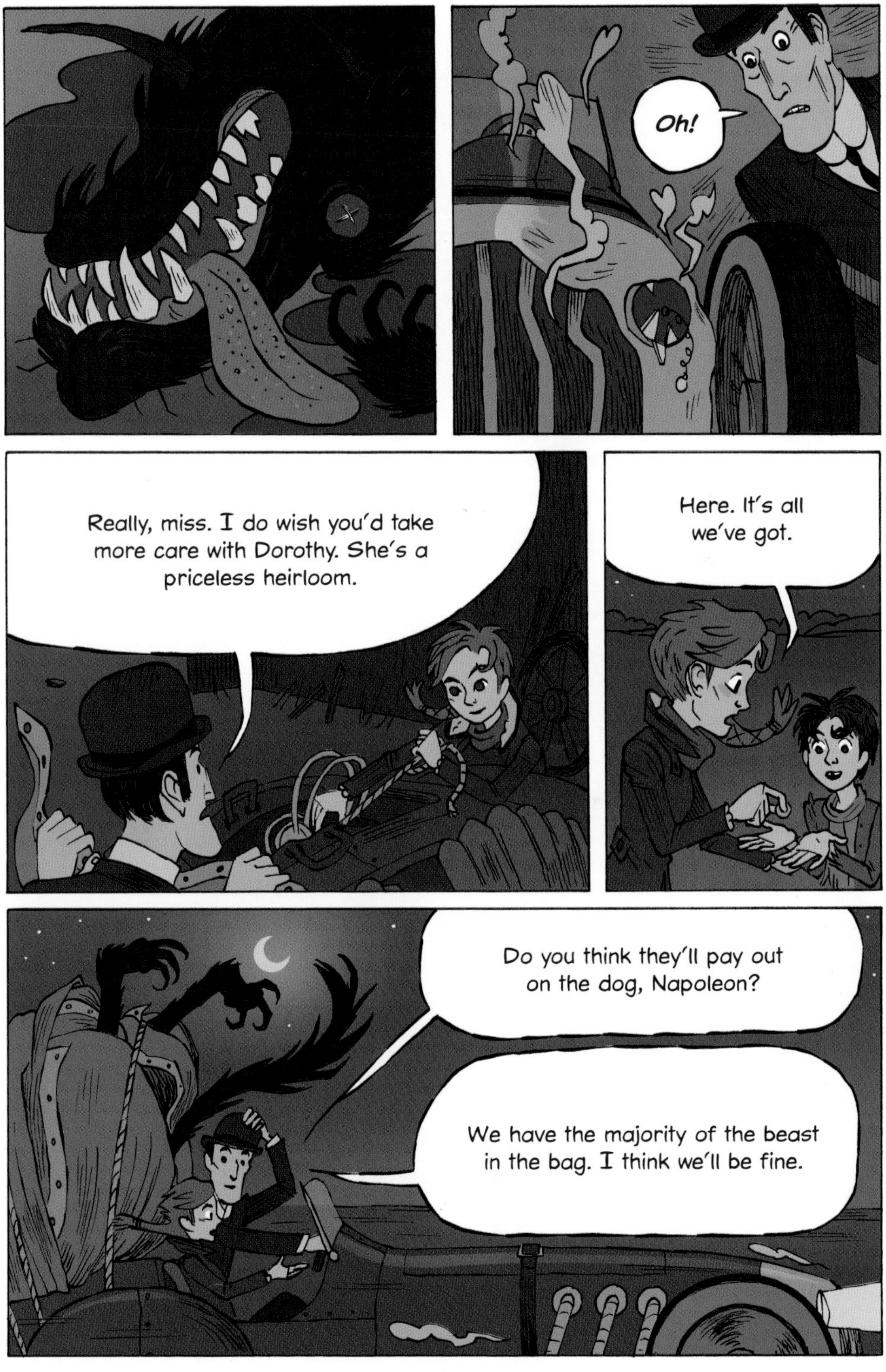
Oh!
Really, miss. I do wish you'd take more care with Dorothy. She's a priceless heirloom.
Here. It's all we've got.
Do you think they'll pay out on the dog, Napoleon?
We have the majority of the beast in the bag. I think we'll be fine.

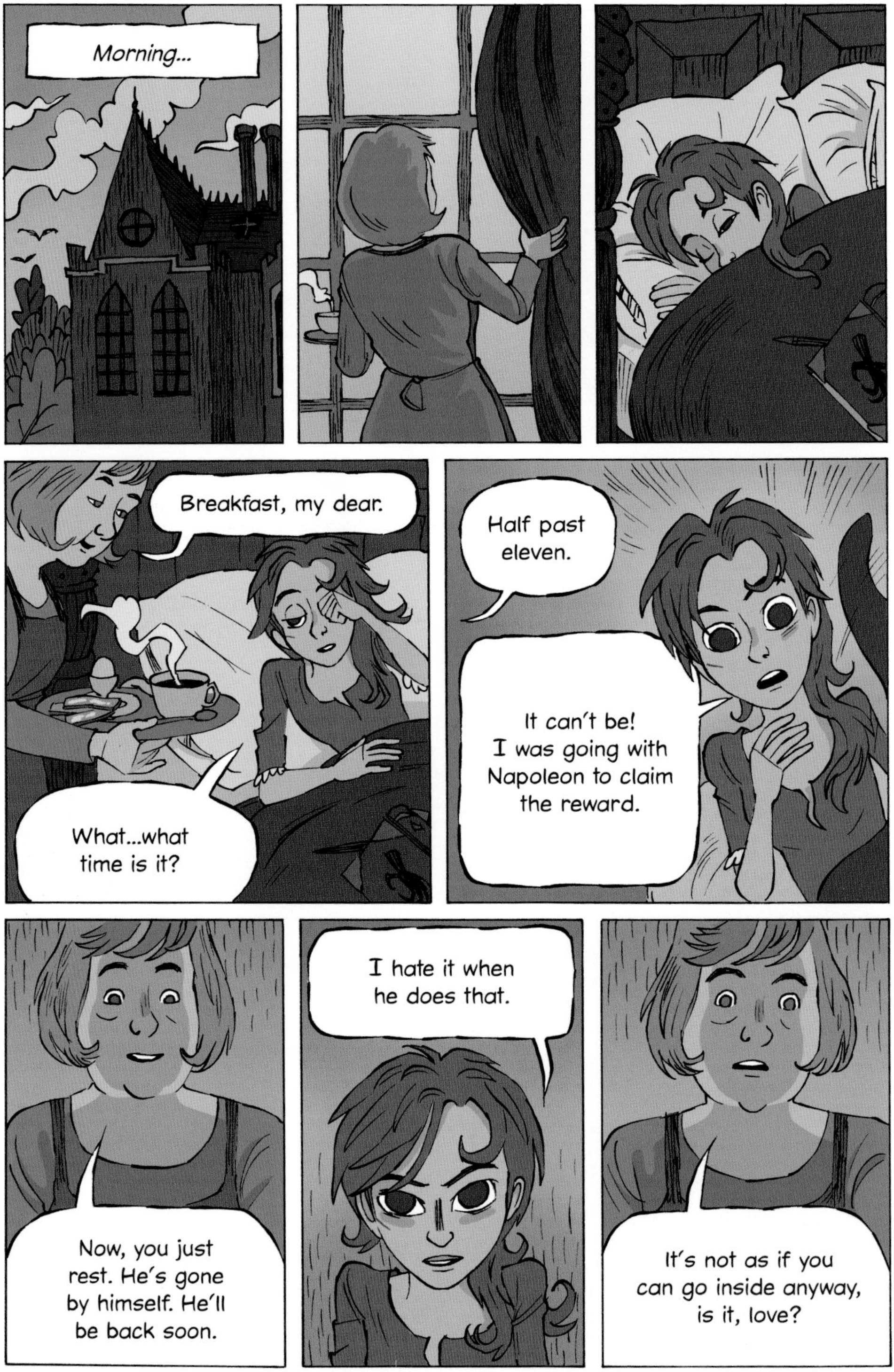
Morning...
Breakfast, my dear.
What...what time is it?
Half past eleven.
It can't be! I was going with Napoleon to claim the reward.
Now, you just rest. He's gone by himself. He'll be back soon.
I hate it when he does that.
It's not as if you can go inside anyway, is it, love?

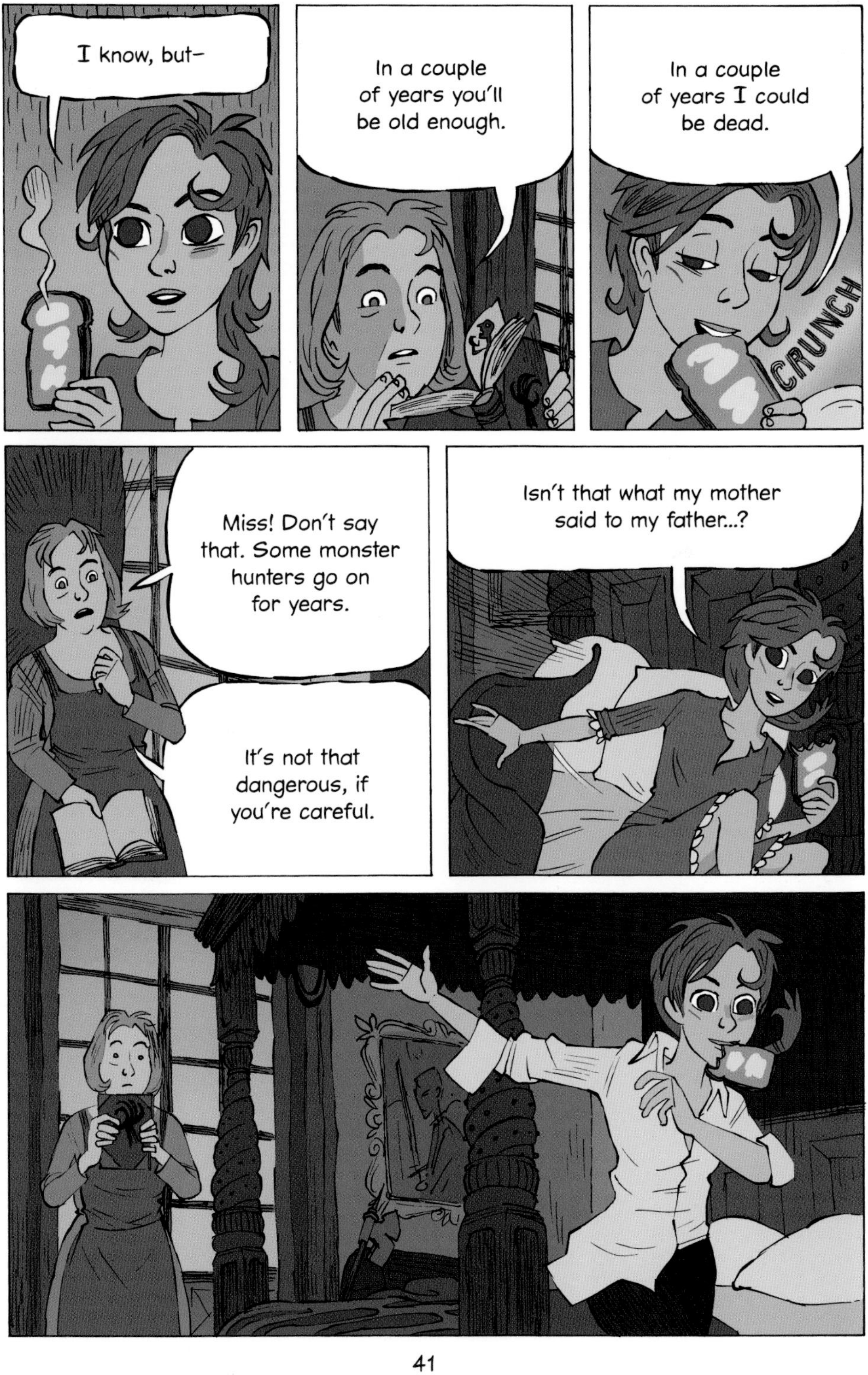
I know, but–
In a couple of years you'll be old enough.
In a couple of years I could be dead.
CRUNCH
Miss! Don't say that. Some monster hunters go on for years.
It's not that dangerous, if you're careful.
Isn't that what my mother said to my father...?

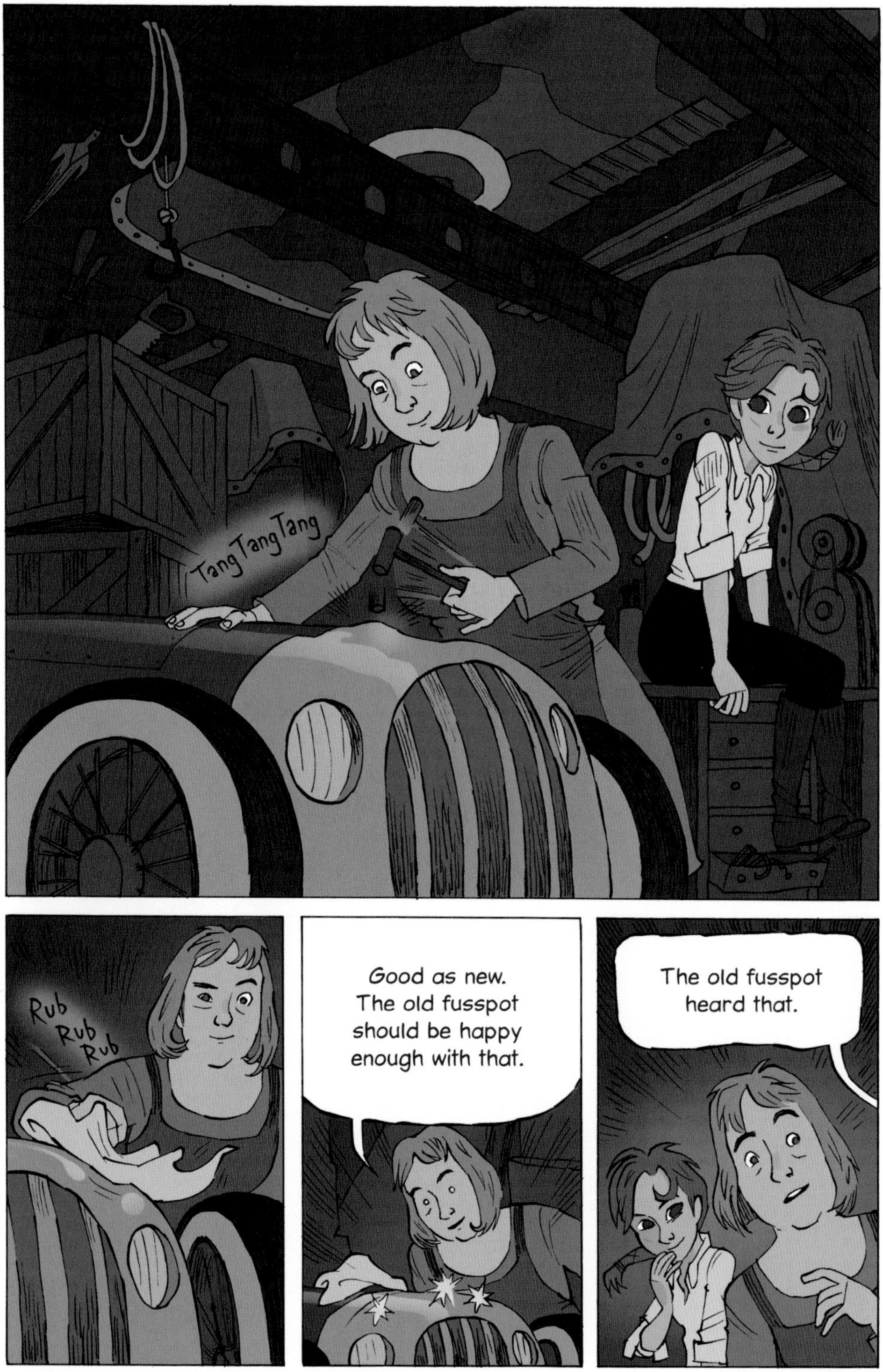
TangTangTang
Rub Rub Rub
Good as new. The old fusspot should be happy enough with that.
The old fusspot heard that.

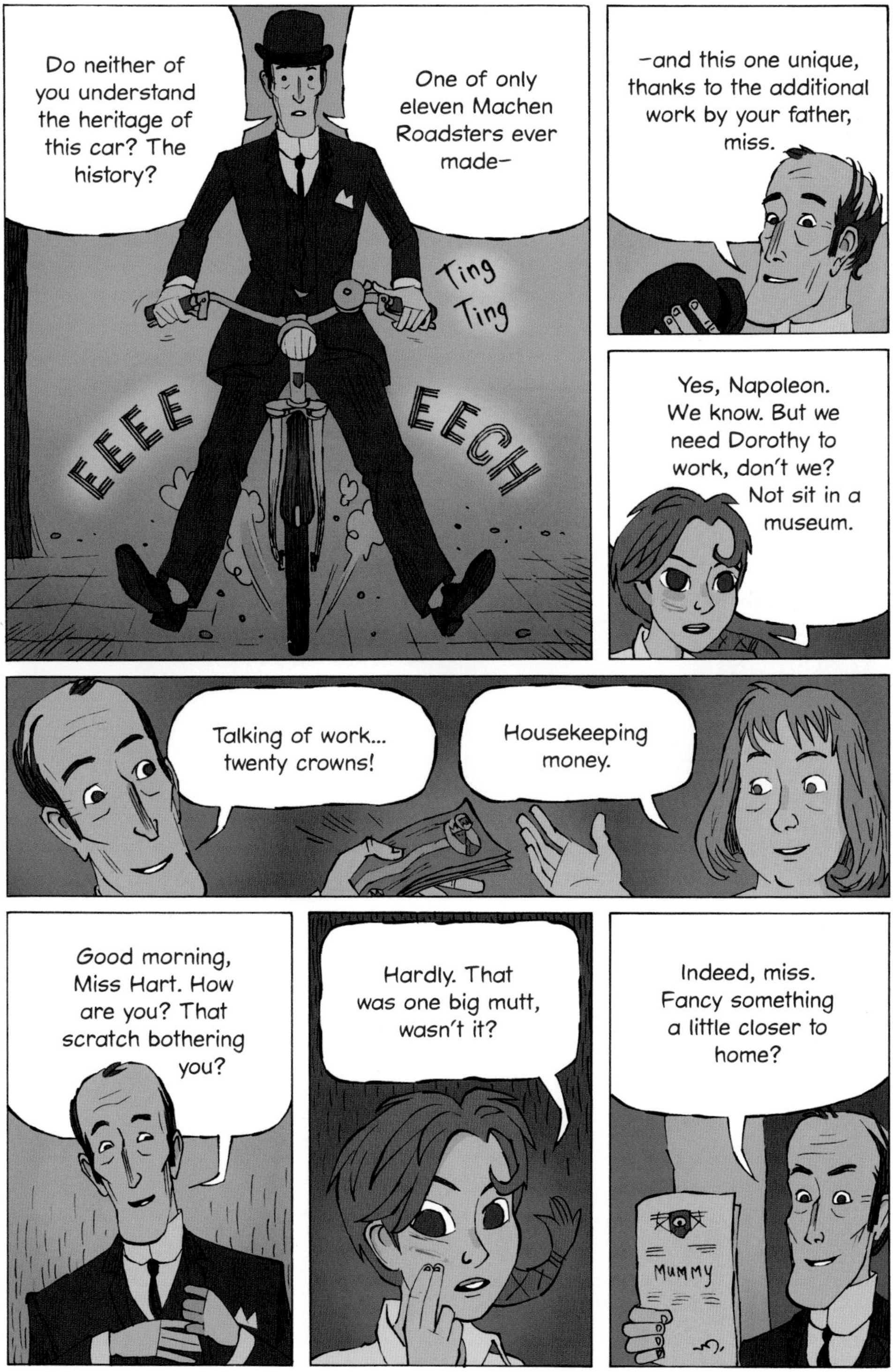
Do neither of you understand the heritage of this car? The history?
One of only eleven Machen Roadsters ever made–
Ting Ting
EEEE EECH
–and this one unique, thanks to the additional work by your father, miss.
Yes, Napoleon. We know. But we need Dorothy to work, don't we? Not sit in a museum.
Talking of work... twenty crowns!
Housekeeping money.
Good morning, Miss Hart. How are you? That scratch bothering you?
Hardly. That was one big mutt, wasn't it?
Indeed, miss. Fancy something a little closer to home?
MUMMY

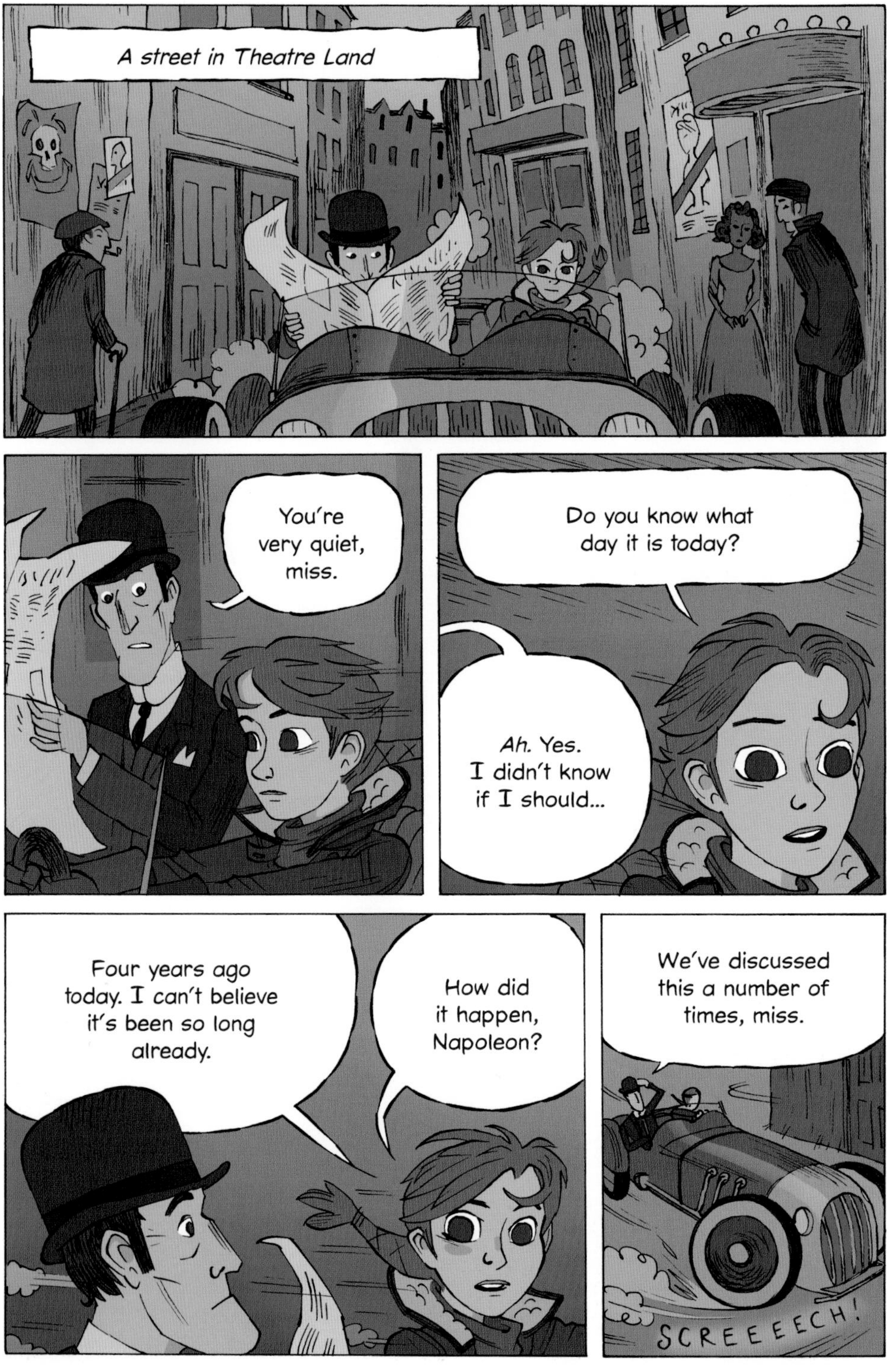
A street in Theatre Land
You're very quiet, miss.
Do you know what day it is today?
Ah. Yes. I didn't know if I should...
Four years ago today. I can't believe it's been so long already.
How did it happen, Napoleon?
We've discussed this a number of times, miss.
SCREEEECH!

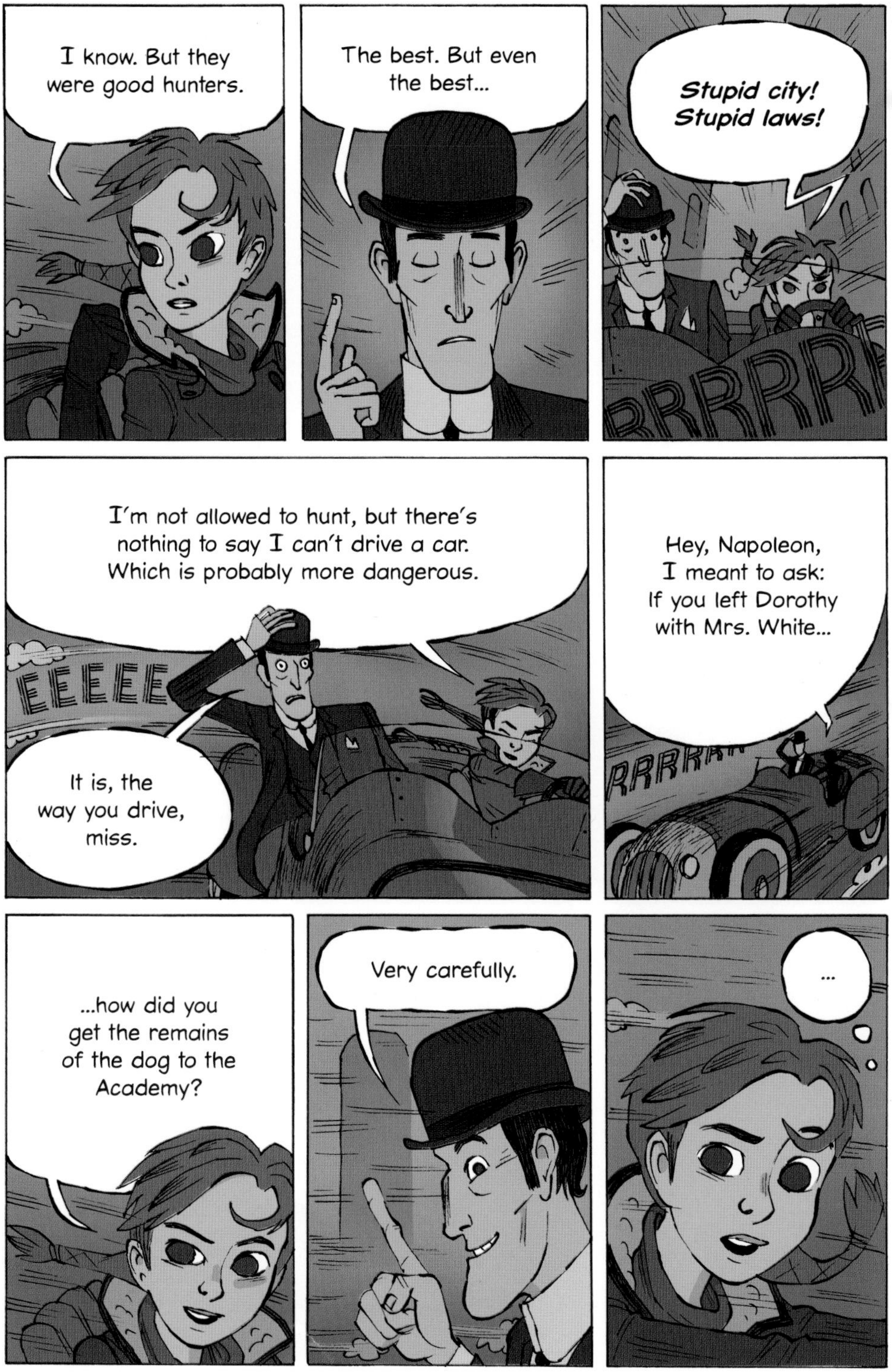
I know. But they were good hunters.
The best. But even the best...
Stupid city! Stupid laws!
BRRRRRR
I'm not allowed to hunt, but there's nothing to say I can't drive a car. Which is probably more dangerous.
EEEEE
It is, the way you drive, miss.
Hey, Napoleon, I meant to ask: If you left Dorothy with Mrs. White...
RRRRRR
...how did you get the remains of the dog to the Academy?
Very carefully.
...

You know, there is one thing.

About your parents.

The day before they... Well, the day before, your father told me about something else.

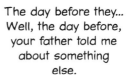

He did?

You know they say there was a time when monsters didn't roam free?

I've heard that, yes.

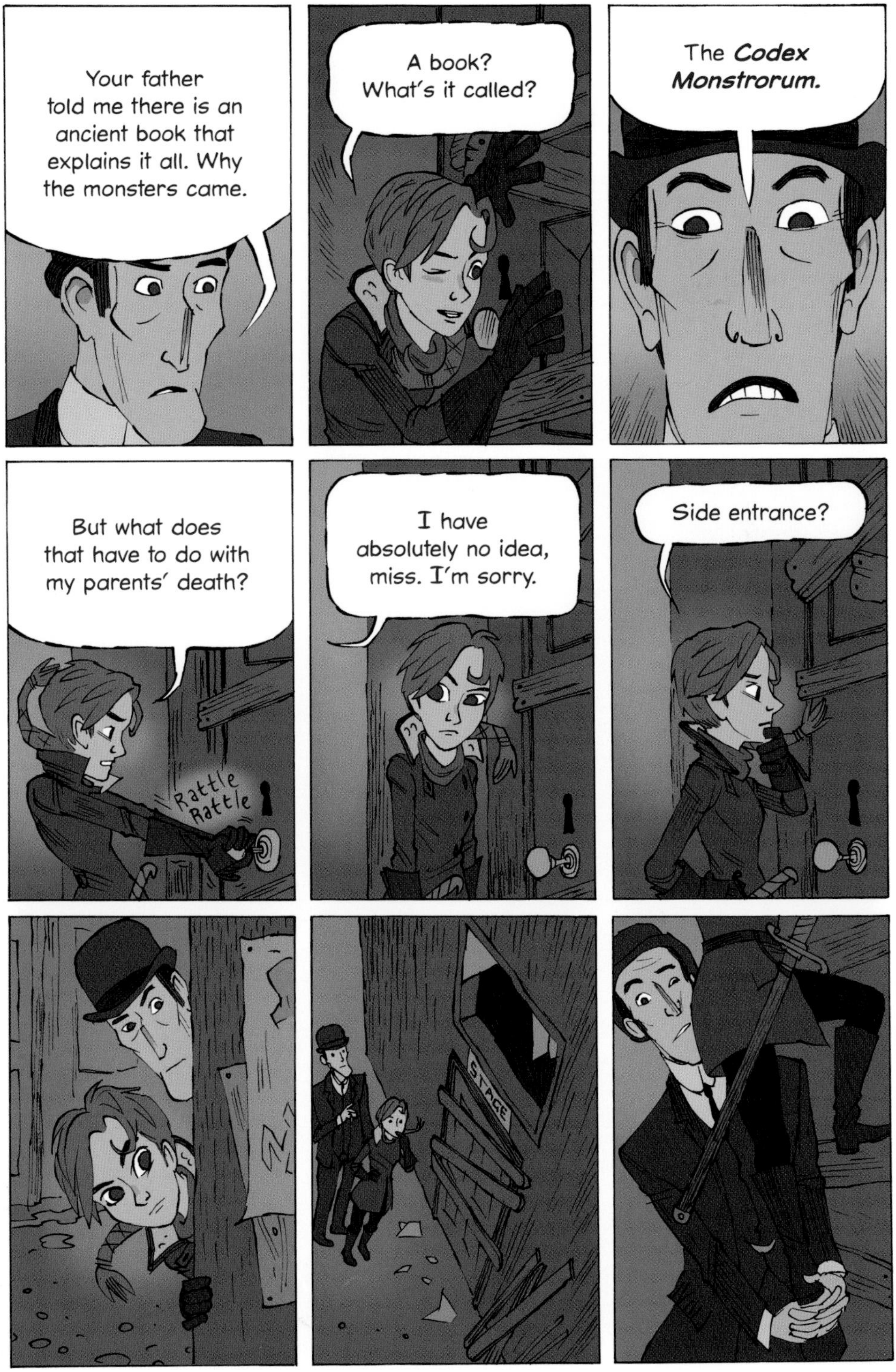
Your father told me there is an ancient book that explains it all. Why the monsters came.
A book? What's it called?
The *Codex Monstrorum.*
But what does that have to do with my parents' death?
Rattle Rattle
I have absolutely no idea, miss. I'm sorry.
Side entrance?
STAGE

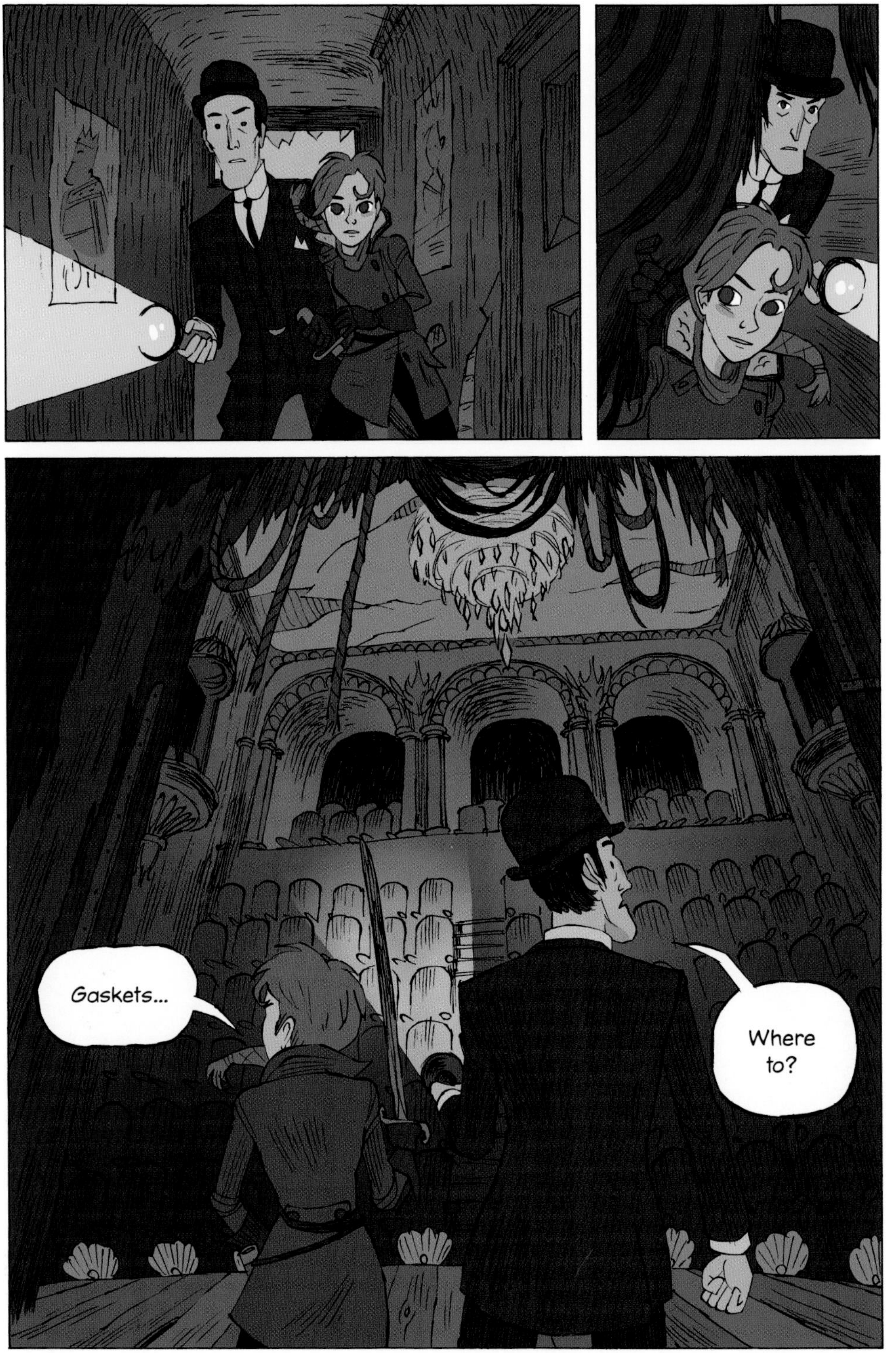
Gaskets...
Where to?

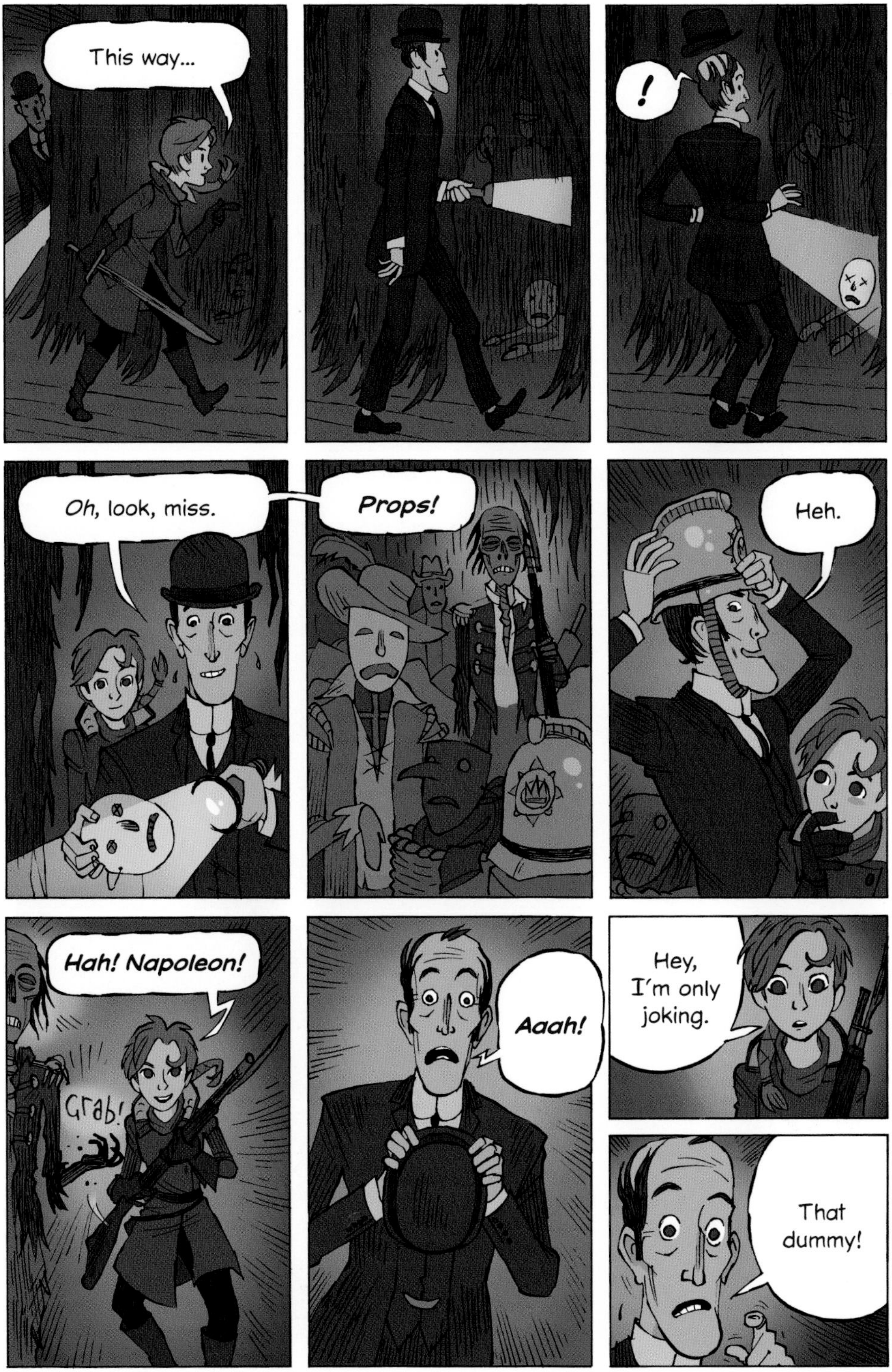
This way...
!
Oh, look, miss.
Props!
Heh.
Hah! Napoleon!
Grab!
Aaah!
Hey, I'm only joking.
That dummy!

UUUUUUUUUR.

That's no dummy. That's the mummy!

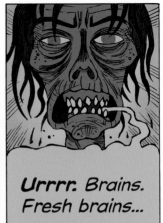

Urrrr. Brains. Fresh brains...

UUUUURRRR...

Run!

!

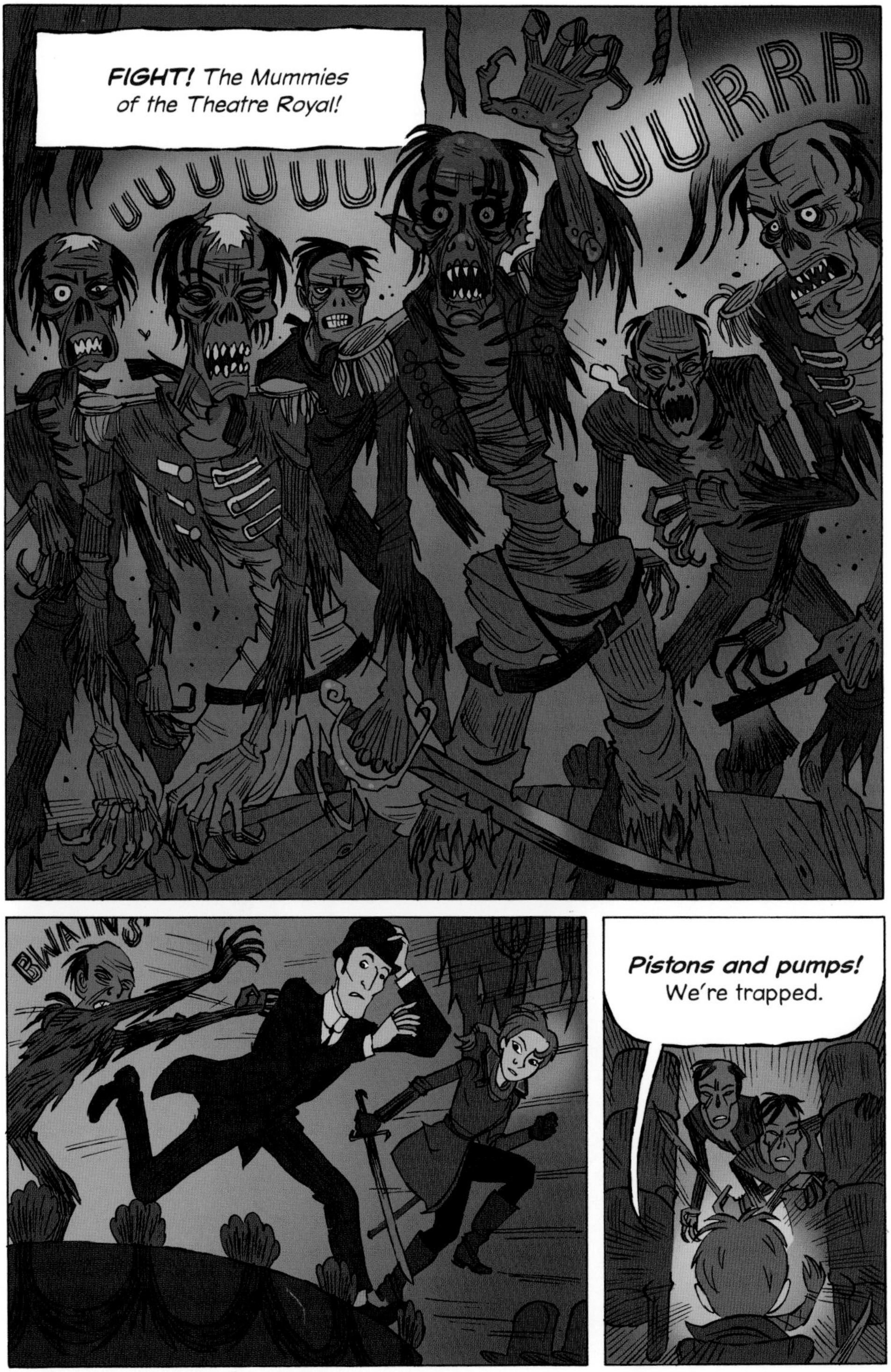
FIGHT! The Mummies of the Theatre Royal!
UUUUUU UUURRRR
BWAINS!
Pistons and pumps! We're trapped.

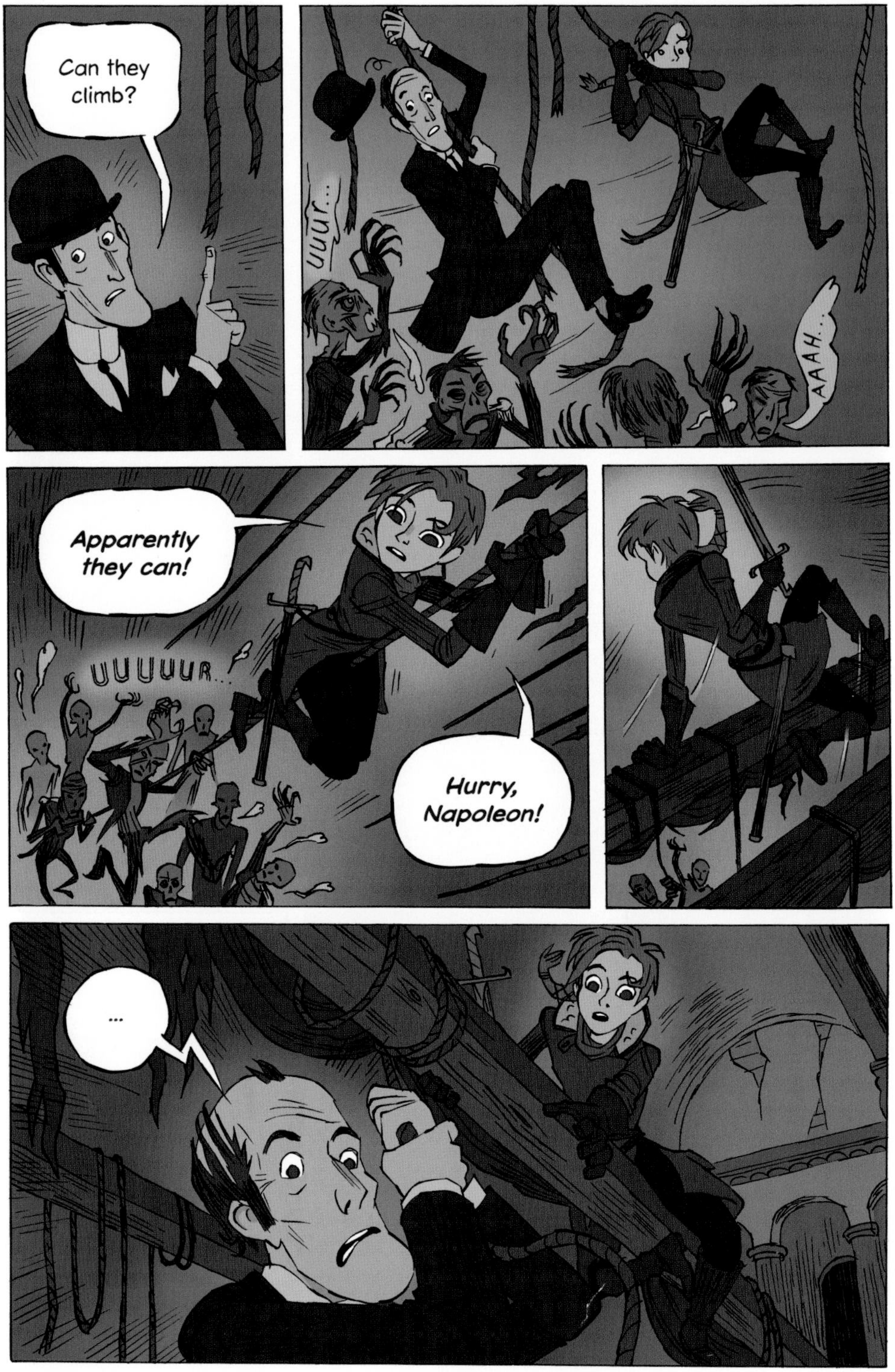
Can they climb?
UUUR...
AAAH...
Apparently they can!
UUUUUR...
Hurry, Napoleon!
...

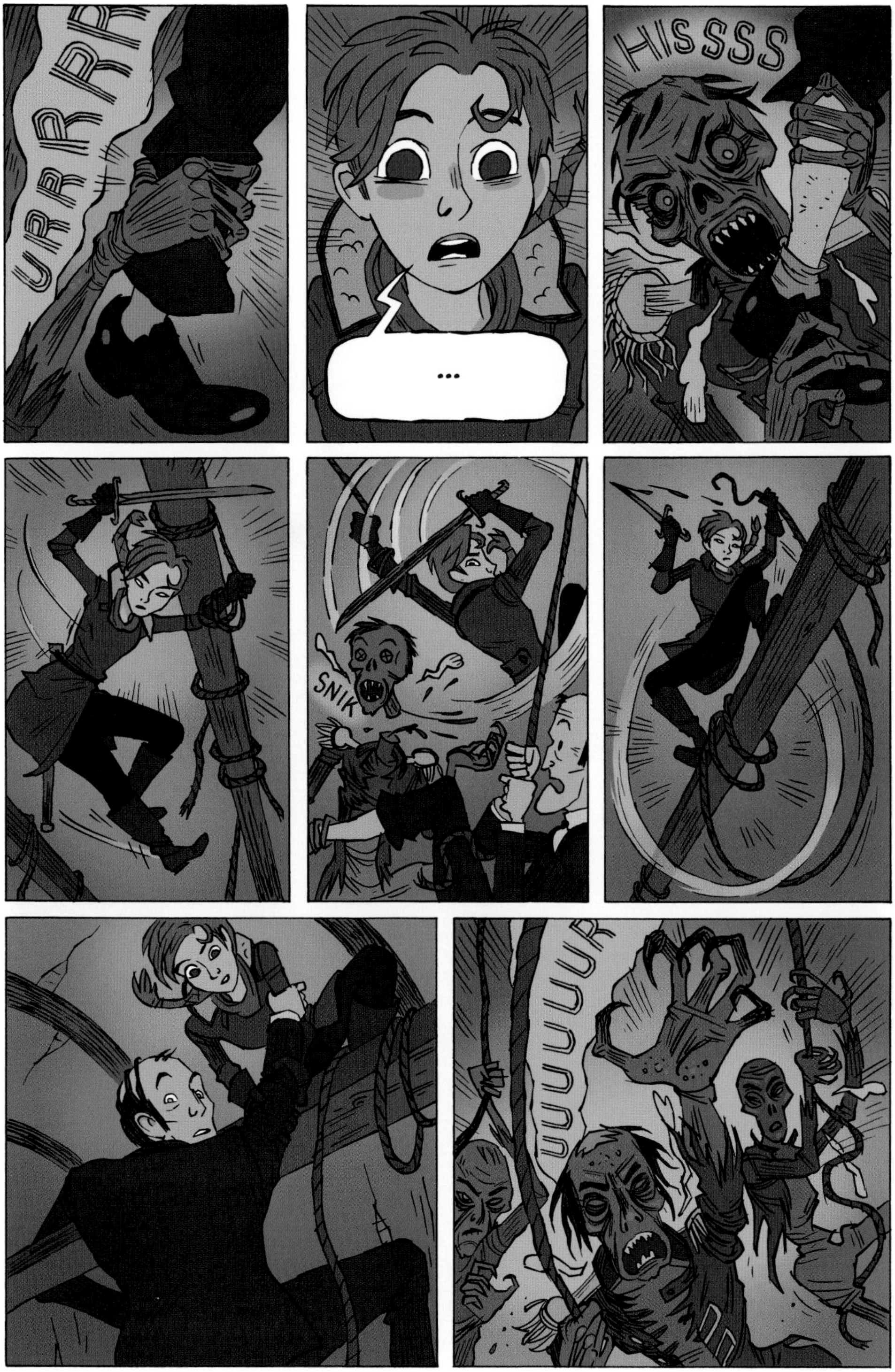
URRRRR
...
HISSSS
SNIK
UUUUUUR

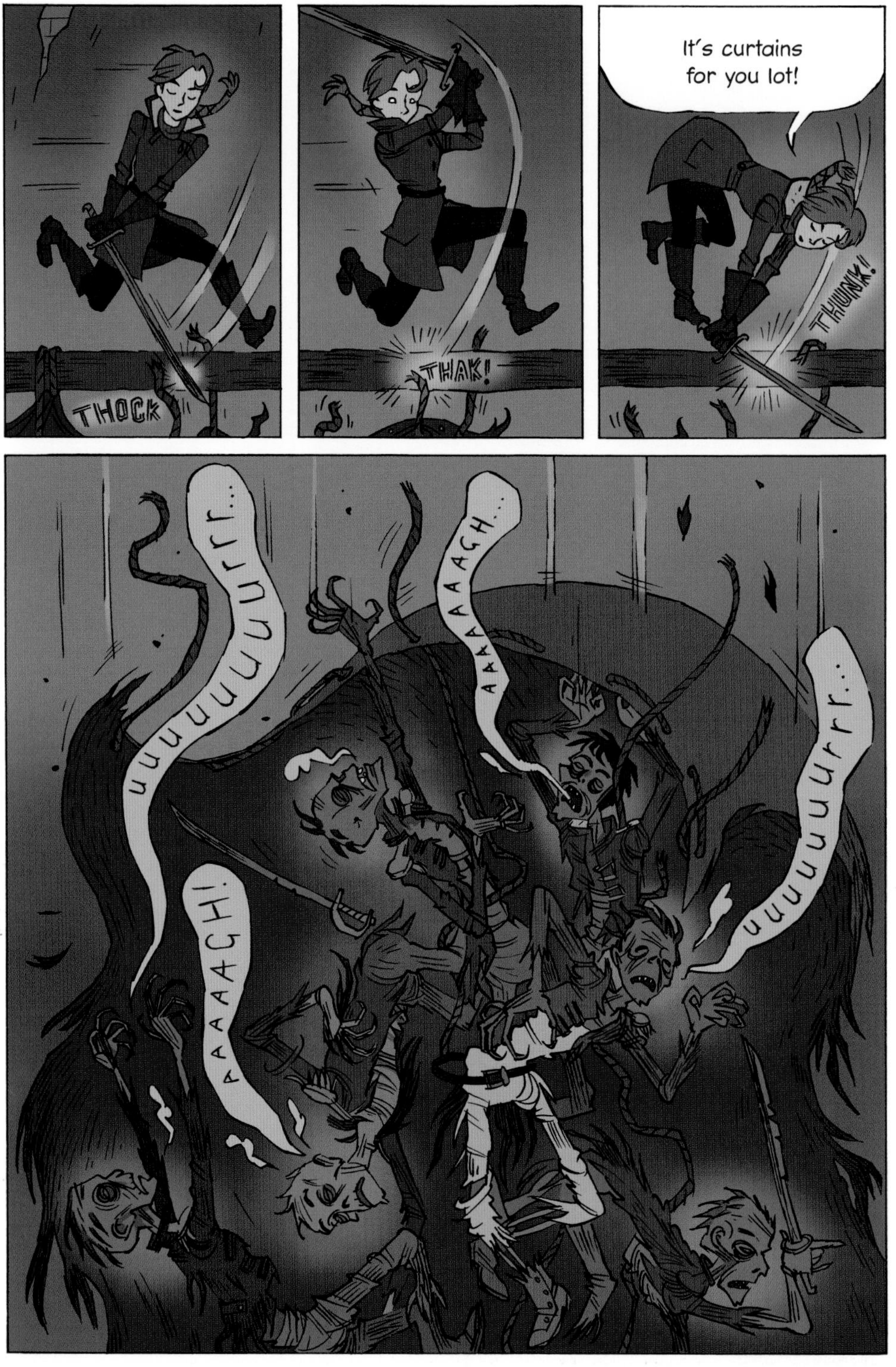
THOCK
THAK!
It's curtains for you lot!
THUNK!
uuuuuuuuuurrr...
AAAAAAAAGH...
AAAAAACH!
uuuuuuuuurrr...

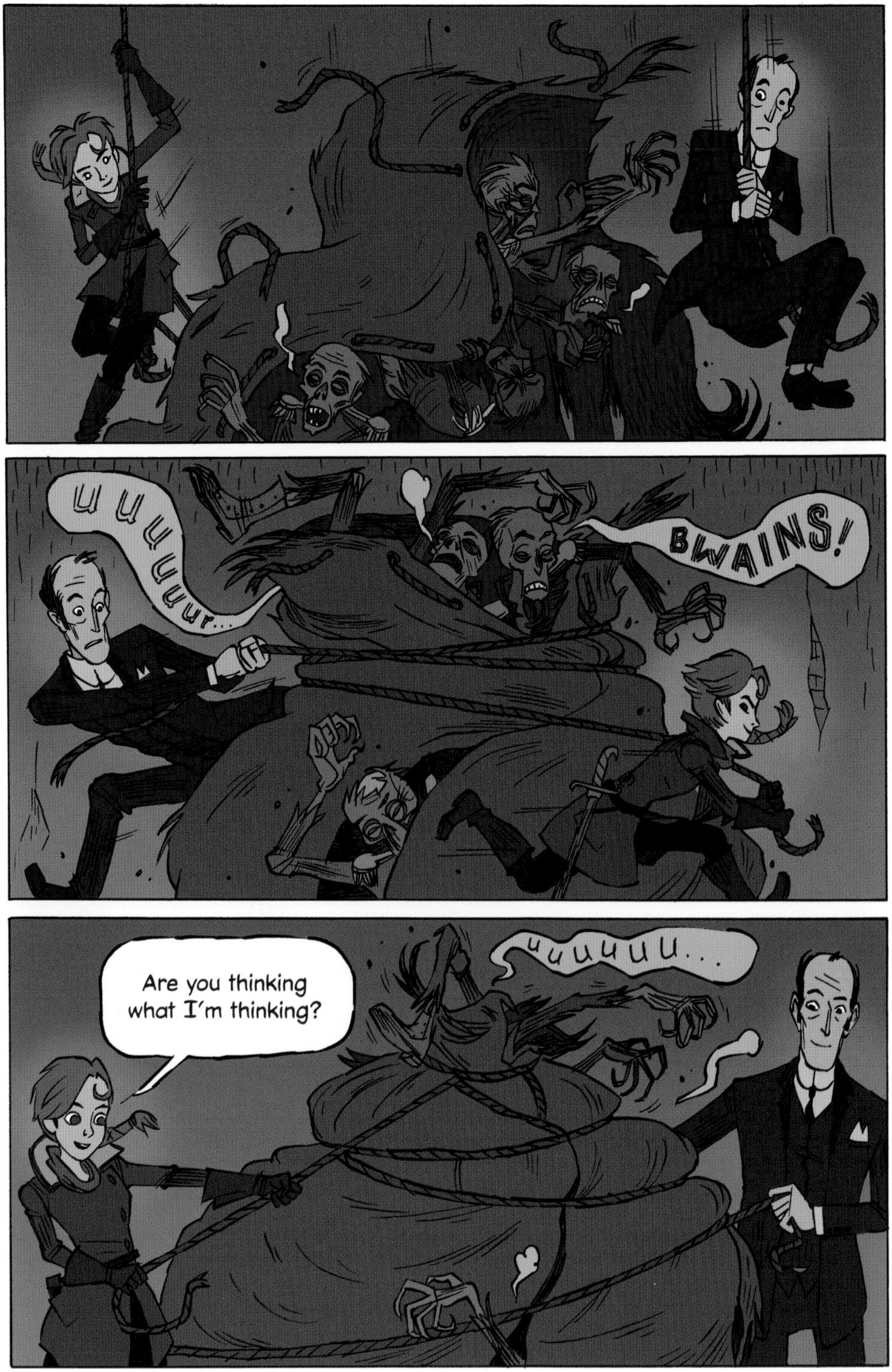
uuuuuuur...
BWAINS!
Are you thinking what I'm thinking?
uuuuuu...

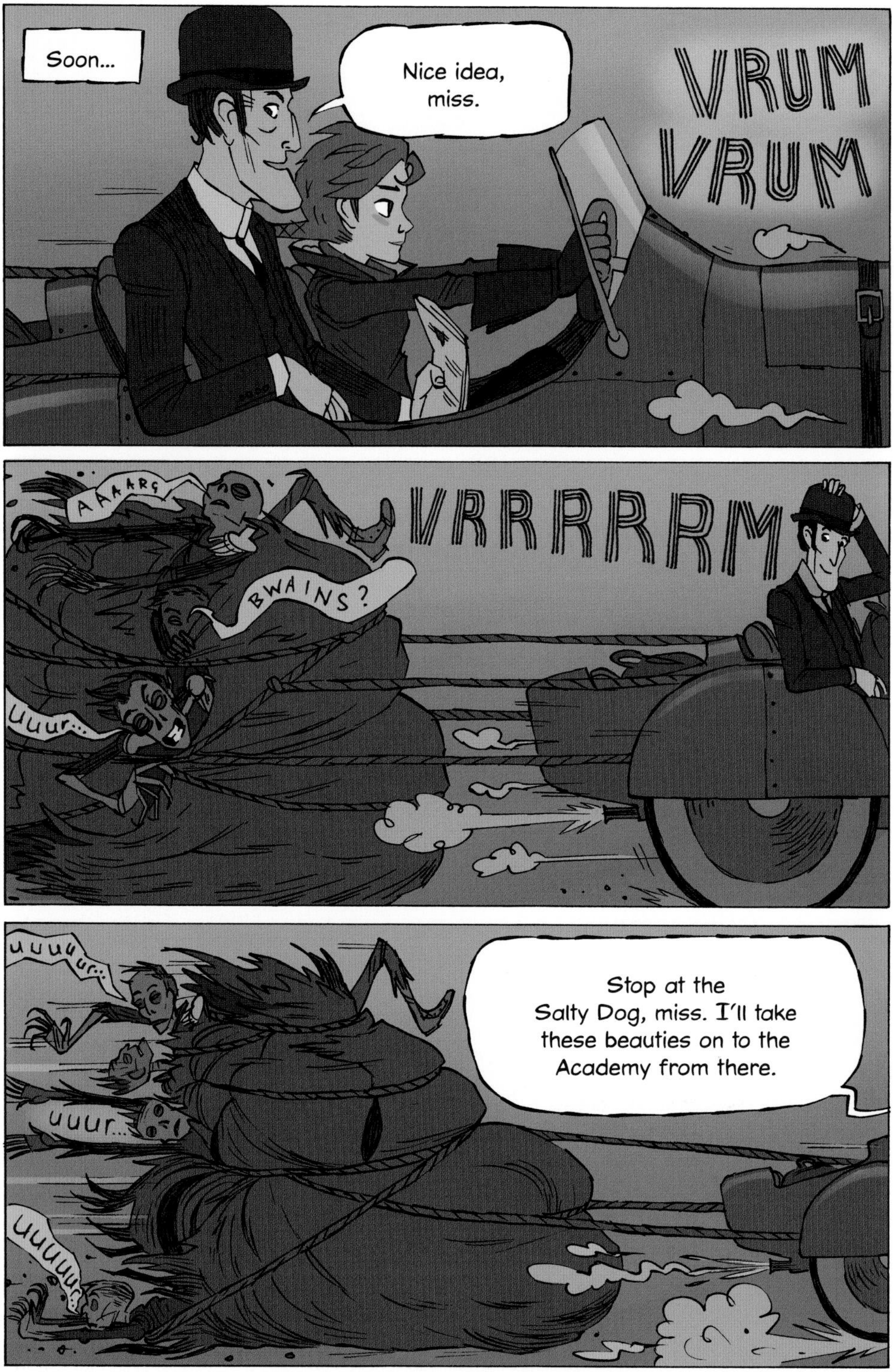
Soon...
Nice idea, miss.
VRUM VRUM
AAAARG
VRRRRRM
BWAINS?
uuur...
uuuur...
uuur...
uuuunn
Stop at the Salty Dog, miss. I'll take these beauties on to the Academy from there.

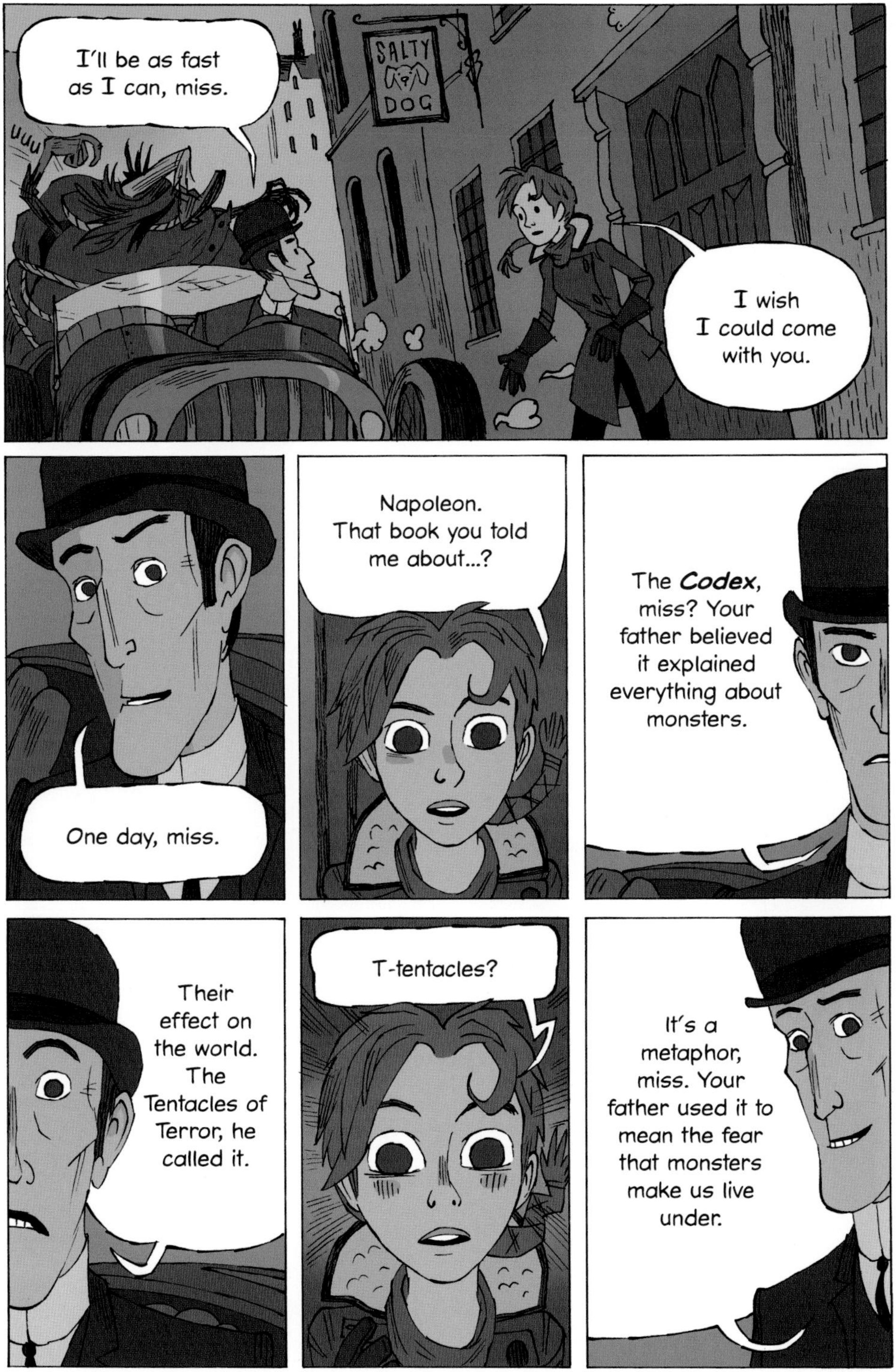
I'll be as fast as I can, miss.
I wish I could come with you.
One day, miss.
Napoleon. That book you told me about...?
The ***Codex***, miss? Your father believed it explained everything about monsters.
Their effect on the world. The Tentacles of Terror, he called it.
T-tentacles?
It's a metaphor, miss. Your father used it to mean the fear that monsters make us live under.
SALTY DOG

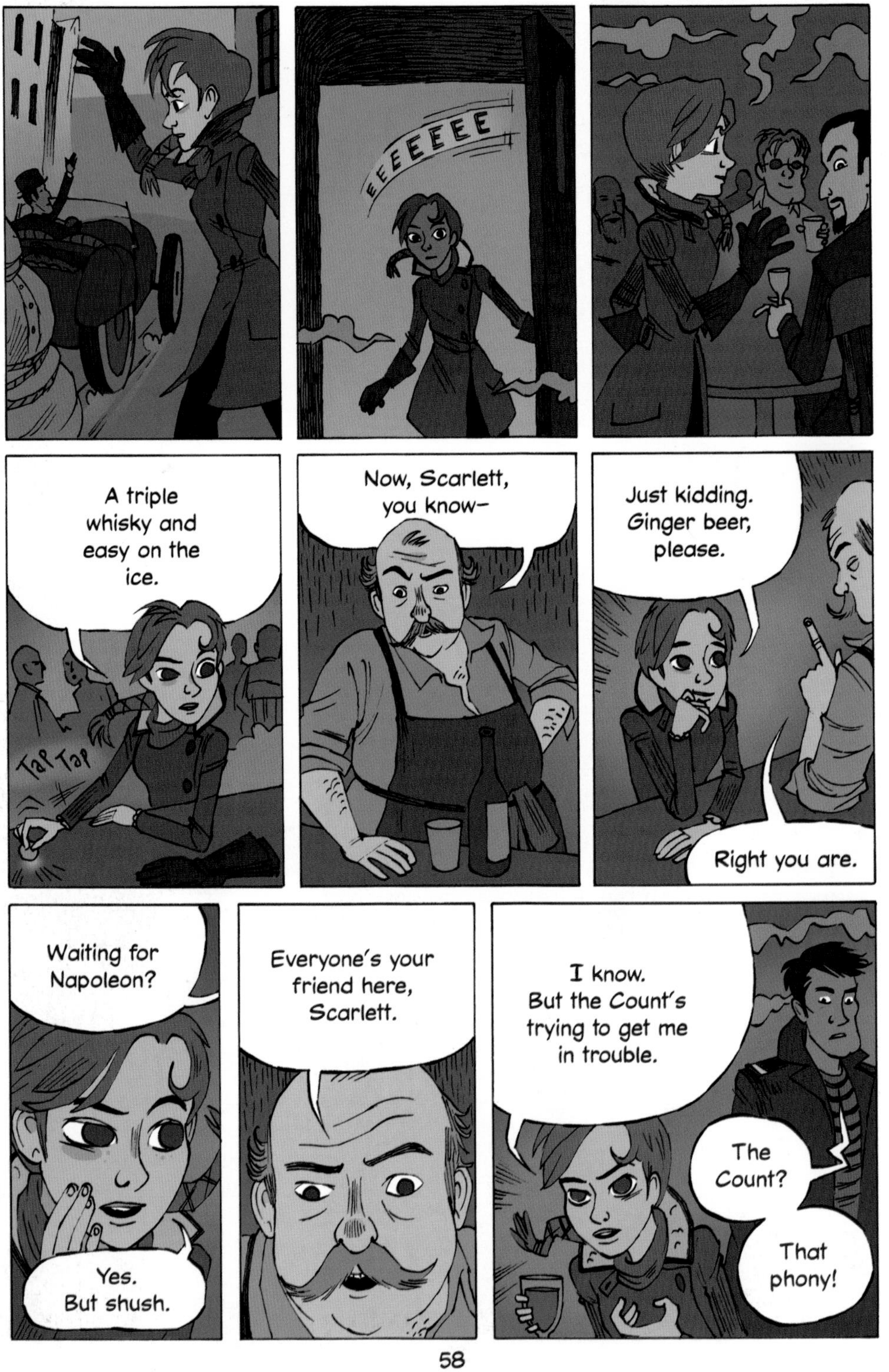
EEEEEEEE
A triple whisky and easy on the ice.
TAP TAP
Now, Scarlett, you know–
Just kidding. Ginger beer, please.
Right you are.
Waiting for Napoleon?
Yes. But shush.
Everyone's your friend here, Scarlett.
I know. But the Count's trying to get me in trouble.
The Count?
That phony!

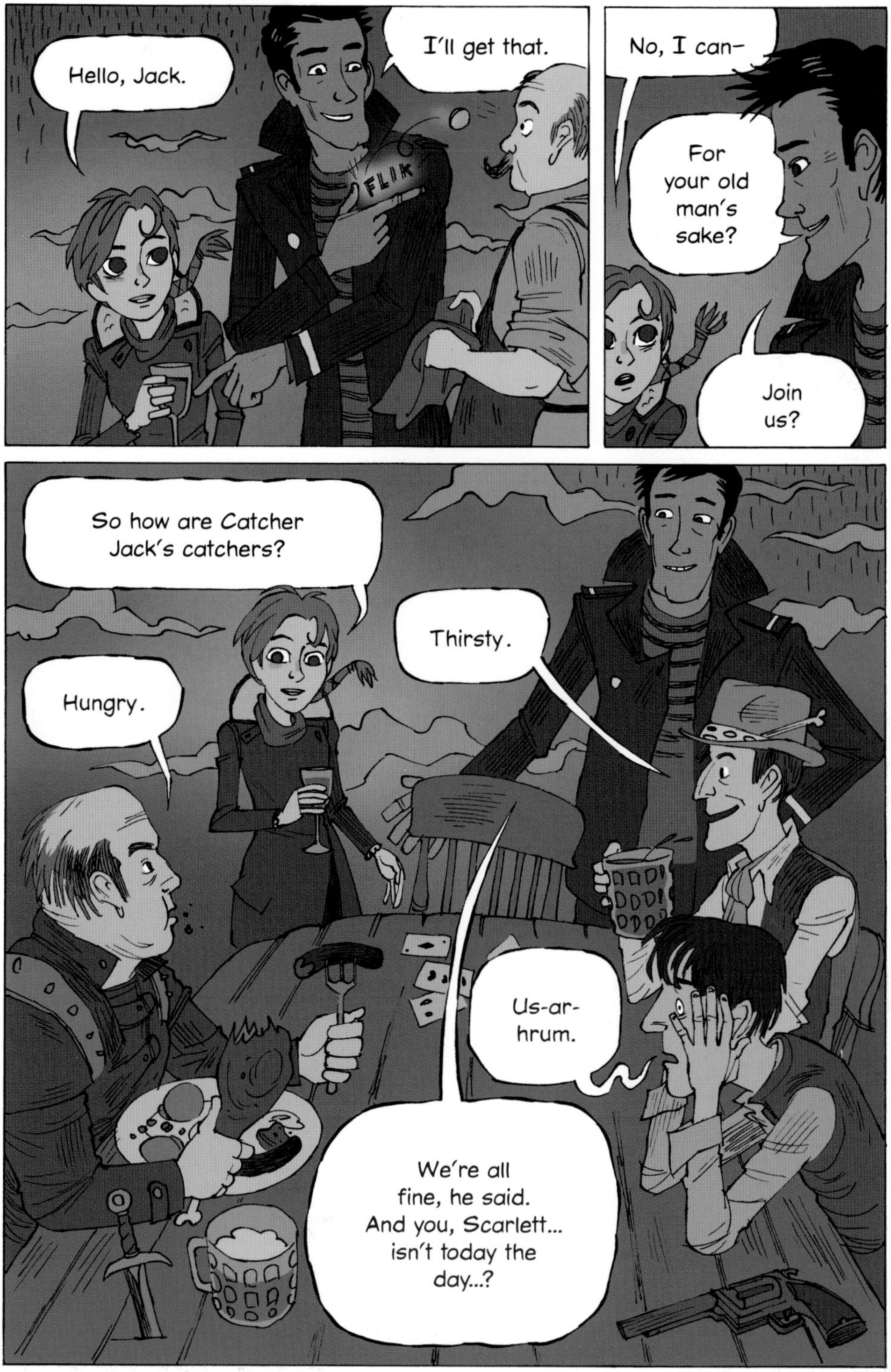
Hello, Jack.
I'll get that.
FLIK
No, I can-
For your old man's sake?
Join us?
So how are Catcher Jack's catchers?
Thirsty.
Hungry.
Us-ar-hrum.
We're all fine, he said. And you, Scarlett... isn't today the day...?

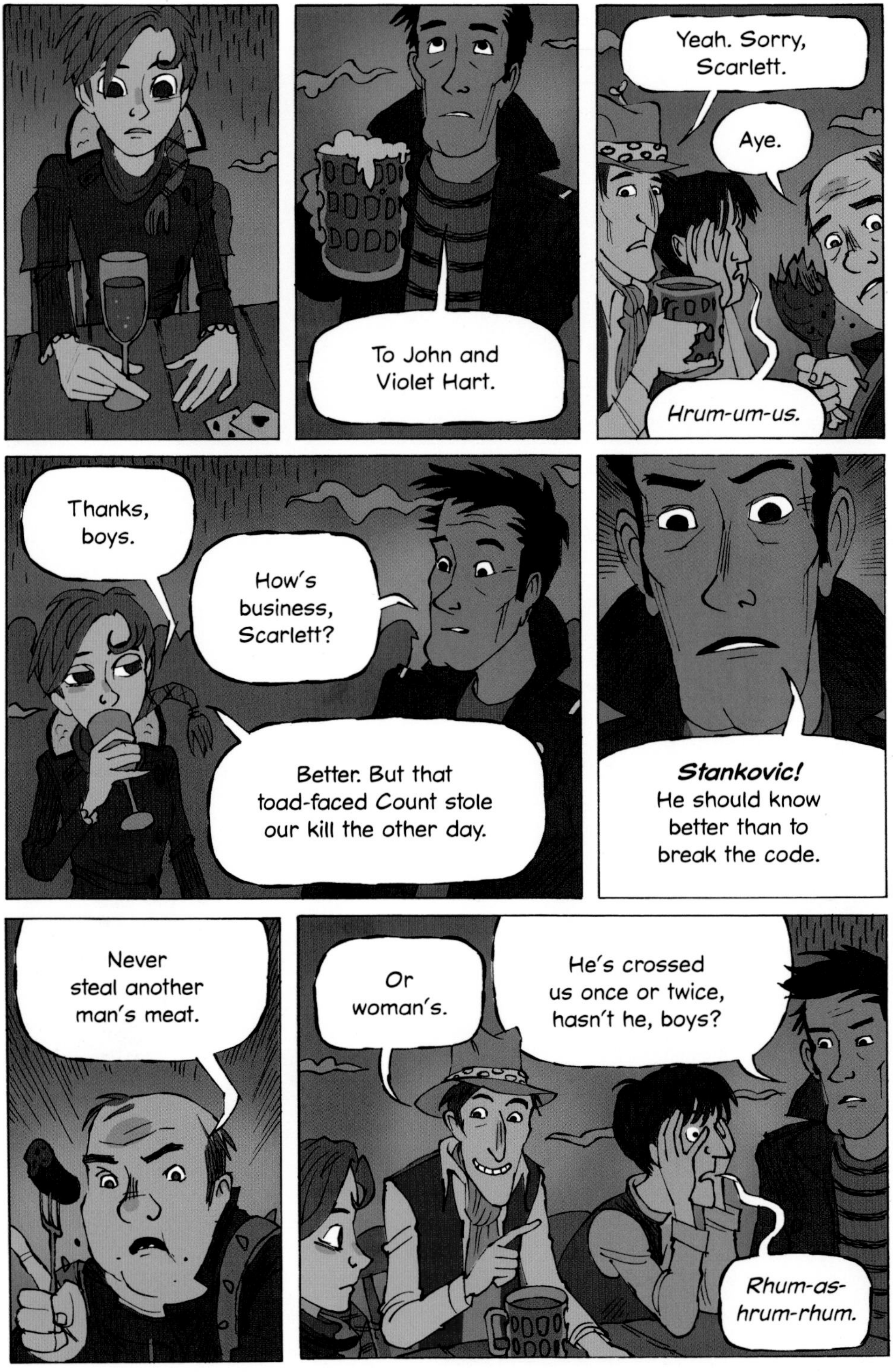
To John and Violet Hart.
Yeah. Sorry, Scarlett.
Aye.
Hrum-um-us.
Thanks, boys.
How's business, Scarlett?
Better. But that toad-faced Count stole our kill the other day.
Stankovic! He should know better than to break the code.
Never steal another man's meat.
Or woman's.
He's crossed us once or twice, hasn't he, boys?
Rhum-as-hrum-rhum.

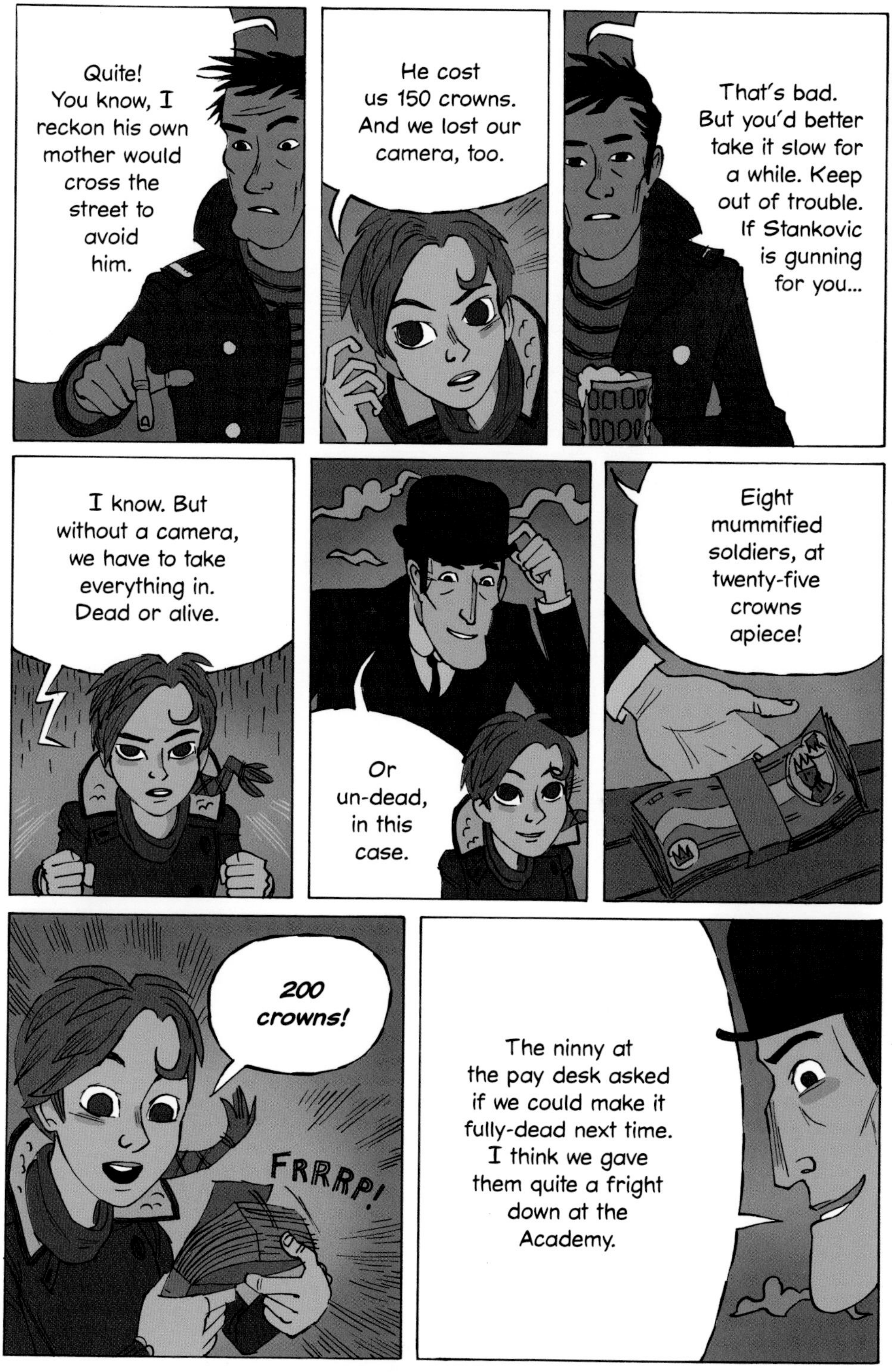

Quite! You know, I reckon his own mother would cross the street to avoid him.
He cost us 150 crowns. And we lost our camera, too.
That's bad. But you'd better take it slow for a while. Keep out of trouble. If Stankovic is gunning for you...
I know. But without a camera, we have to take everything in. Dead or alive.
Or un-dead, in this case.
Eight mummified soldiers, at twenty-five crowns apiece!
200 crowns!
FRRRP!
The ninny at the pay desk asked if we could make it fully-dead next time. I think we gave them quite a fright down at the Academy.

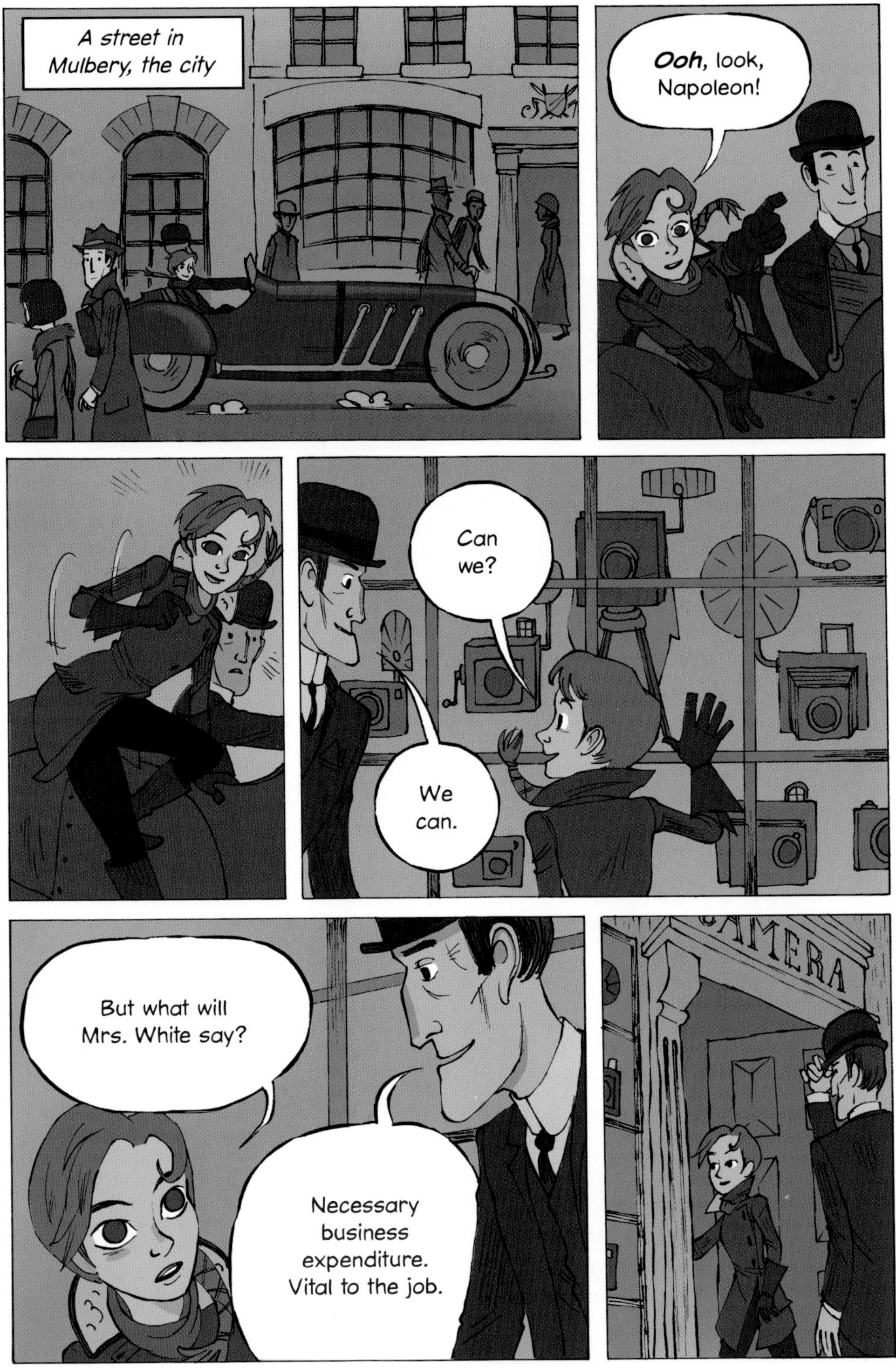
A street in Mulbery, the city
Ooh, look, Napoleon!
Can we?
We can.
But what will Mrs. White say?
Necessary business expenditure. Vital to the job.

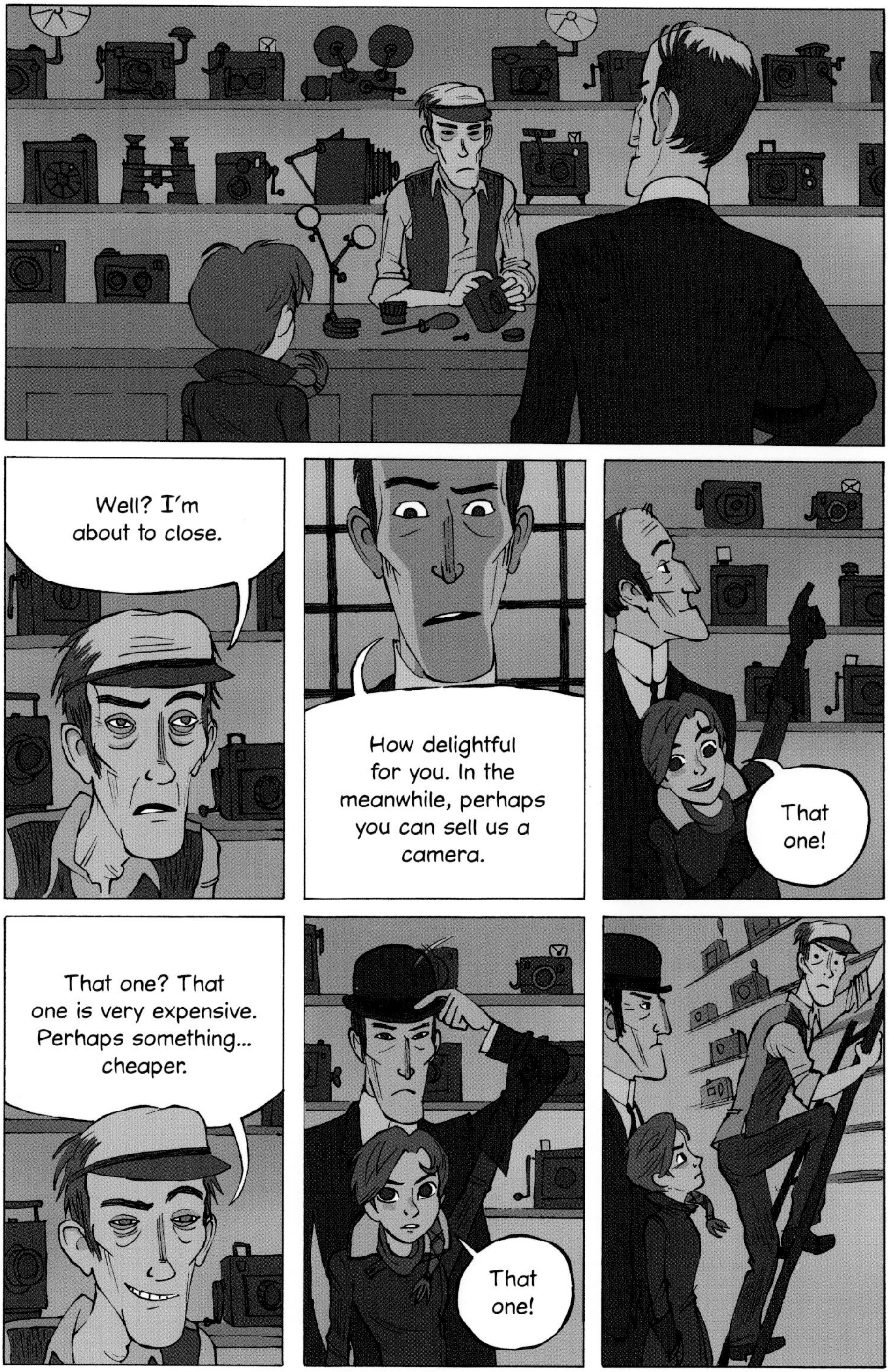
Well? I'm about to close.
How delightful for you. In the meanwhile, perhaps you can sell us a camera.
That one!
That one? That one is very expensive. Perhaps something... cheaper.
That one!

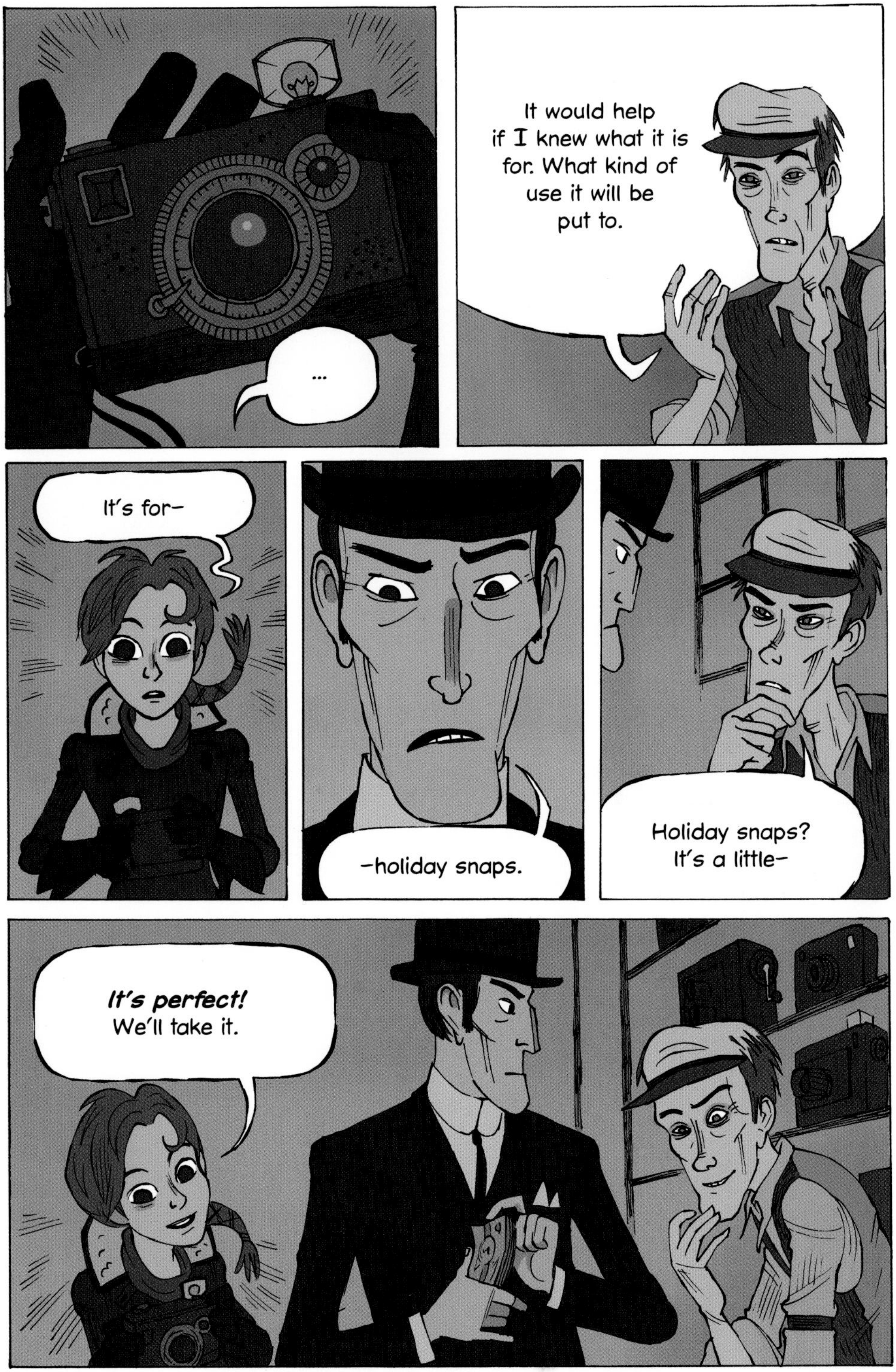
...
It would help if I knew what it is for. What kind of use it will be put to.
It's for–
–holiday snaps.
Holiday snaps? It's a little–
It's perfect! We'll take it.

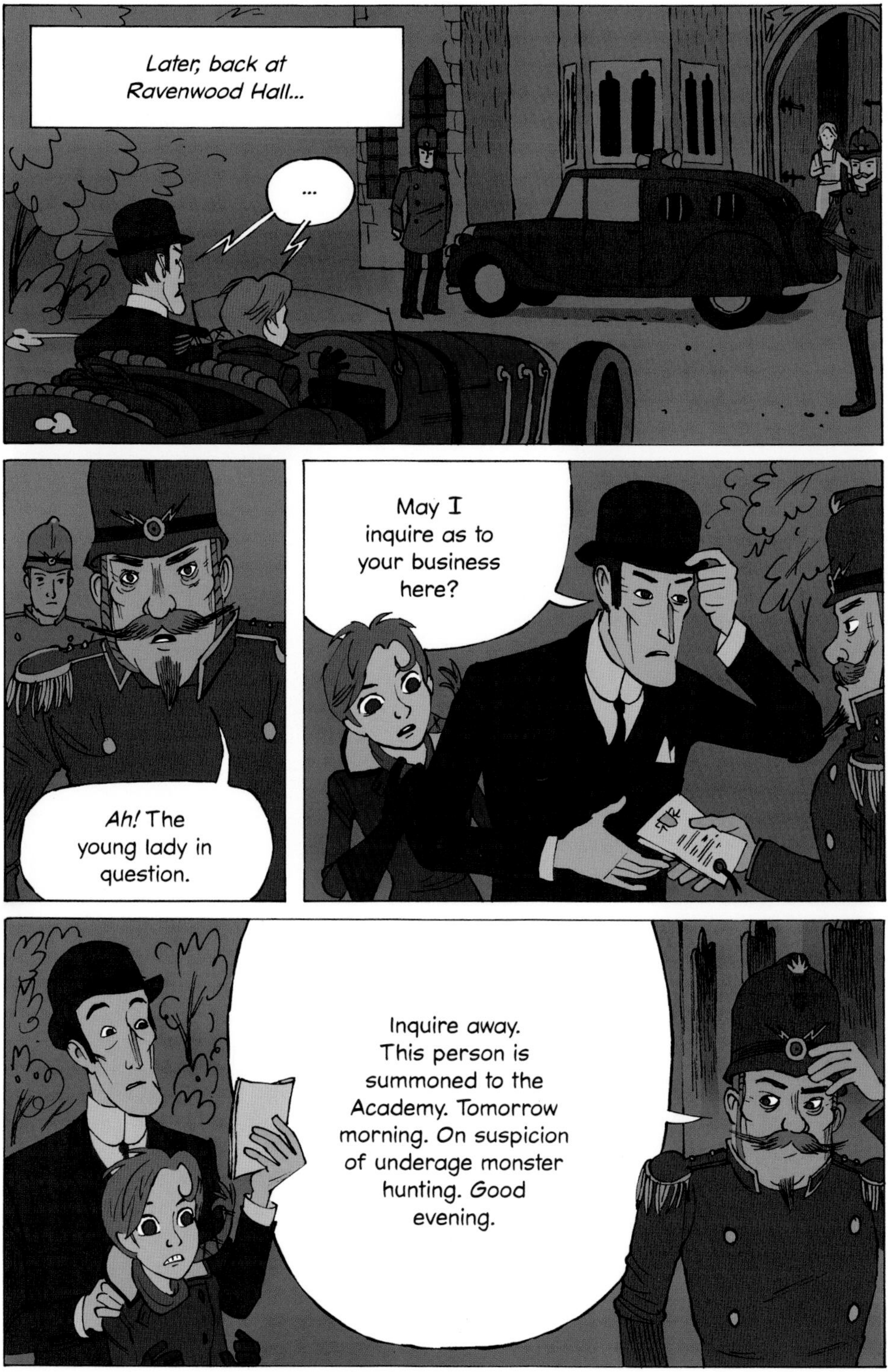
Later, back at Ravenwood Hall...
...
Ah! The young lady in question.
May I inquire as to your business here?
Inquire away. This person is summoned to the Academy. Tomorrow morning. On suspicion of underage monster hunting. Good evening.

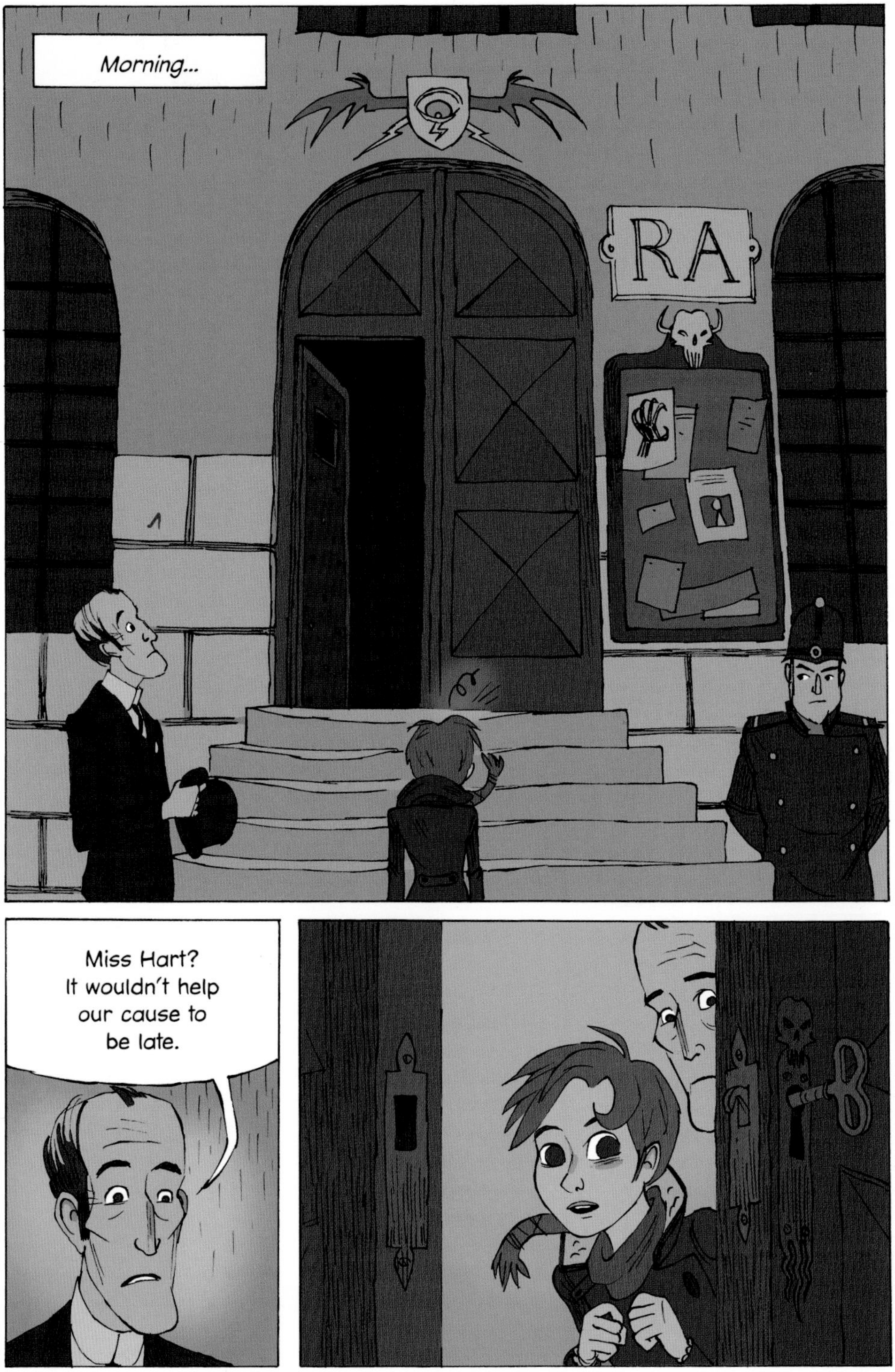
Morning...
RA
Miss Hart? It wouldn't help our cause to be late.

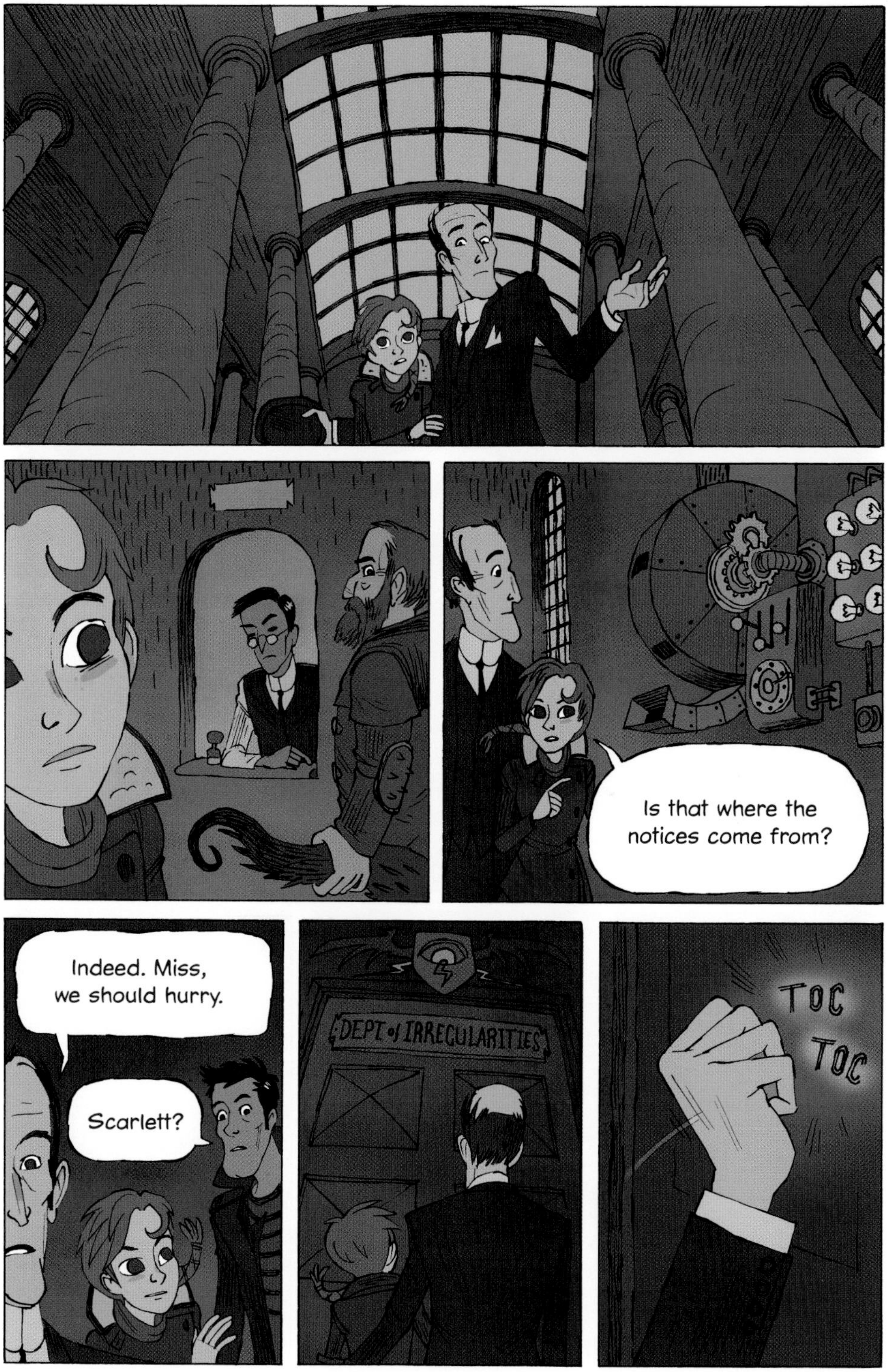

Is that where the notices come from?
Indeed. Miss, we should hurry.
Scarlett?
DEPT. of IRREGULARITIES
TOC
TOC

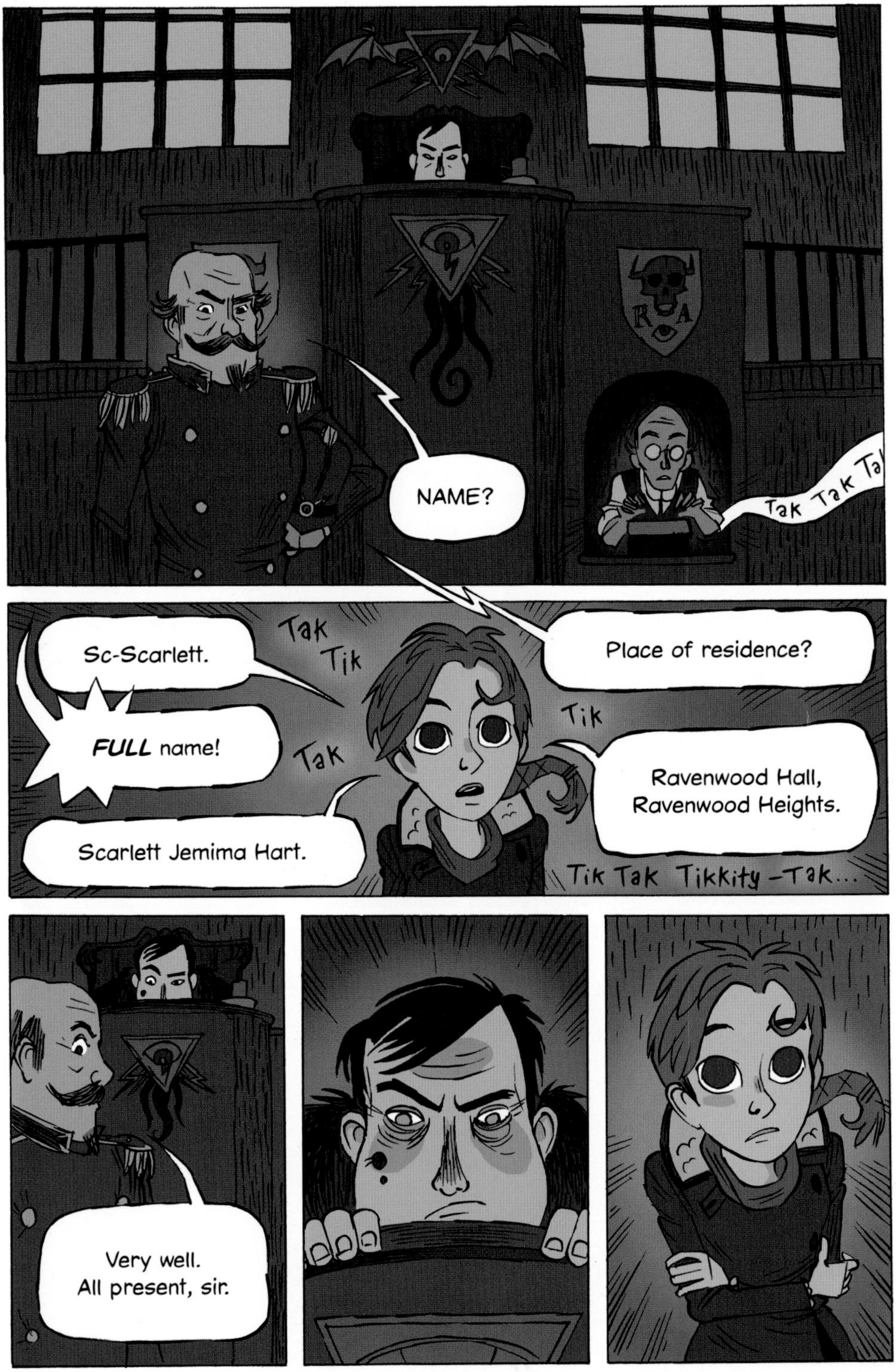
NAME?
Tak Tak Tak
Sc-Scarlett.
Tak
Tik
FULL name!
Tak
Scarlett Jemima Hart.
Place of residence?
Tik
Ravenwood Hall,
Ravenwood Heights.
Tik Tak Tikkity -Tak...
Very well.
All present, sir.

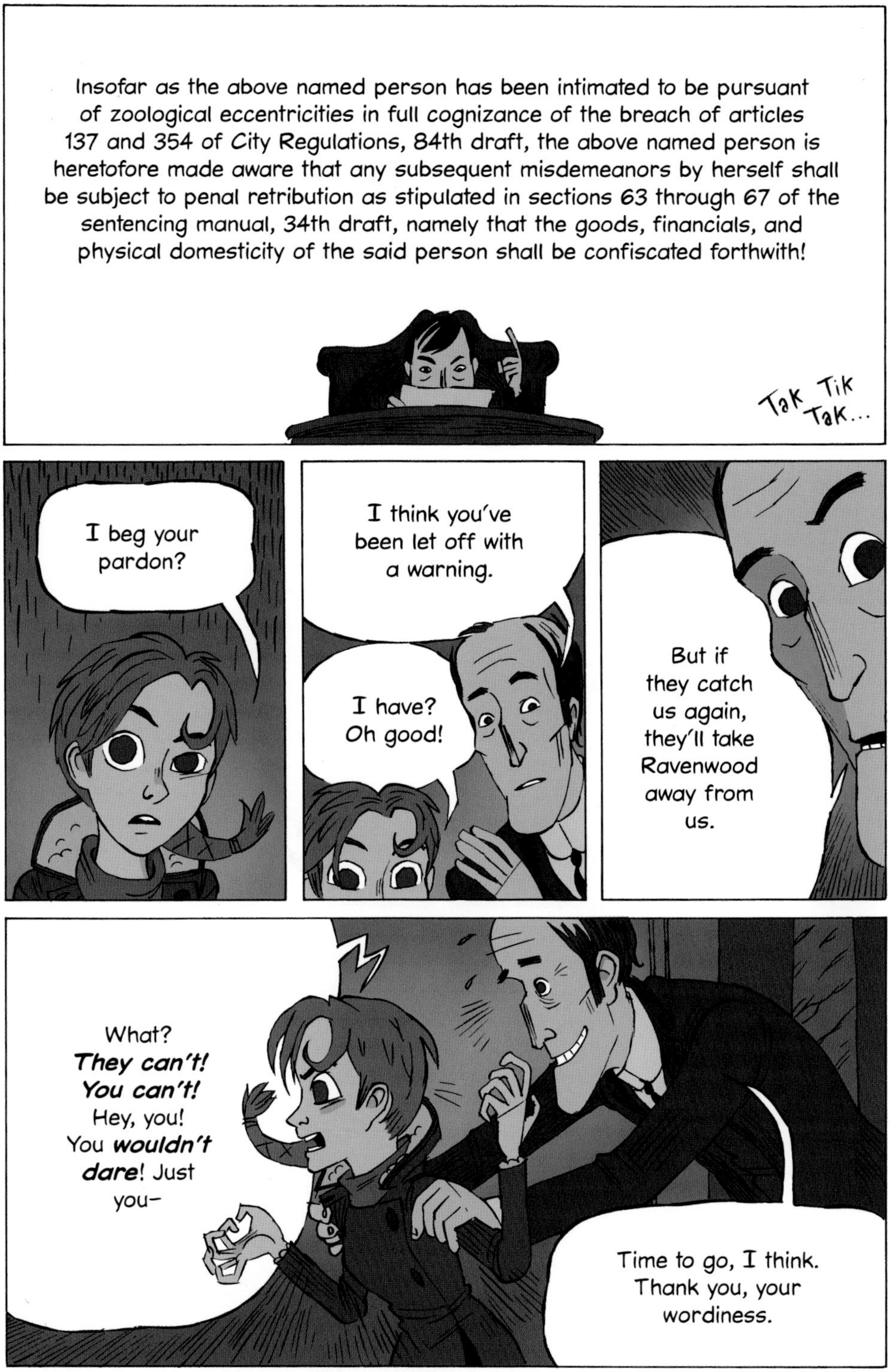
Insofar as the above named person has been intimated to be pursuant of zoological eccentricities in full cognizance of the breach of articles 137 and 354 of City Regulations, 84th draft, the above named person is heretofore made aware that any subsequent misdemeanors by herself shall be subject to penal retribution as stipulated in sections 63 through 67 of the sentencing manual, 34th draft, namely that the goods, financials, and physical domesticity of the said person shall be confiscated forthwith!
Tak Tik Tak...
I beg your pardon?
I think you've been let off with a warning.
I have? Oh good!
But if they catch us again, they'll take Ravenwood away from us.
What? ***They can't! You can't!*** Hey, you! You ***wouldn't dare***! Just you–
Time to go, I think. Thank you, your wordiness.

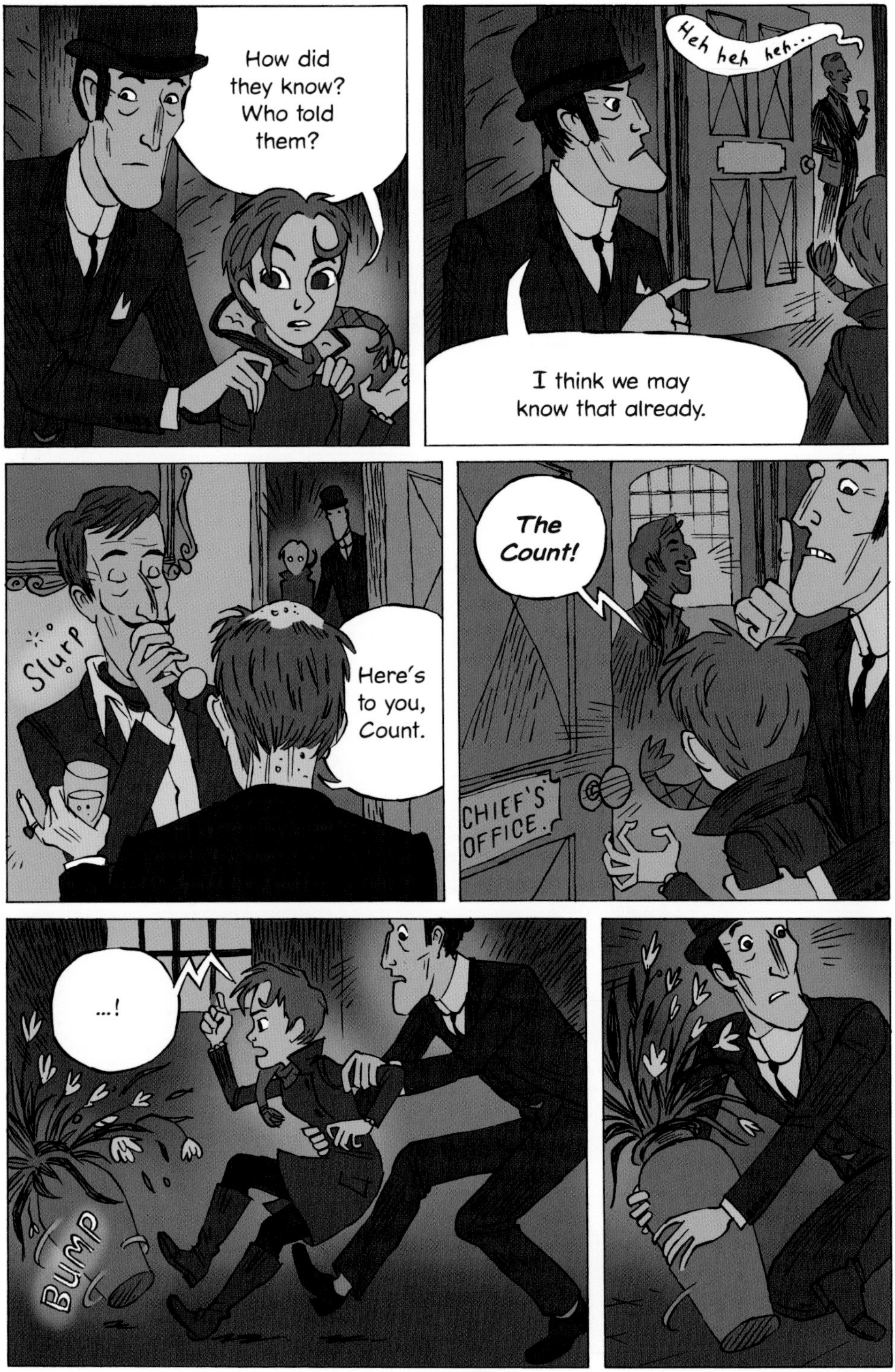
How did they know? Who told them?
Heh heh heh...
I think we may know that already.
Slurp
Here's to you, Count.
The Count!
CHIEF'S OFFICE.
...!
BUMP

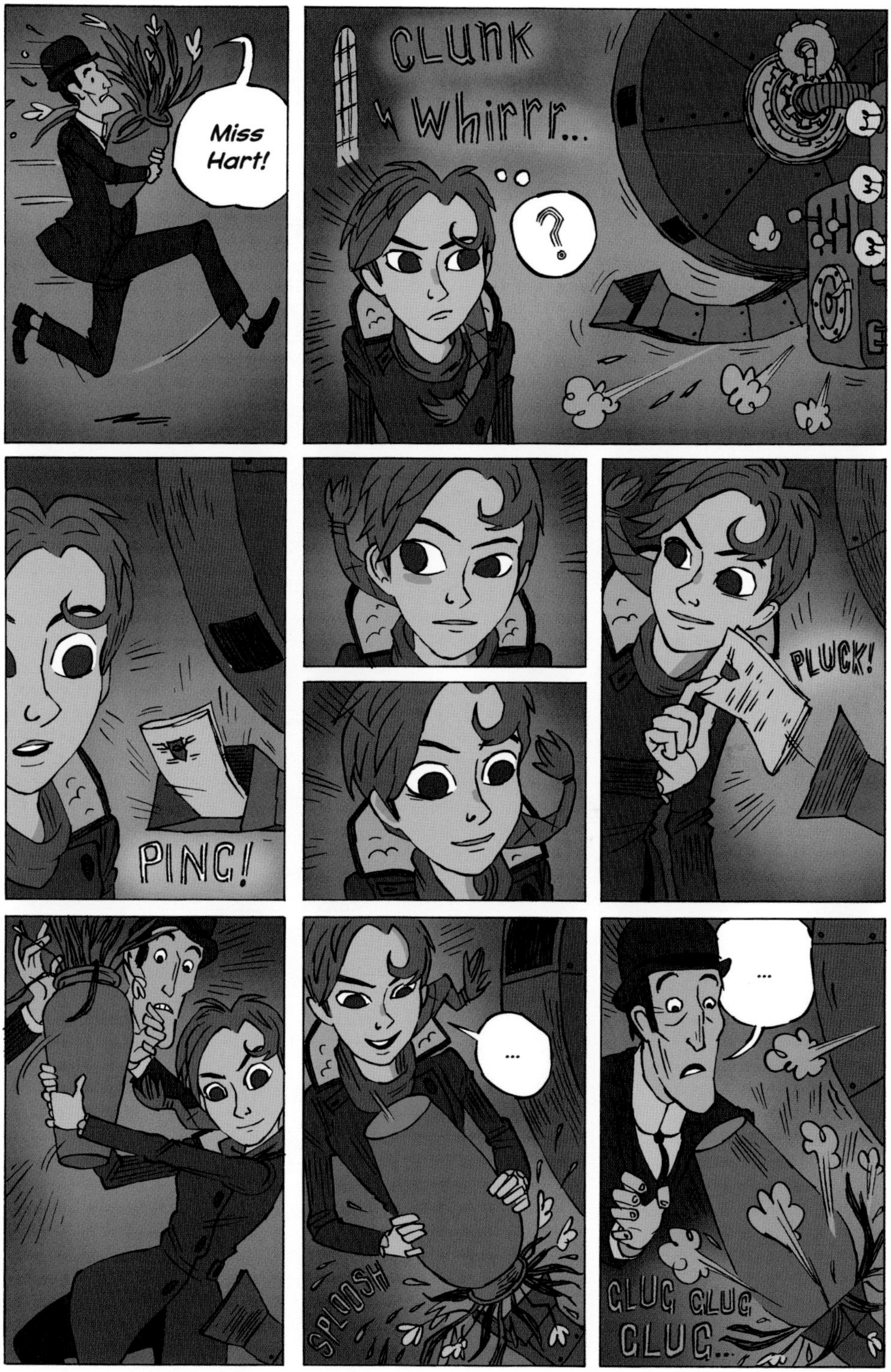
Miss Hart!
CLUNK
Whirrr...
?
PING!
PLUCK!
...
SPLOOSH
...
CLUG CLUG
CLUG...

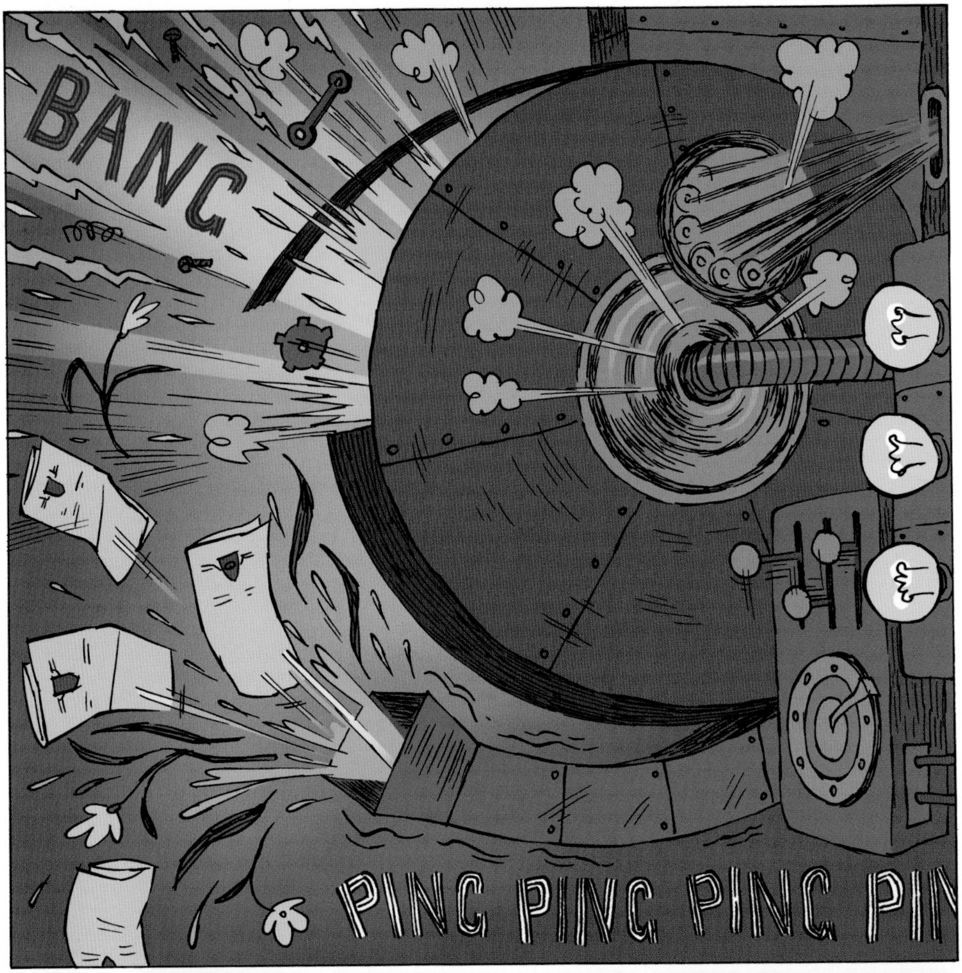
BANG
PING PING PING PI

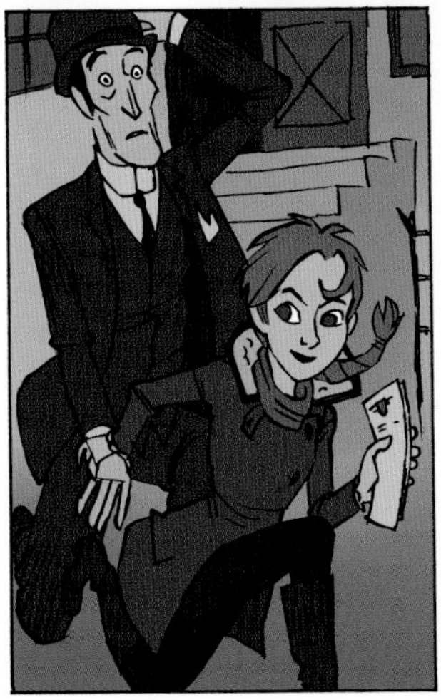

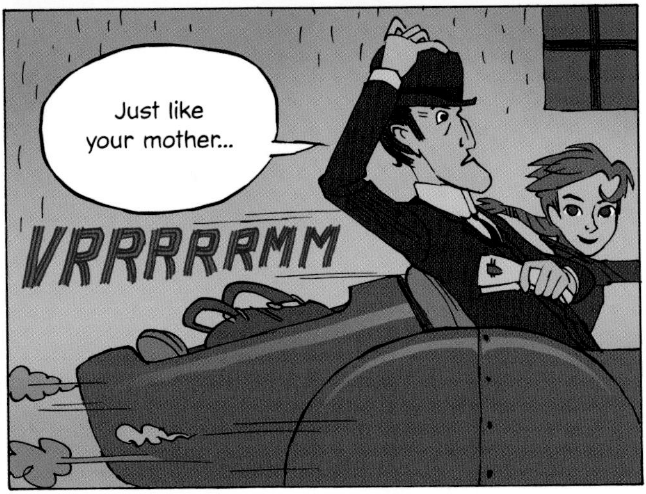
Just like your mother...
VRRRRRMM

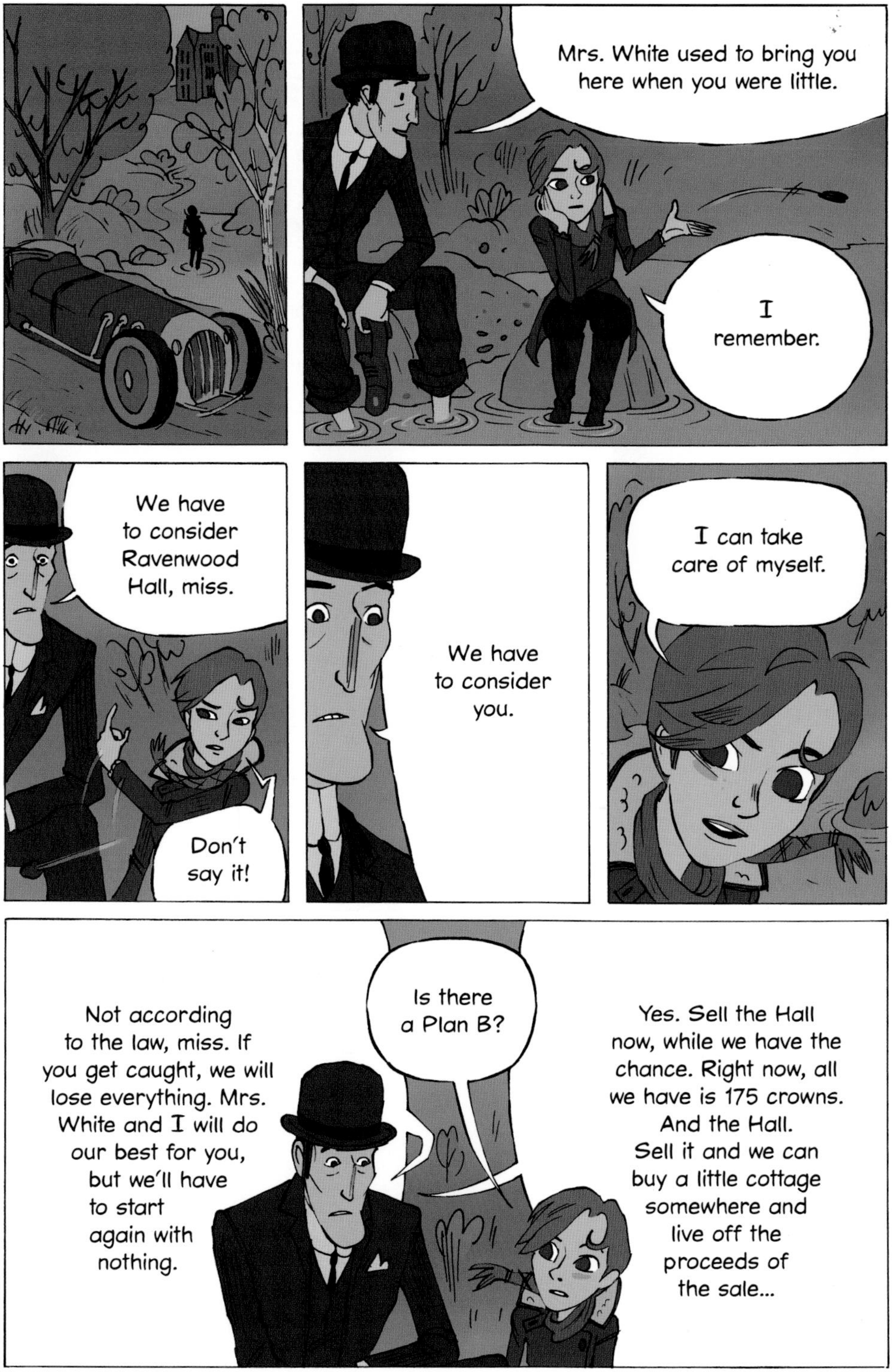

Mrs. White used to bring you here when you were little.
I remember.
We have to consider Ravenwood Hall, miss.
Don't say it!
We have to consider you.
I can take care of myself.
Not according to the law, miss. If you get caught, we will lose everything. Mrs. White and I will do our best for you, but we'll have to start again with nothing.
Is there a Plan B?
Yes. Sell the Hall now, while we have the chance. Right now, all we have is 175 crowns. And the Hall. Sell it and we can buy a little cottage somewhere and live off the proceeds of the sale...

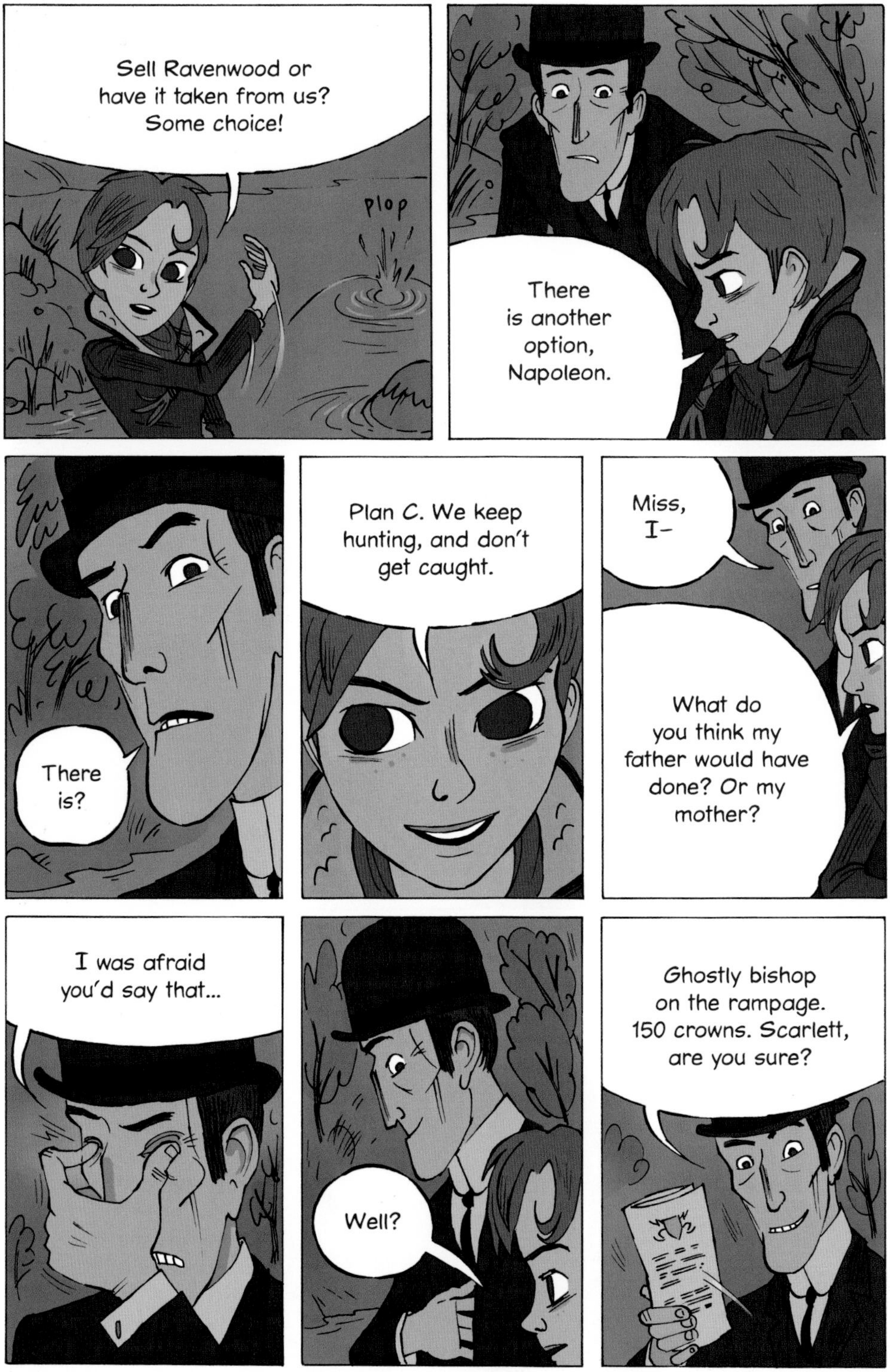
Sell Ravenwood or have it taken from us? Some choice!
plop
There is another option, Napoleon.
There is?
Plan C. We keep hunting, and don't get caught.
Miss, I-
What do you think my father would have done? Or my mother?
I was afraid you'd say that...
Well?
Ghostly bishop on the rampage. 150 crowns. Scarlett, are you sure?

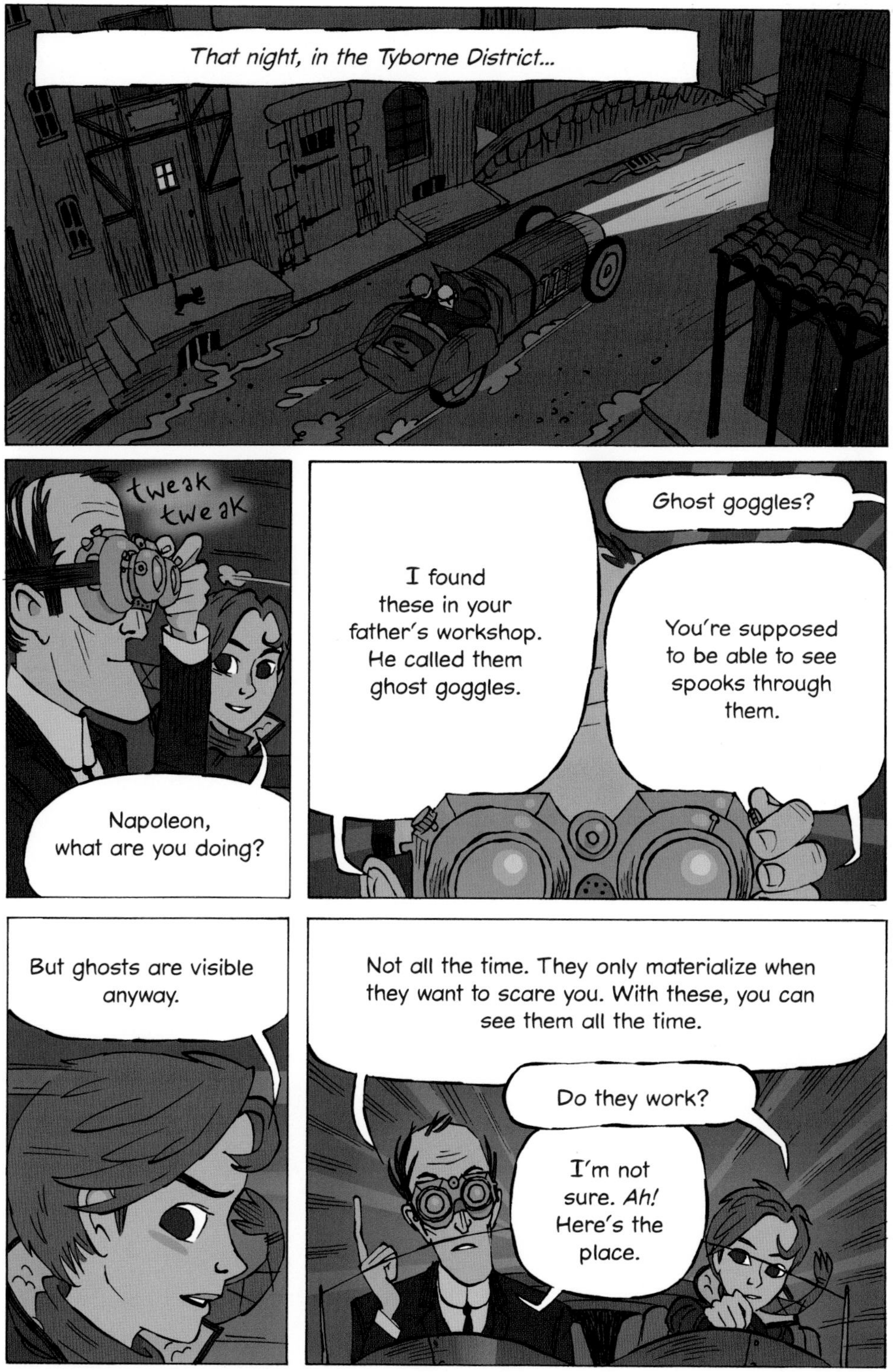
That night, in the Tyborne District...
tweak tweak
Napoleon, what are you doing?
I found these in your father's workshop. He called them ghost goggles.
Ghost goggles?
You're supposed to be able to see spooks through them.
But ghosts are visible anyway.
Not all the time. They only materialize when they want to scare you. With these, you can see them all the time.
Do they work?
I'm not sure. *Ah!* Here's the place.

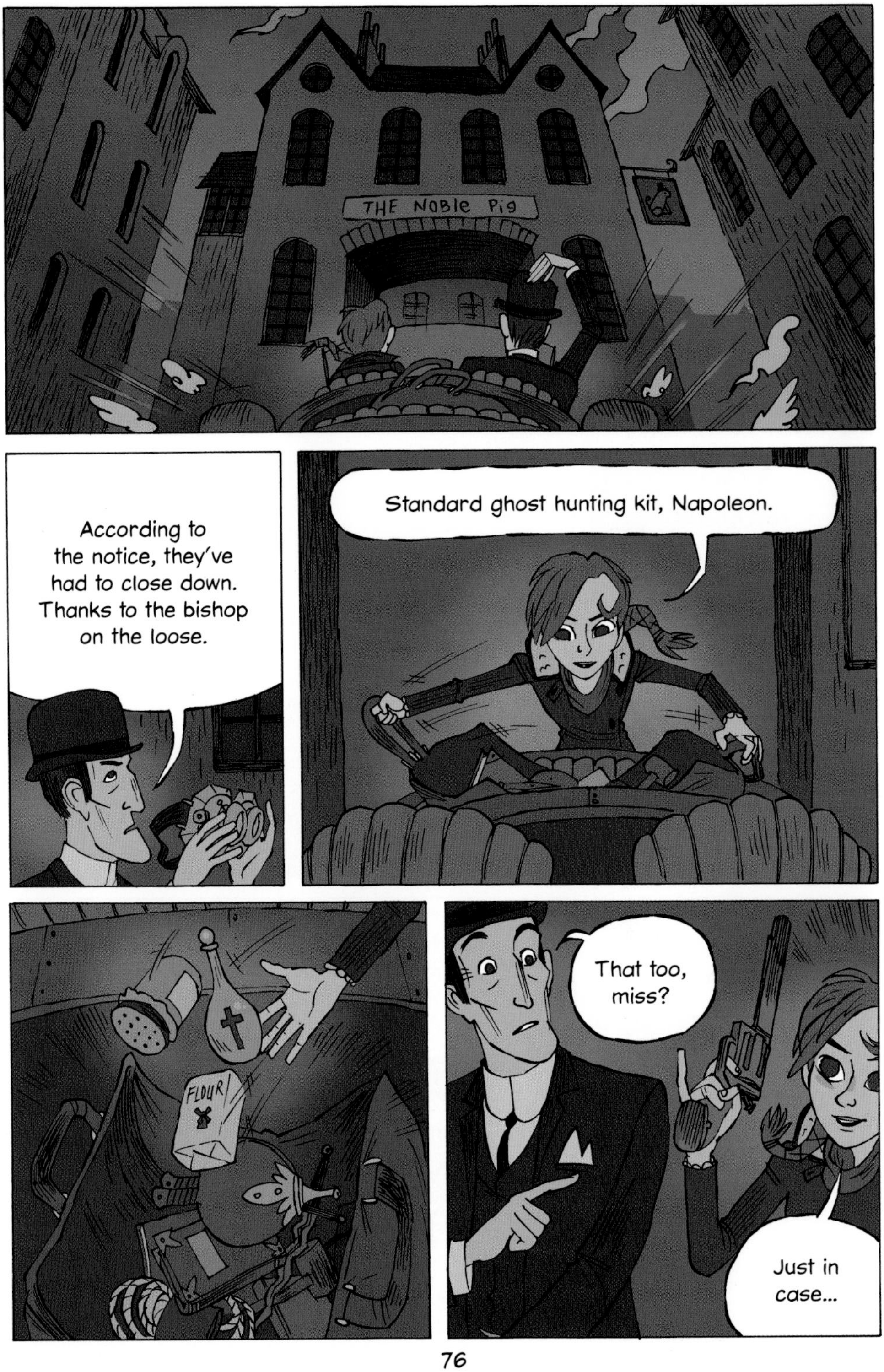
THE NOBLE PIG
According to the notice, they've had to close down. Thanks to the bishop on the loose.
Standard ghost hunting kit, Napoleon.
FLOUR
That too, miss?
Just in case...

The trouble with ghost hunting is you have to do it at night.

Scared, miss?

Of course not!

Nor I.

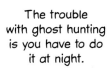

Whirrrr......

All clear.

Let's try upstairs.

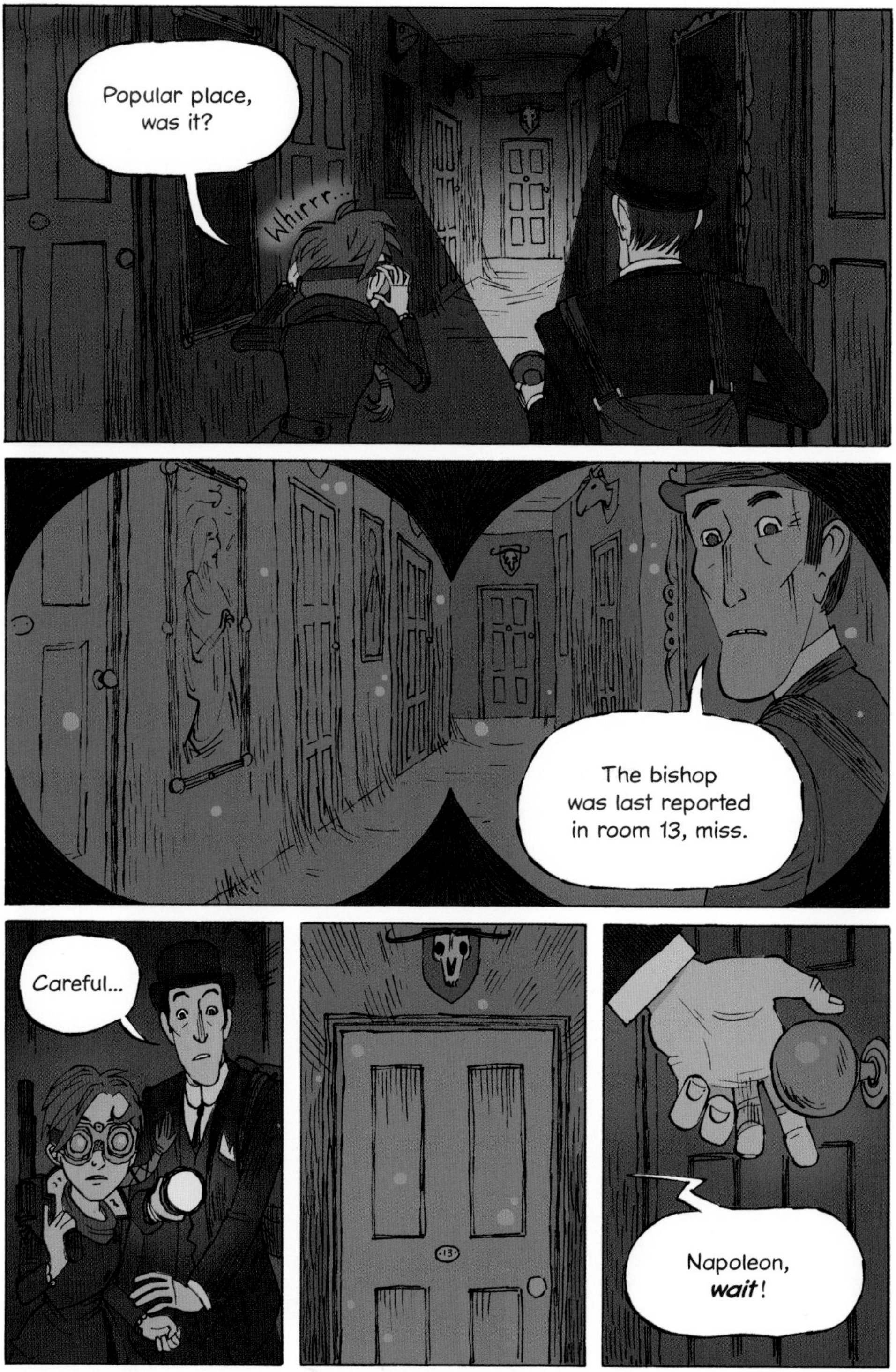
Popular place, was it?
Whirrr...
The bishop was last reported in room 13, miss.
Careful...
13
Napoleon, ***wait***!

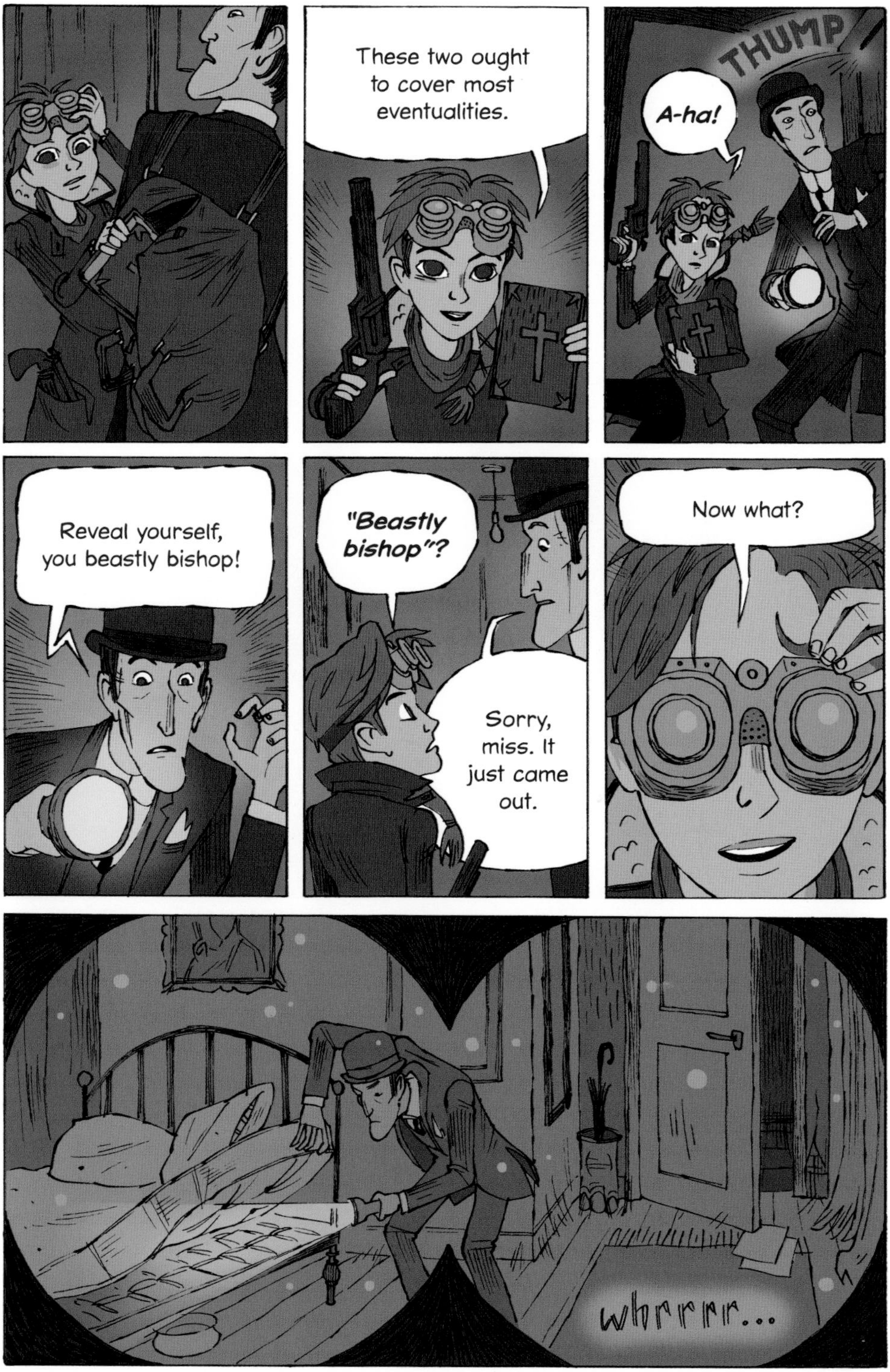
These two ought to cover most eventualities.
THUMP
A-ha!
Reveal yourself, you beastly bishop!
"Beastly bishop"?
Sorry, miss. It just came out.
Now what?
whrrrr...

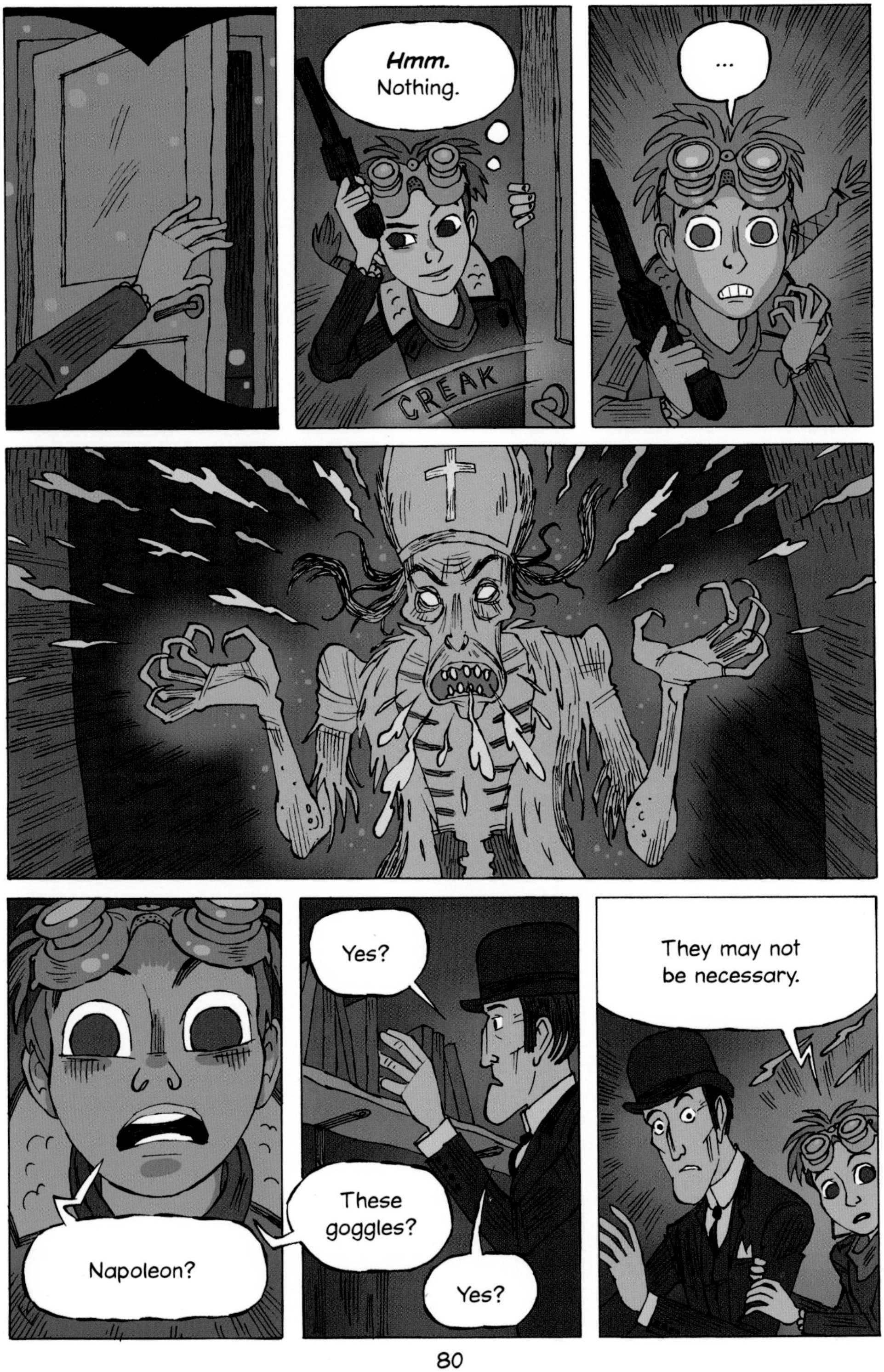
Hmm. Nothing.
CREAK
...
Napoleon?
Yes?
These goggles?
Yes?
They may not be necessary.

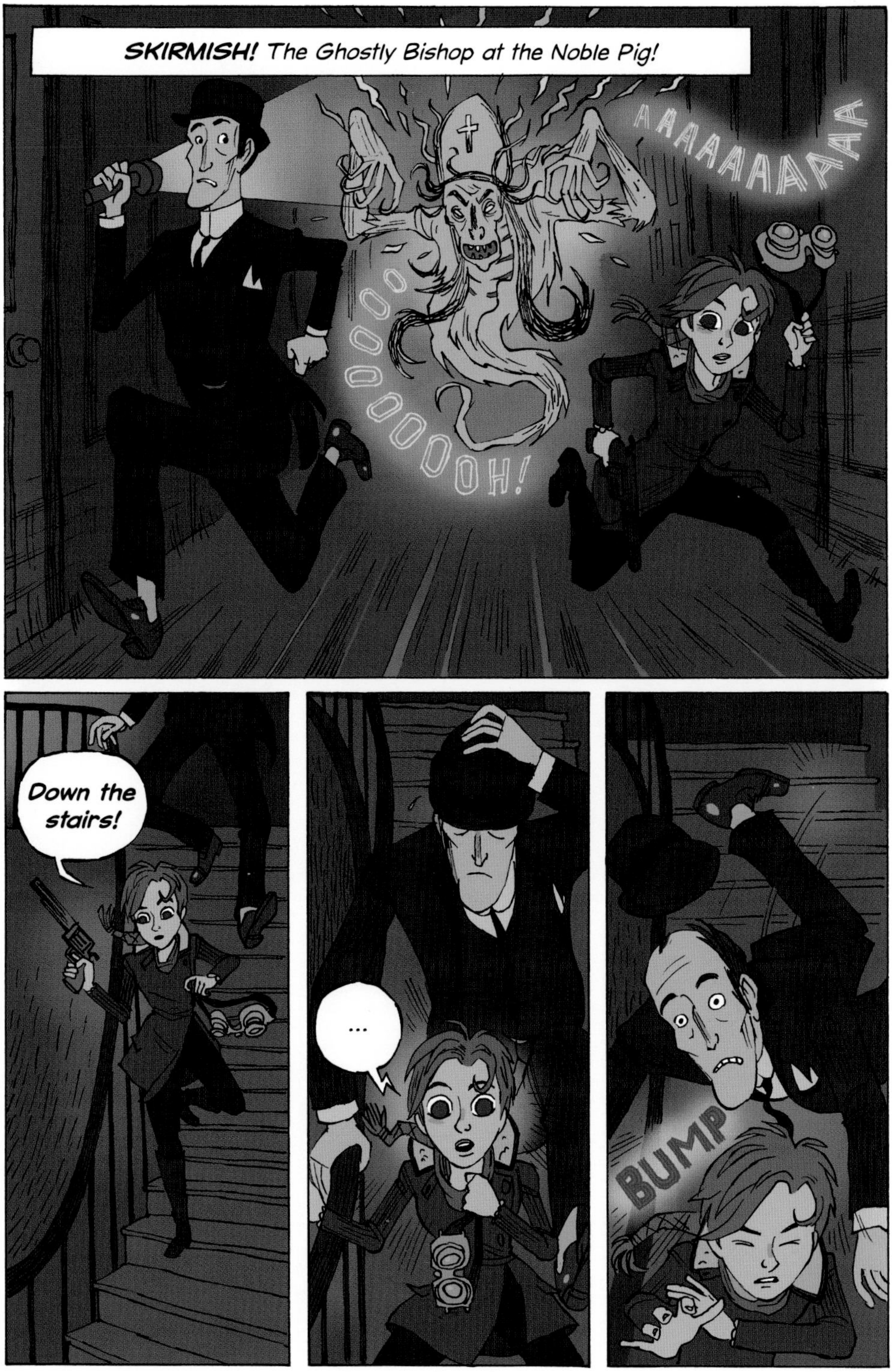
SKIRMISH! The Ghostly Bishop at the Noble Pig!
AAAAAAAAAAAA
OOOOOOOOOOOOH!
Down the stairs!
...
BUMP

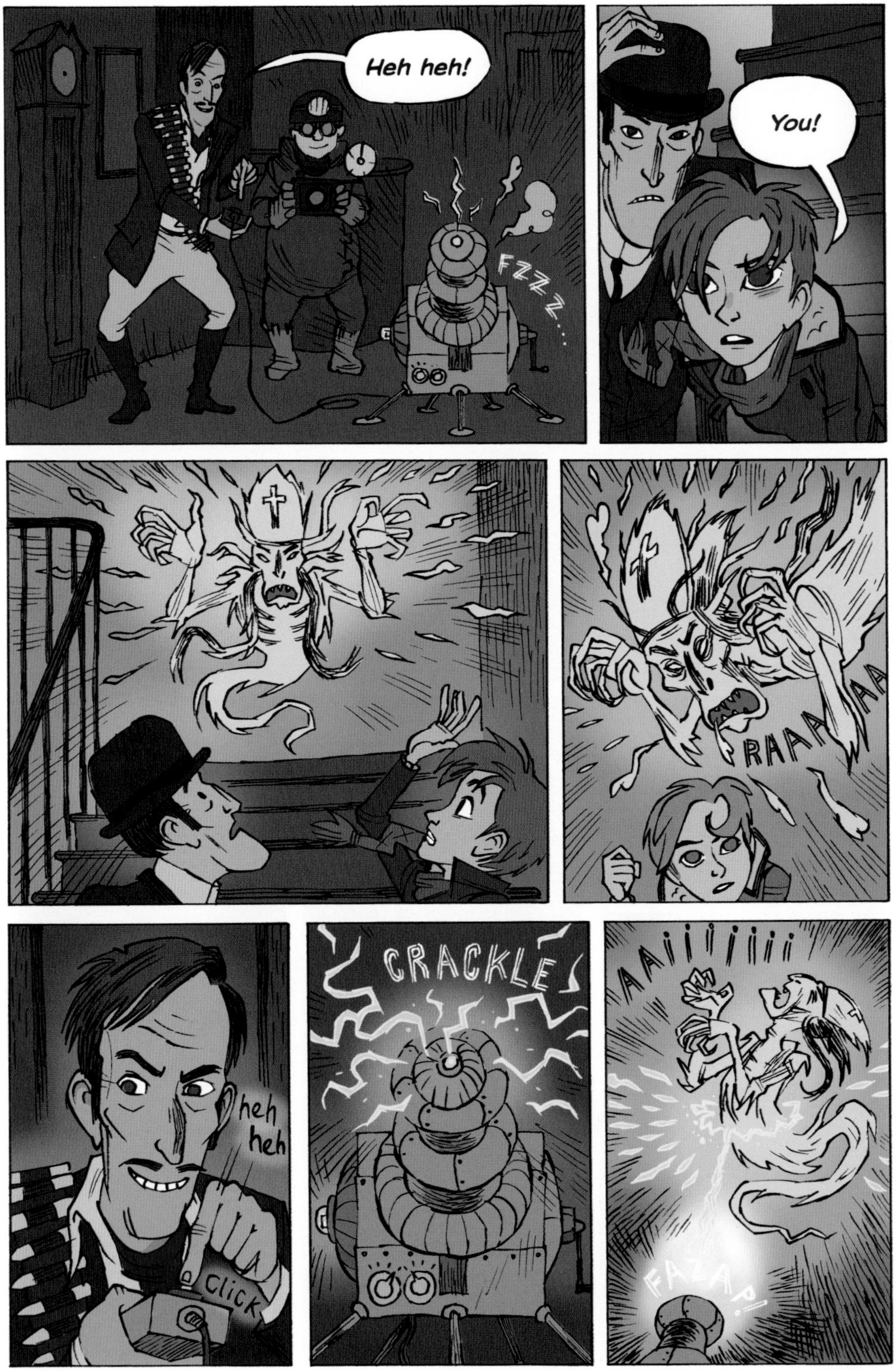
Heh heh!
FZZZZ...
You!
RAAAAA
heh heh
CLICK
CRACKLE
AAiiiiiiii
FAZAP!

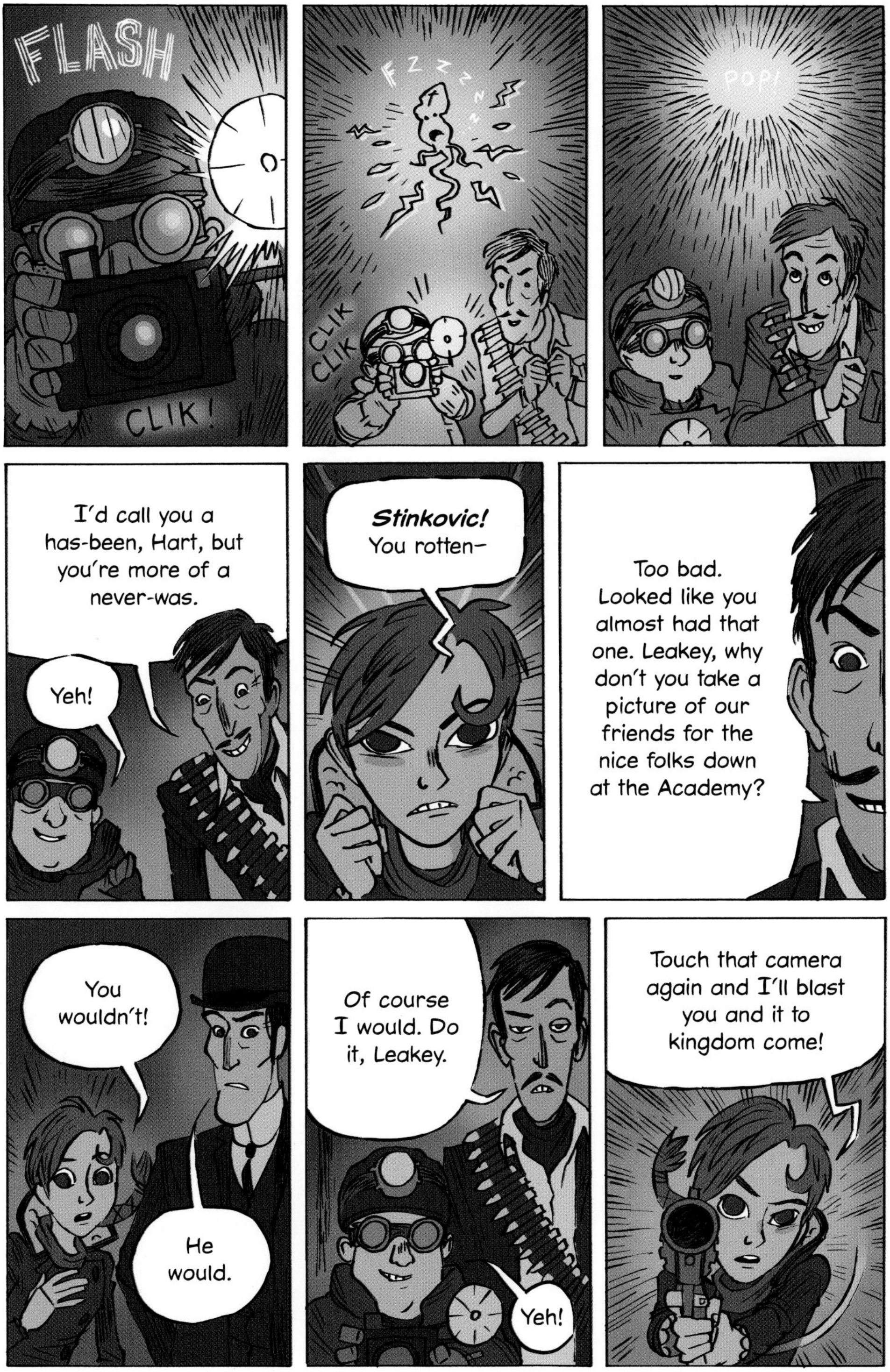
FLASH
CLIK!
FZZZZZ
CLIK
CLIK
POP!
I'd call you a has-been, Hart, but you're more of a never-was.
Yeh!
Stinkovic! You rotten–
Too bad. Looked like you almost had that one. Leakey, why don't you take a picture of our friends for the nice folks down at the Academy?
You wouldn't!
He would.
Of course I would. Do it, Leakey.
Yeh!
Touch that camera again and I'll blast you and it to kingdom come!

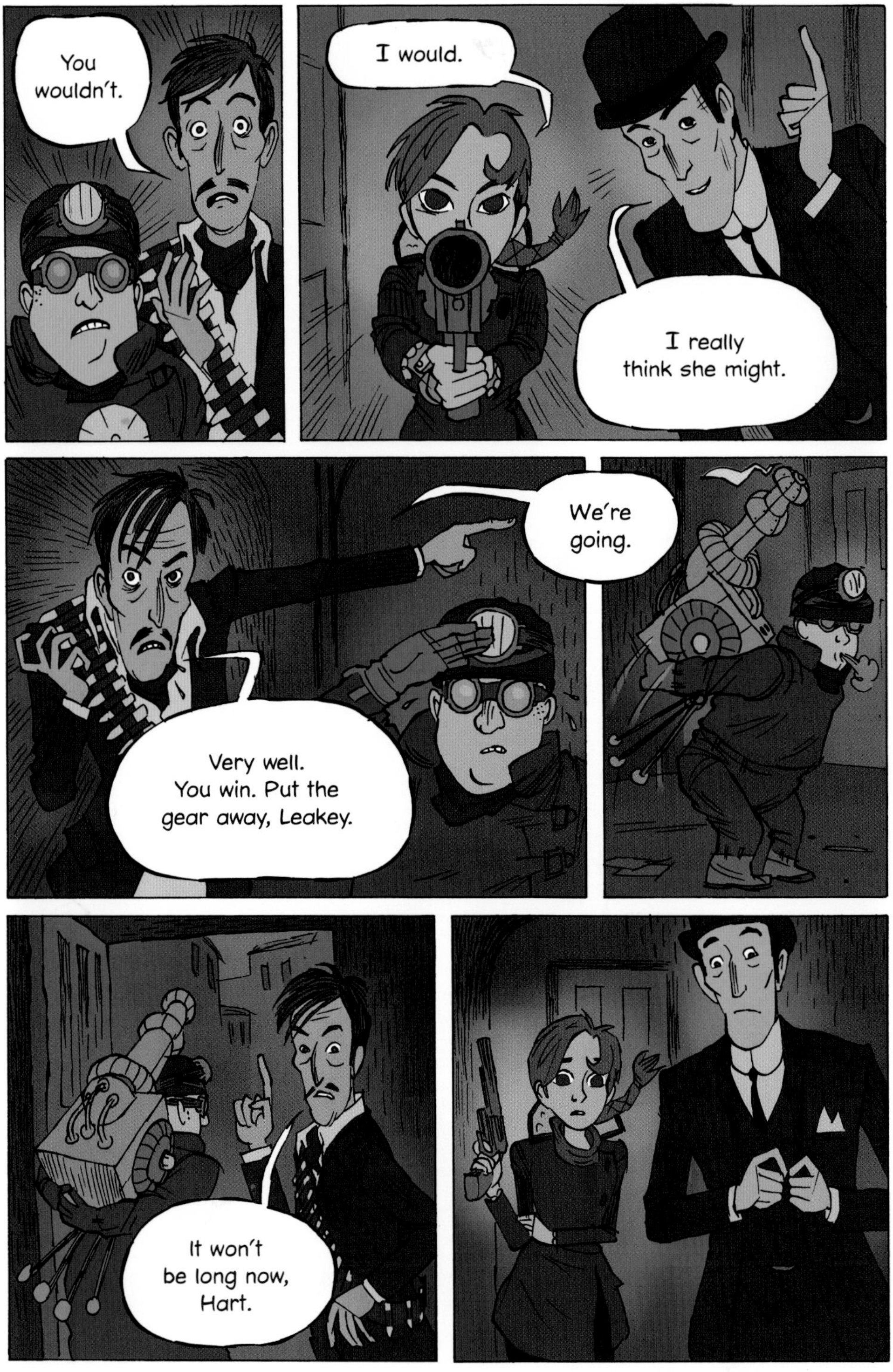
You wouldn't.
I would.
I really think she might.
We're going.
Very well. You win. Put the gear away, Leakey.
It won't be long now, Hart.

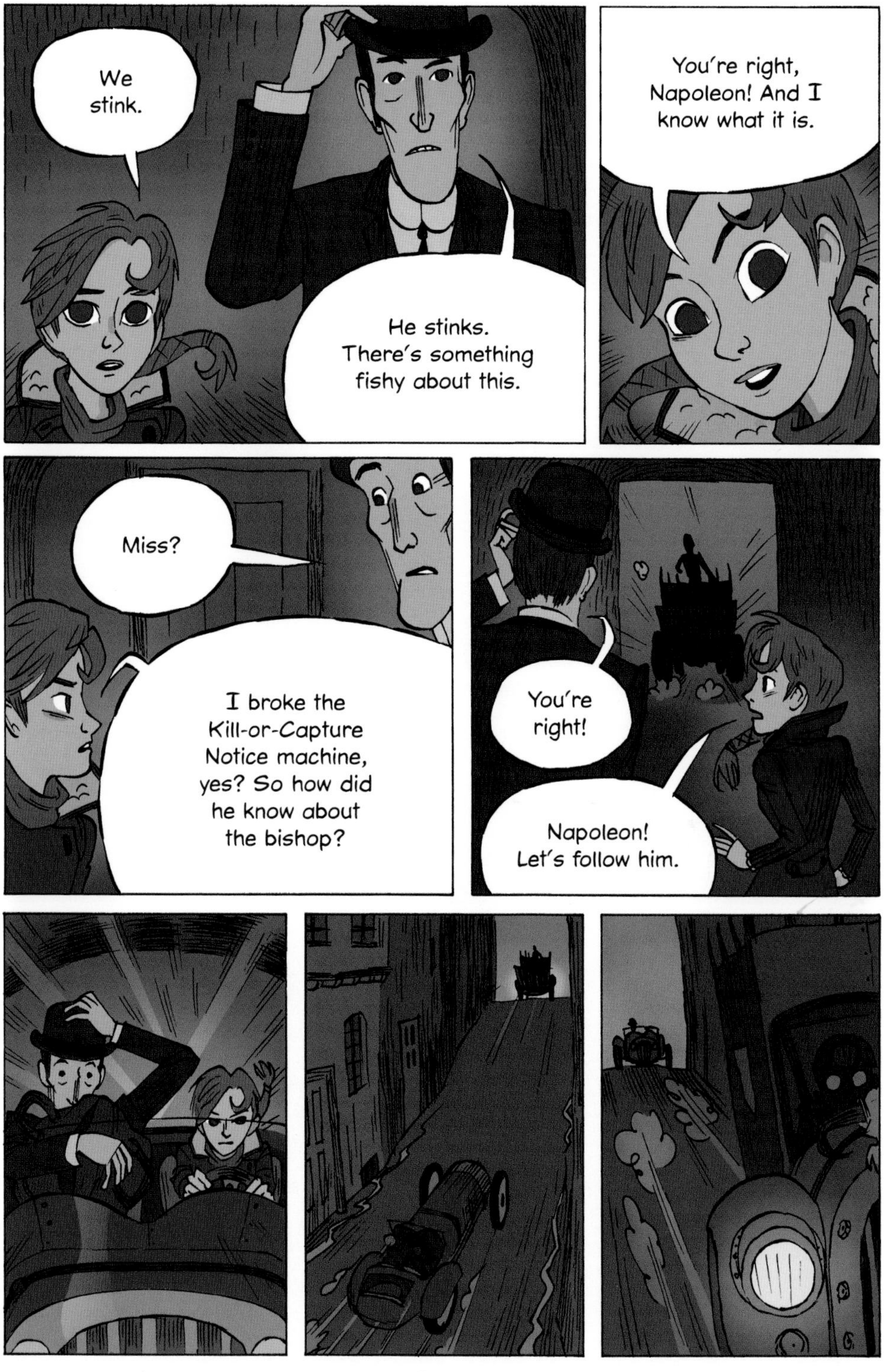
We stink.
He stinks. There's something fishy about this.
You're right, Napoleon! And I know what it is.
Miss?
I broke the Kill-or-Capture Notice machine, yes? So how did he know about the bishop?
You're right!
Napoleon! Let's follow him.

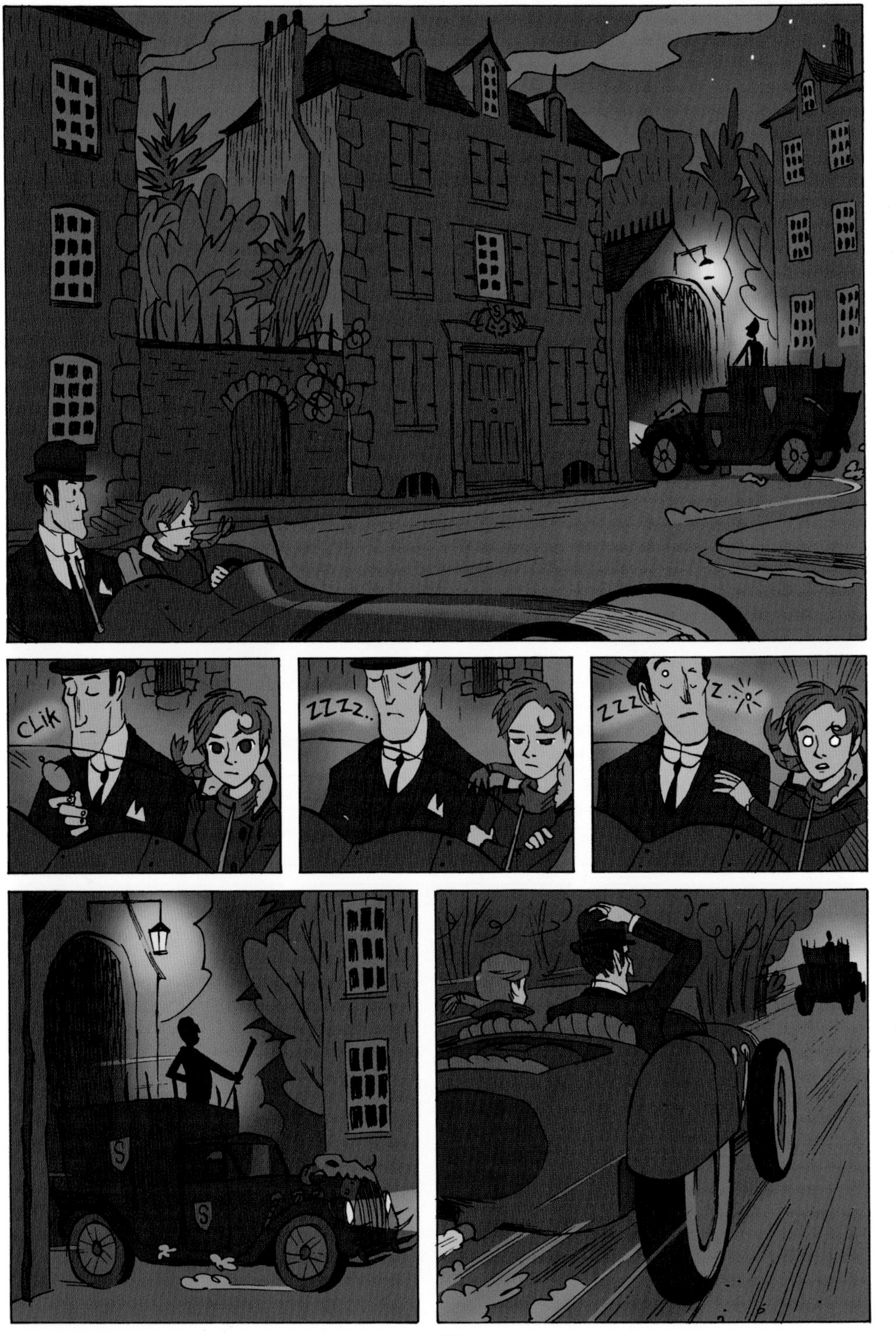
CLik
ZZZZ..
ZZZ
Z..

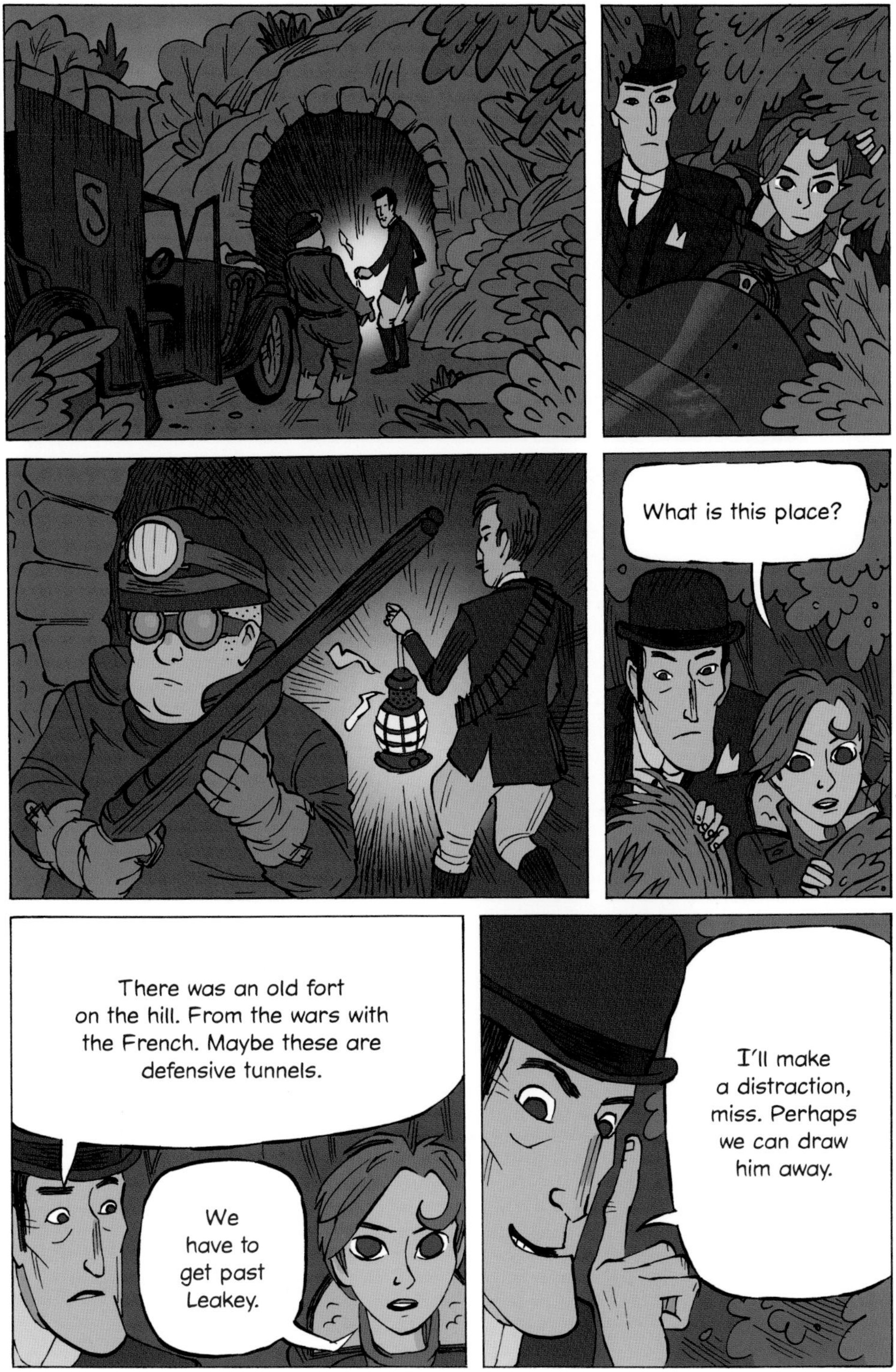
What is this place?
There was an old fort on the hill. From the wars with the French. Maybe these are defensive tunnels.
We have to get past Leakey.
I'll make a distraction, miss. Perhaps we can draw him away.

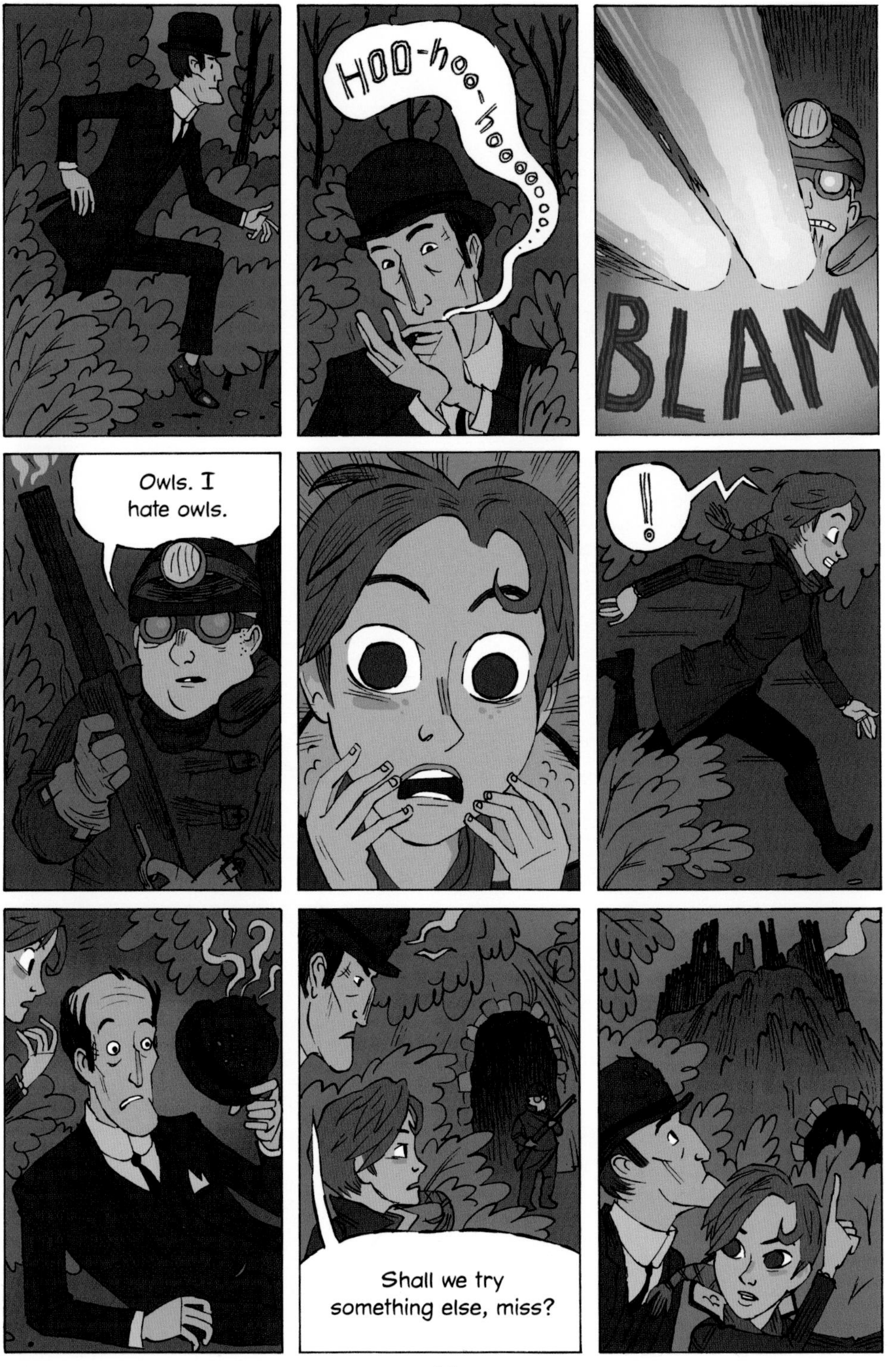
HOO-hoo-hoooooo...
BLAM
Owls. I hate owls.
!!
Shall we try something else, miss?

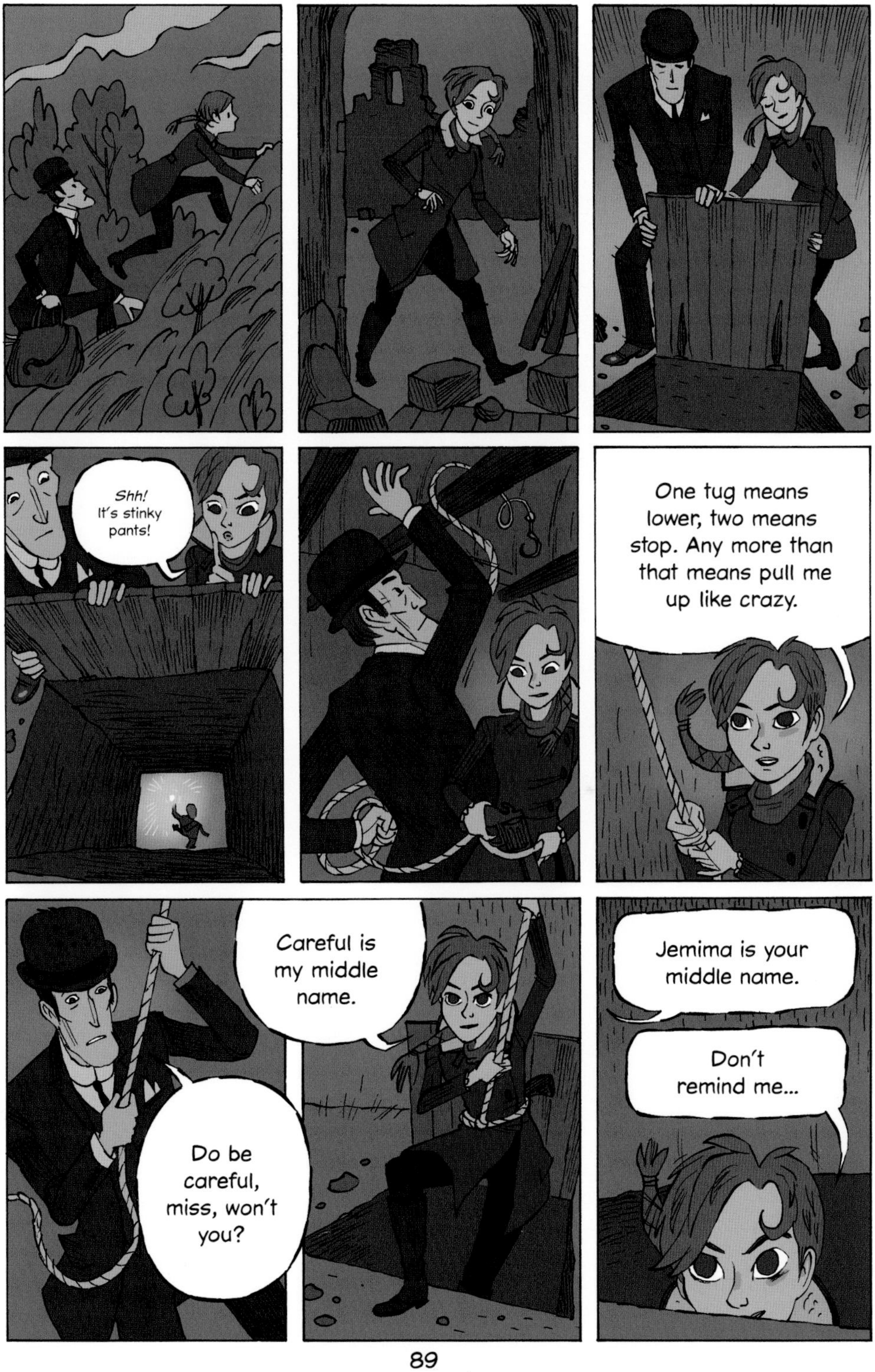
Shh! It's stinky pants!
One tug means lower, two means stop. Any more than that means pull me up like crazy.
Careful is my middle name.
Do be careful, miss, won't you?
Jemima is your middle name.
Don't remind me...

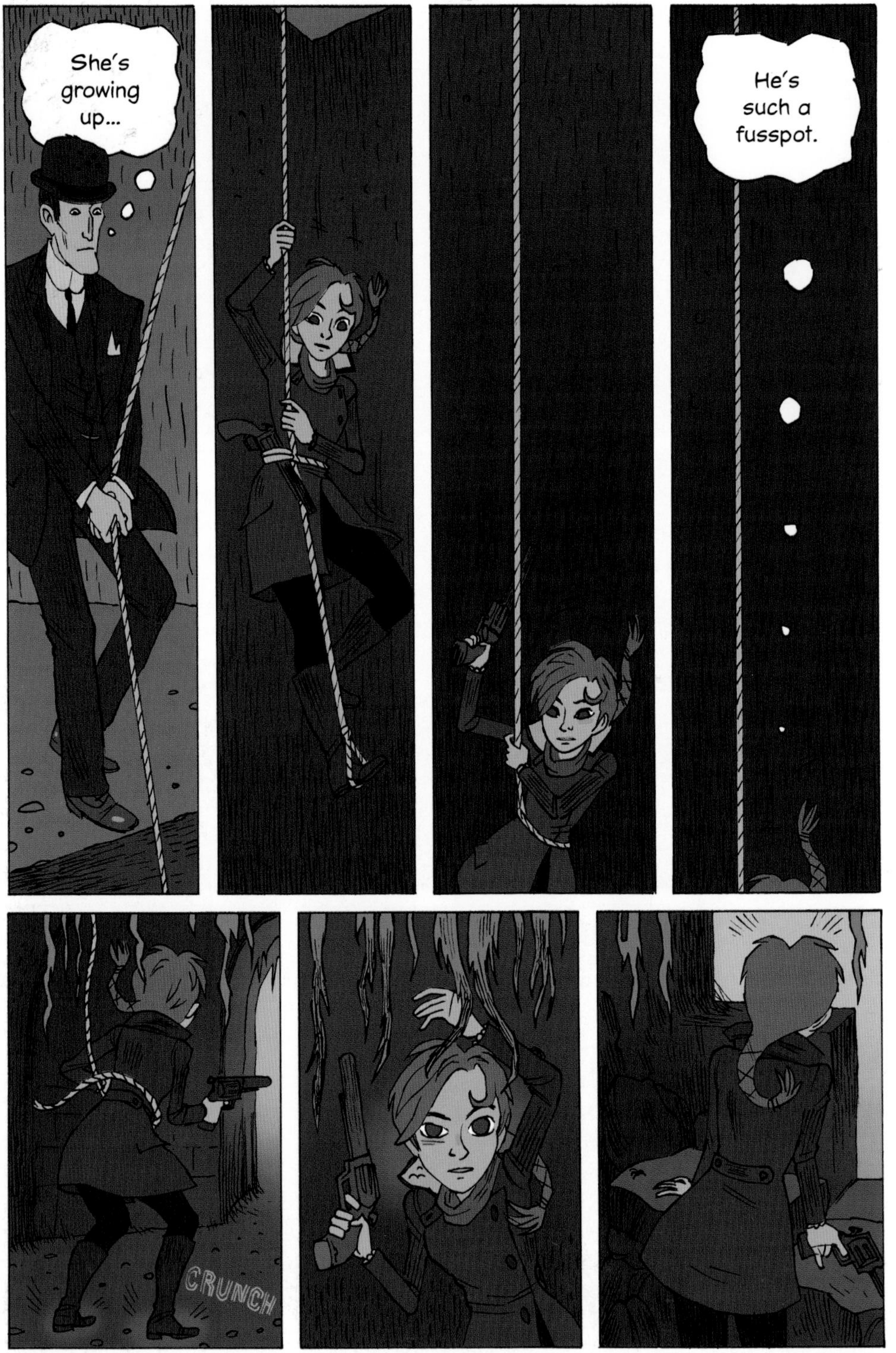
She's growing up...
He's such a fusspot.
CRUNCH

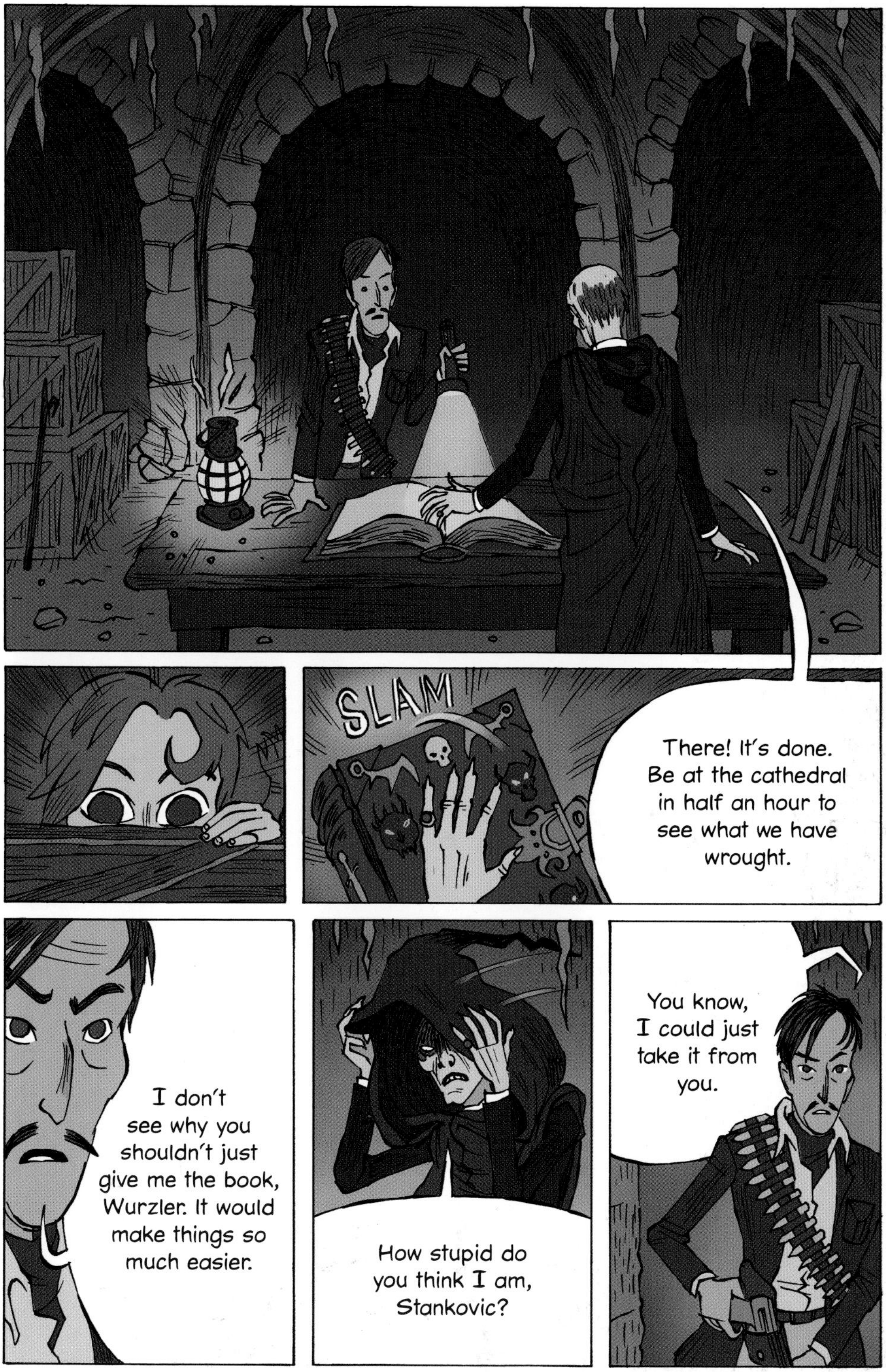
SLAM
There! It's done. Be at the cathedral in half an hour to see what we have wrought.
I don't see why you shouldn't just give me the book, Wurzler. It would make things so much easier.
How stupid do you think I am, Stankovic?
You know, I could just take it from you.

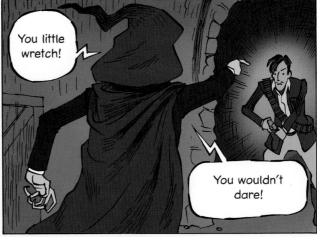

You little wretch!

You wouldn't dare!

One word from me and you'll be sent back to the gutter you came from!

Just stick to the bargain, Stankovic. And be at the cathedral.

CRASH!

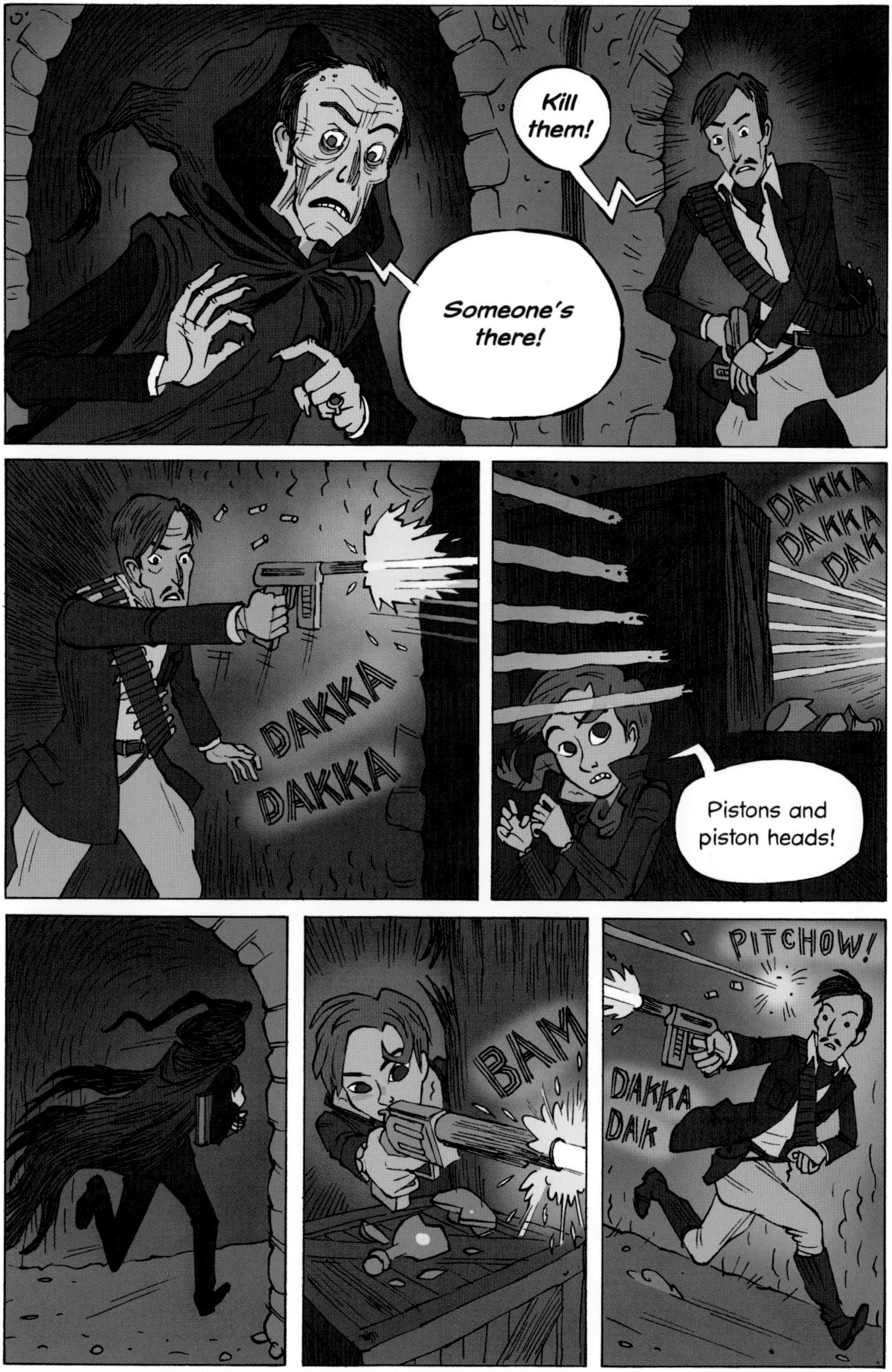
Kill them!
Someone's there!
DAKKA DAKKA
DAKKA DAKKA DAK
Pistons and piston heads!
BAM
PITCHOW!
DAKKA DAK

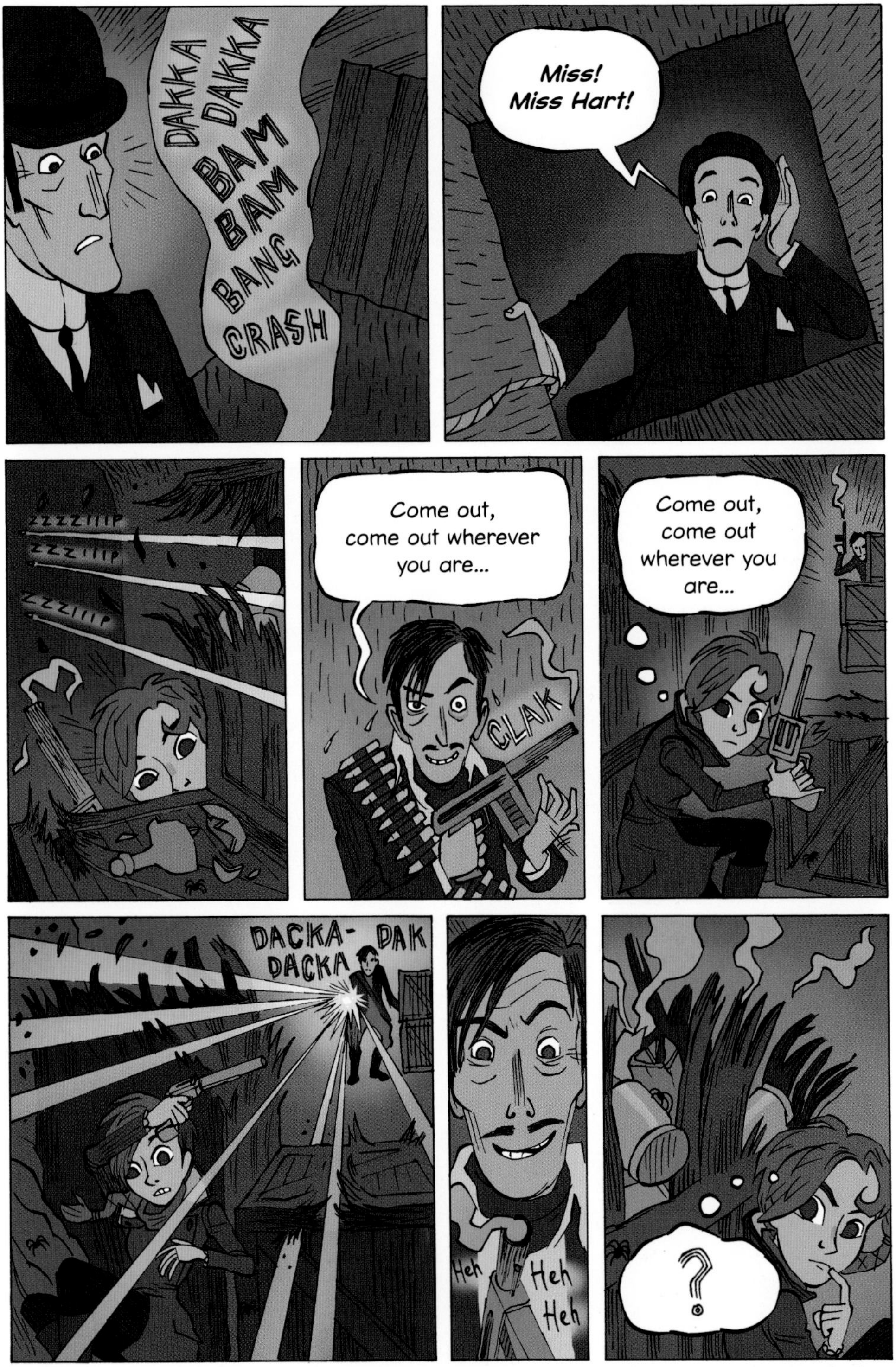
DAKKA DAKKA
BAM BAM
BANG
CRASH
Miss!
Miss Hart!
ZZZZIIIP
ZZZIIIP
ZZZIIIP
Come out, come out wherever you are...
CLAK
Come out, come out wherever you are...
DACKA-DACKA
DAK
Heh
Heh
Heh
?

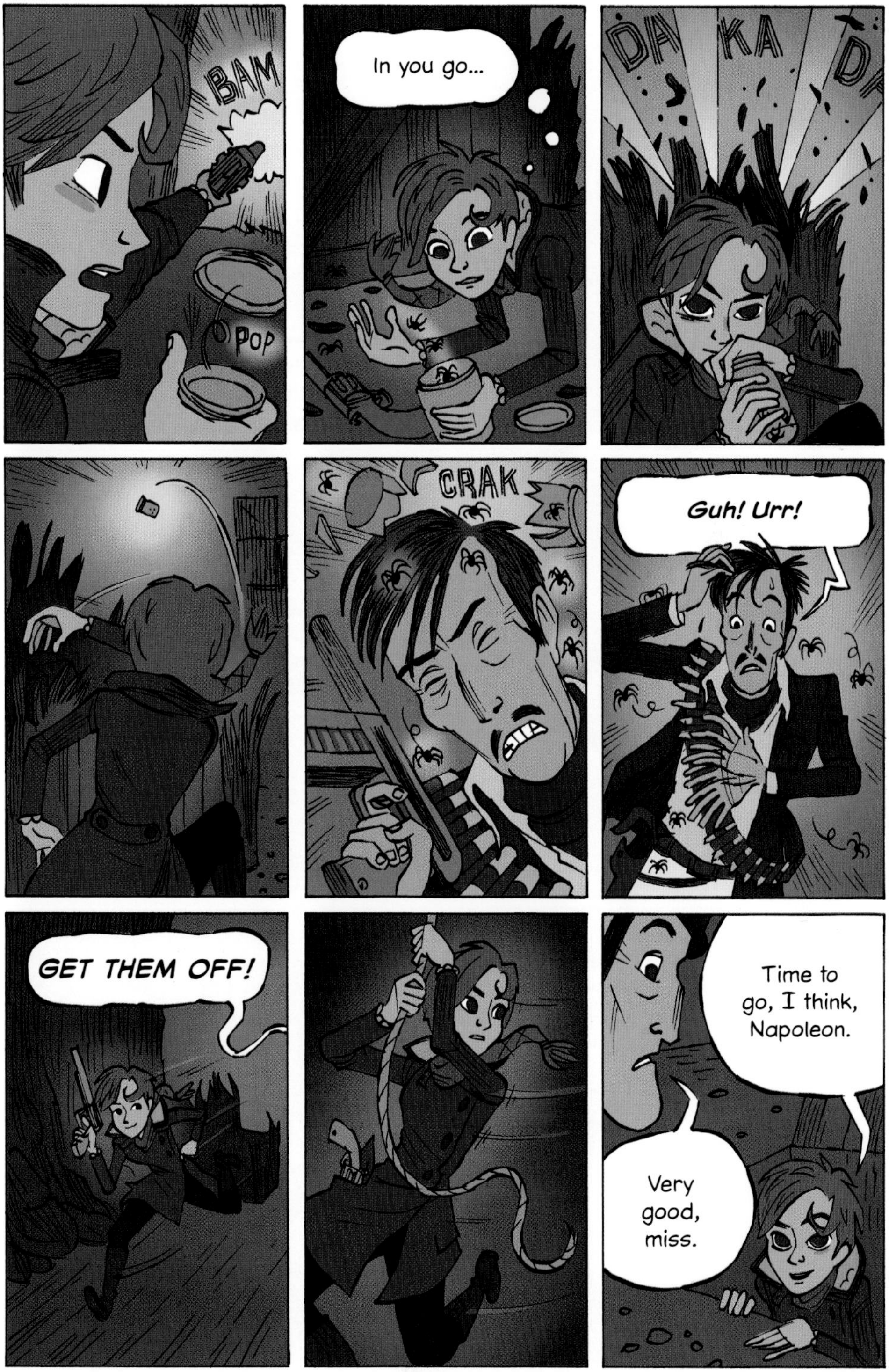
BAM
POP
In you go...
DA KA
CRAK
Guh! Urr!
GET THEM OFF!
Time to go, I think, Napoleon.
Very good, miss.

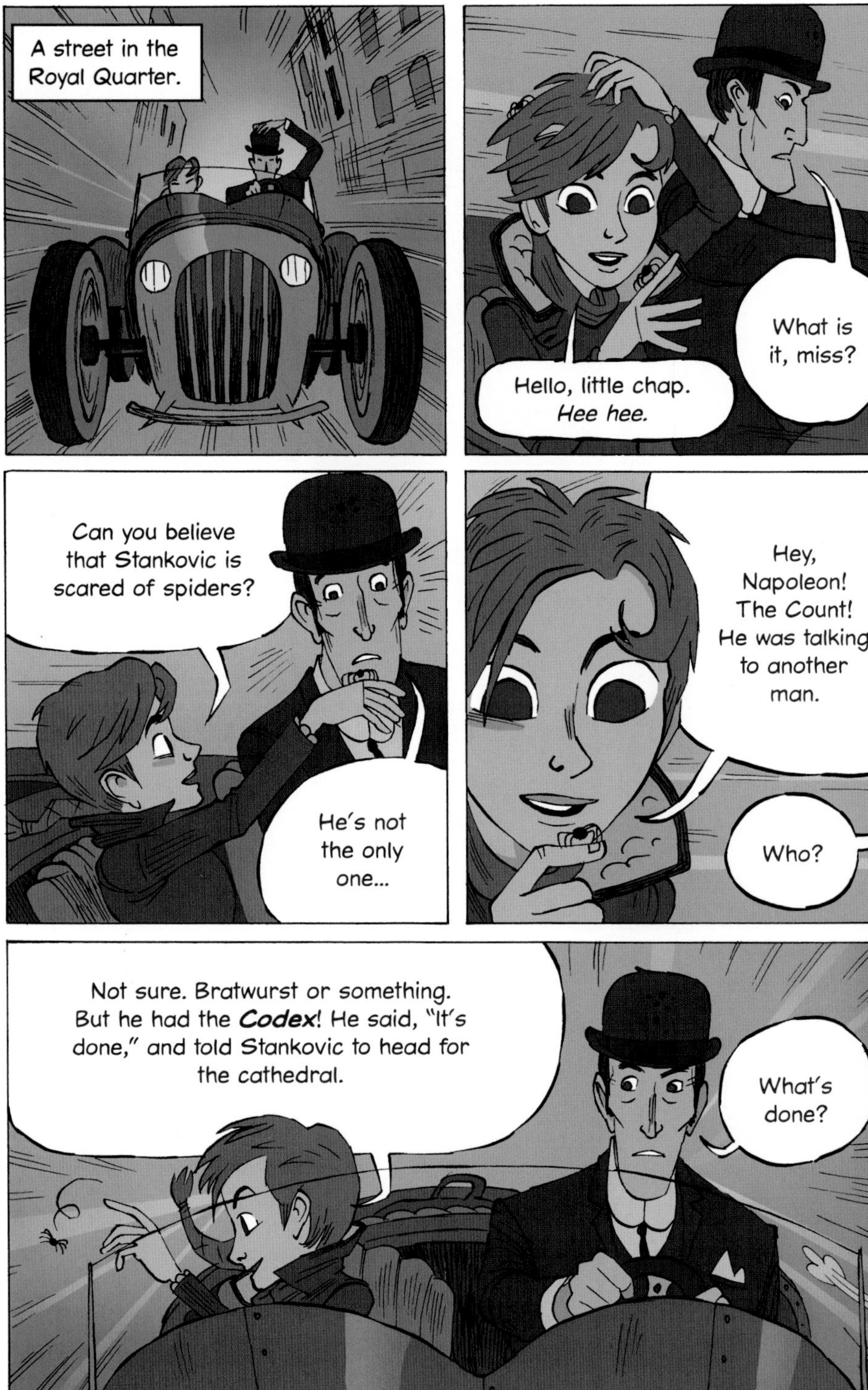
A street in the Royal Quarter.
Hello, little chap. *Hee hee.*
What is it, miss?
Can you believe that Stankovic is scared of spiders?
He's not the only one...
Hey, Napoleon! The Count! He was talking to another man.
Who?
Not sure. Bratwurst or something. But he had the ***Codex***! He said, "It's done," and told Stankovic to head for the cathedral.
What's done?

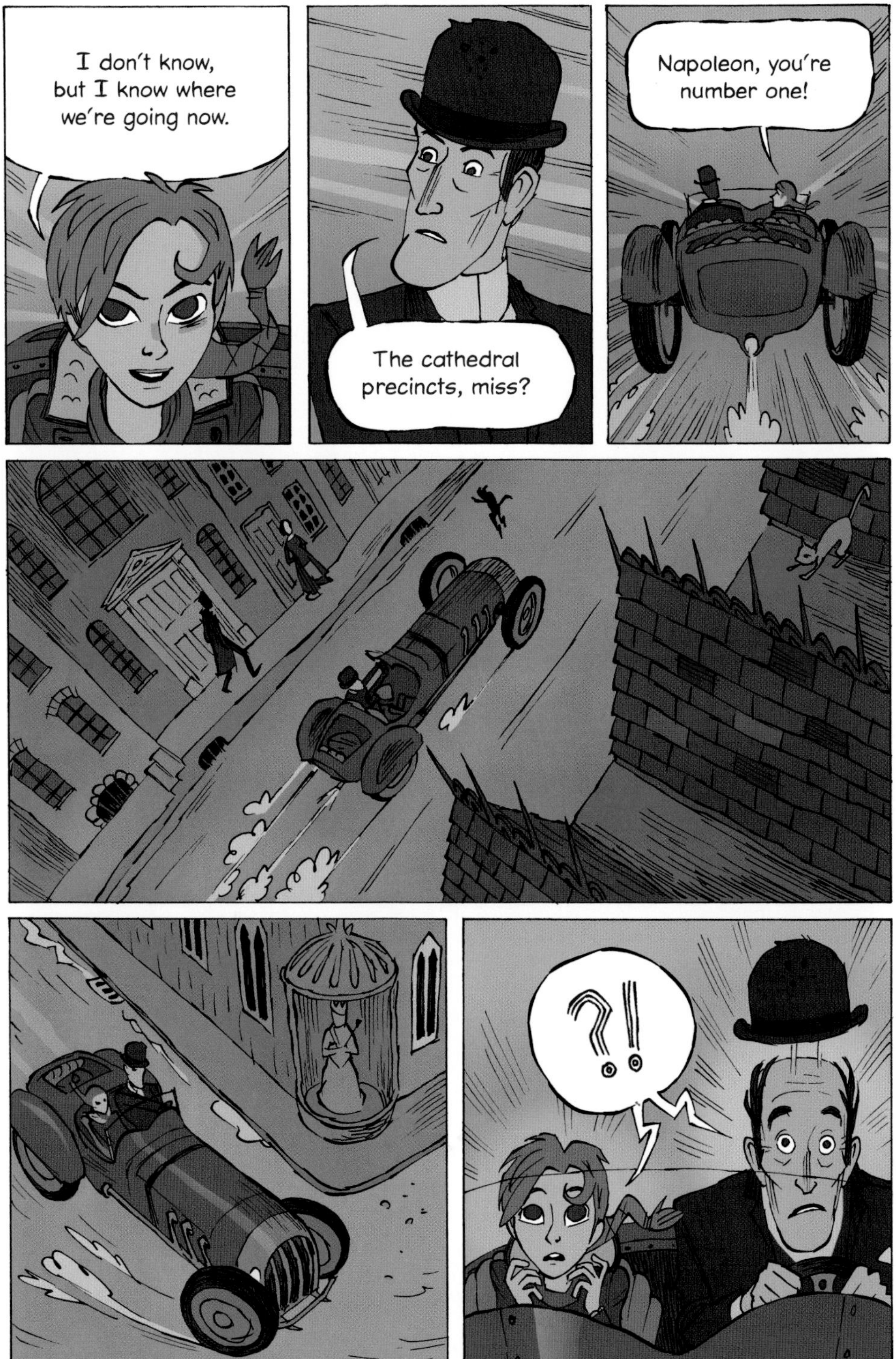
I don't know, but I know where we're going now.
The cathedral precincts, miss?
Napoleon, you're number one!
?!

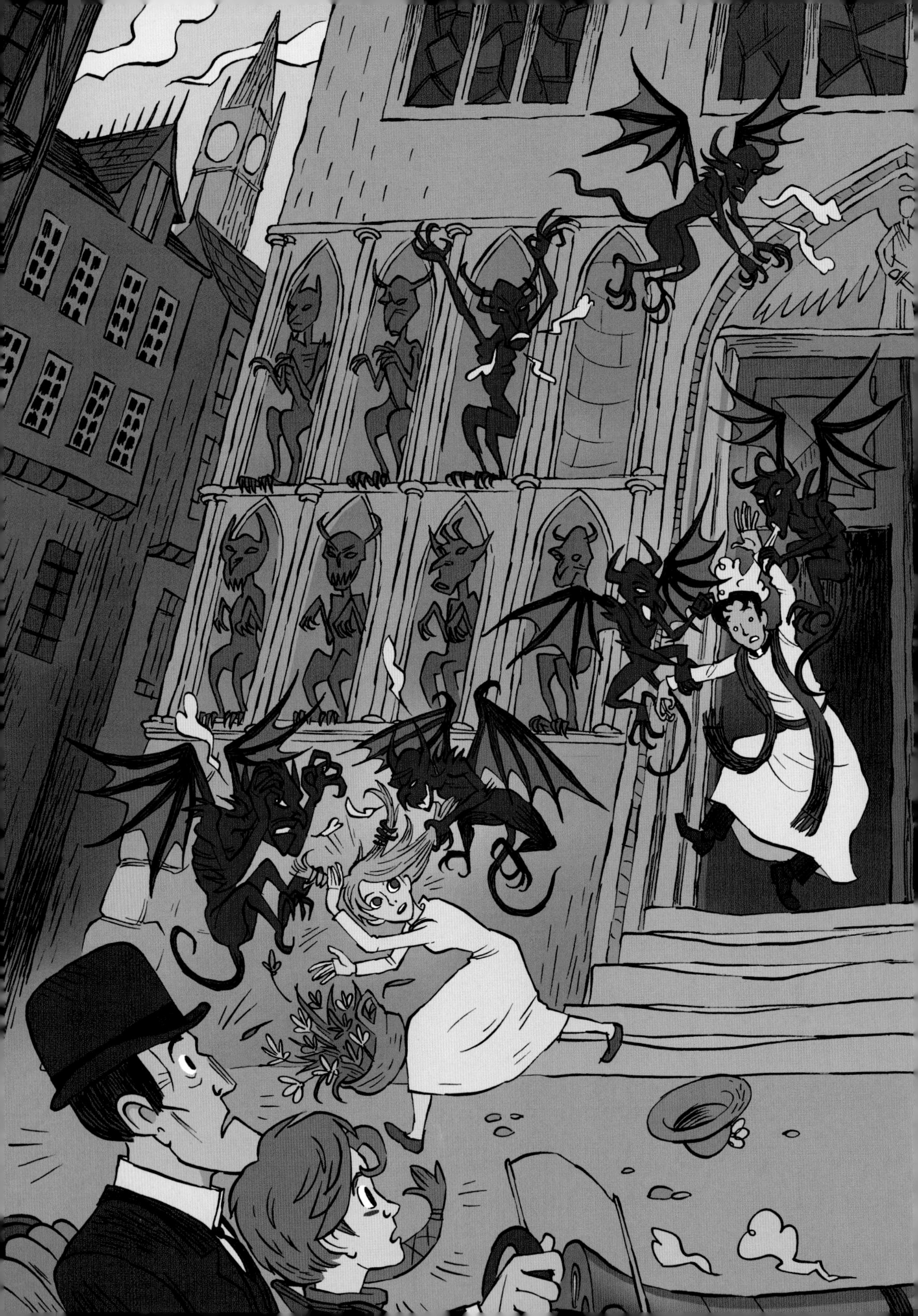

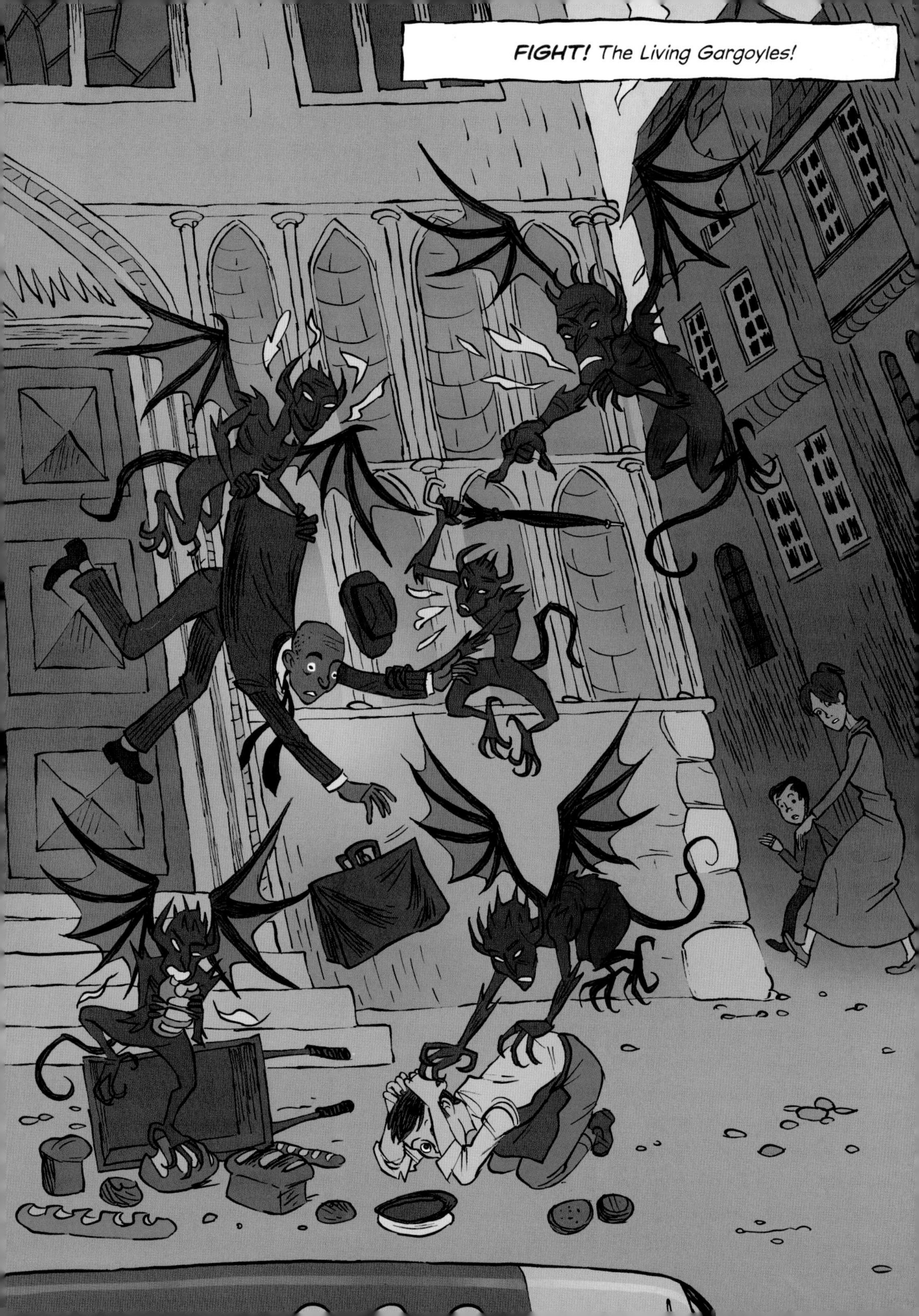
FIGHT! The Living Gargoyles!

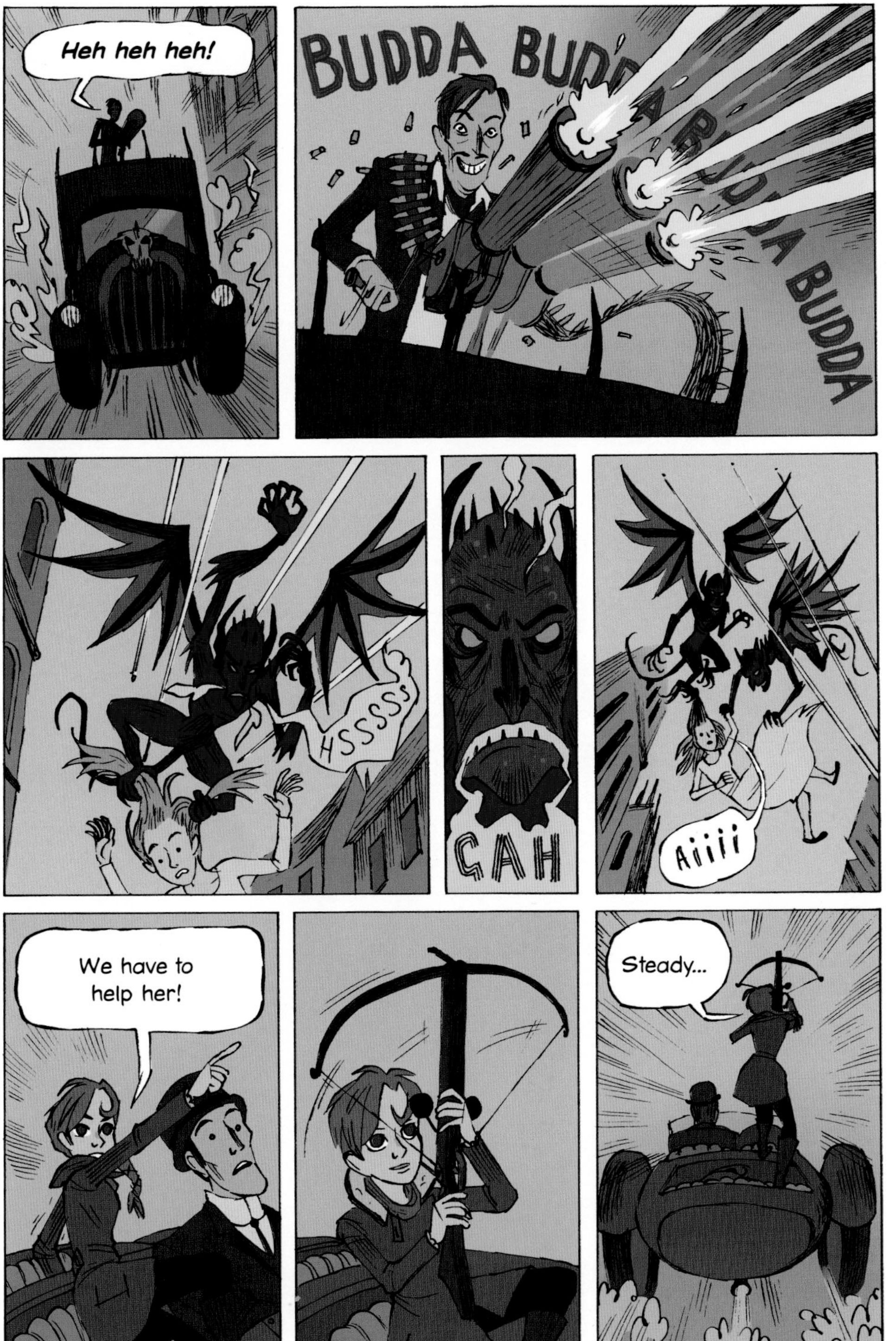
Heh heh heh!
BUDDA BUDDA BUDDA BUDDA
HSSSSS
GAH
Aiiii
We have to help her!
Steady...

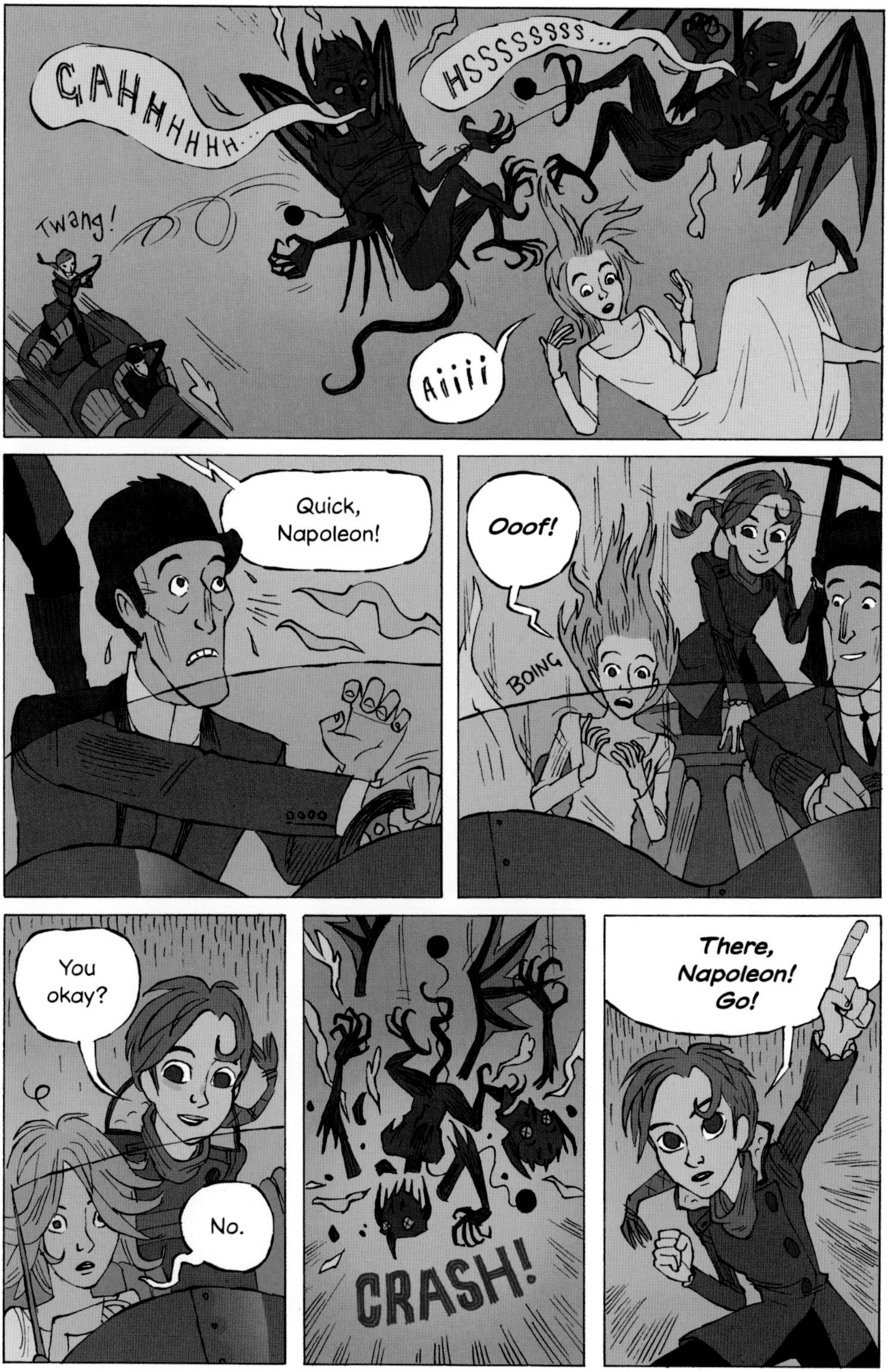
GAHHHHHH...
HSSSSSSSS...
Twang!
Aiiii
Quick, Napoleon!
Ooof!
BOING
You okay?
No.
CRASH!
There, Napoleon! Go!

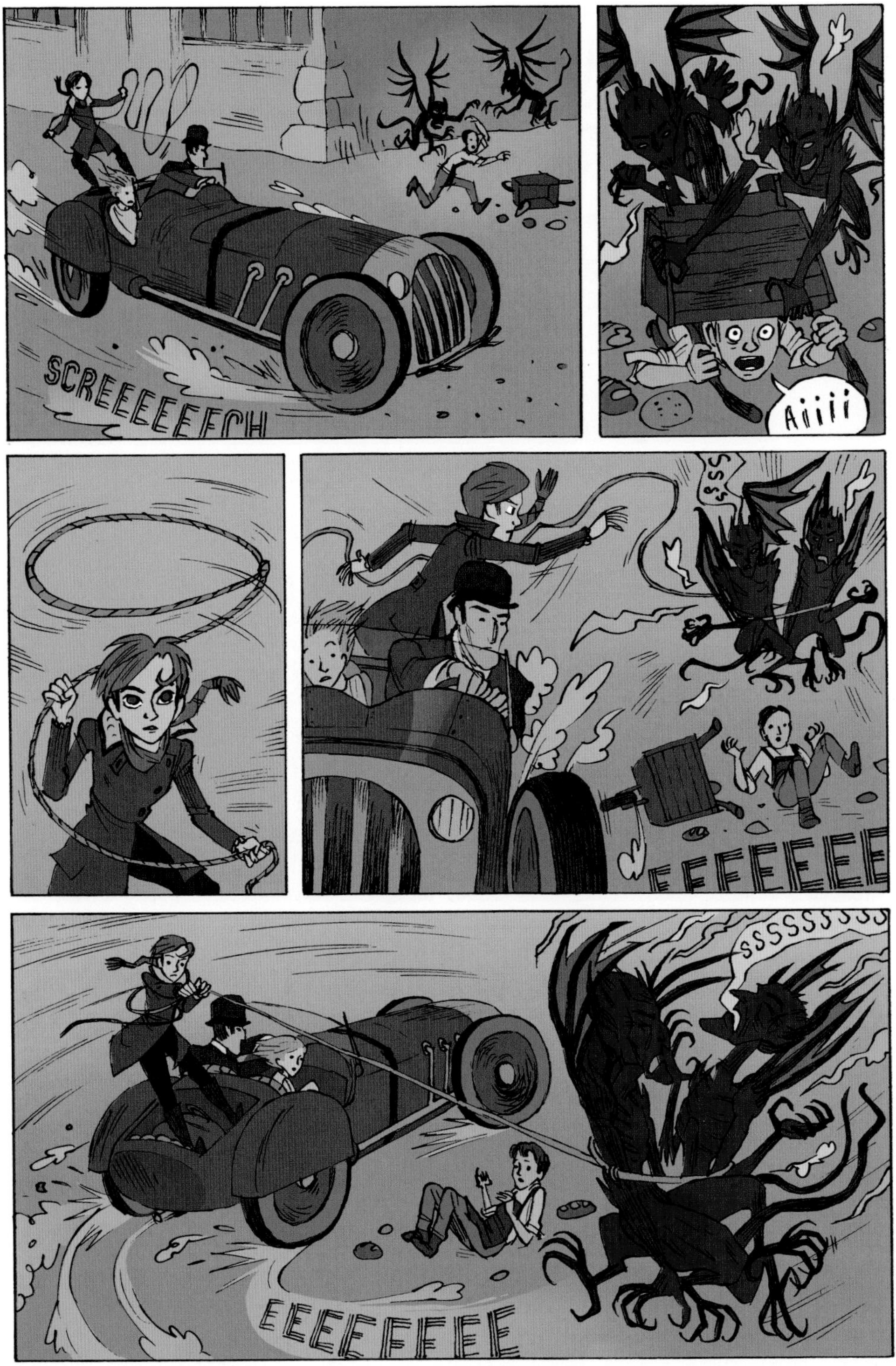
SCREEEEEEECH
Aiiii
SSS
EEEEEEE
SSSSSSSSS
EEEEEEEE

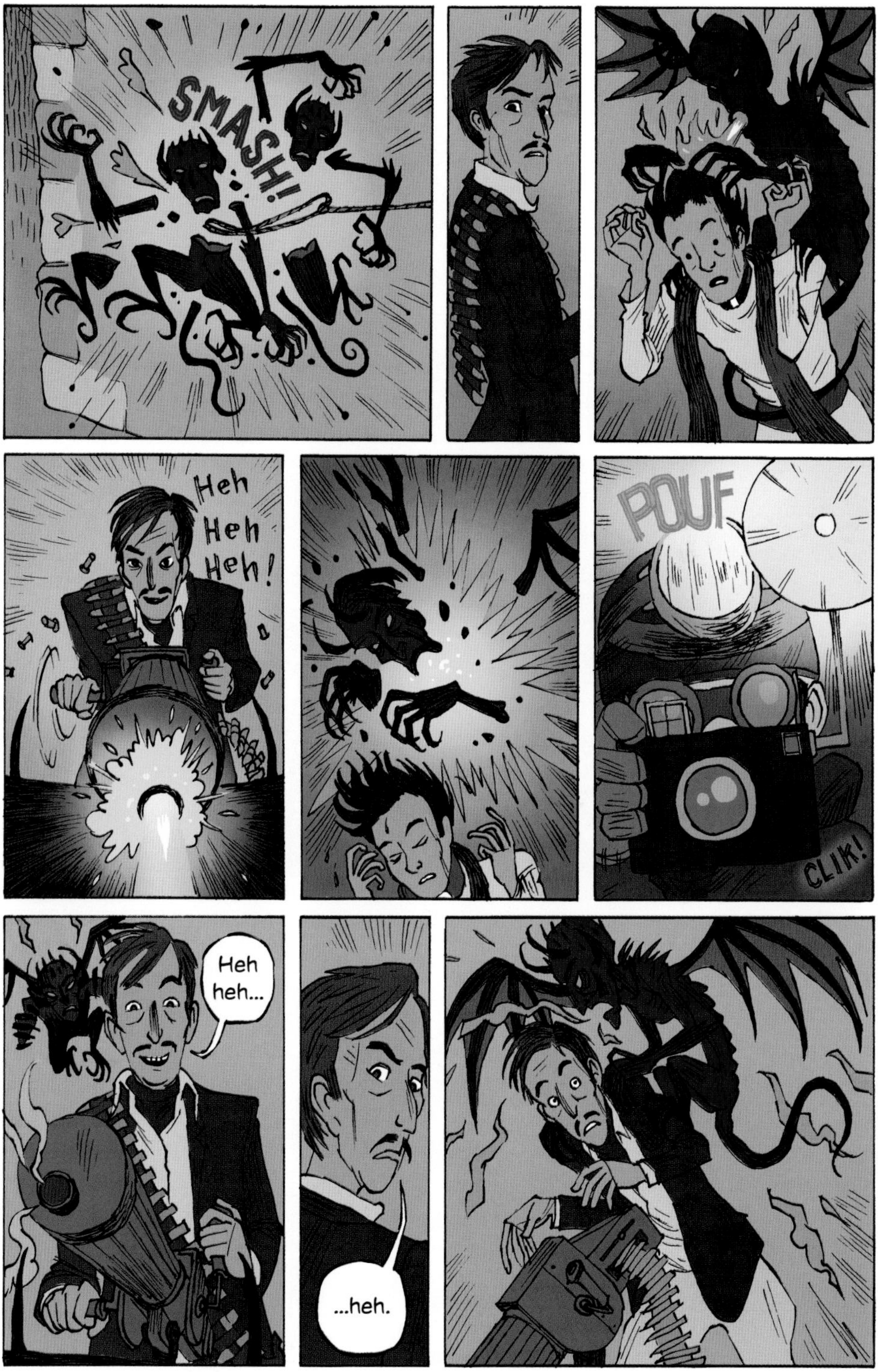
SMASH!
Heh
Heh
Heh!
POUF
CLIK!
Heh heh...
...heh.

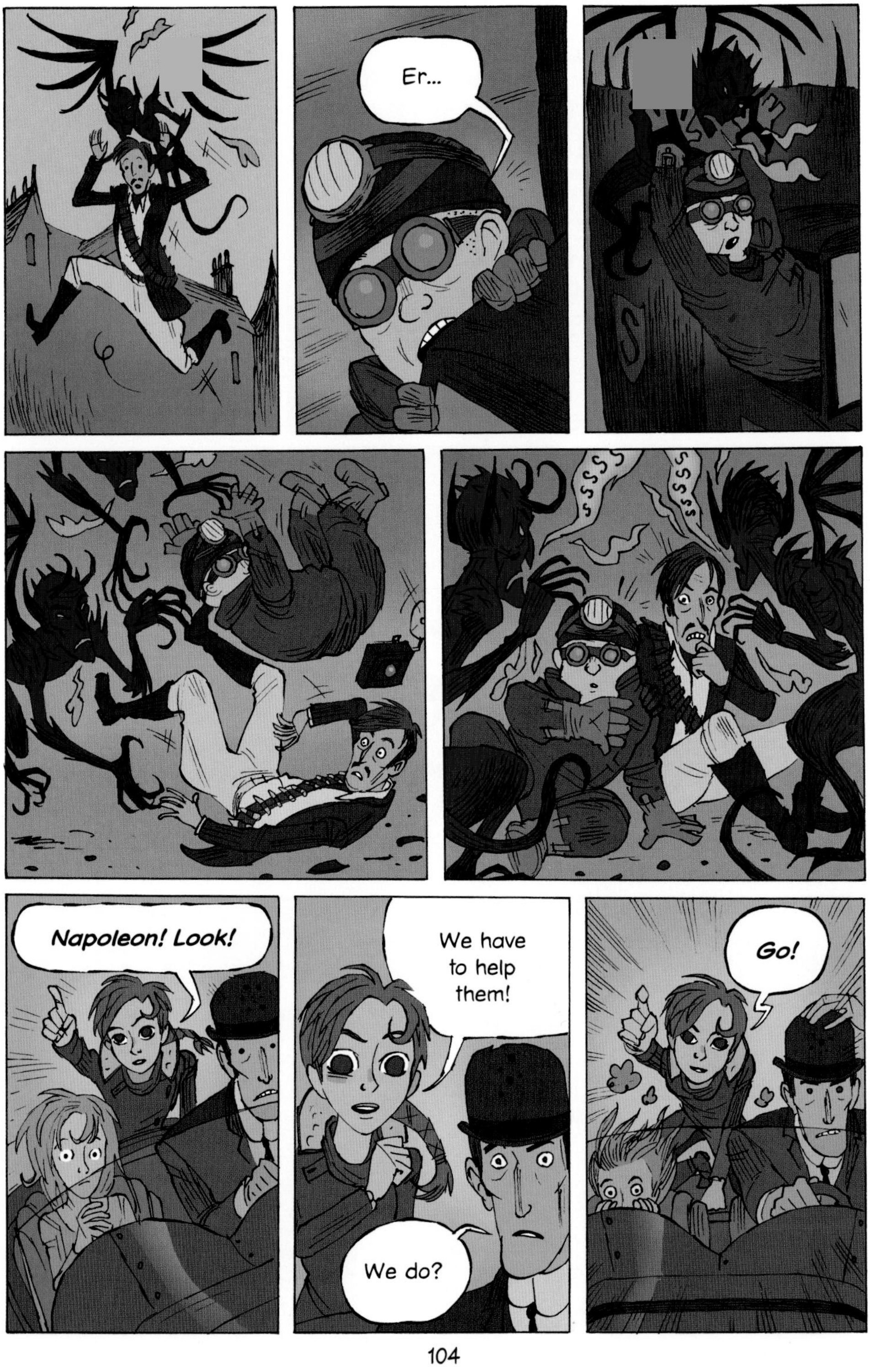
Er...
SSSS
SSSS
Napoleon! Look!
We have to help them!
We do?
Go!

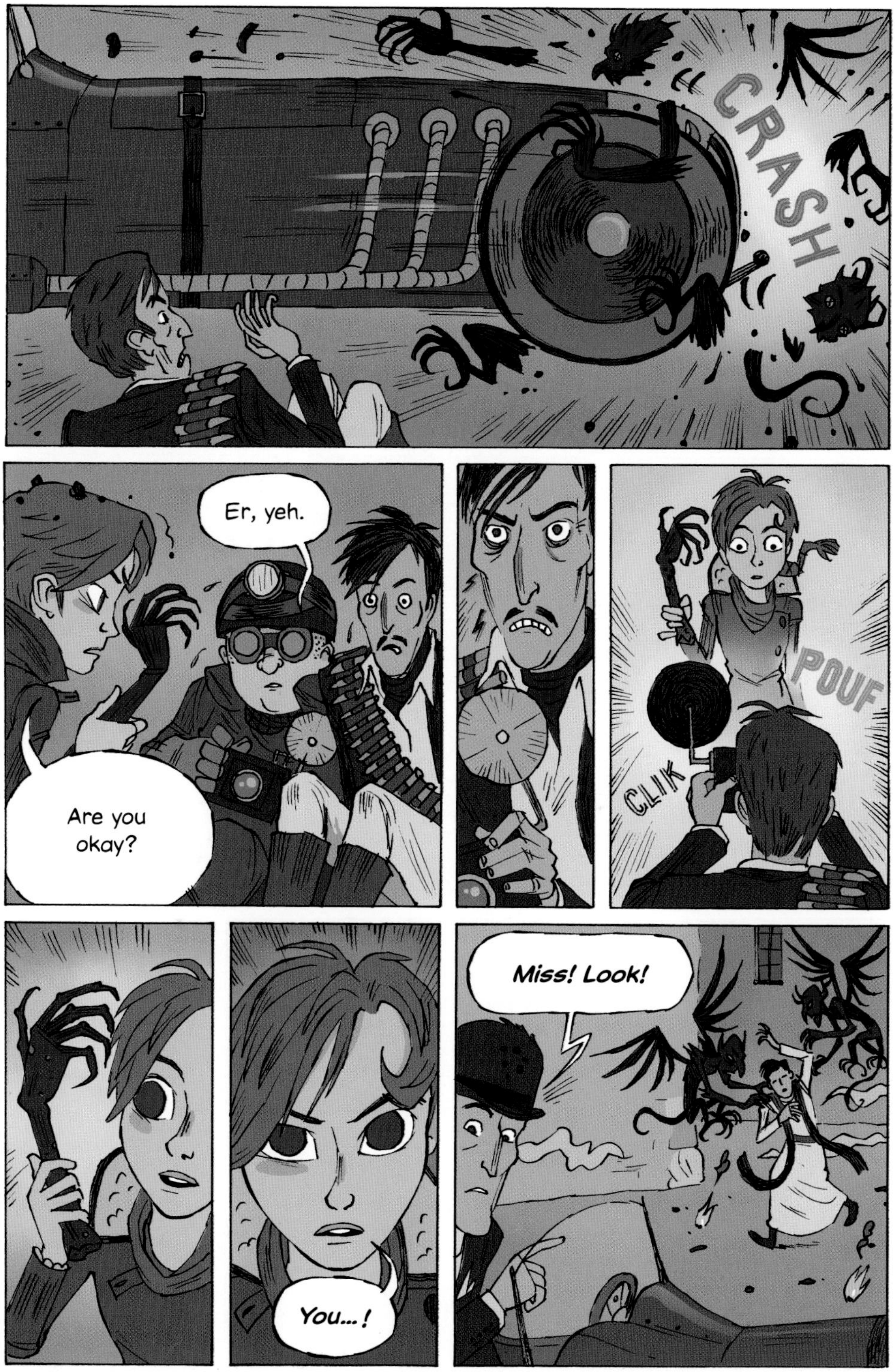

CRASH
Er, yeh.
Are you okay?
POUF
CLIK
You...!
Miss! Look!

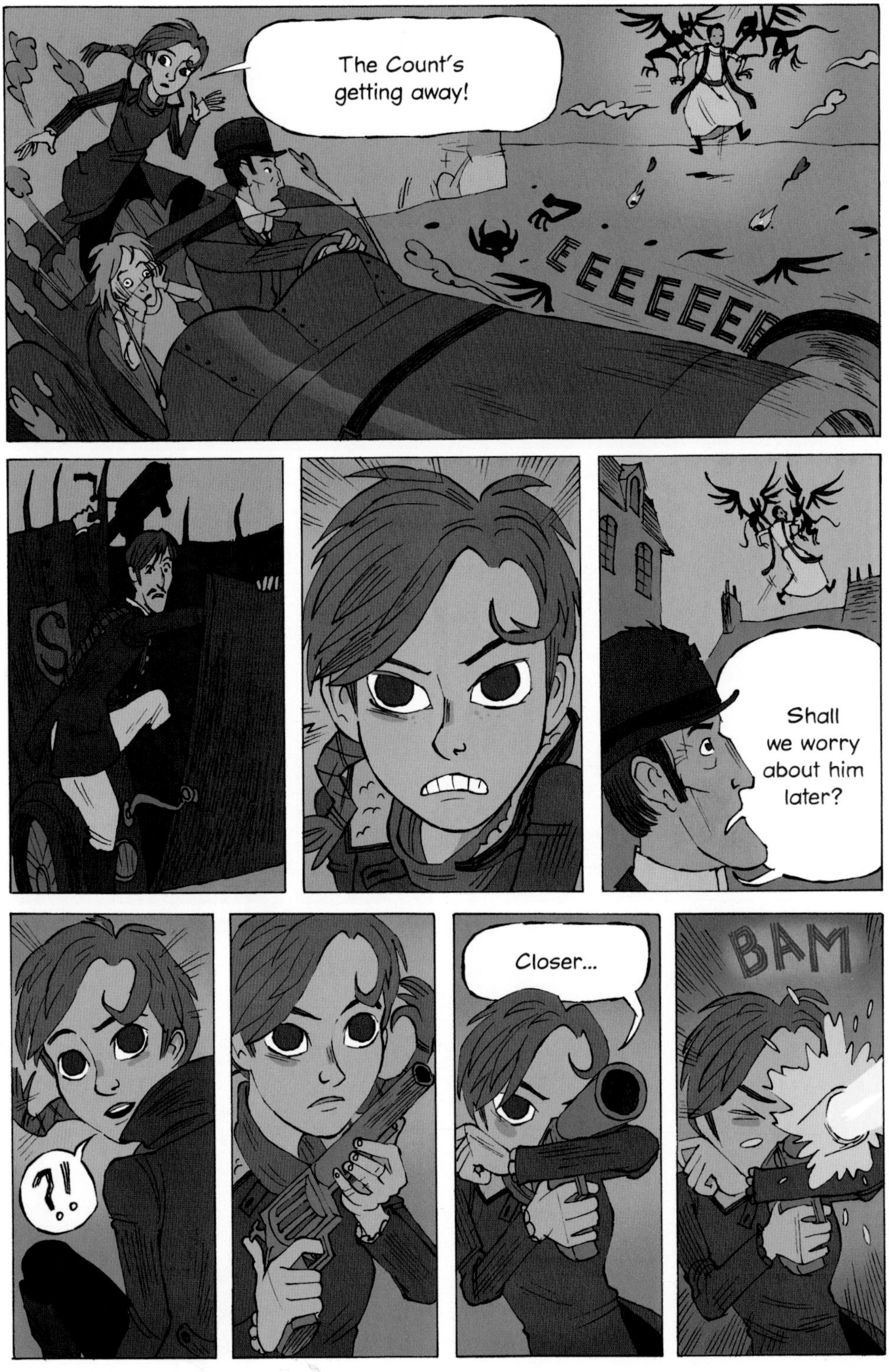

The Count's getting away!
EEEEEEE
Shall we worry about him later?
?!
Closer...
BAM

That Count!

We saved his miserable skin, and not so much as a thank you.

Never mind that, Napoleon. We know he's a complete cad. But we know something else now, too.

Namely?

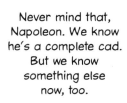

The **Codex**. It doesn't just **explain** monsters. It can **summon** them! That's how Stankovic knew to come to the cathedral! They're **making** monsters!

Why?

For the bounty. Stankovic gets there first, makes the kill, takes the money.

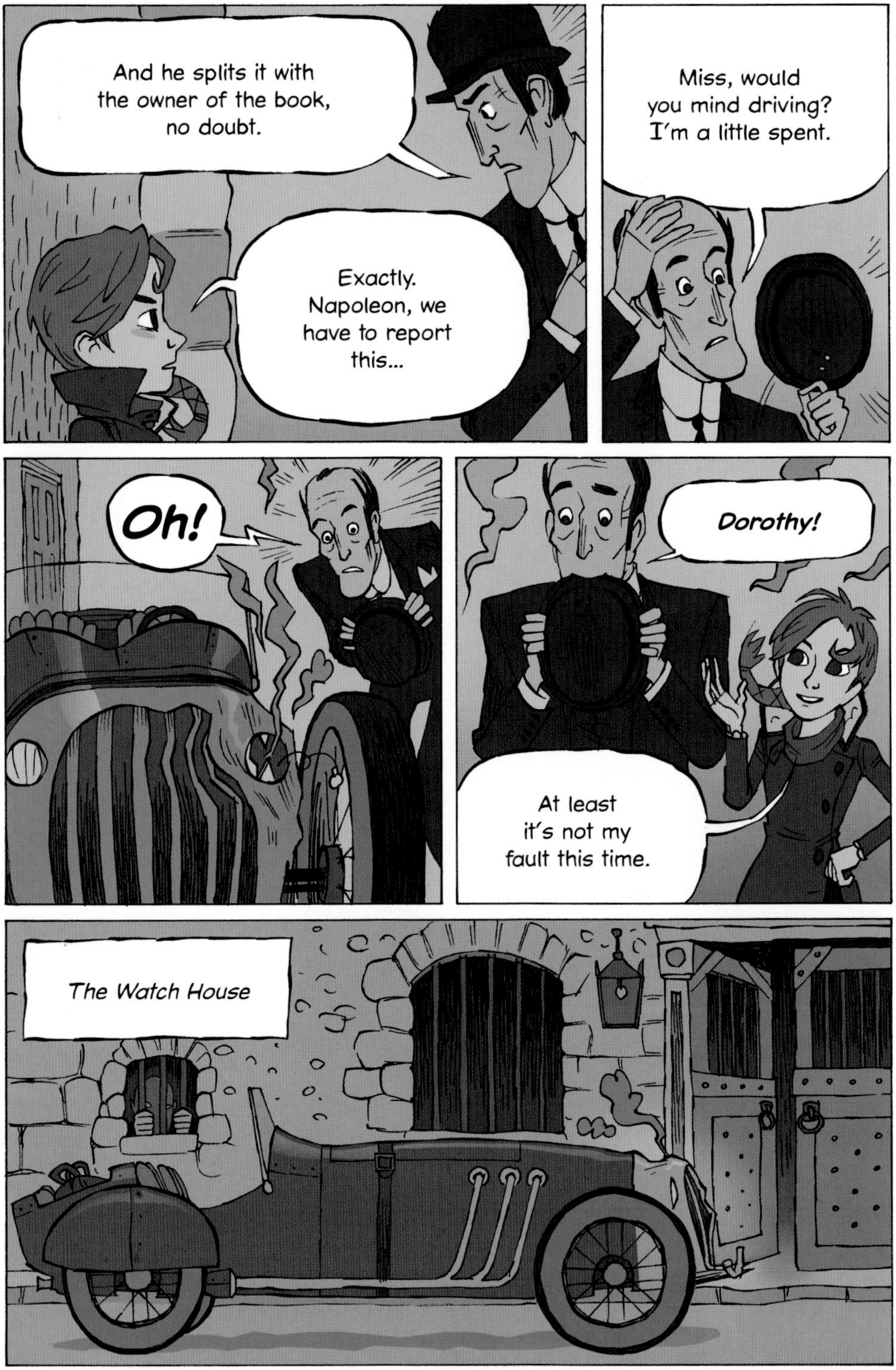
And he splits it with the owner of the book, no doubt.
Exactly. Napoleon, we have to report this...
Miss, would you mind driving? I'm a little spent.
Oh!
Dorothy!
At least it's not my fault this time.
The Watch House

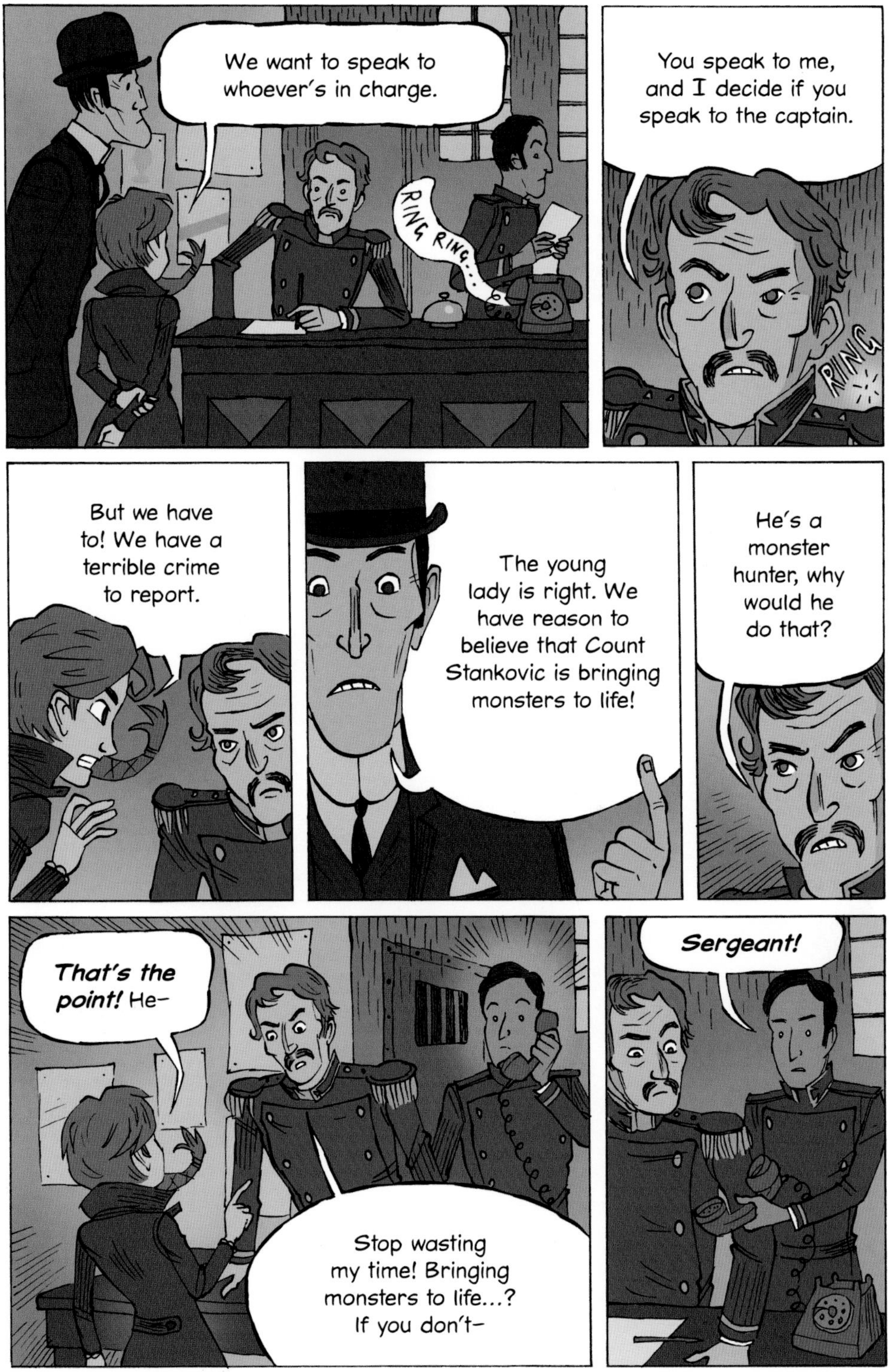
We want to speak to whoever's in charge.
RING RING...
You speak to me, and I decide if you speak to the captain.
RING
But we have to! We have a terrible crime to report.
The young lady is right. We have reason to believe that Count Stankovic is bringing monsters to life!
He's a monster hunter, why would he do that?
That's the point! He-
Stop wasting my time! Bringing monsters to life...? If you don't-
Sergeant!

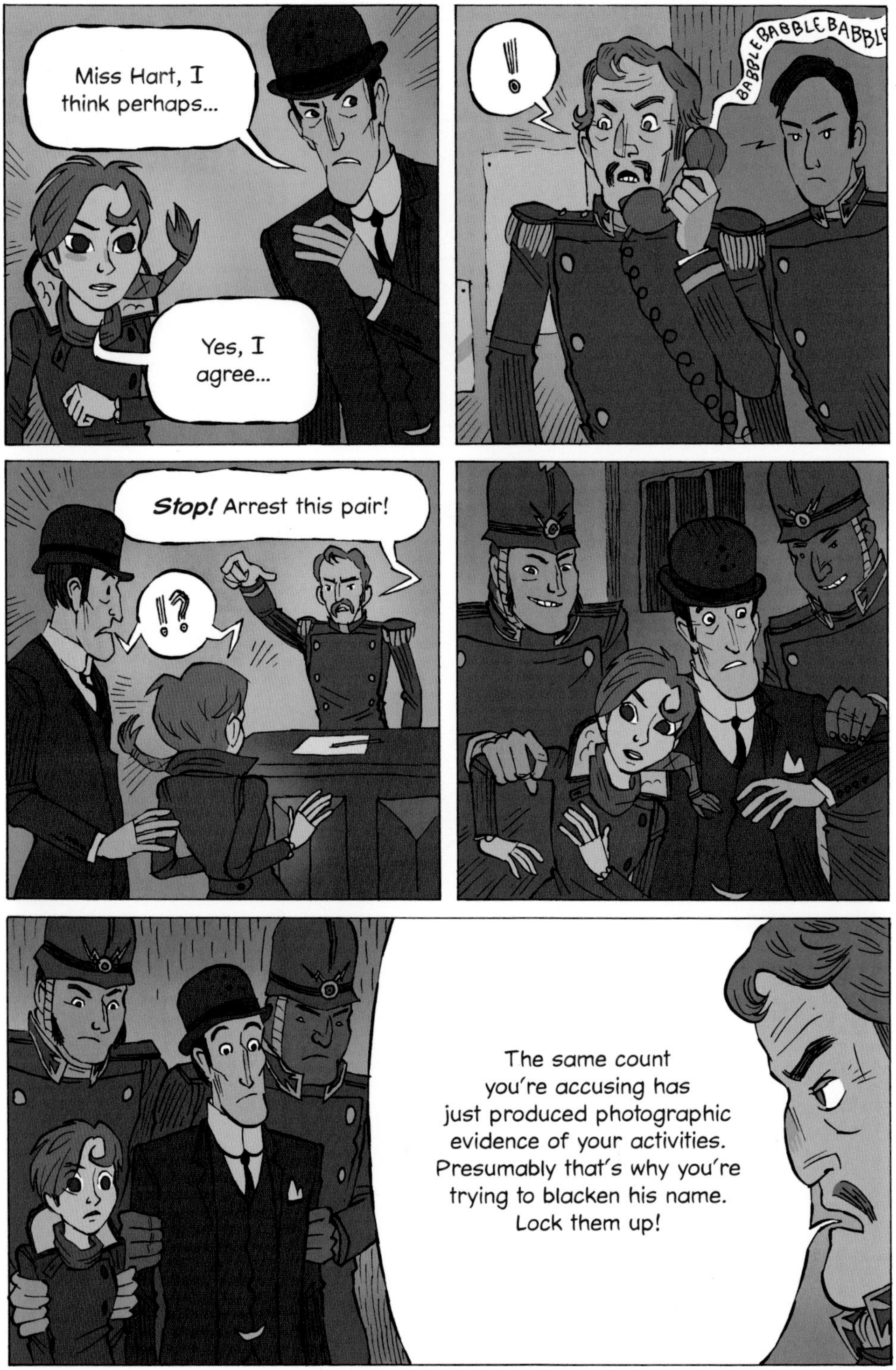
Miss Hart, I think perhaps...
Yes, I agree...
!!
BABBLE BABBLE BABBLE BABBLE
Stop! Arrest this pair!
!?
The same count you're accusing has just produced photographic evidence of your activities. Presumably that's why you're trying to blacken his name. Lock them up!

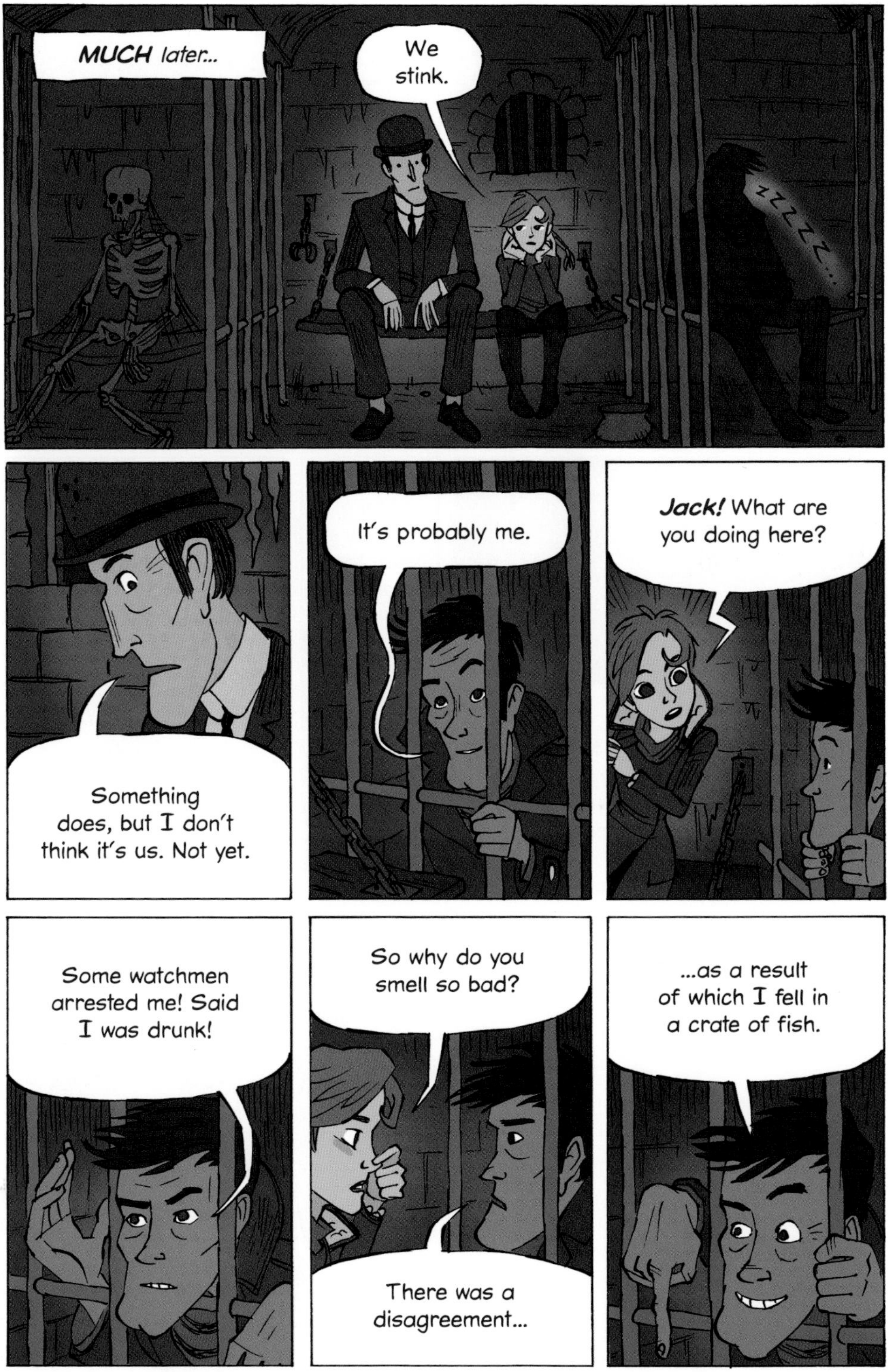

MUCH later...
We stink.
Something does, but I don't think it's us. Not yet.
It's probably me.
Jack! What are you doing here?
Some watchmen arrested me! Said I was drunk!
So why do you smell so bad?
There was a disagreement...
...as a result of which I fell in a crate of fish.

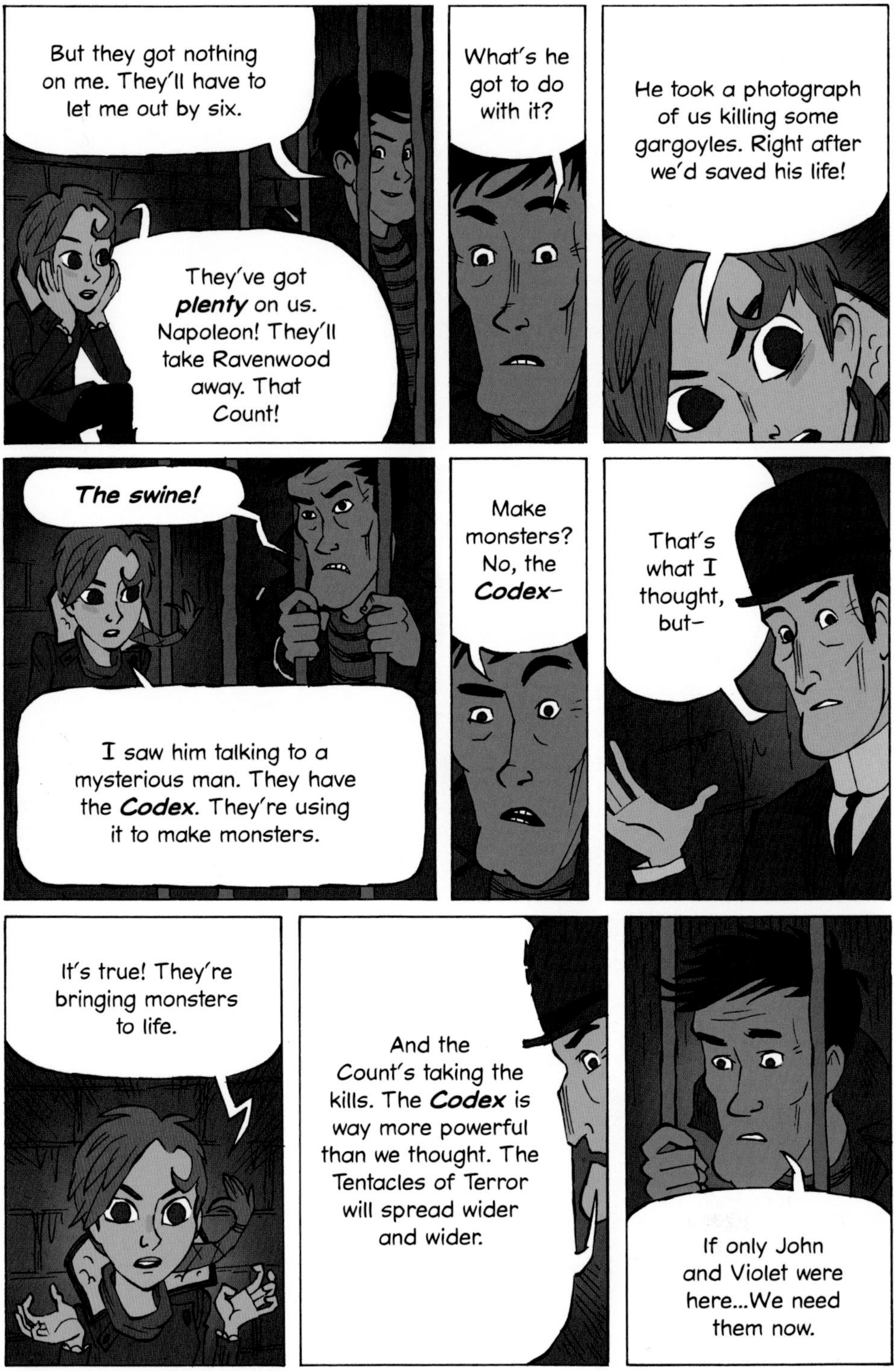

But they got nothing on me. They'll have to let me out by six.
They've got *plenty* on us. Napoleon! They'll take Ravenwood away. That Count!
What's he got to do with it?
He took a photograph of us killing some gargoyles. Right after we'd saved his life!
The swine!
I saw him talking to a mysterious man. They have the *Codex*. They're using it to make monsters.
Make monsters? No, the *Codex*–
That's what I thought, but–
It's true! They're bringing monsters to life.
And the Count's taking the kills. The *Codex* is way more powerful than we thought. The Tentacles of Terror will spread wider and wider.
If only John and Violet were here...We need them now.

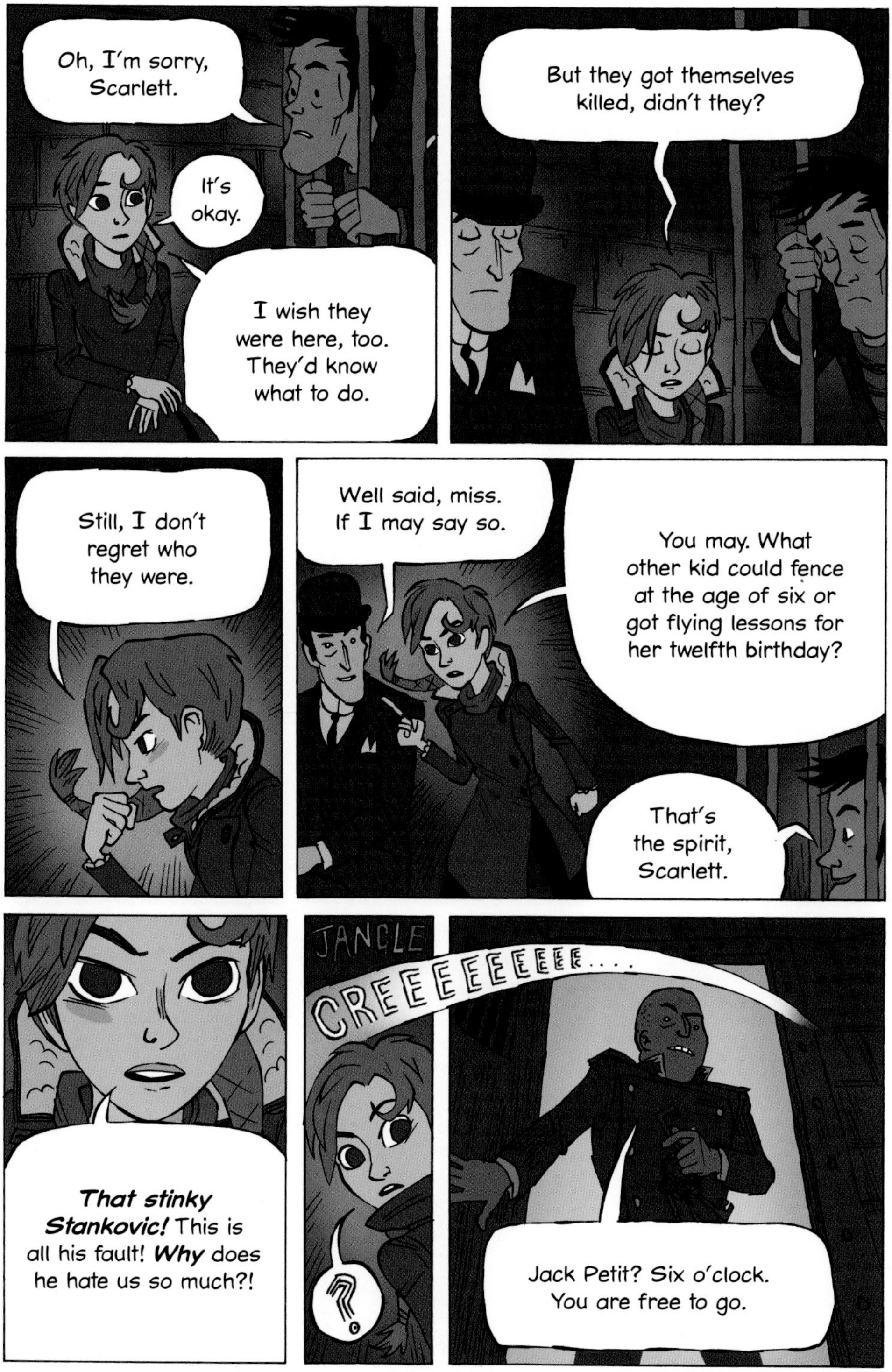

Oh, I'm sorry, Scarlett.
It's okay.
I wish they were here, too. They'd know what to do.
But they got themselves killed, didn't they?
Still, I don't regret who they were.
Well said, miss. If I may say so.
You may. What other kid could fence at the age of six or got flying lessons for her twelfth birthday?
That's the spirit, Scarlett.
That stinky Stankovic! This is all his fault! ***Why*** does he hate us so much?!
JANGLE
CREEEEEEEEEE....
?
Jack Petit? Six o'clock. You are free to go.

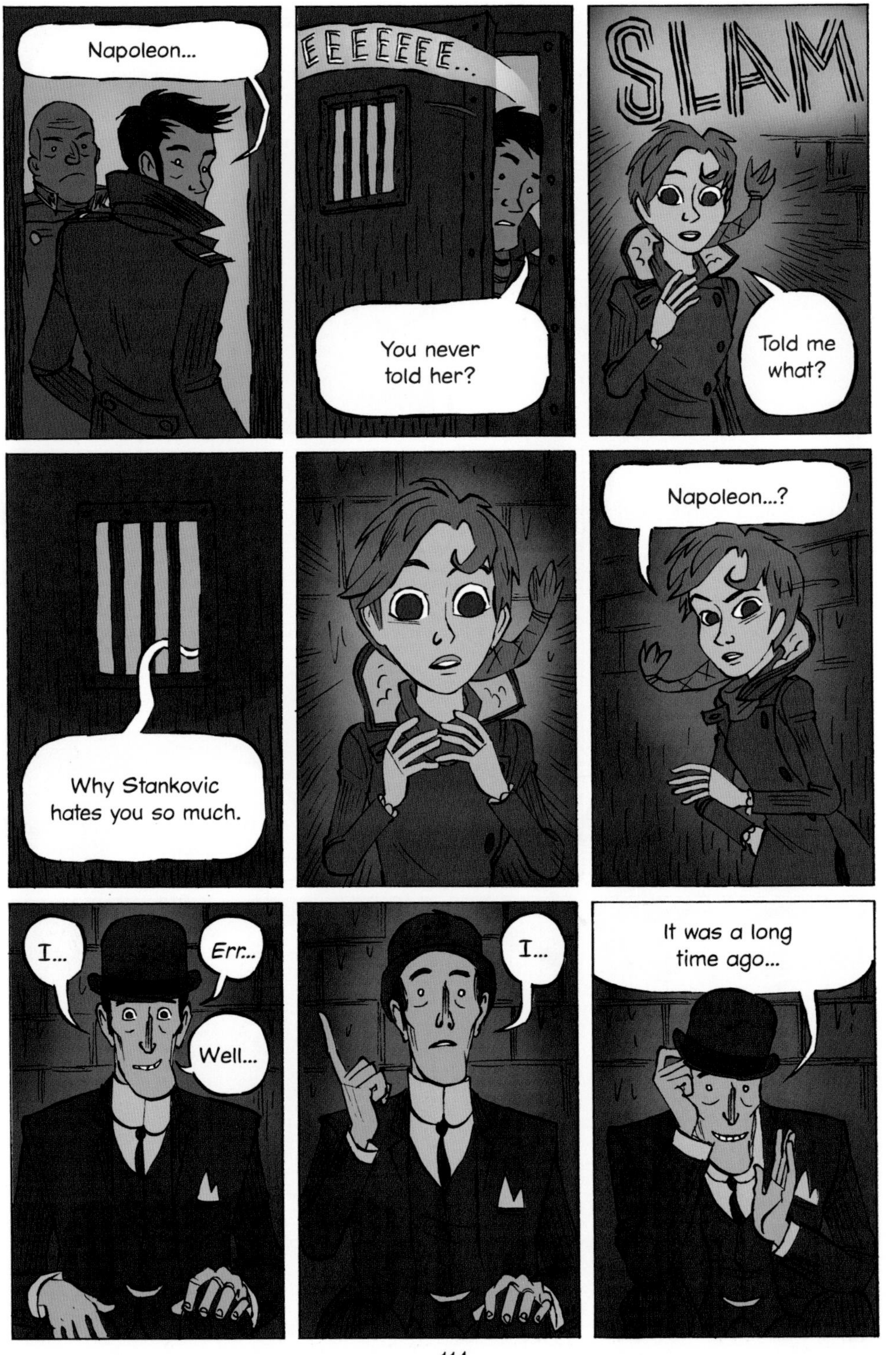

Napoleon...
EEEEEEE...
You never told her?
SLAM
Told me what?
Why Stankovic hates you so much.
Napoleon...?
I...
Err...
Well...
I...
It was a long time ago...

...a very long time ago, when you were only a dream that was yet to be had by your parents.

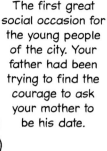The first great social occasion for the young people of the city. Your father had been trying to find the courage to ask your mother to be his date.

It was the debutante's ball.

Dad? Nervous? Never!

Don't you believe it. He was smitten by your mother the first time he saw her. But finally he asked her, and she said yes.

The trouble was, Stankovic had already asked your mother to go with him.

Stankovic? **Ugh, no!**

I'm afraid so. At the ball, there was a terrible scene. Stankovic called your mother something awful.

You said you'd go with **me**!

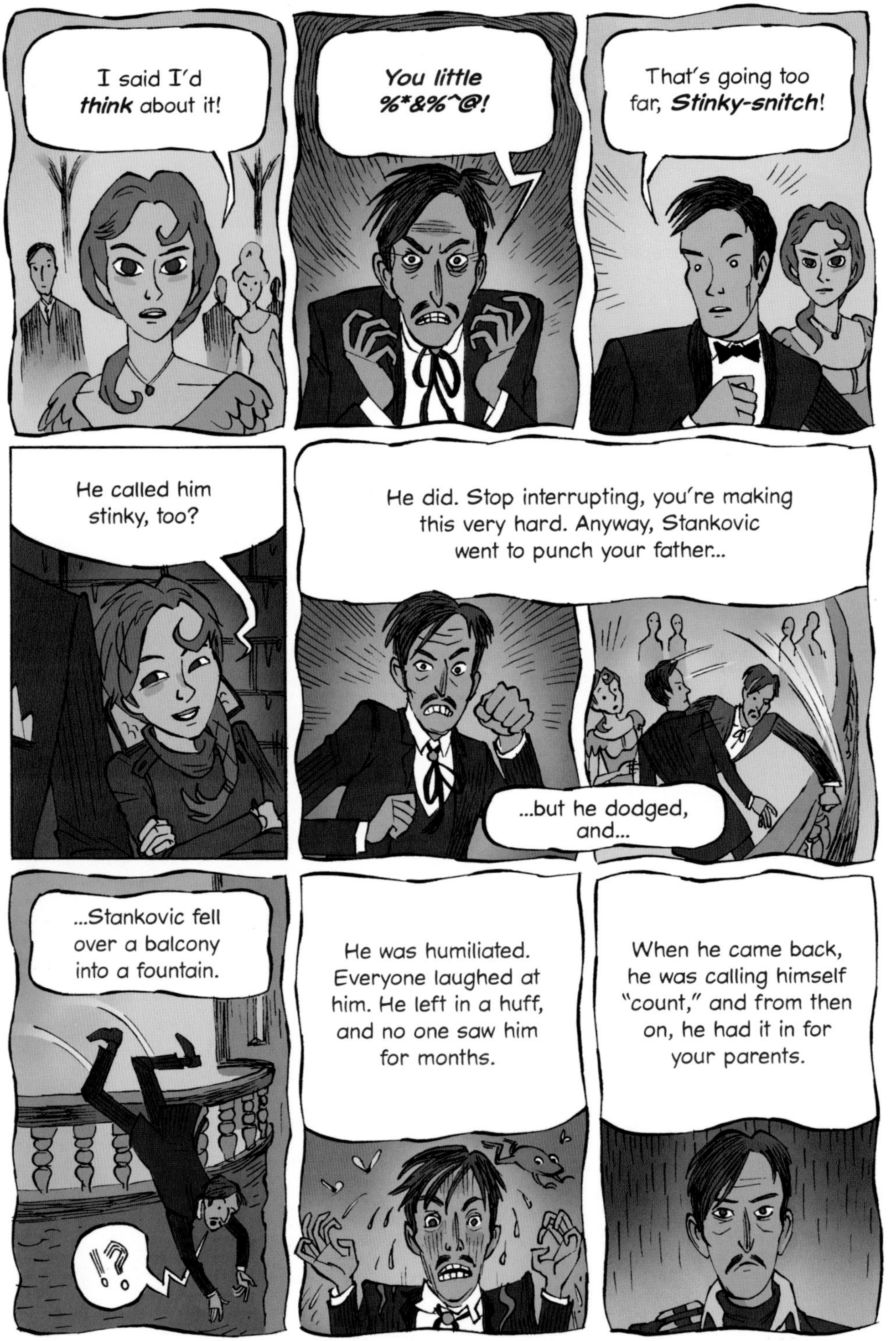
I said I'd *think* about it!
You little %&%^@!*
That's going too far, ***Stinky-snitch***!
He called him stinky, too?
He did. Stop interrupting, you're making this very hard. Anyway, Stankovic went to punch your father...
...but he dodged, and...
...Stankovic fell over a balcony into a fountain.
!?
He was humiliated. Everyone laughed at him. He left in a huff, and no one saw him for months.
When he came back, he was calling himself "count," and from then on, he had it in for your parents.

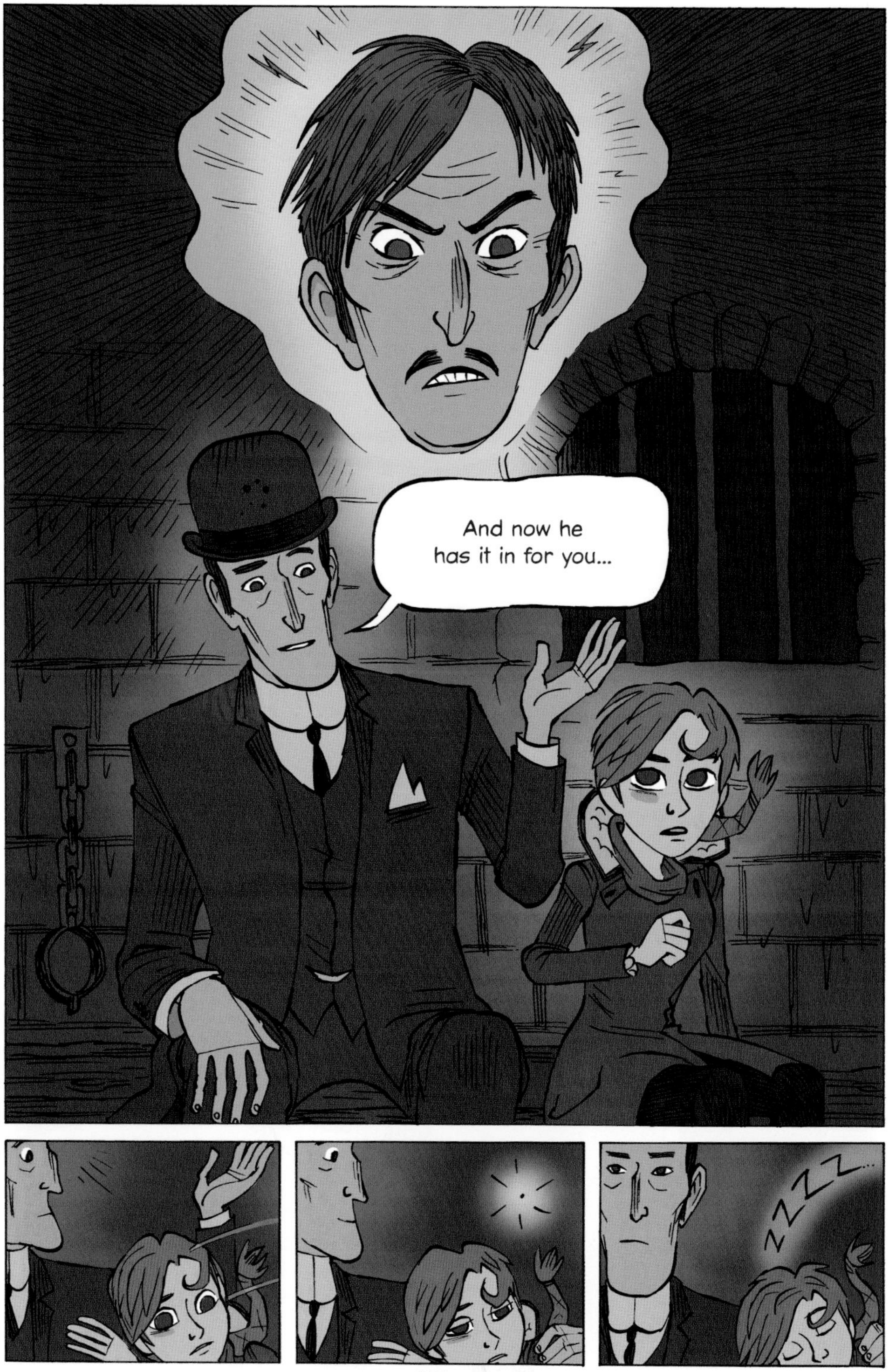
And now he has it in for you...
ZZZZ...

Later...

What time is it, Napoleon?

Around four in the morning.

Can't sleep?

You know, if it's true about what the Count is up to... It's very dangerous. He doesn't know what he's doing. He could do anything.

He could **summon** anything. Napoleon, you're right. We have to stop him.

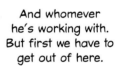

And whomever he's working with. But first we have to get out of here.

Oh, yes. I'd forgotten.

Don't worry, miss. While you were asleep I took the liberty of arranging an escape plan.

You did?

I did. Catcher Jack returned to the window, just here. I gave him the keys to Dorothy and instructions for Mrs. White.

118

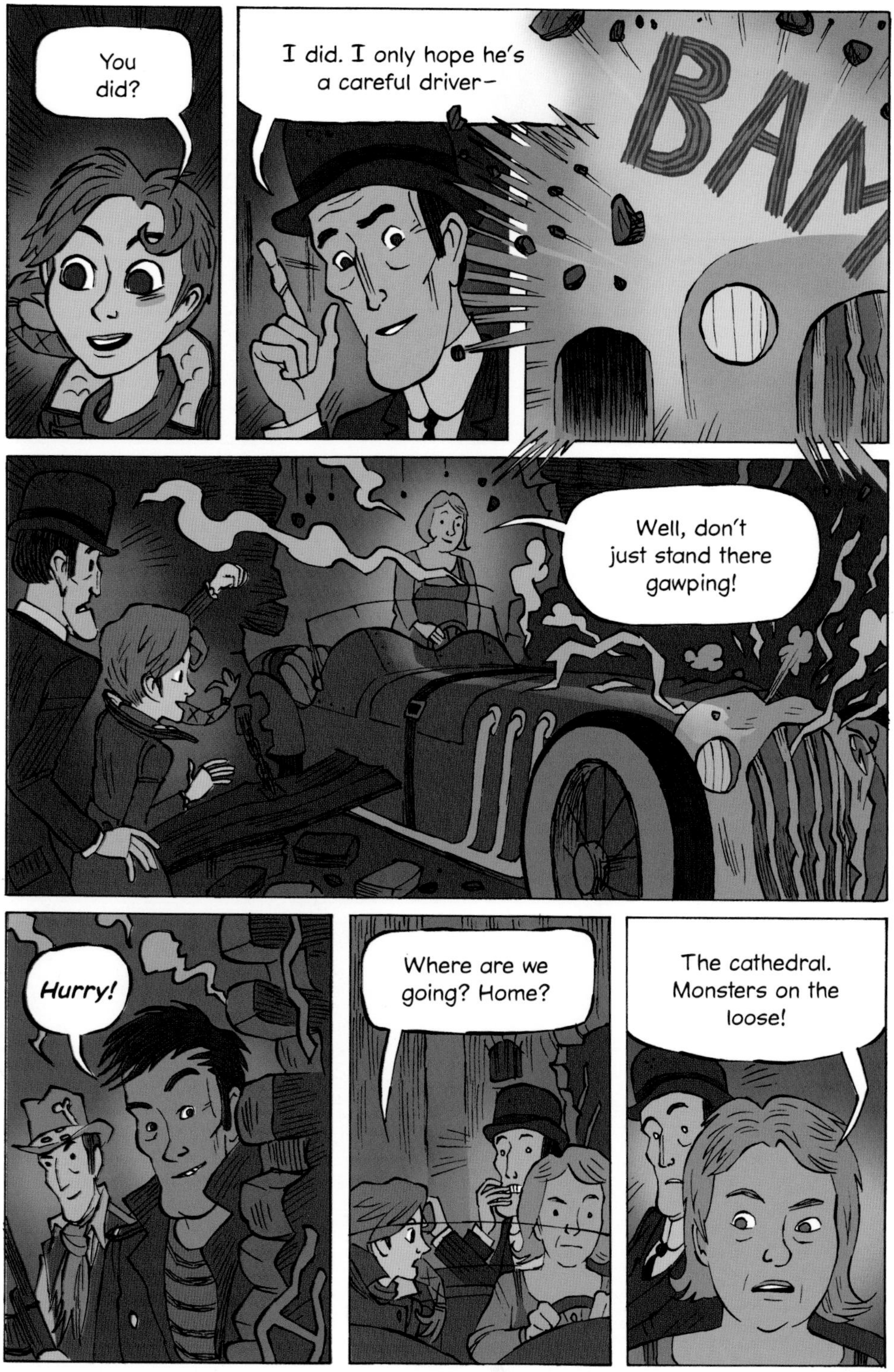
You did?
I did. I only hope he's a careful driver–
BAM
Well, don't just stand there gawping!
Hurry!
Where are we going? Home?
The cathedral. Monsters on the loose!

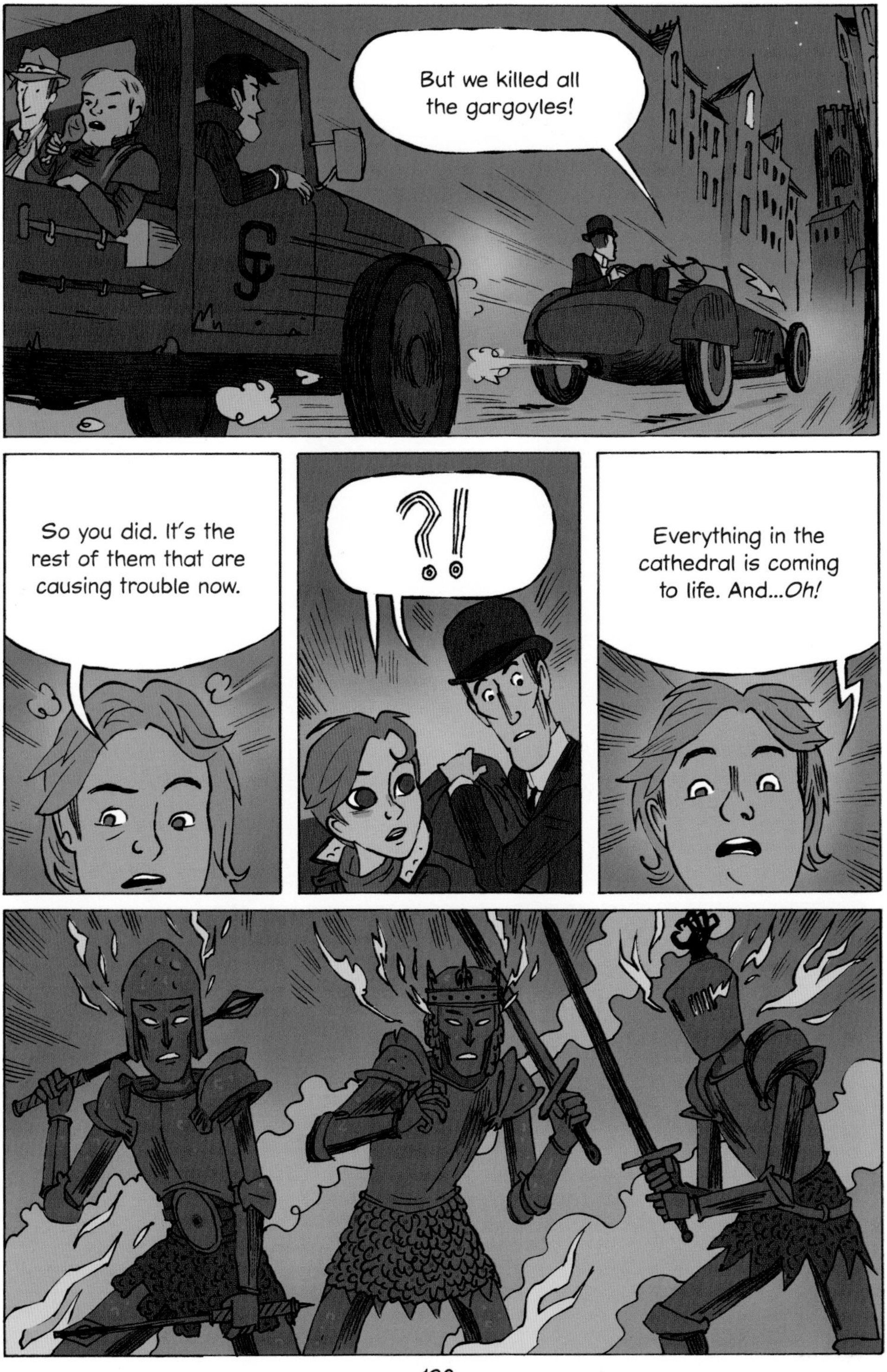
But we killed all the gargoyles!
So you did. It's the rest of them that are causing trouble now.
?!
Everything in the cathedral is coming to life. And...*Oh!*

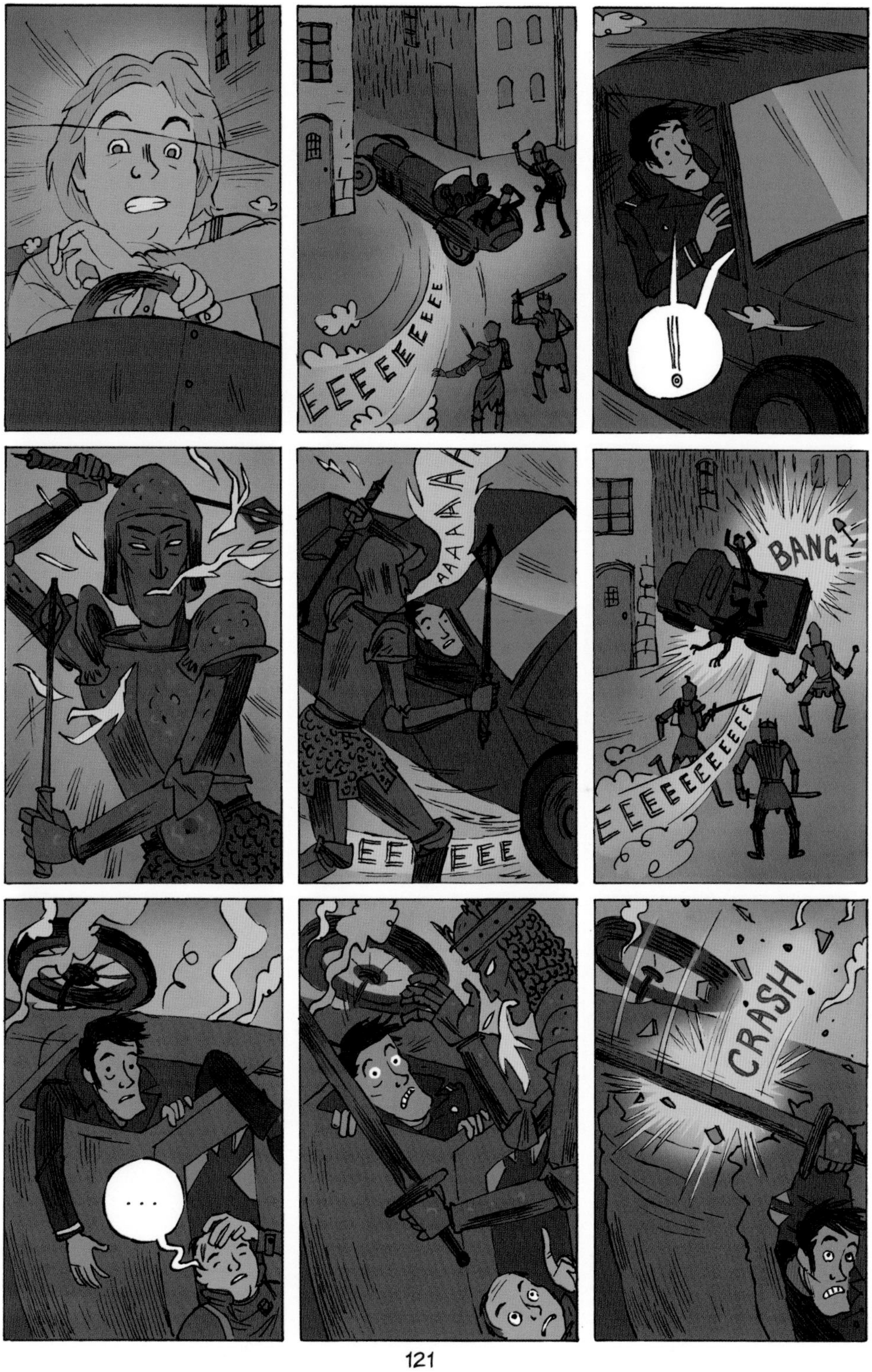
EEEEEEEEEEEE
!!
AAAAAAAAH
EEEEEEE
BANG
EEEEEEEEEEEE
...
CRASH

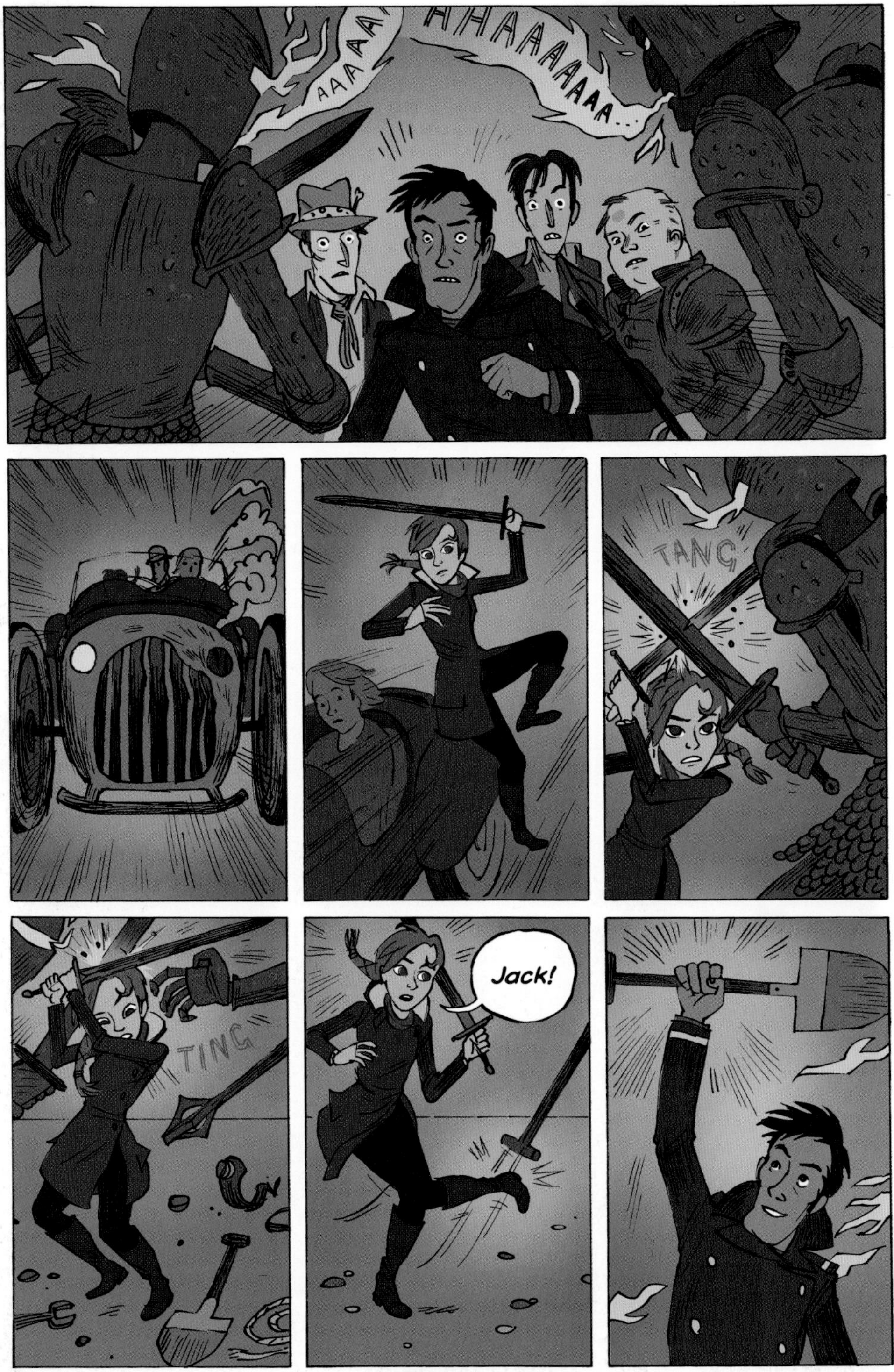
AAAAAAHHAAAAAAAAAAA...
TANG
TING
Jack!

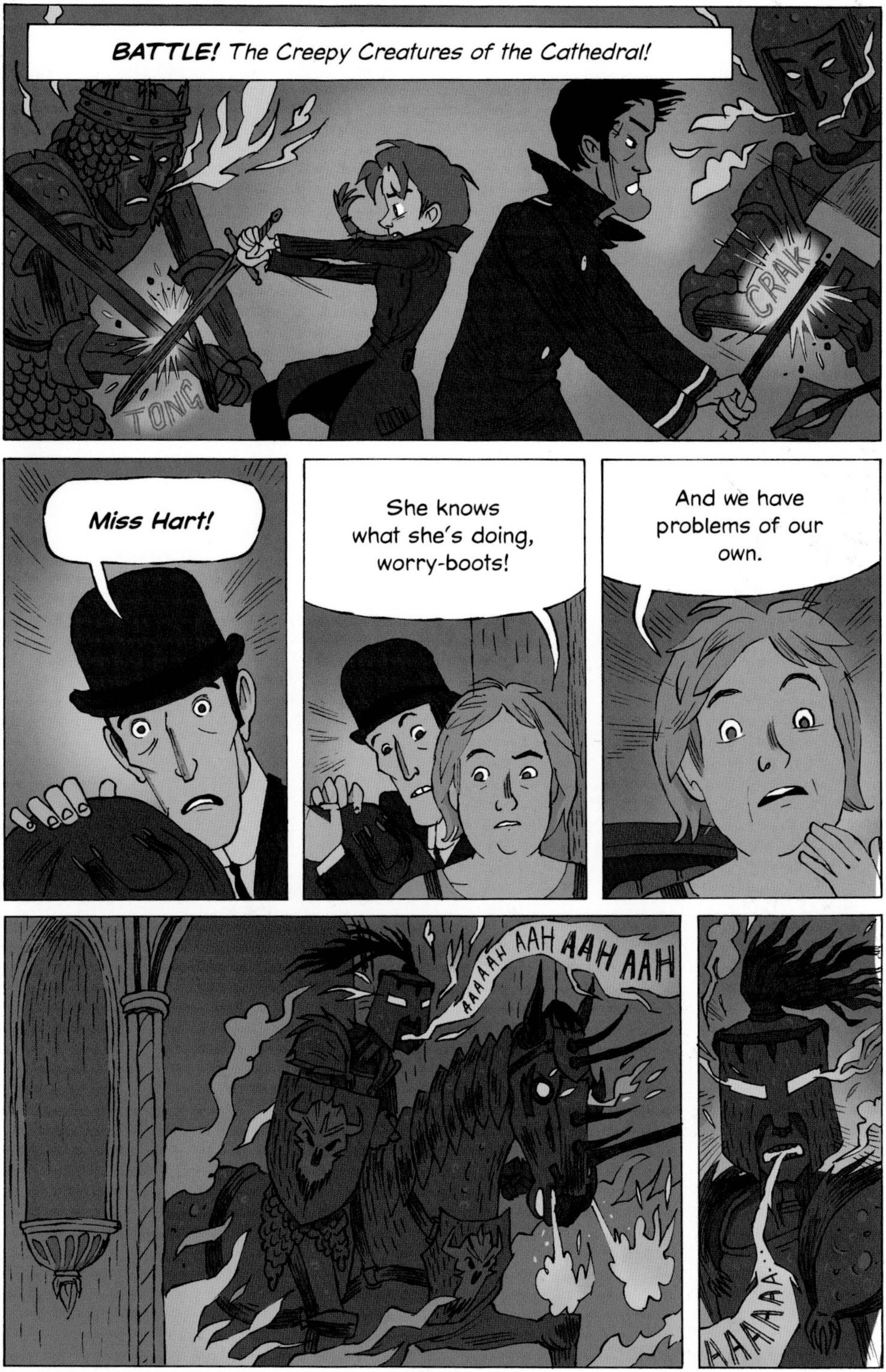

BATTLE! The Creepy Creatures of the Cathedral!
TONG
CRAK
Miss Hart!
She knows what she's doing, worry-boots!
And we have problems of our own.
AAAAAH AAH AAH AAH
AAAAAAA...

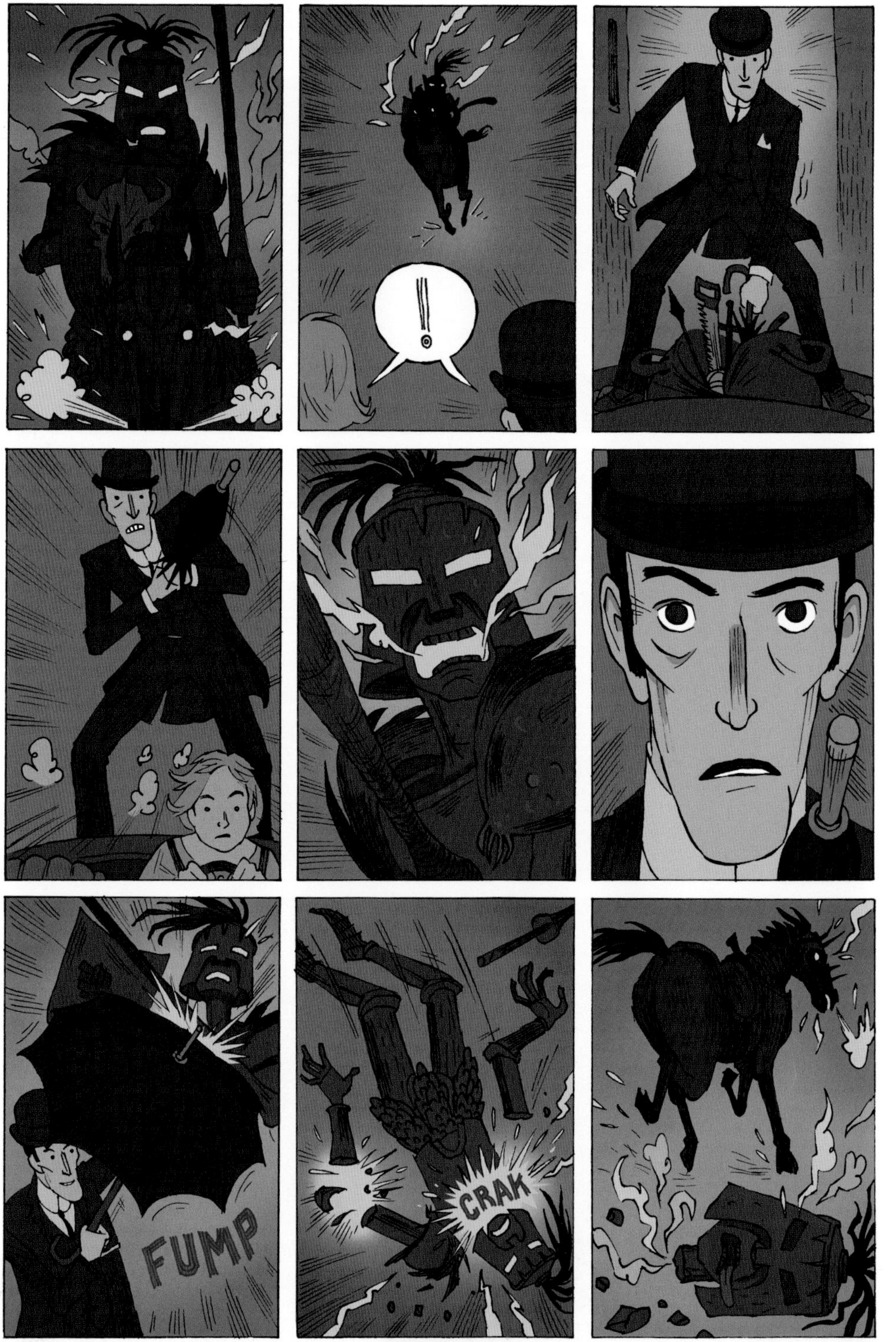
!
FUMP
CRAK

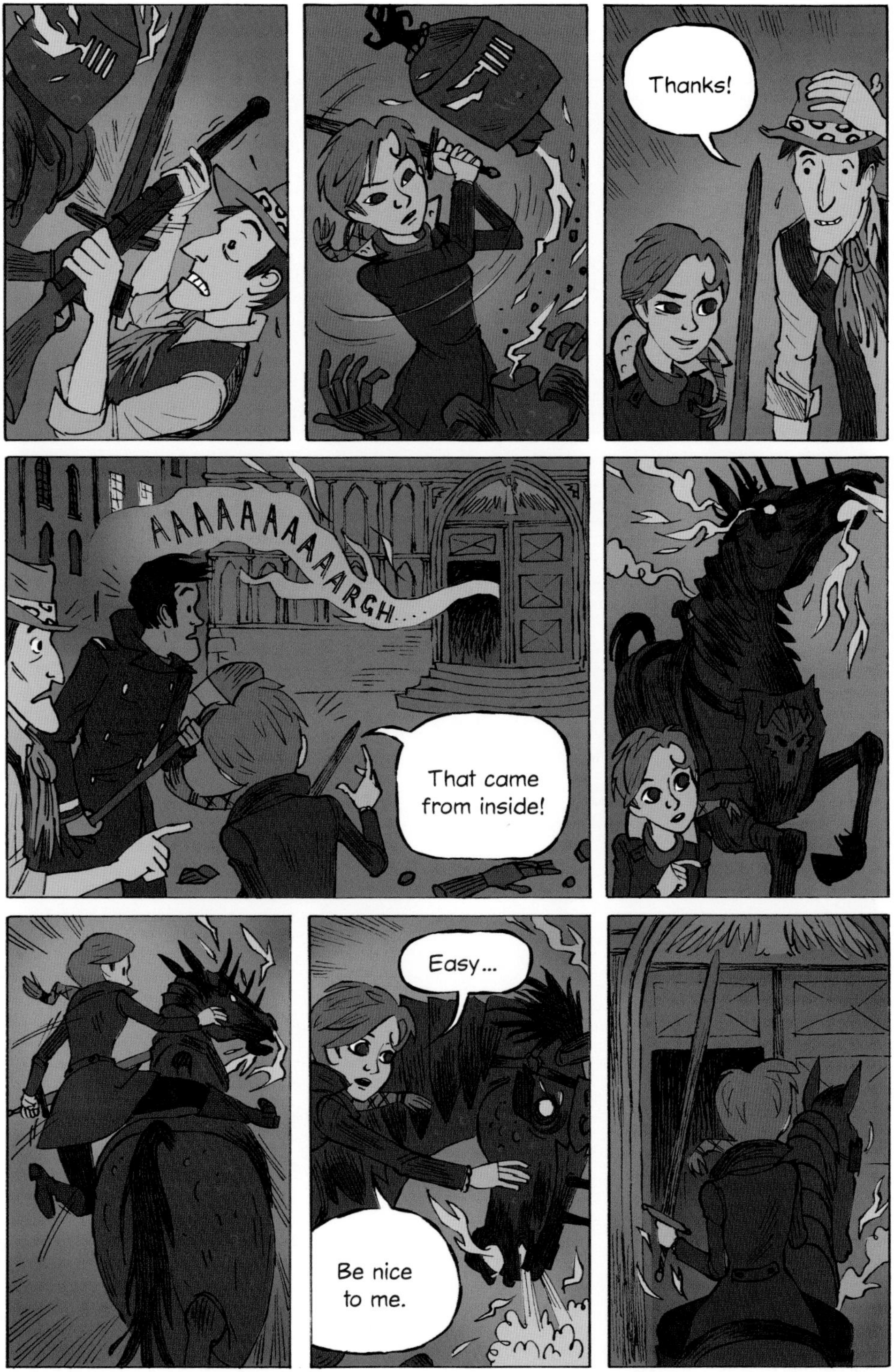
Thanks!
AAAAAAAAAAAARGH
That came from inside!
Easy...
Be nice to me.

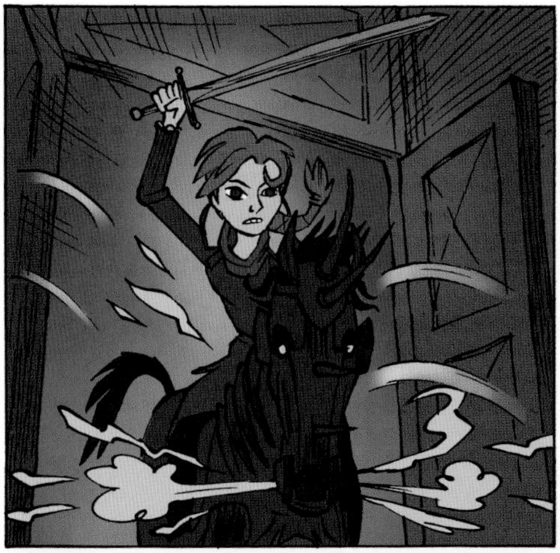

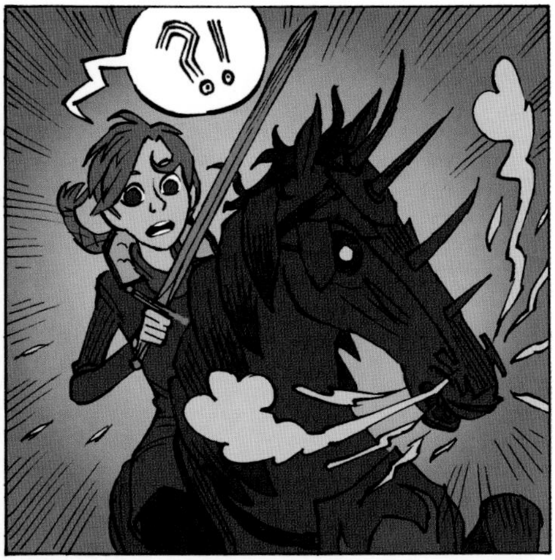
?!

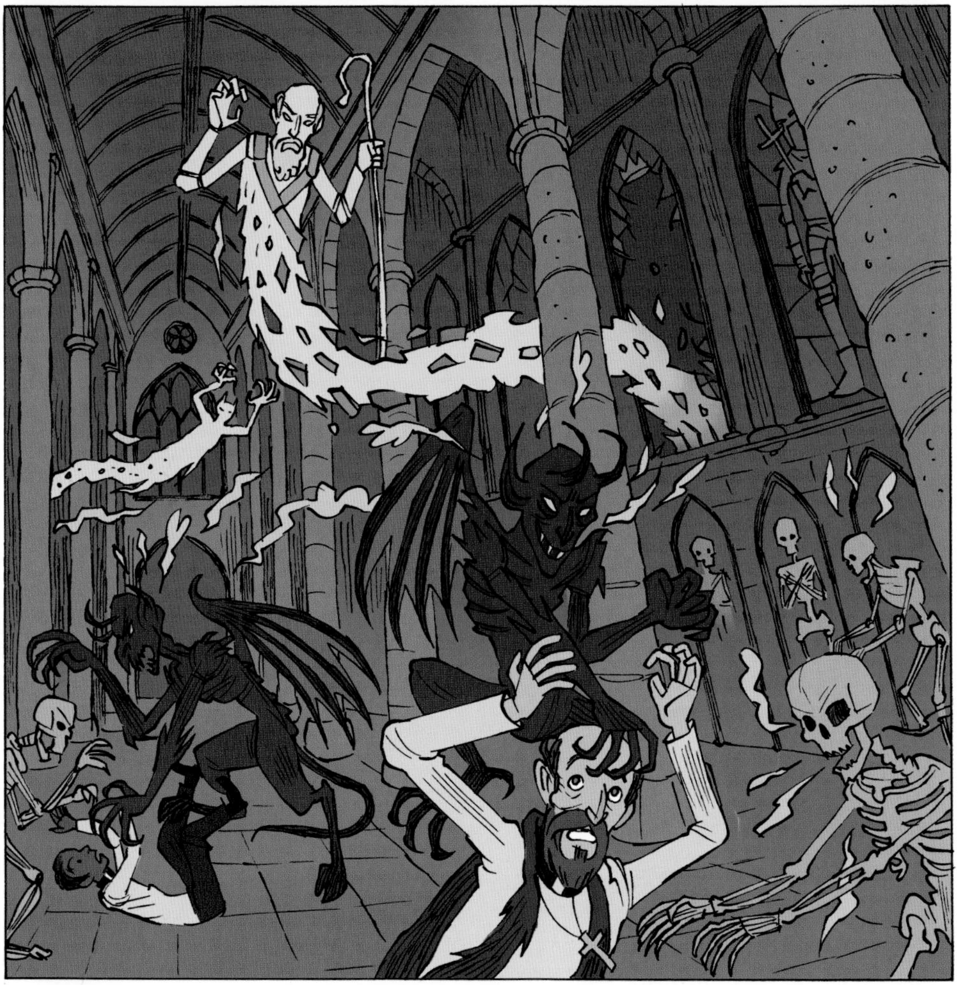

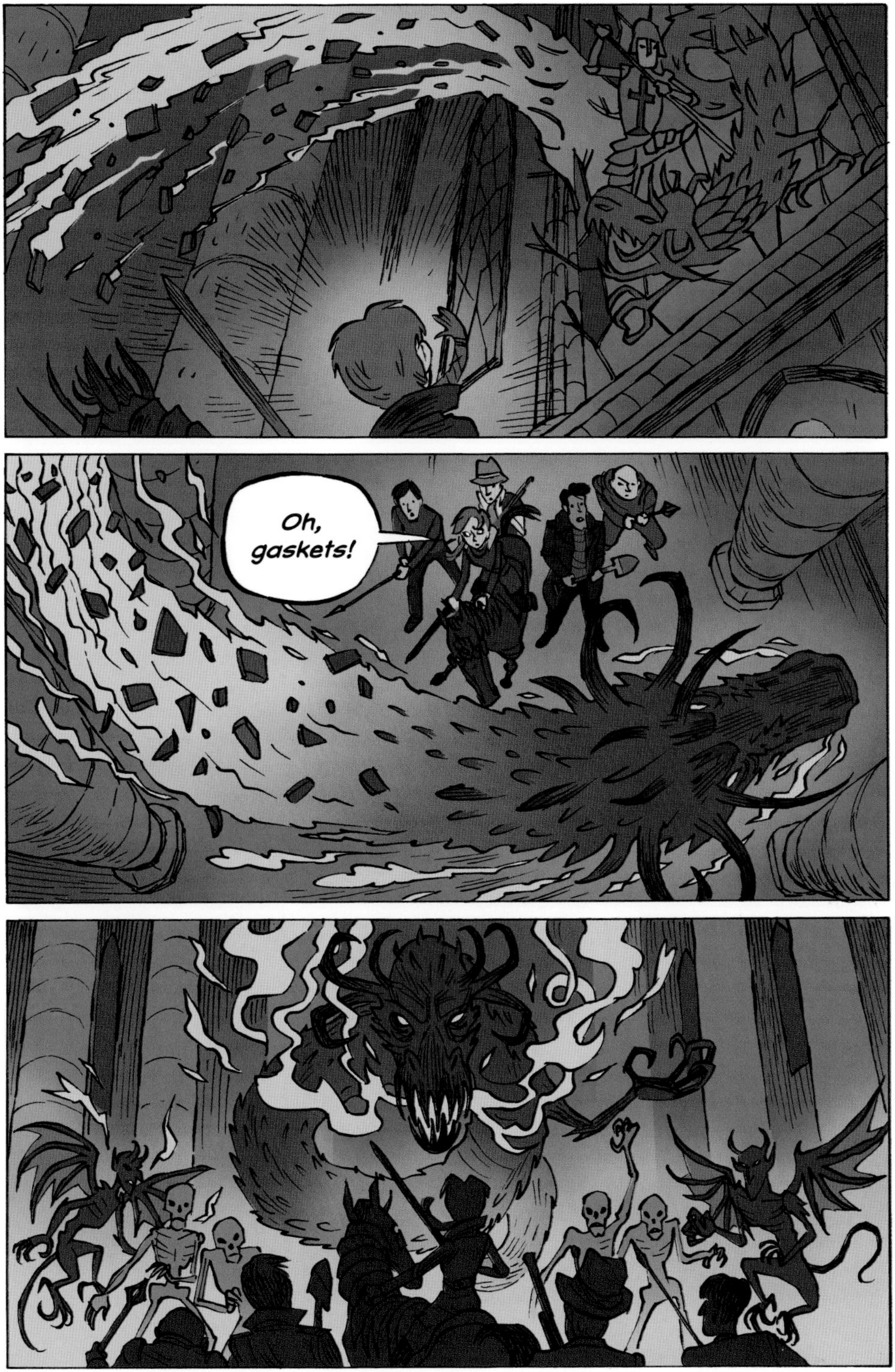
Oh, gaskets!

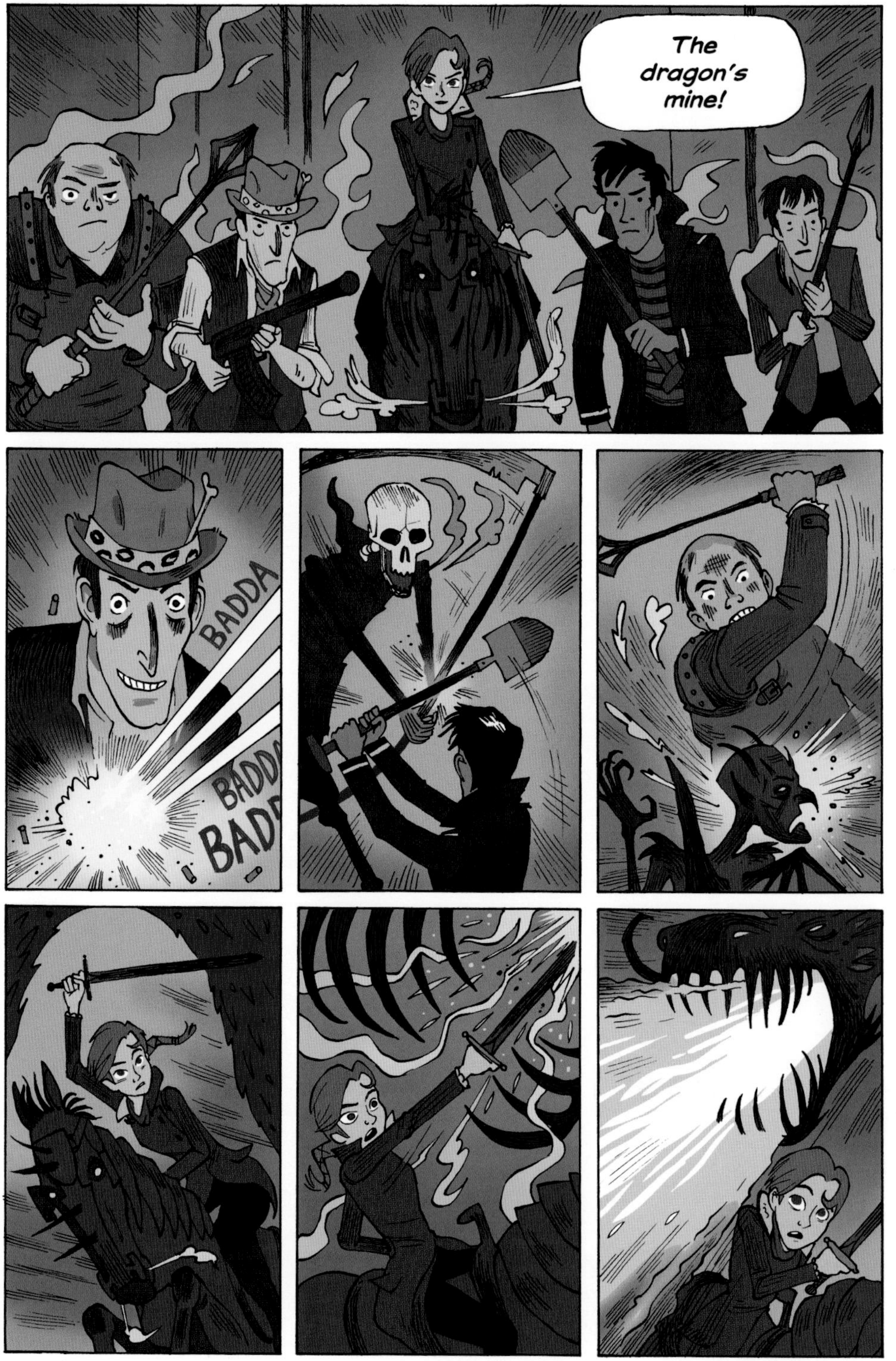
The dragon's mine!
BADDA
BADDA
BADD

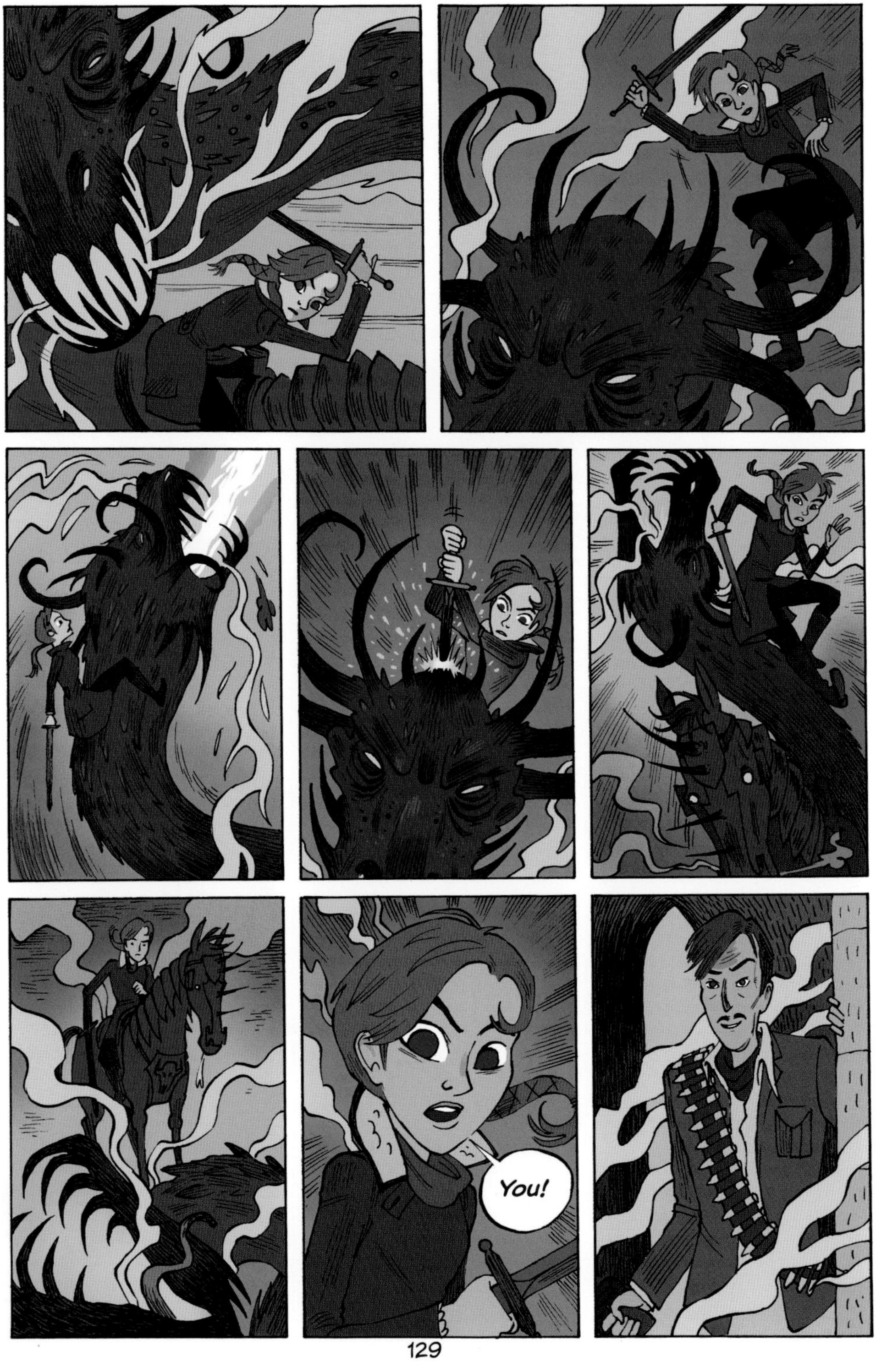
You!

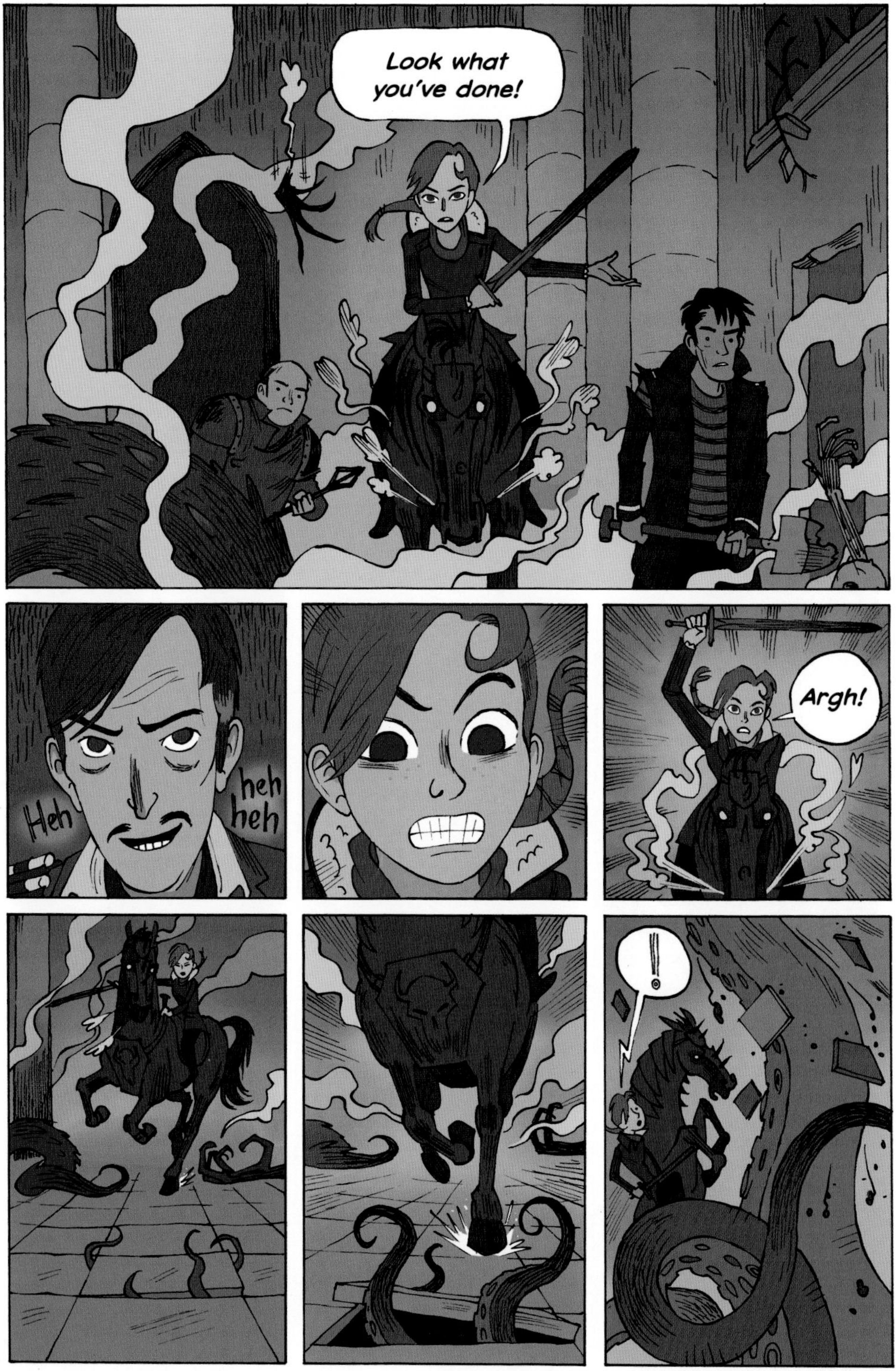
Look what you've done!
Heh
heh heh
Argh!
!

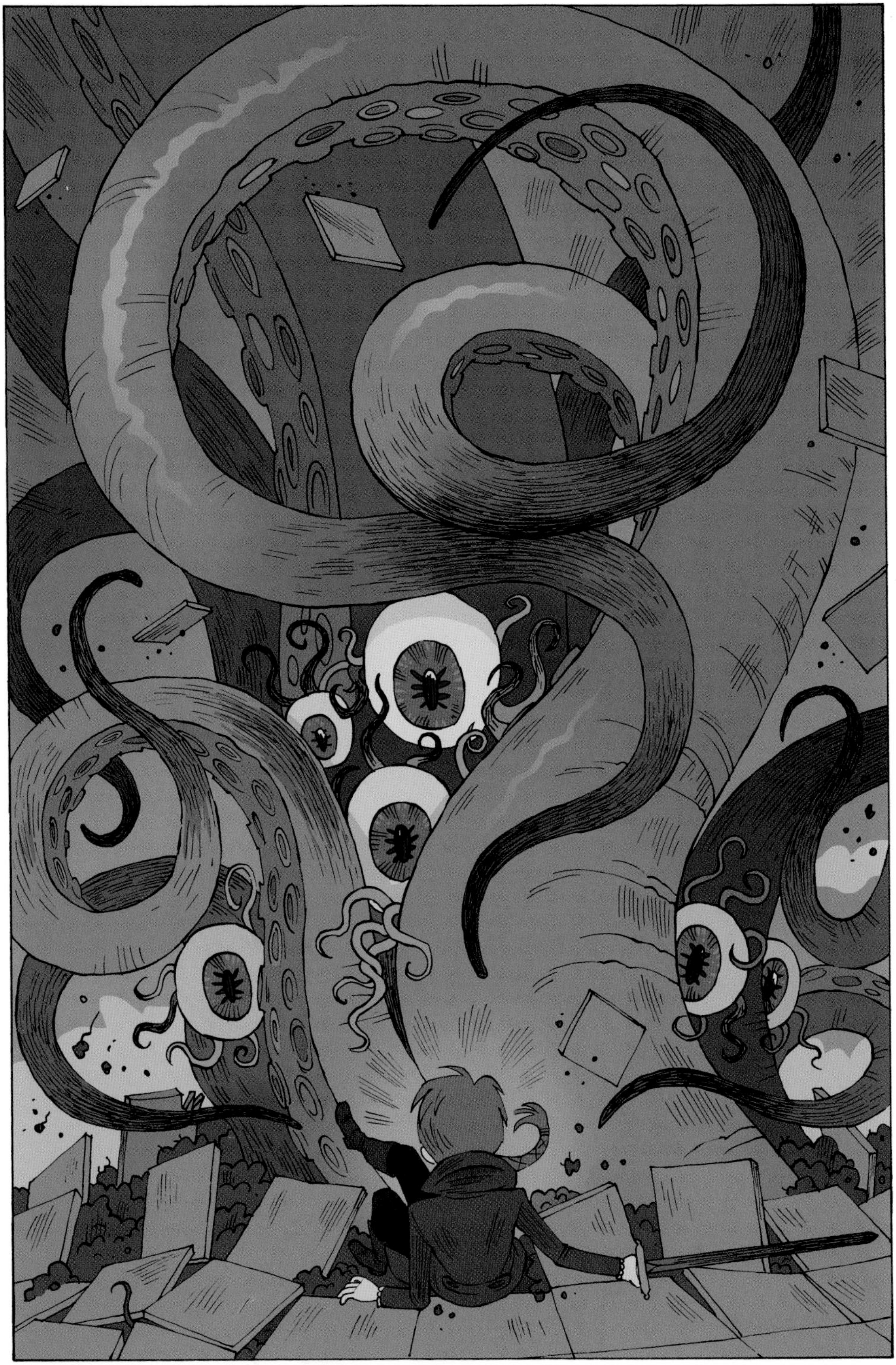

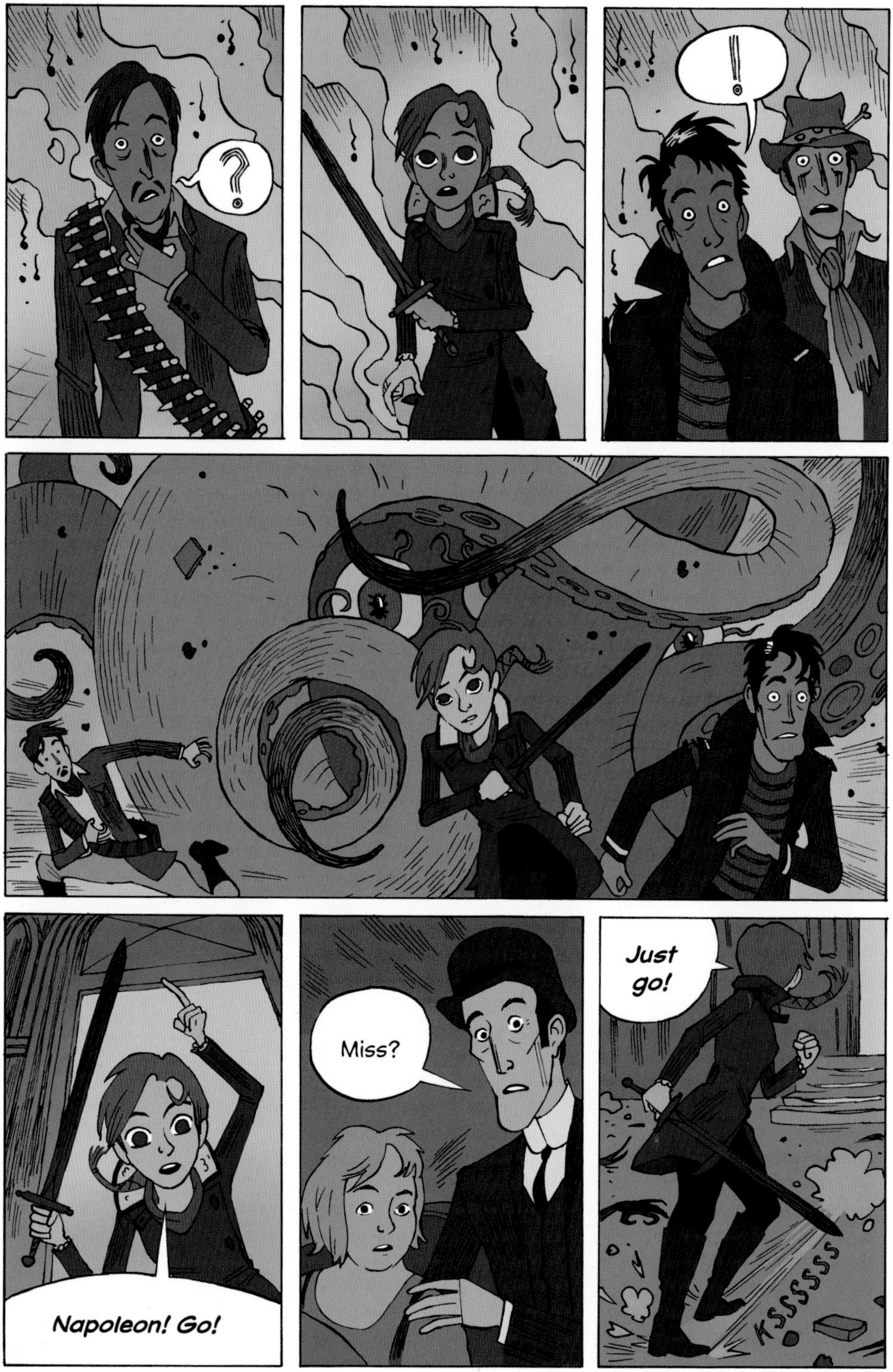
?
!
Napoleon! Go!
Miss?
Just go!
KSSSSSS

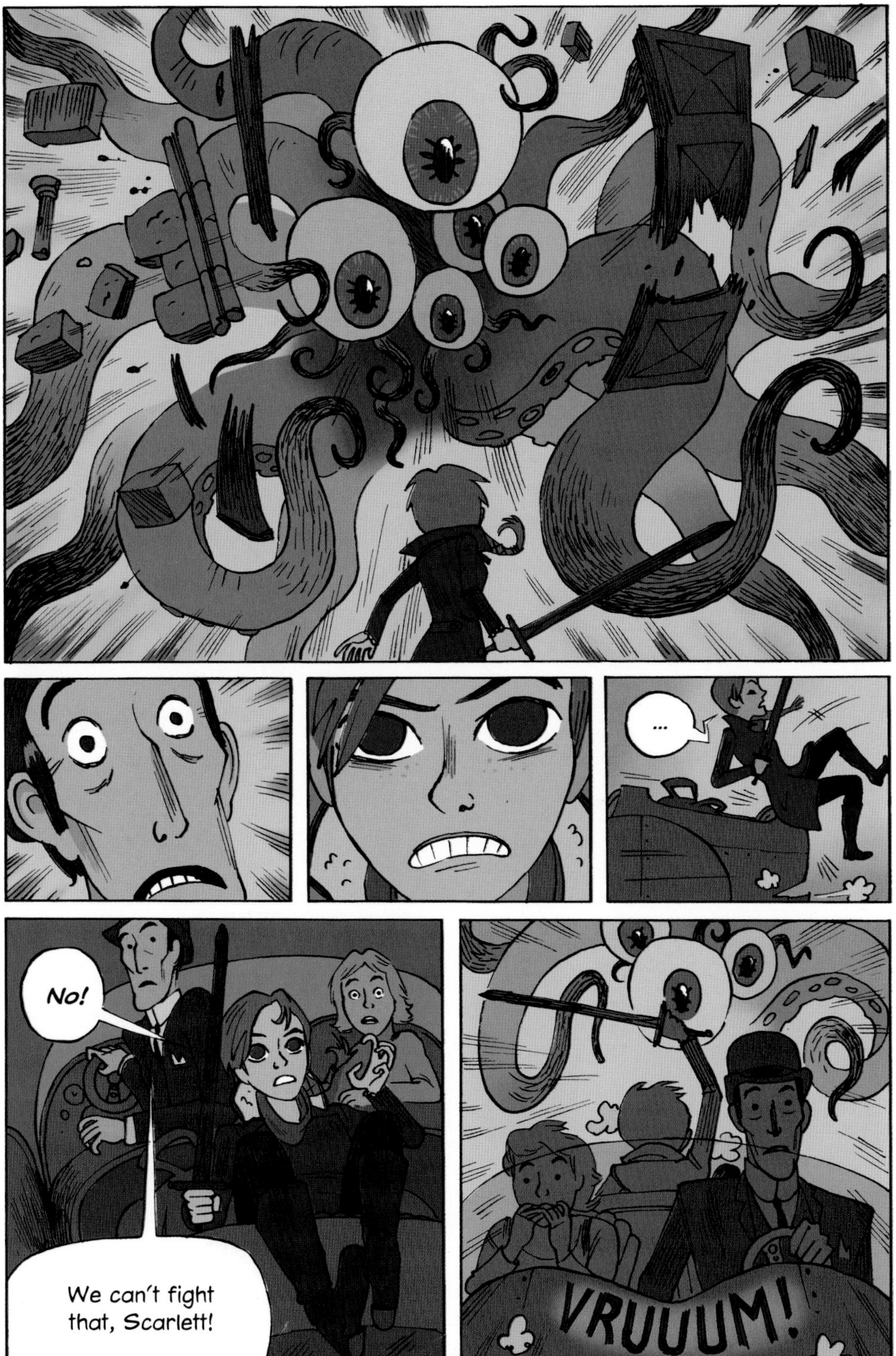
...
No!
We can't fight that, Scarlett!
VRUUUM!

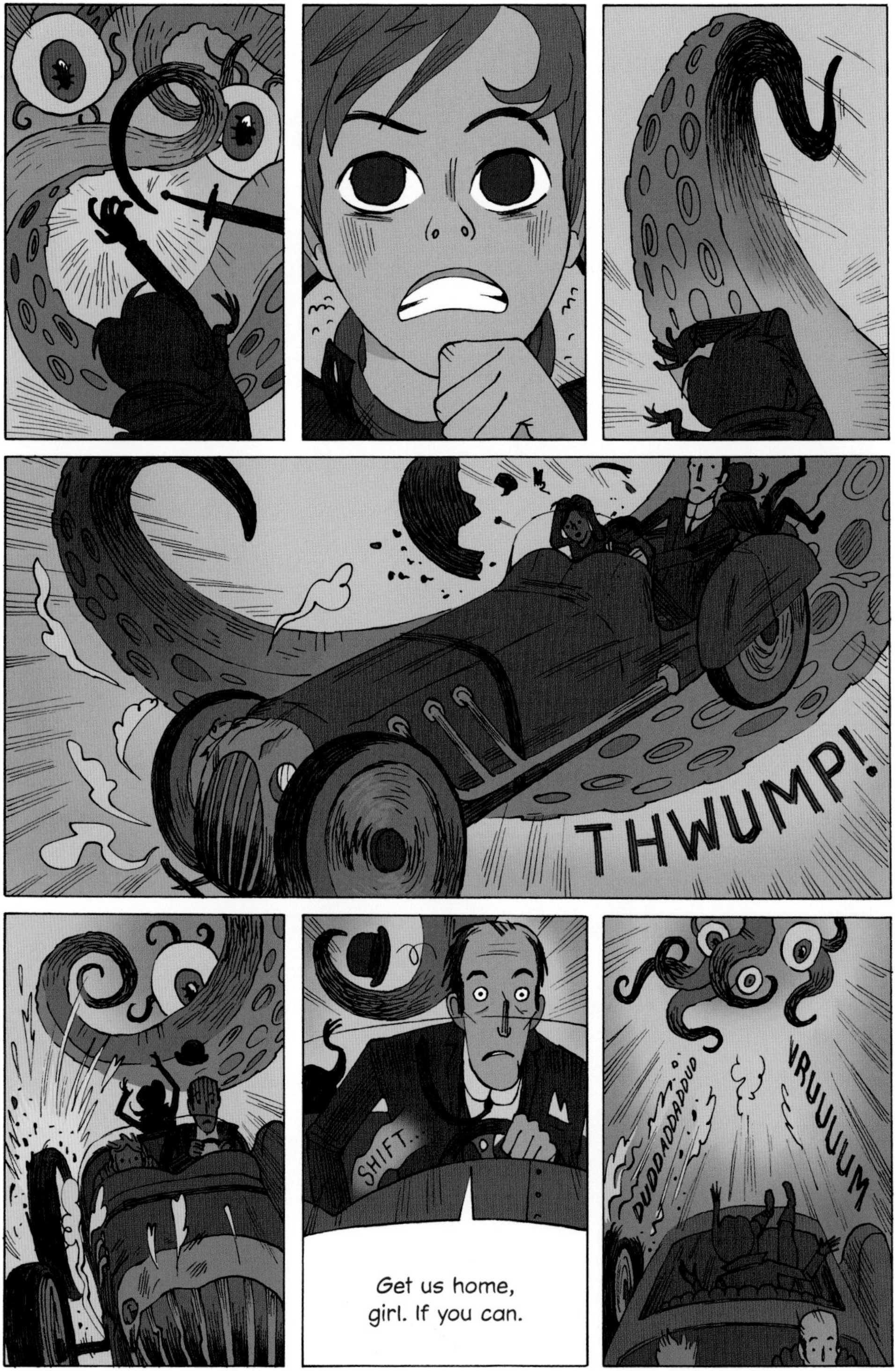
THWUMP!
SHIFT.
Get us home, girl. If you can.
DUDDADDADDUD
VRUUUUUM

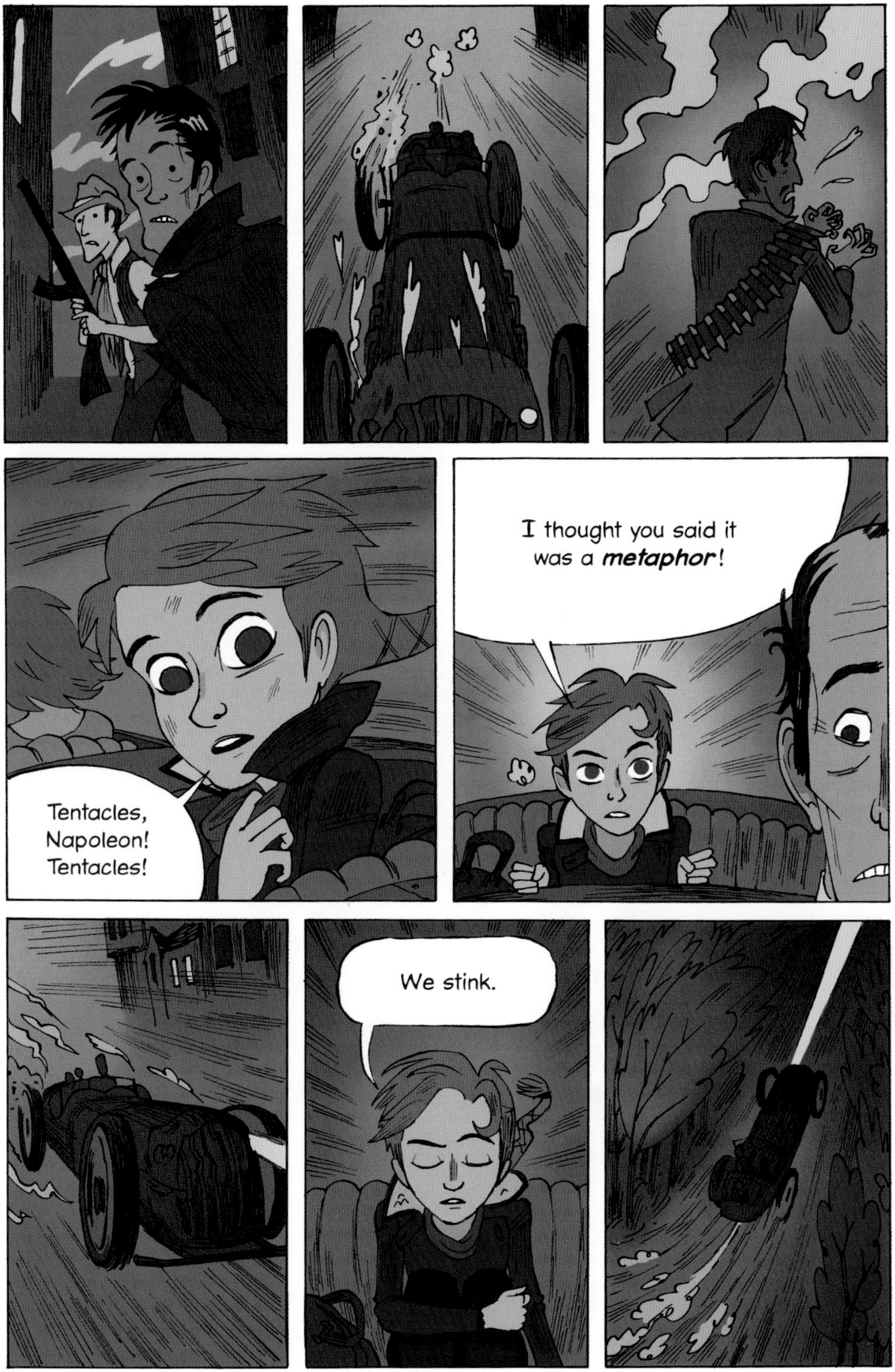
Tentacles, Napoleon! Tentacles!
I thought you said it was a ***metaphor***!
We stink.

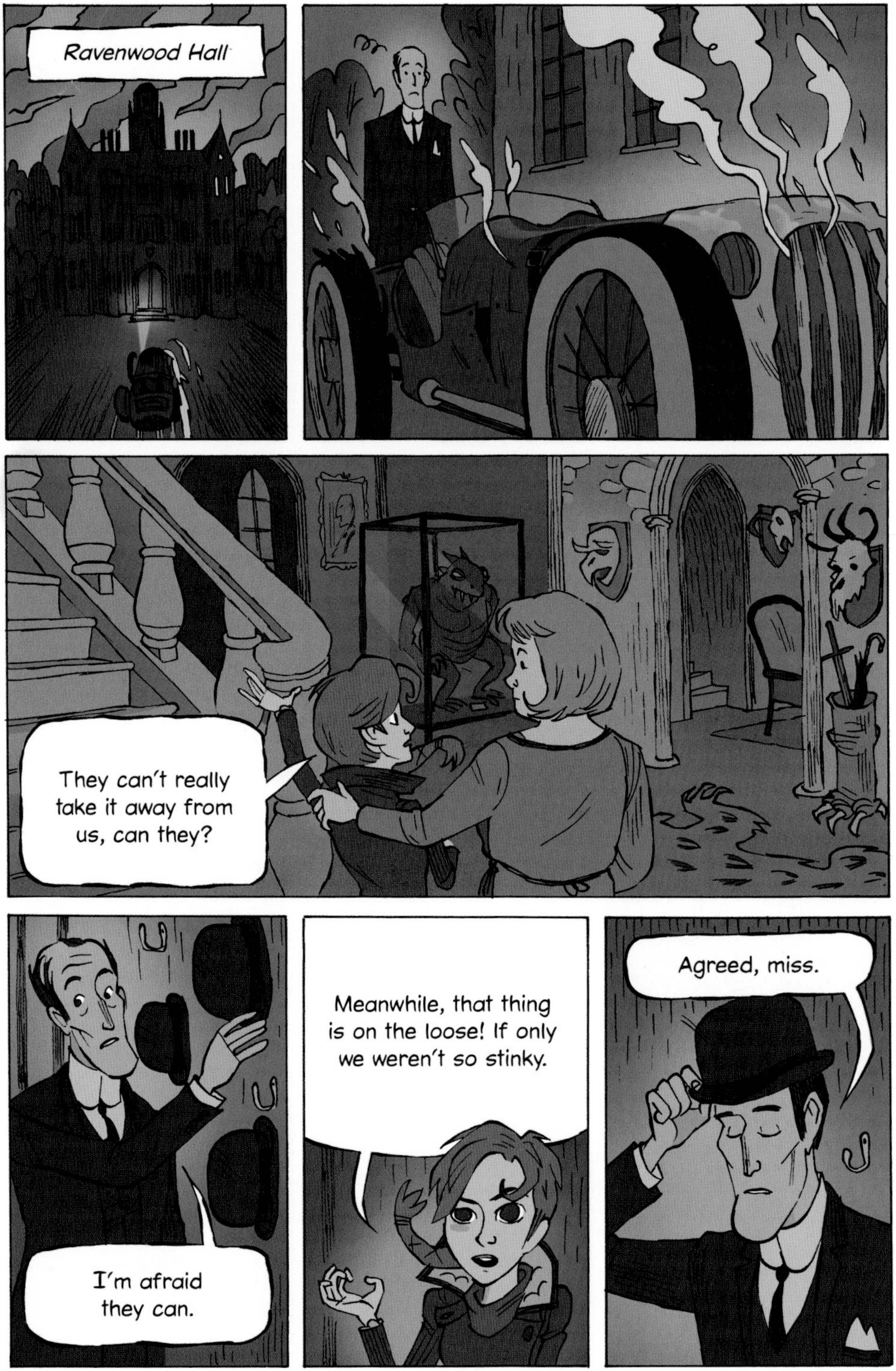
Ravenwood Hall
They can't really take it away from us, can they?
I'm afraid they can.
Meanwhile, that thing is on the loose! If only we weren't so stinky.
Agreed, miss.

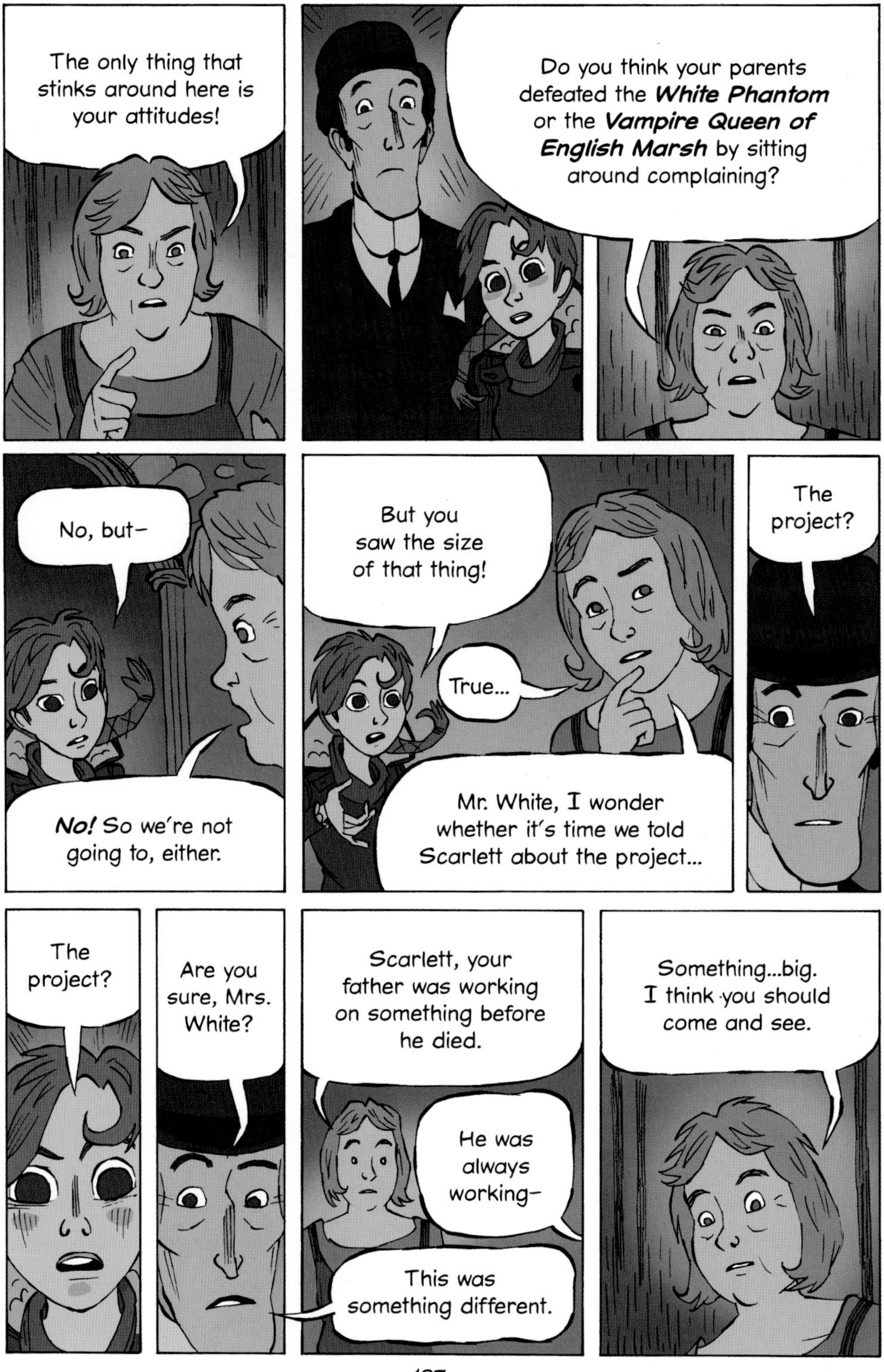
The only thing that stinks around here is your attitudes!
Do you think your parents defeated the ***White Phantom*** or the ***Vampire Queen of English Marsh*** by sitting around complaining?
No, but–
No! So we're not going to, either.
But you saw the size of that thing!
True...
Mr. White, I wonder whether it's time we told Scarlett about the project...
The project?
The project?
Are you sure, Mrs. White?
Scarlett, your father was working on something before he died.
He was always working–
This was something different.
Something...big. I think you should come and see.

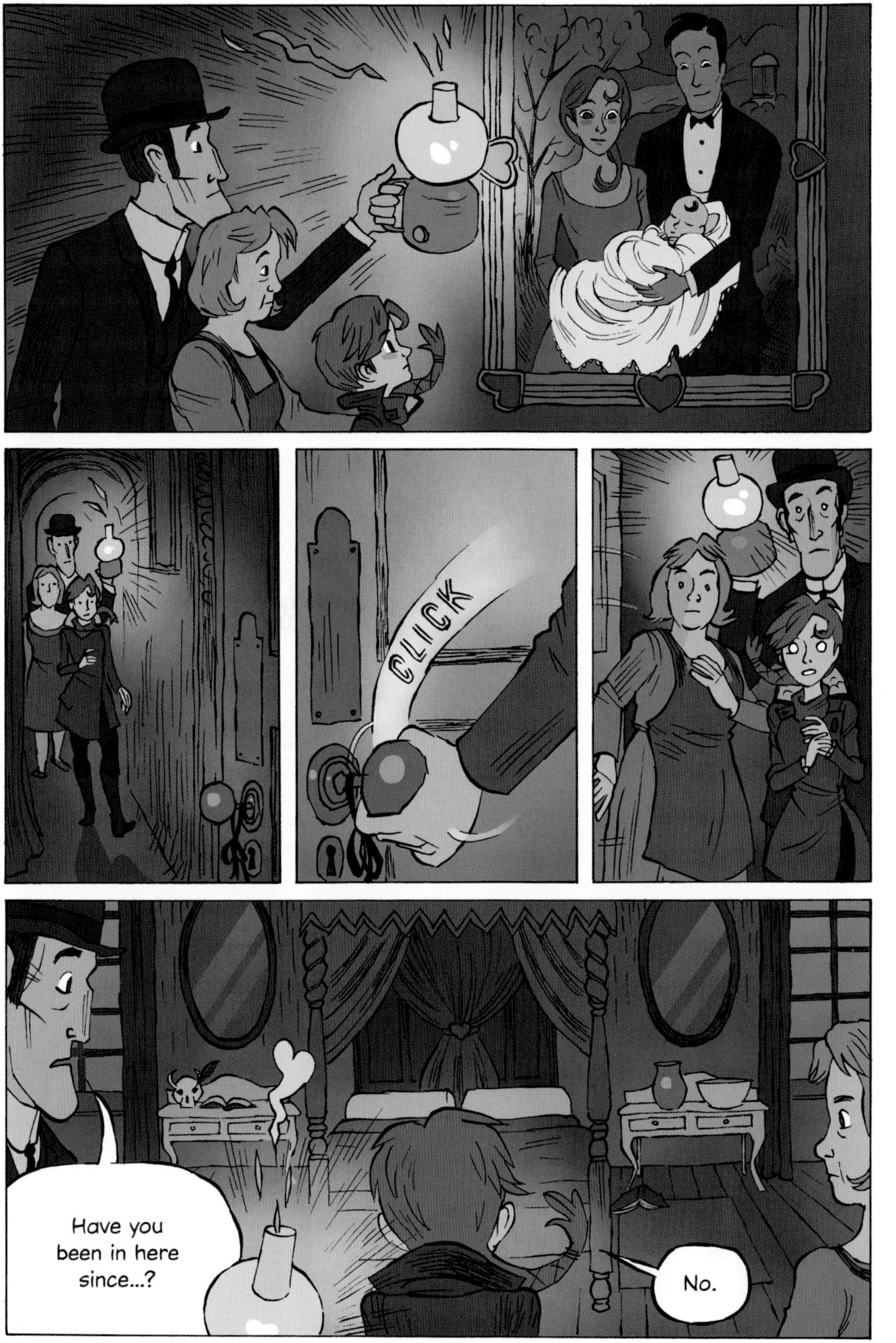
CLICK
Have you been in here since...?
No.

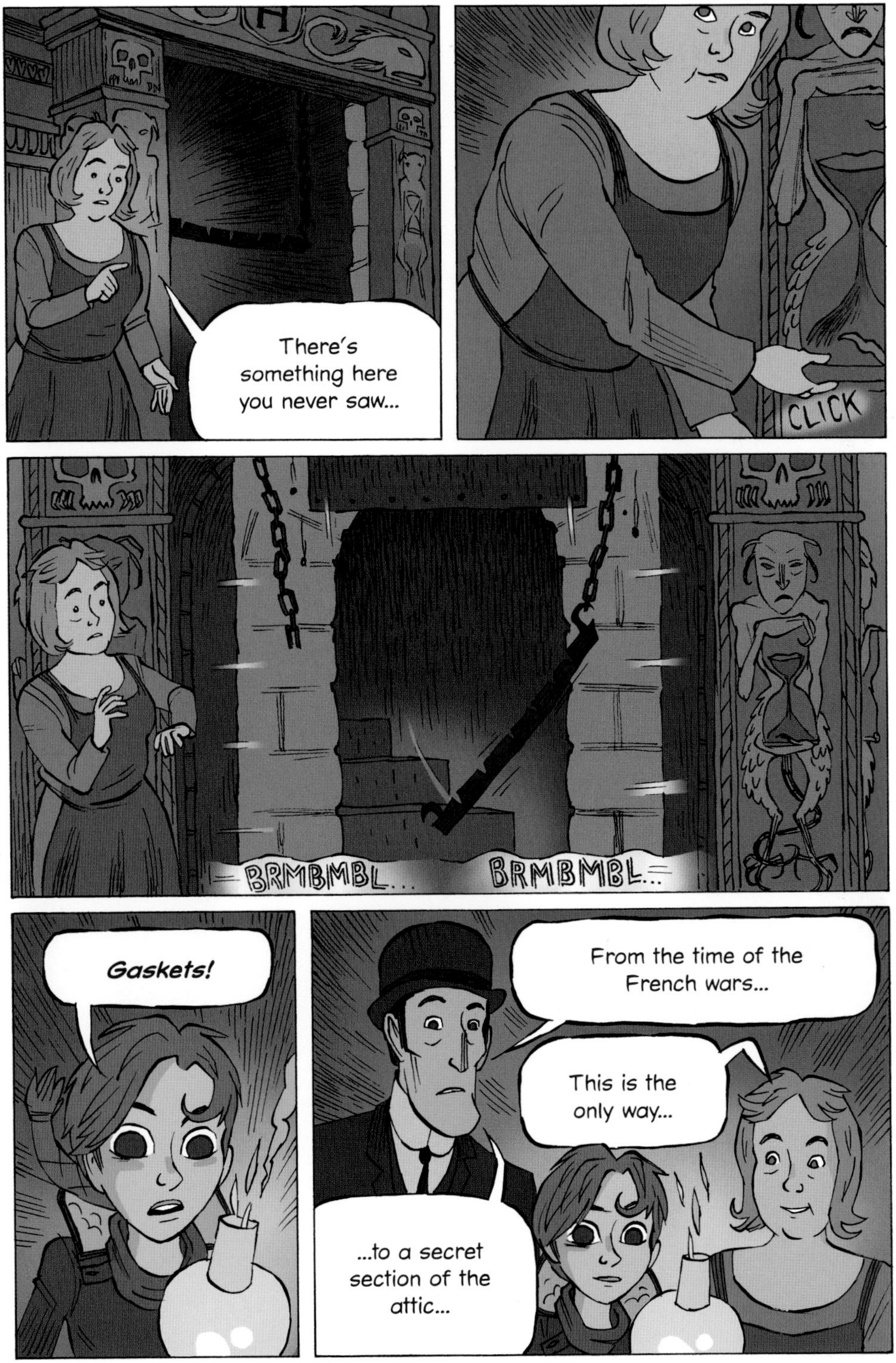

There's something here you never saw...
CLICK
BRMBMBL... BRMBMBL...
Gaskets!
From the time of the French wars...
This is the only way...
...to a secret section of the attic...

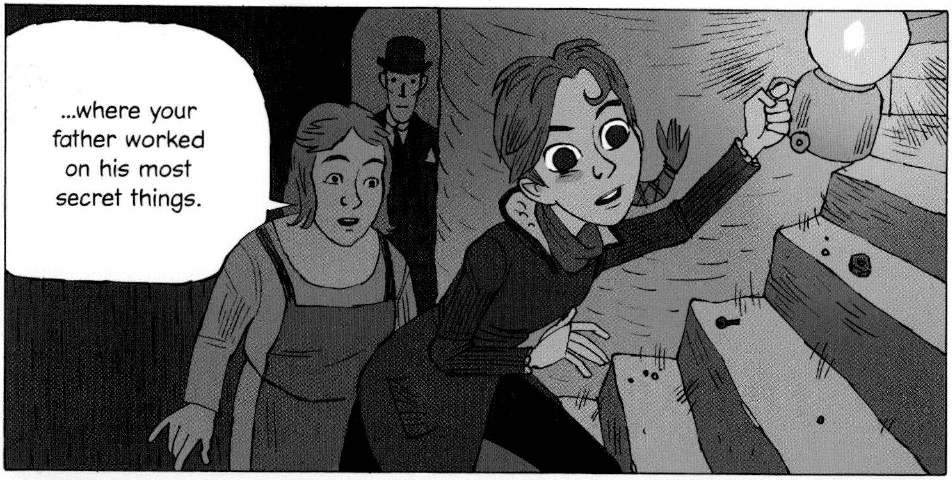
...where your father worked on his most secret things.

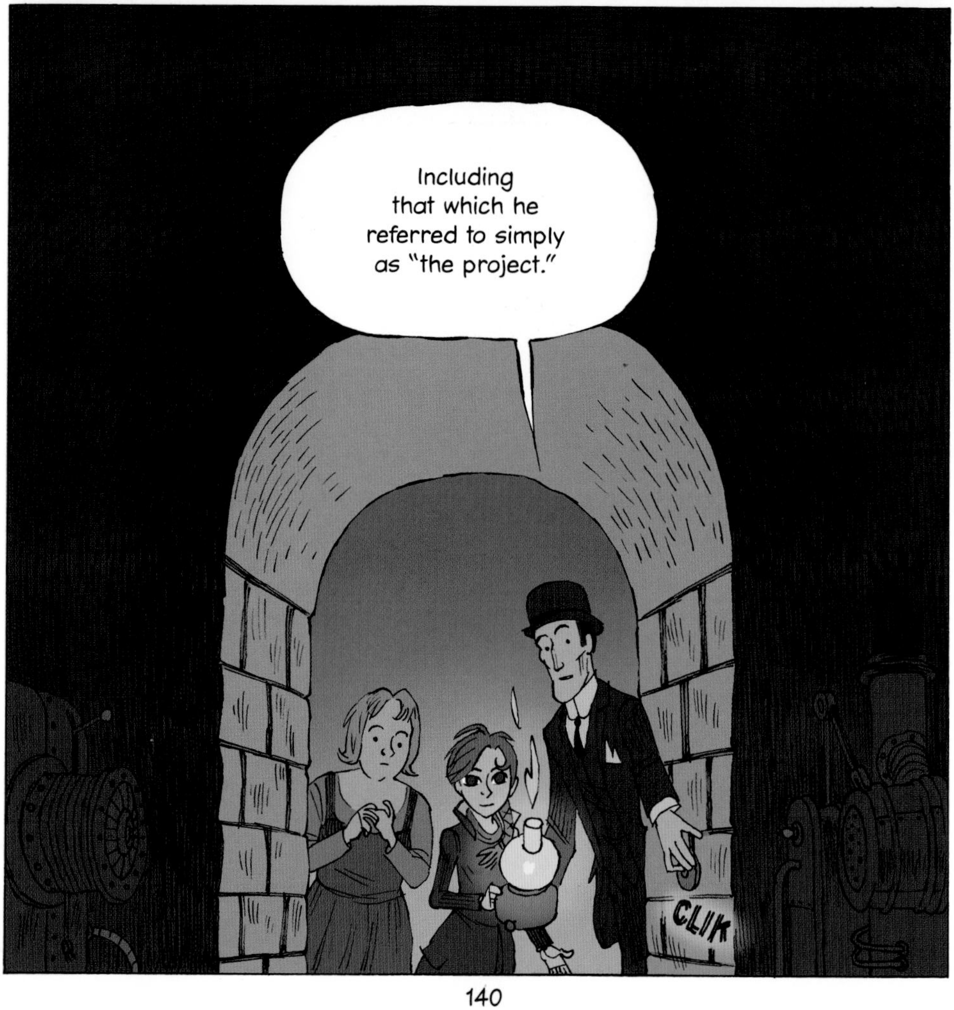
Including that which he referred to simply as "the project."
CLIK

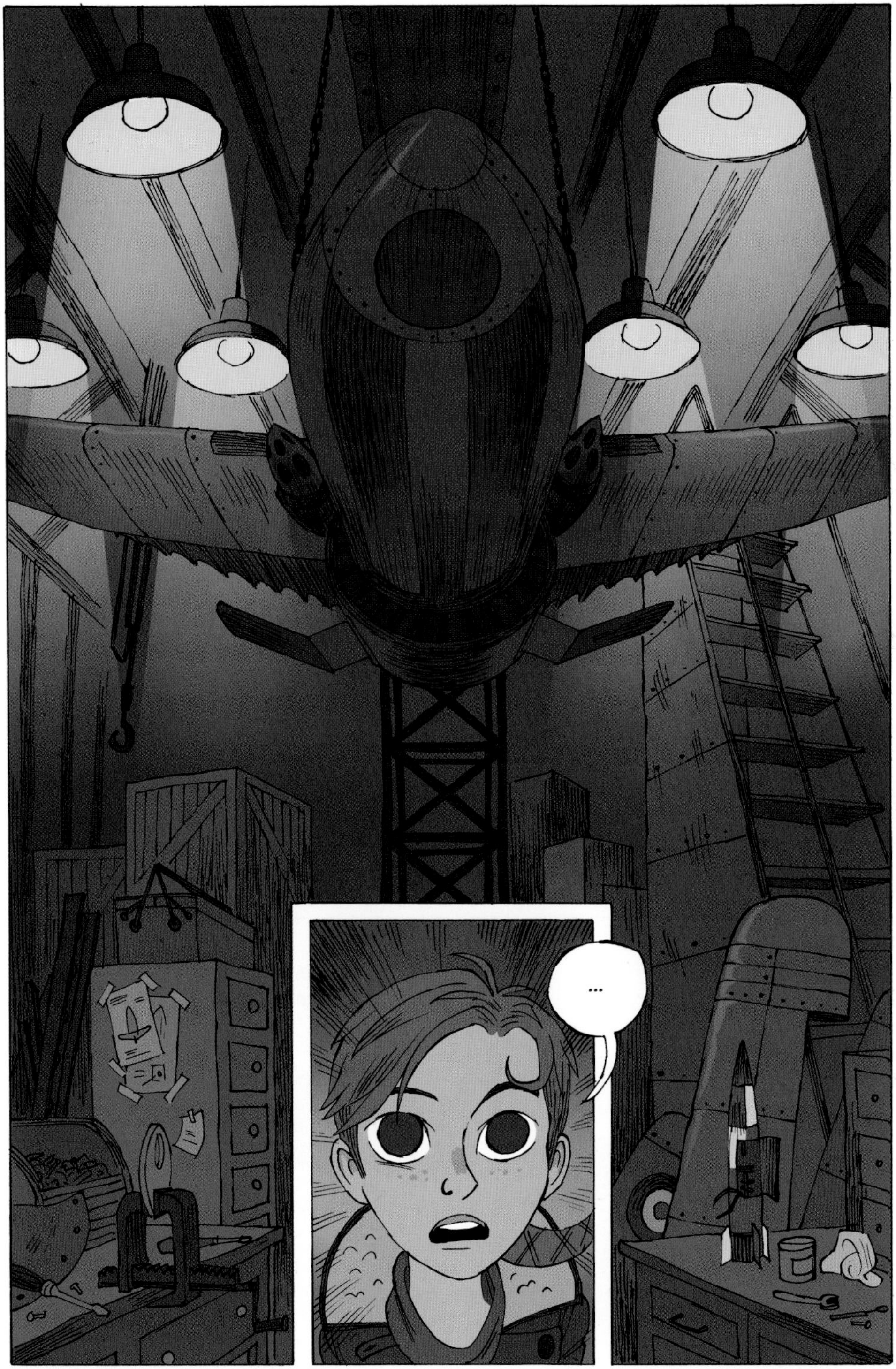
...

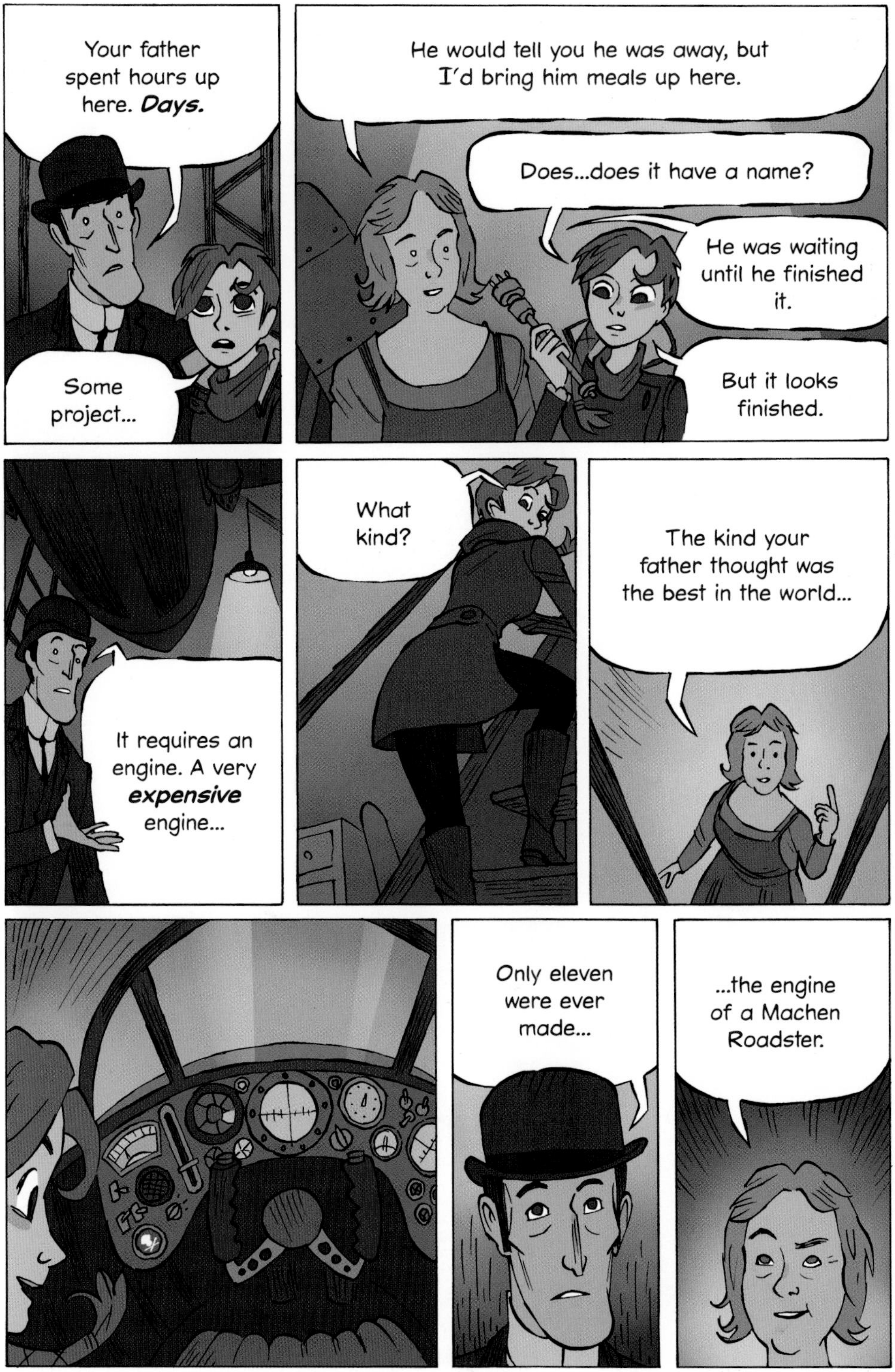
Your father spent hours up here. *Days.*
Some project...
He would tell you he was away, but I'd bring him meals up here.
Does...does it have a name?
He was waiting until he finished it.
But it looks finished.
It requires an engine. A very *expensive* engine...
What kind?
The kind your father thought was the best in the world...
Only eleven were ever made...
...the engine of a Machen Roadster.

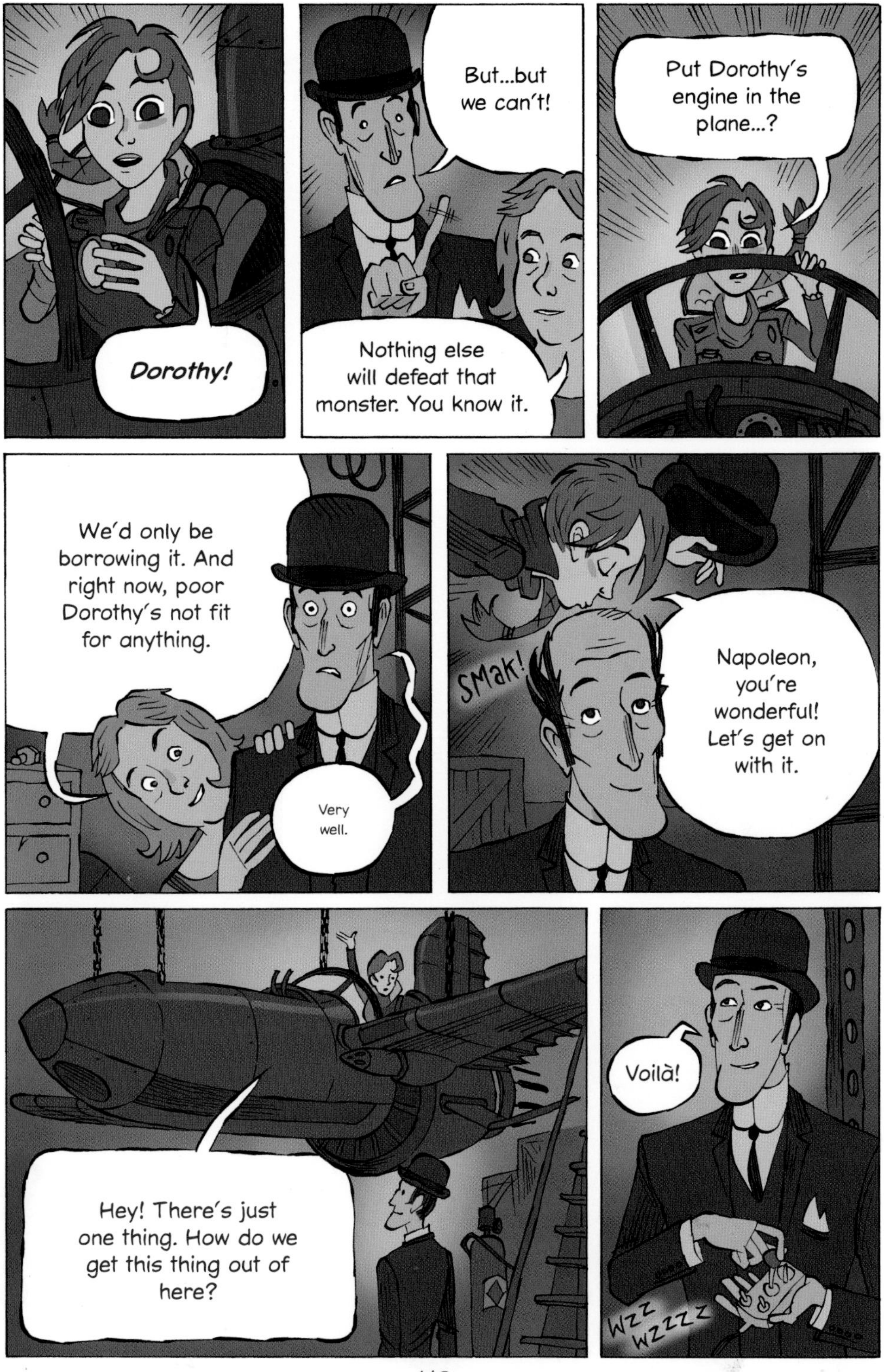
Dorothy!
But...but we can't!
Nothing else will defeat that monster. You know it.
Put Dorothy's engine in the plane...?
We'd only be borrowing it. And right now, poor Dorothy's not fit for anything.
Very well.
SMAK!
Napoleon, you're wonderful! Let's get on with it.
Hey! There's just one thing. How do we get this thing out of here?
Voilà!
WZZ WZZZZ

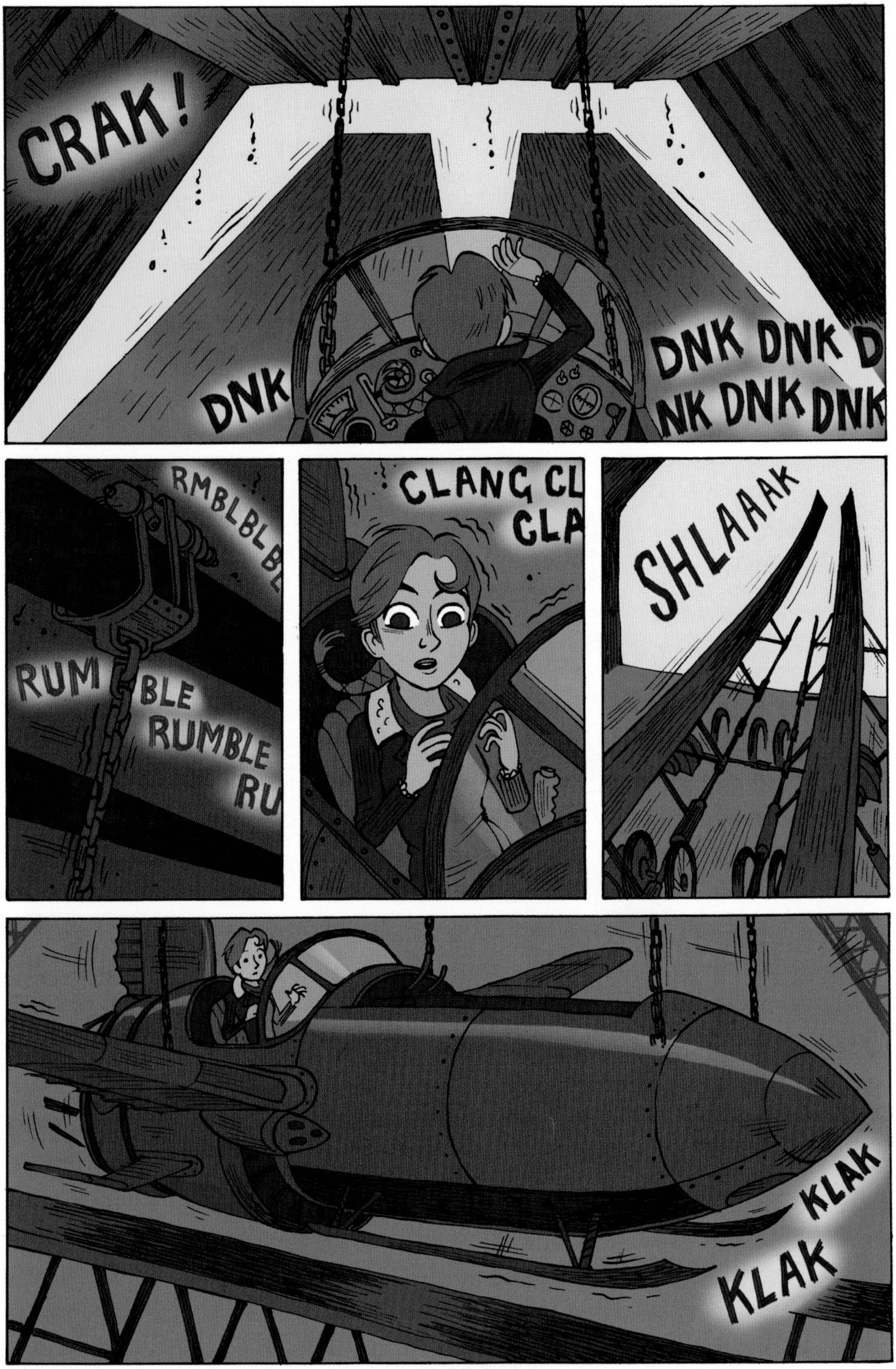
CRAK!
DNK
DNK DNK D
NK DNK DNK
RMBLBLBLBL
RUM BLE
RUMBLE
RU
CLANG CL
CLA
SHLAAAK
KLAK
KLAK

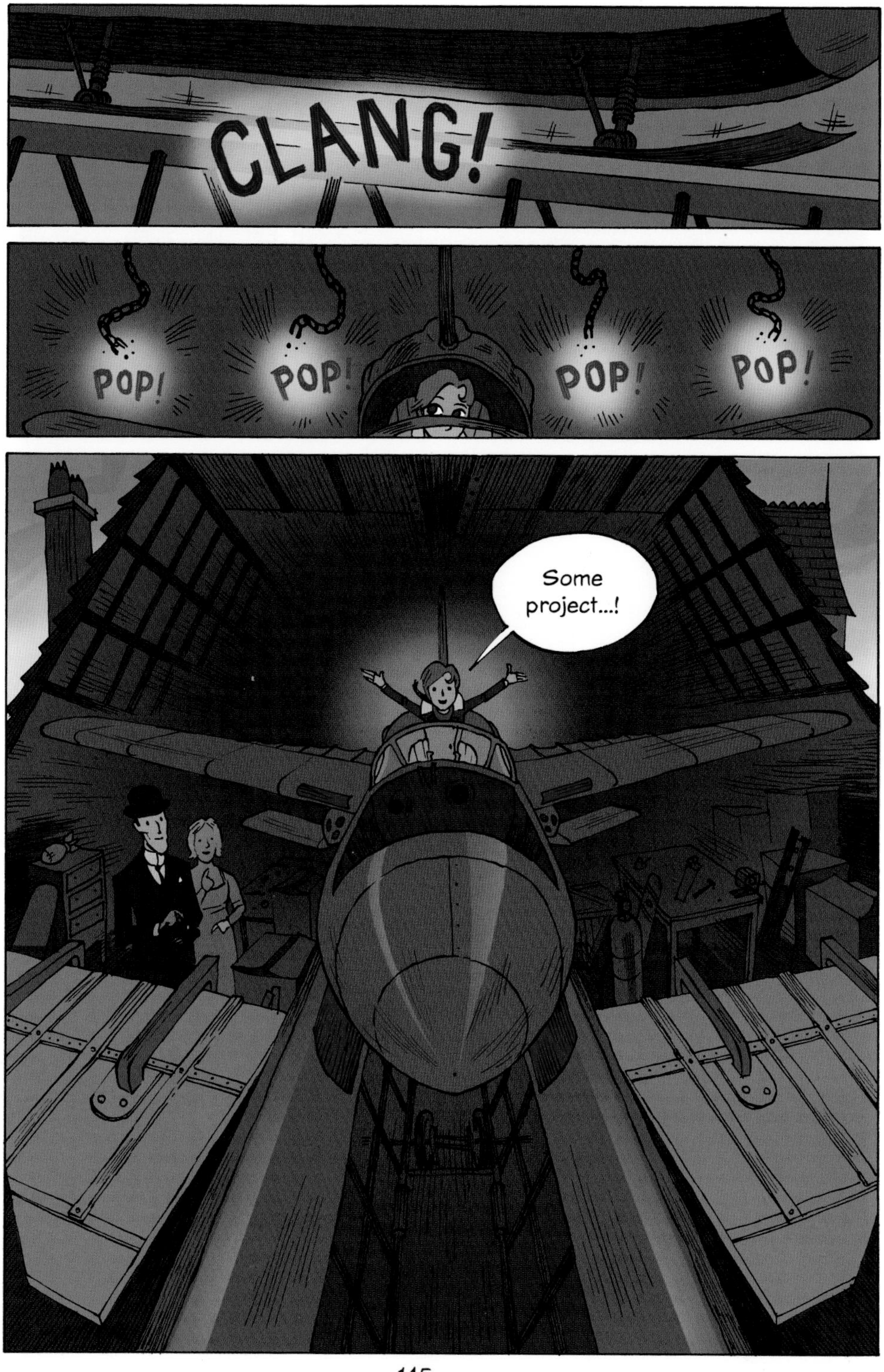
CLANG!
POP!
POP!
POP!
POP!
Some project...!

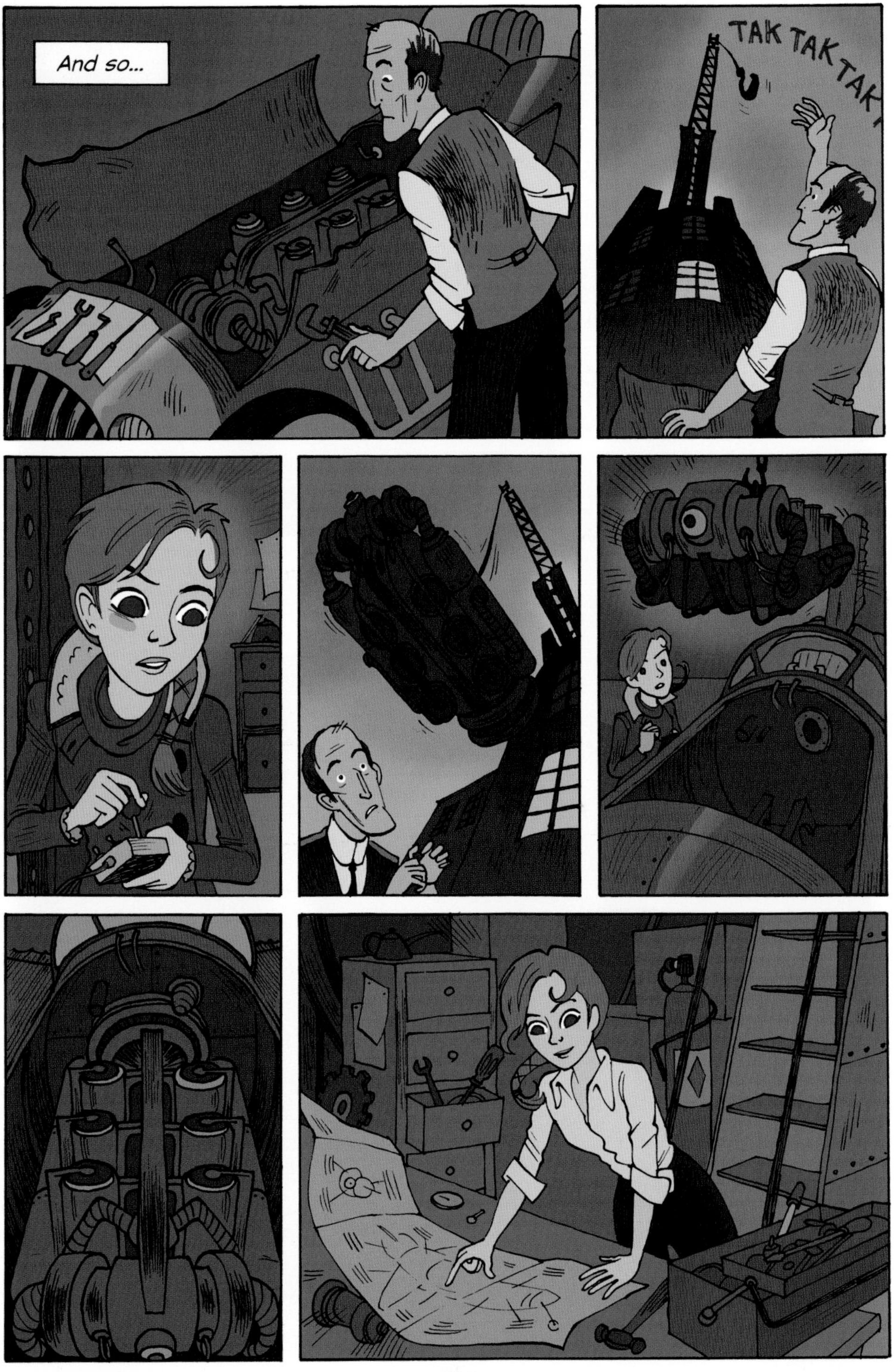
And so...
TAK TAK TAK

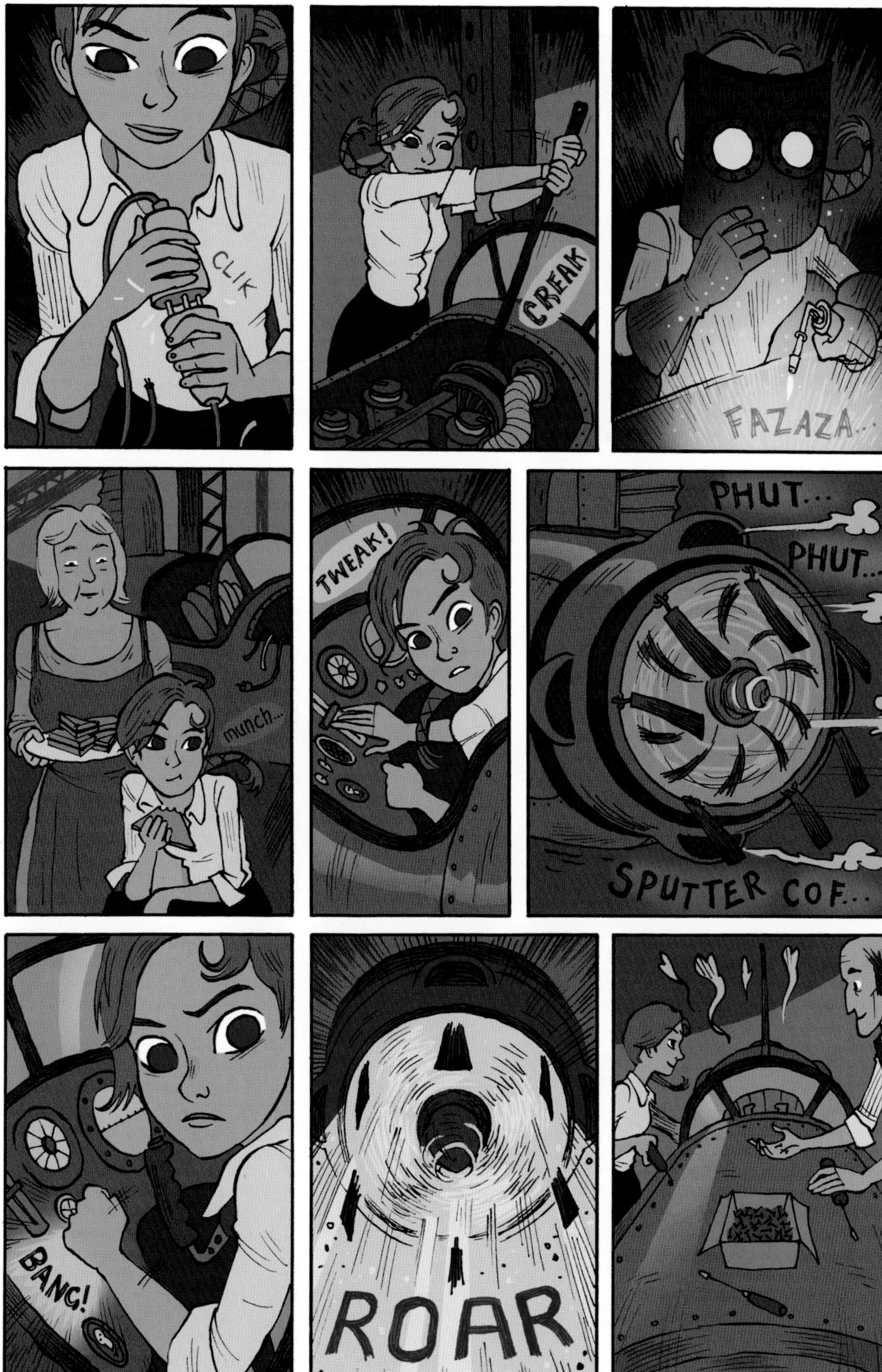
CLIK
CREAK
FAZAZA...
munch...
TWEAK!
PHUT...
PHUT...
SPUTTER COF...
BANG!
ROAR

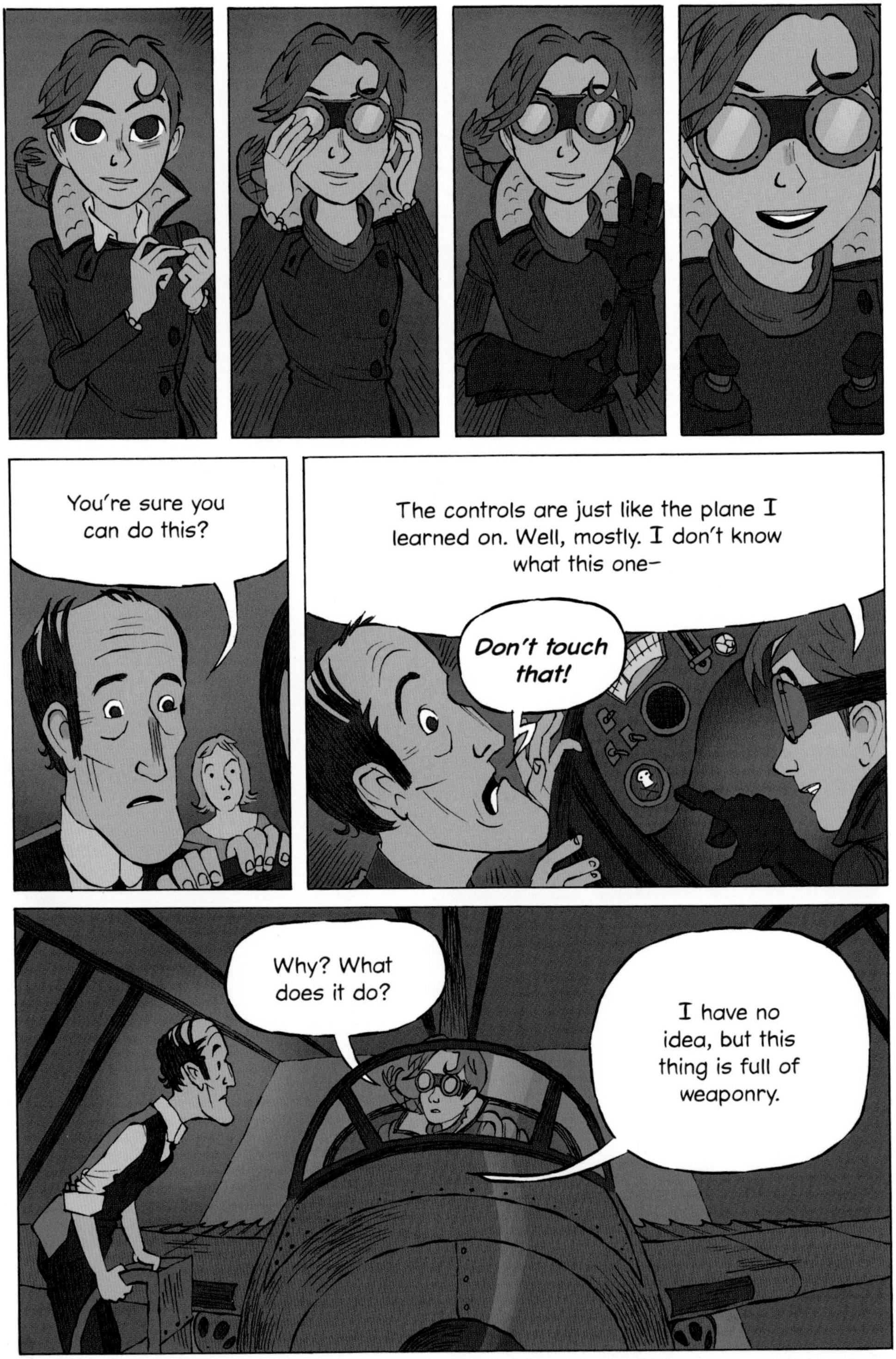
You're sure you can do this?
The controls are just like the plane I learned on. Well, mostly. I don't know what this one–
Don't touch that!
Why? What does it do?
I have no idea, but this thing is full of weaponry.

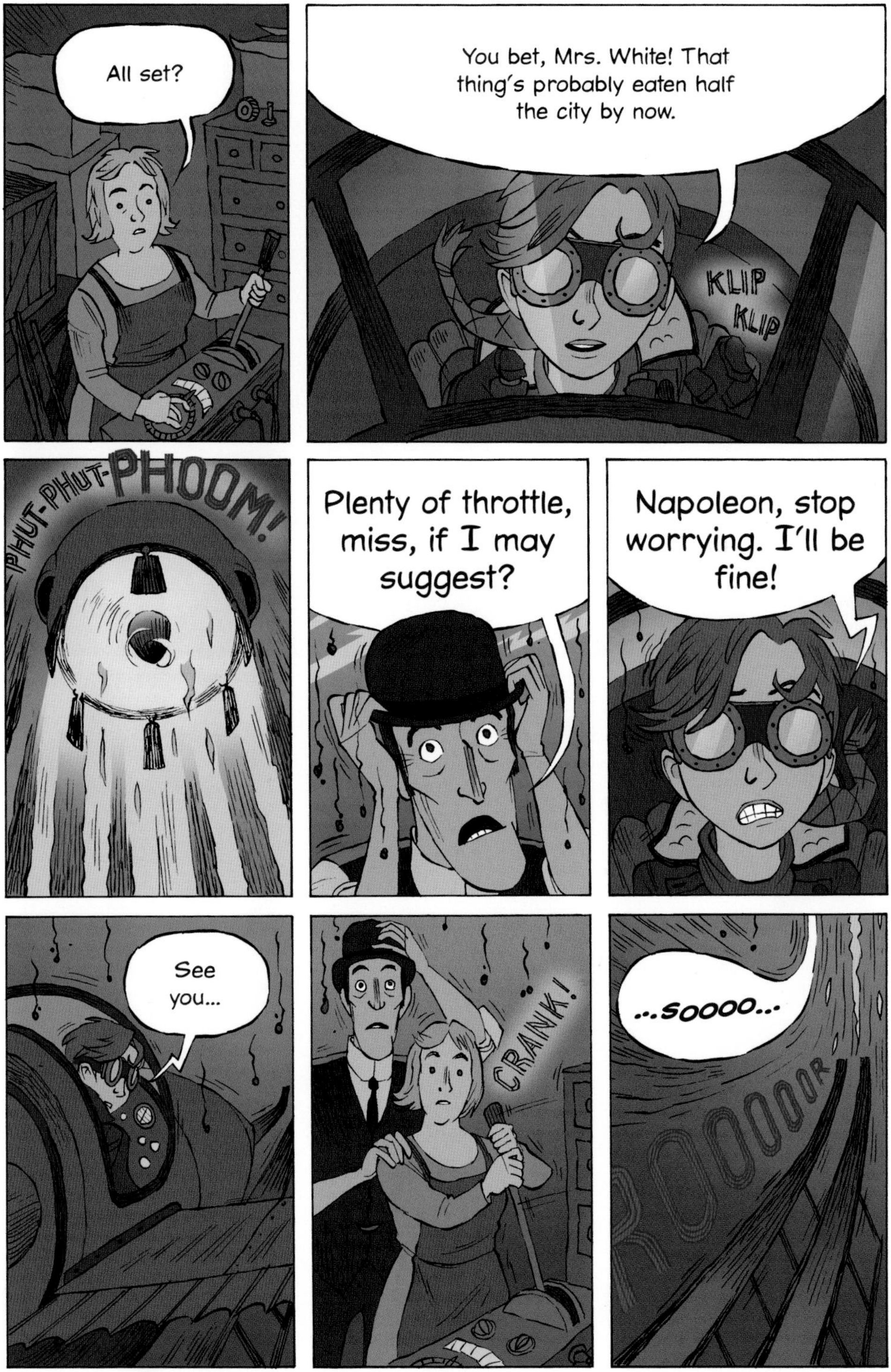
All set?
You bet, Mrs. White! That thing's probably eaten half the city by now.
KLIP KLIP
PHUT-PHUT-PHOOM!
Plenty of throttle, miss, if I may suggest?
Napoleon, stop worrying. I'll be fine!
See you...
CRANK!
...SOOOO...
ROOOOOOOR

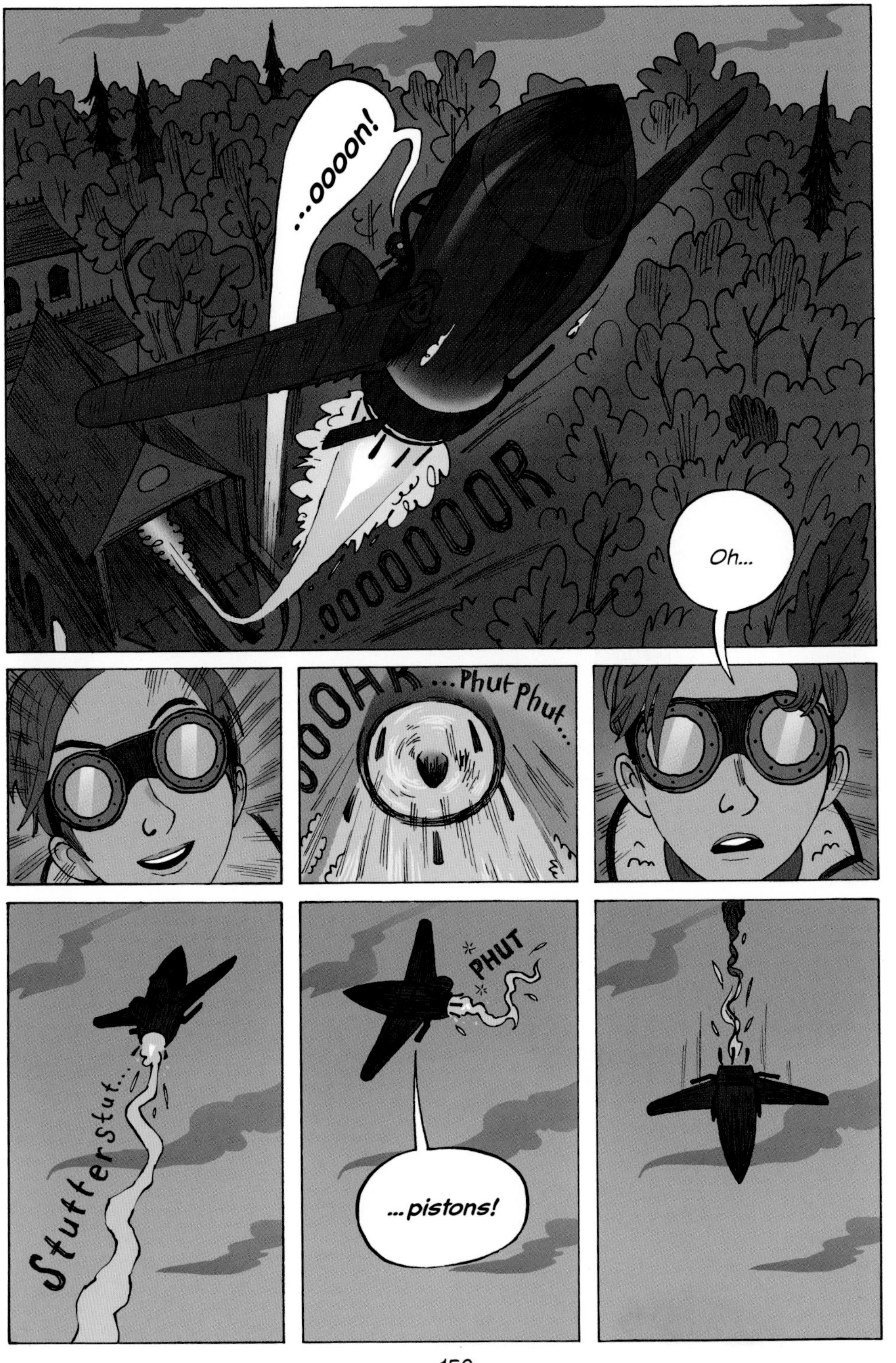

...oooon!
...ooooooooOR
Oh...
OOOAR ...Phut Phut...
Stutterstut...
PHUT
...pistons!

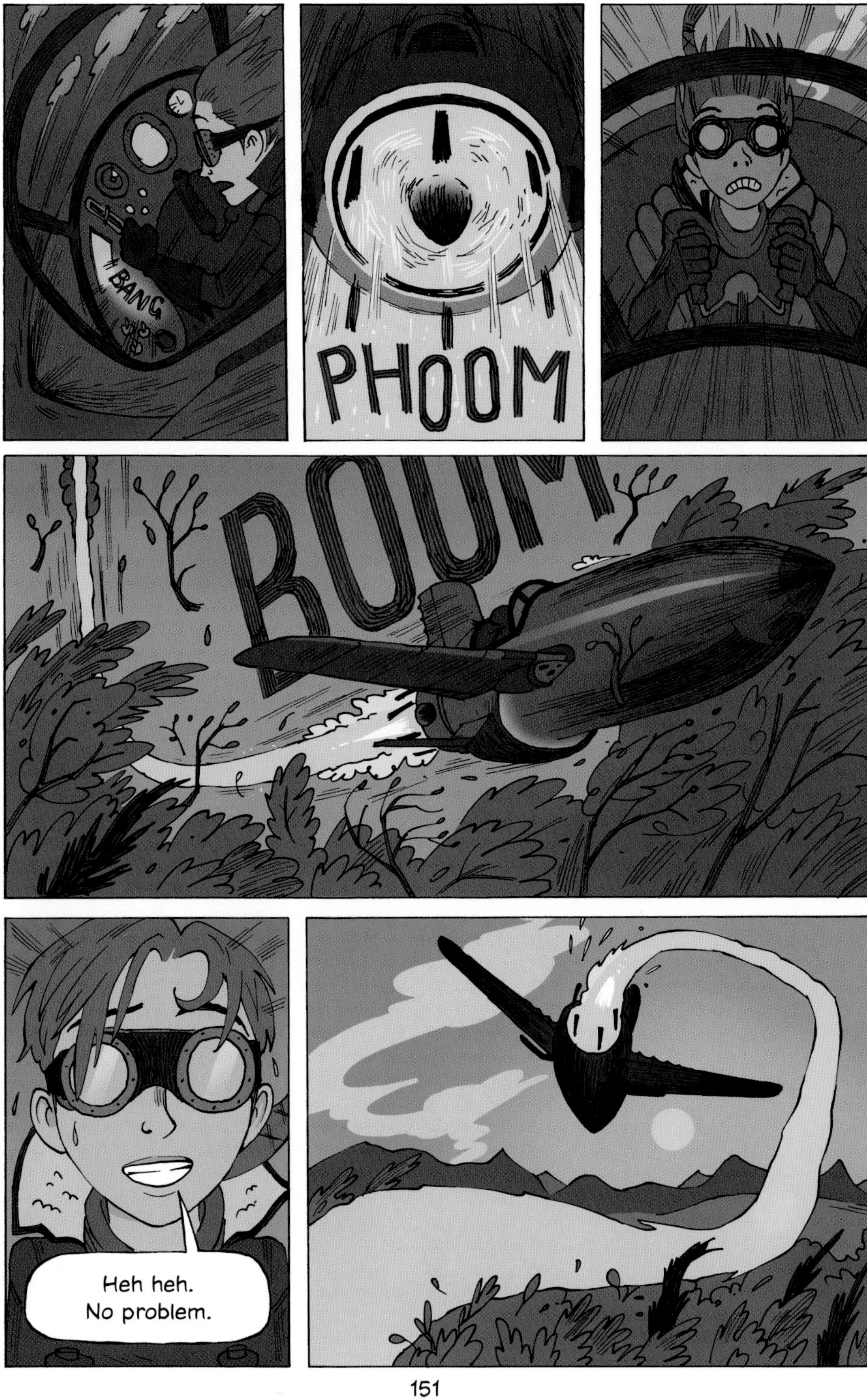
BANG
PHOOM
ROOM
Heh heh.
No problem.

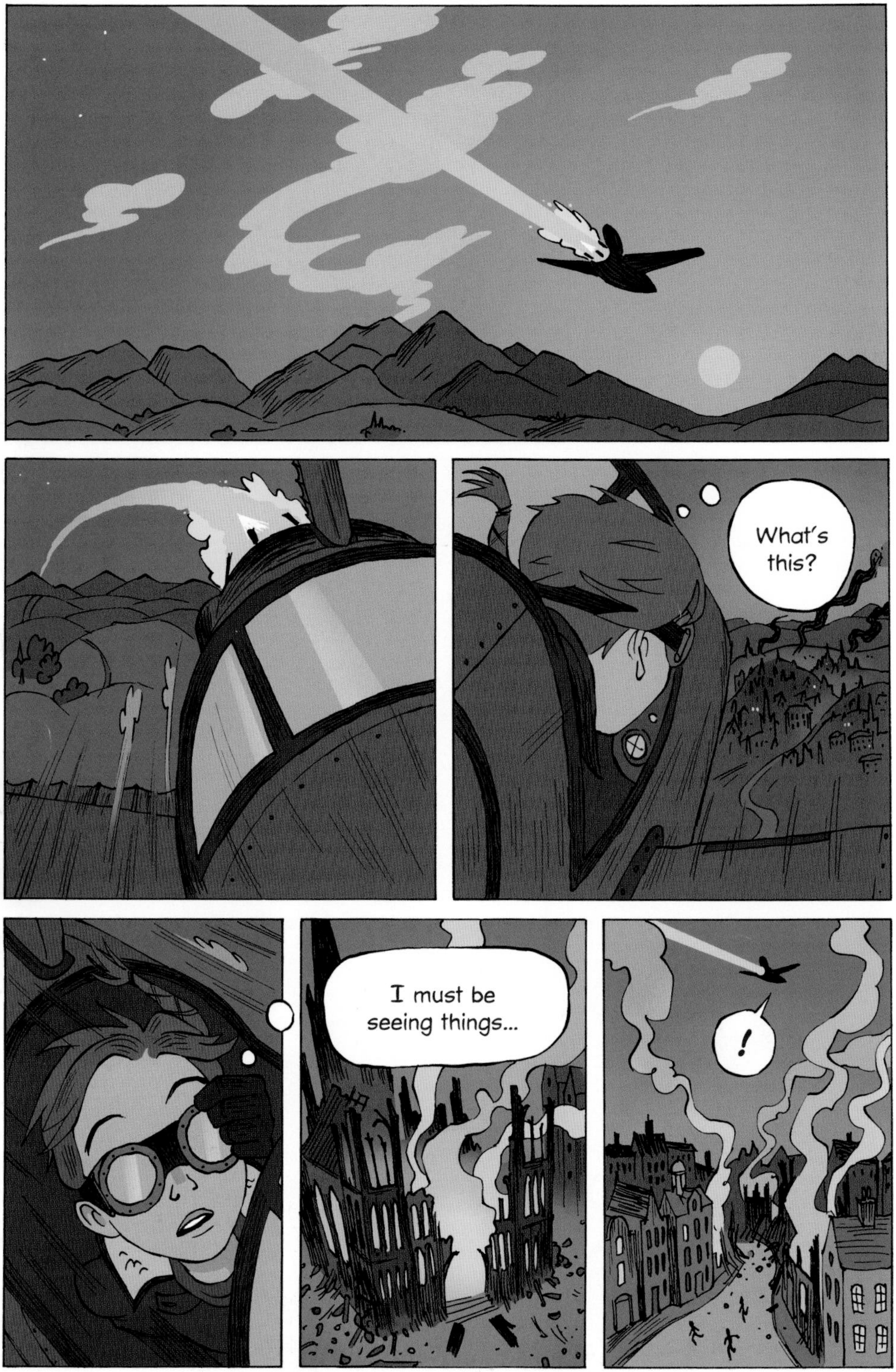
What's this?
I must be seeing things...
!

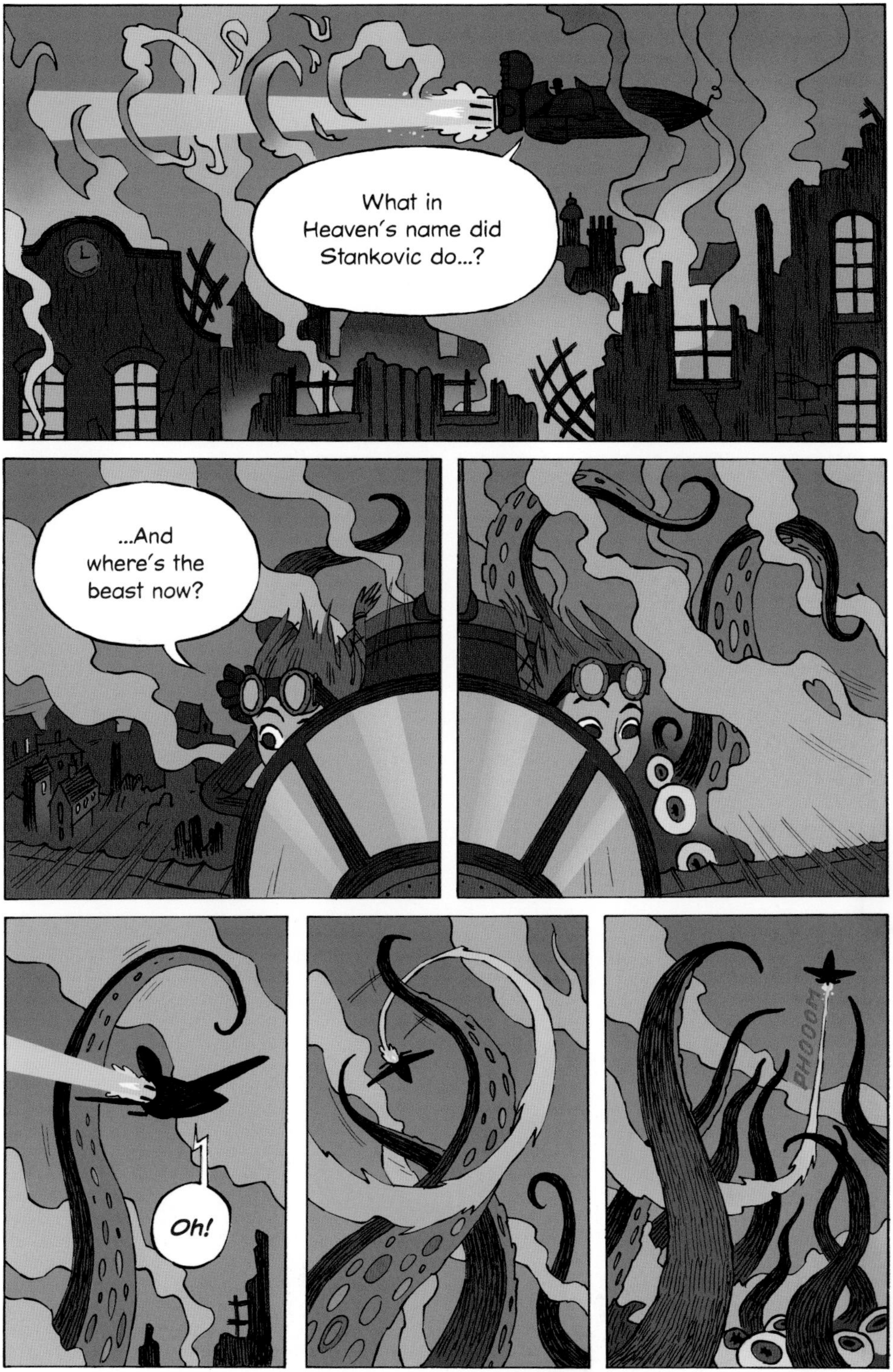
What in Heaven's name did Stankovic do...?
...And where's the beast now?
Oh!
PHOOOM

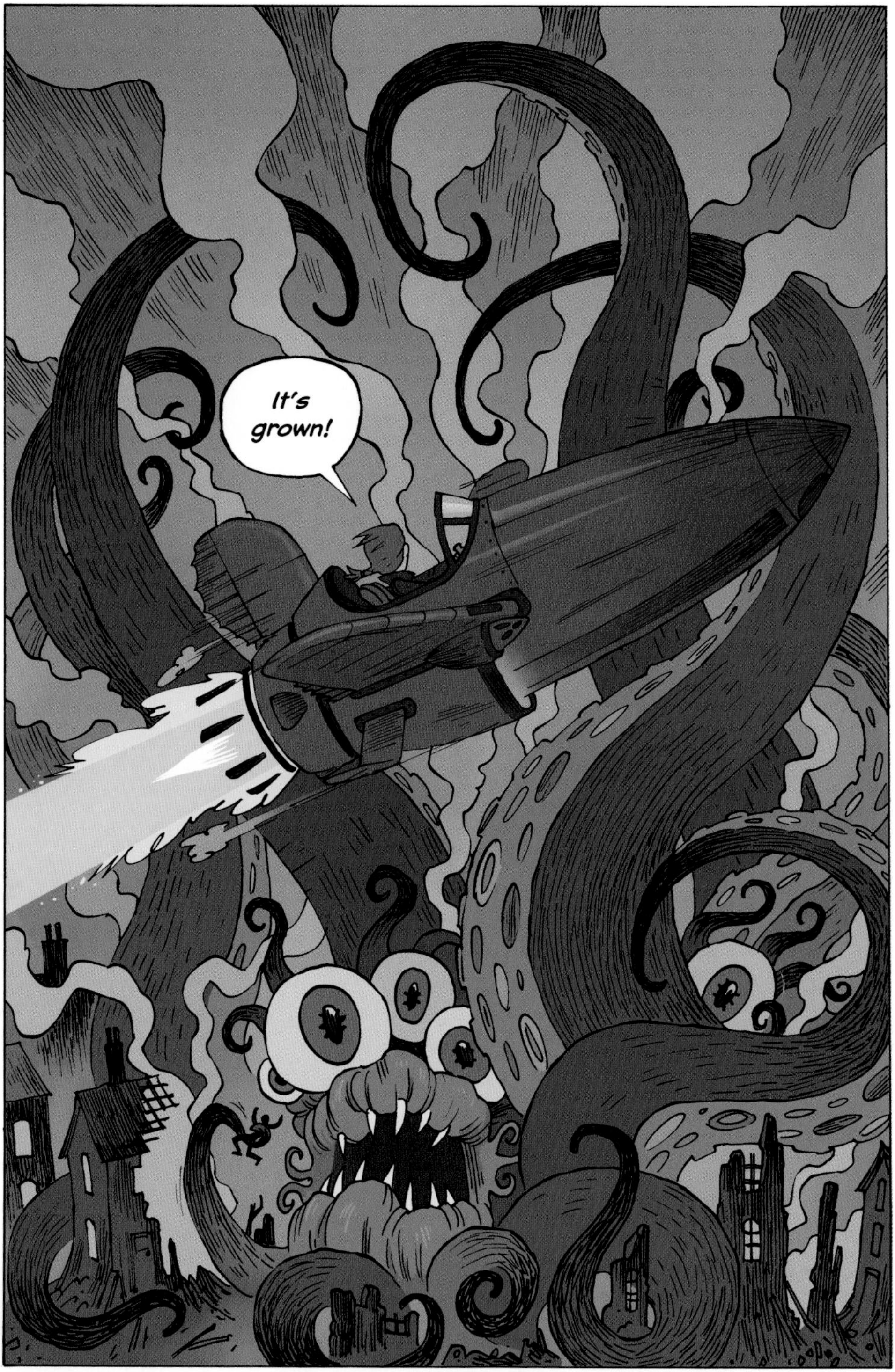
It's grown!

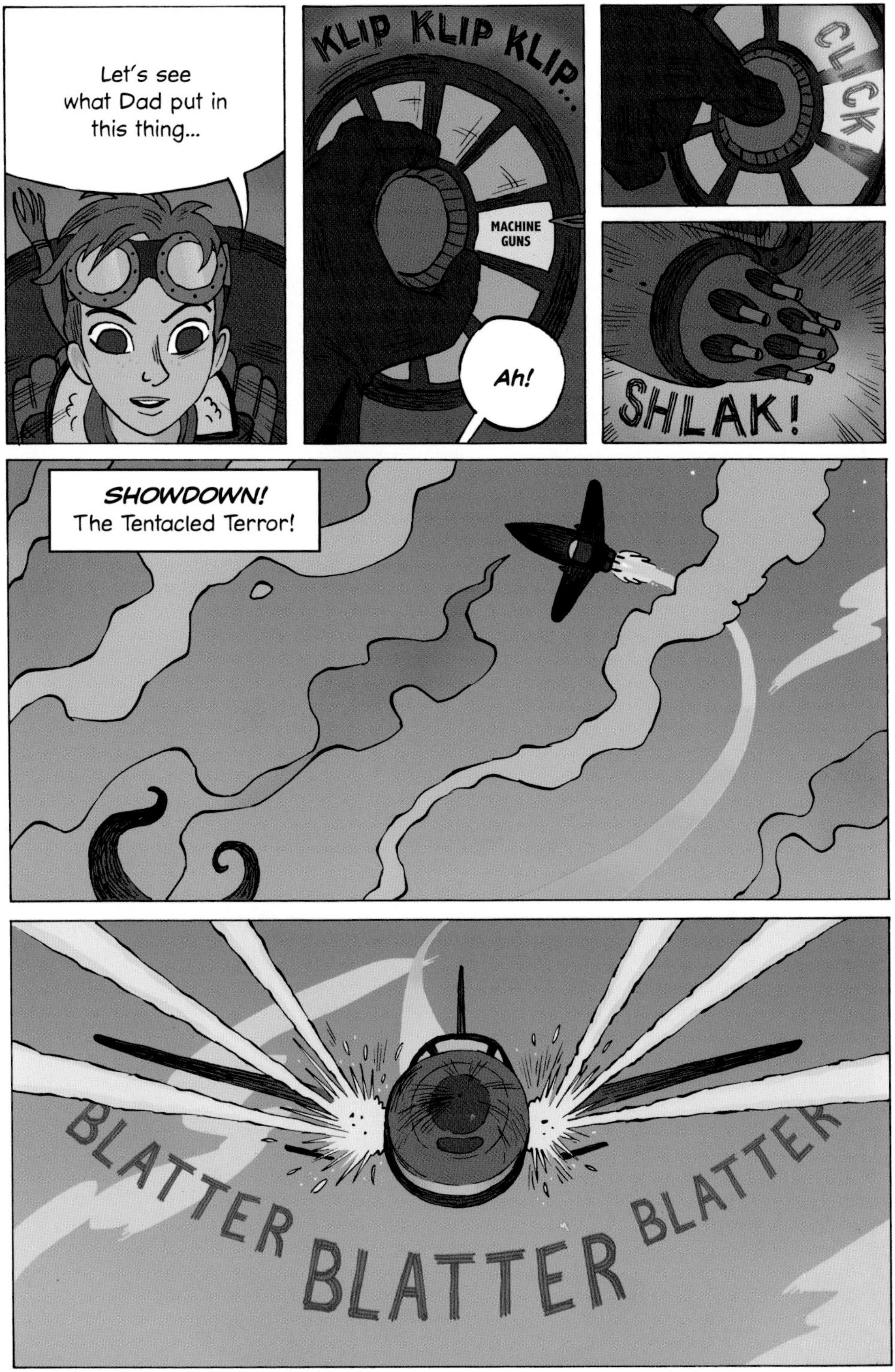
Let's see what Dad put in this thing...
KLIP KLIP KLIP...
MACHINE GUNS
Ah!
CLICK
SHLAK!
SHOWDOWN!
The Tentacled Terror!
BLATTER
BLATTER
BLATTER
BLATTER

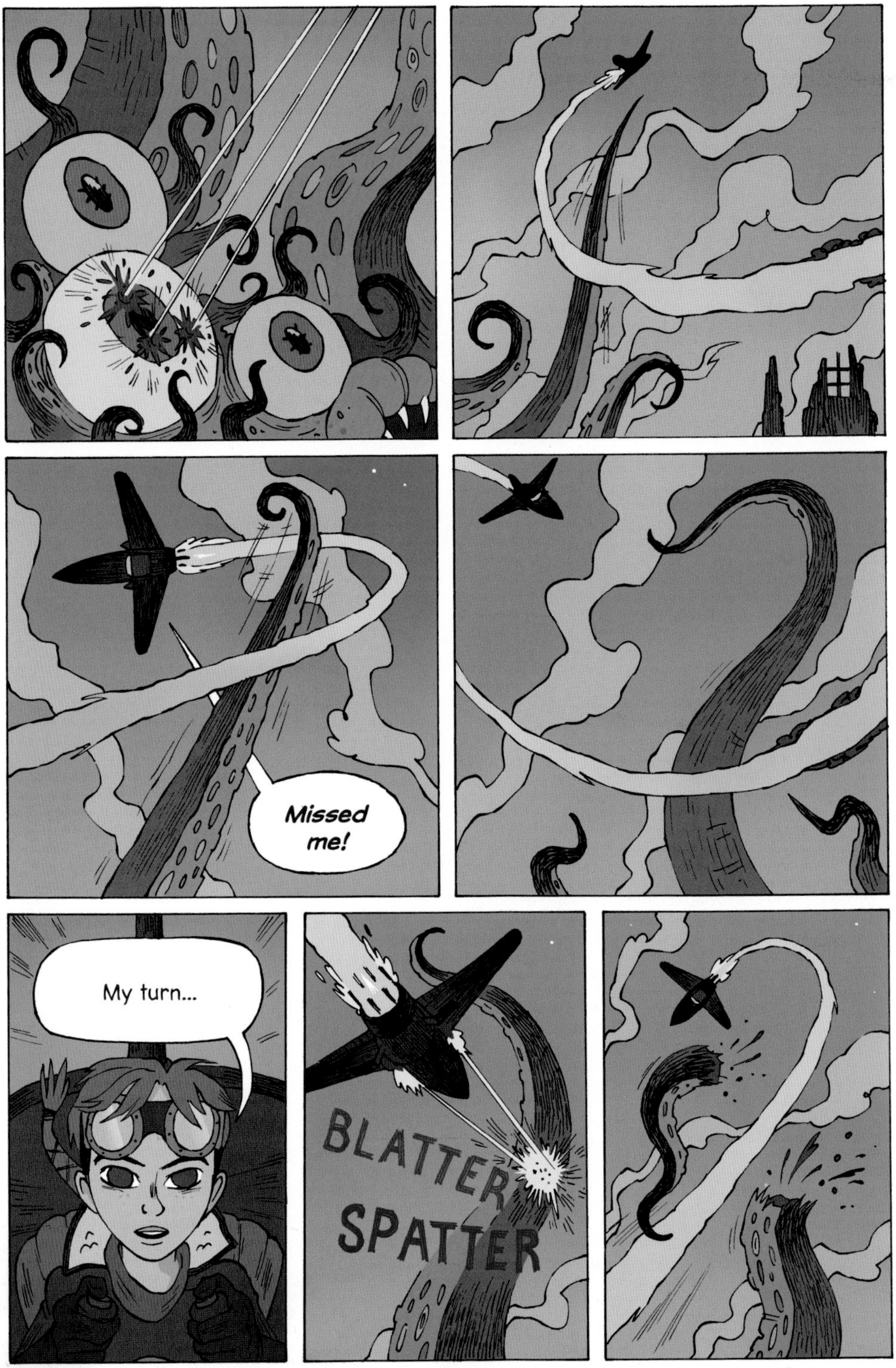
Missed me!
My turn...
BLATTER
SPATTER

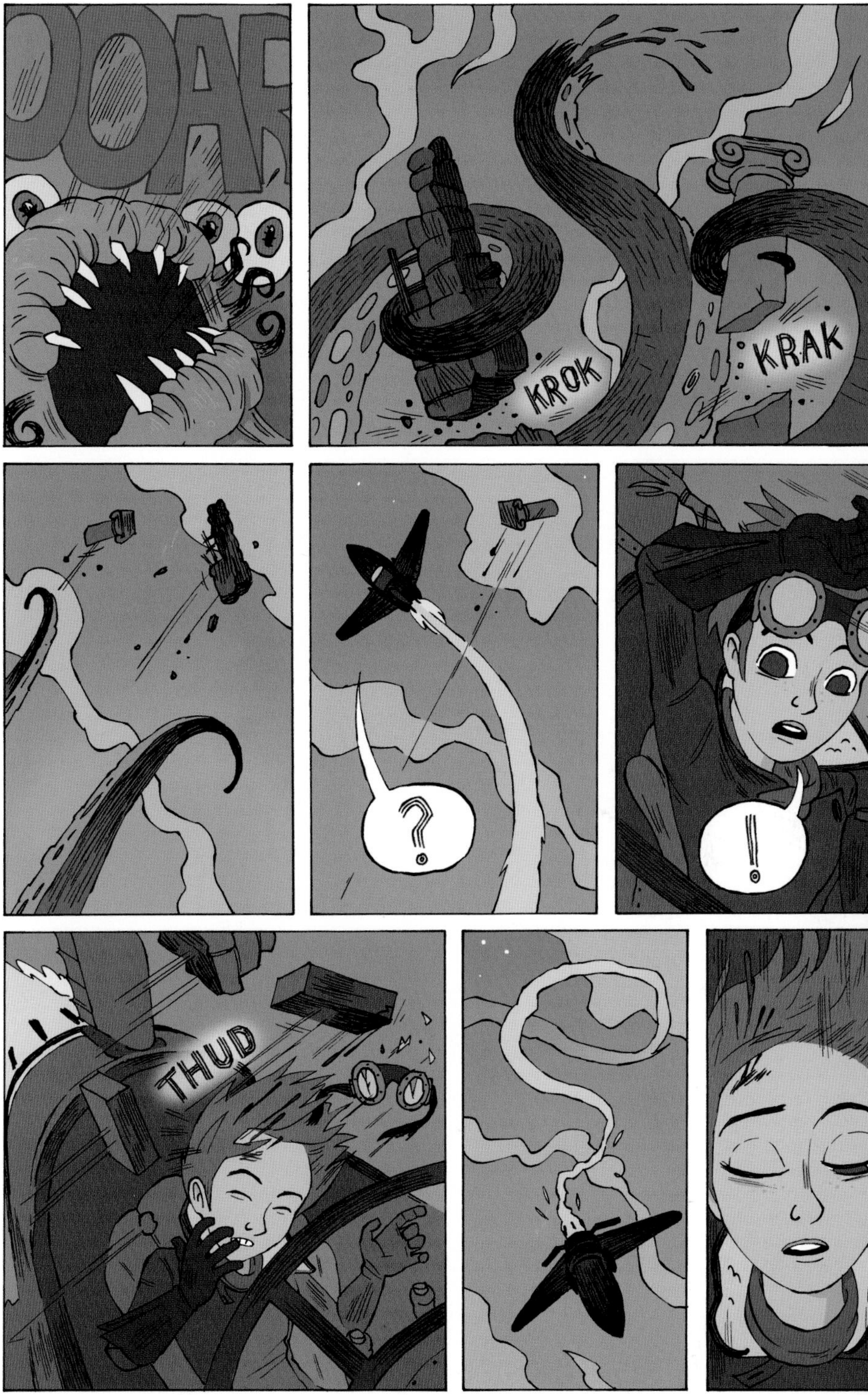
OOAR
KROK
KRAK
?
!
THUD

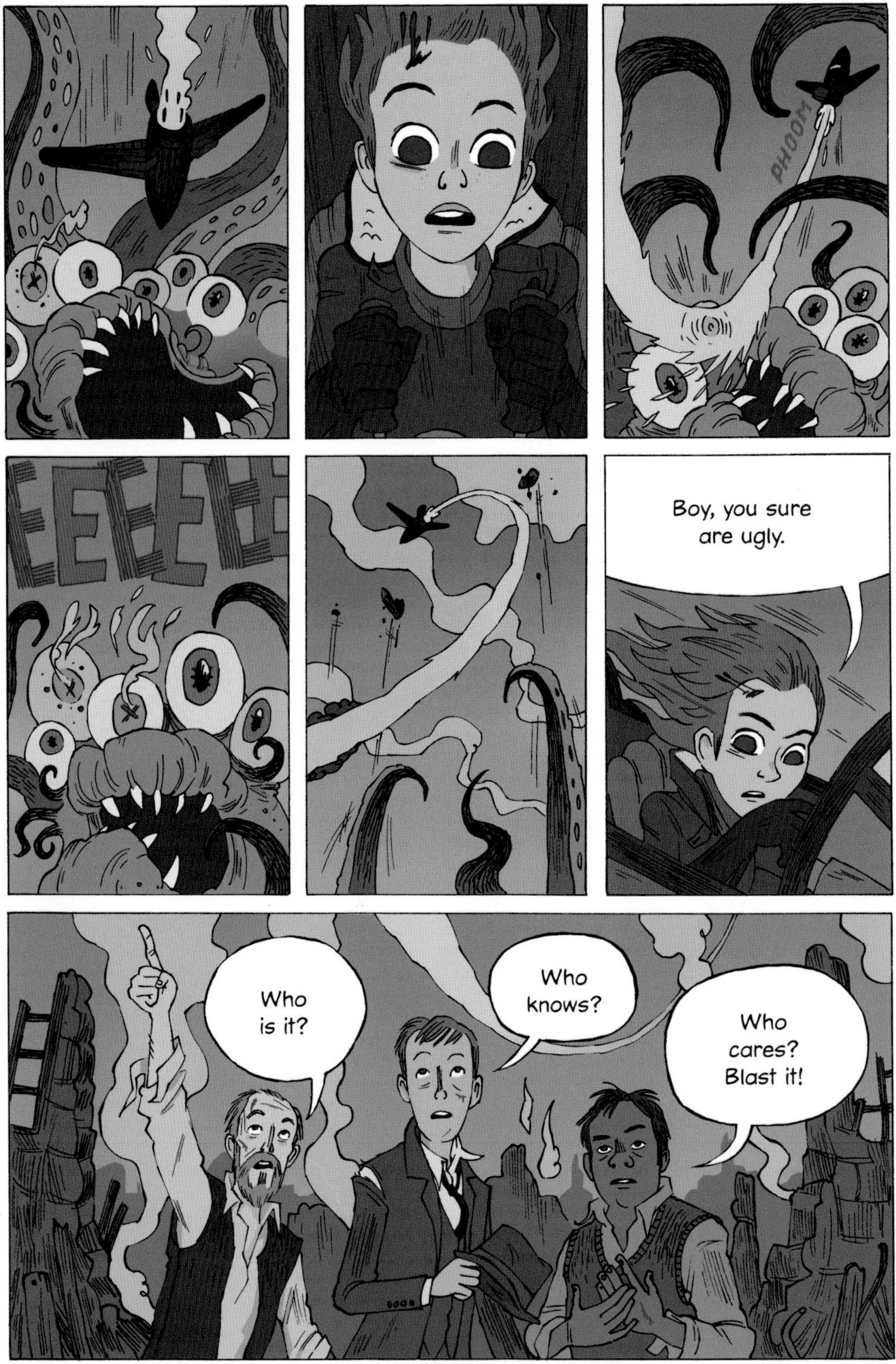
PHOOM
Boy, you sure are ugly.
Who is it?
Who knows?
Who cares? Blast it!

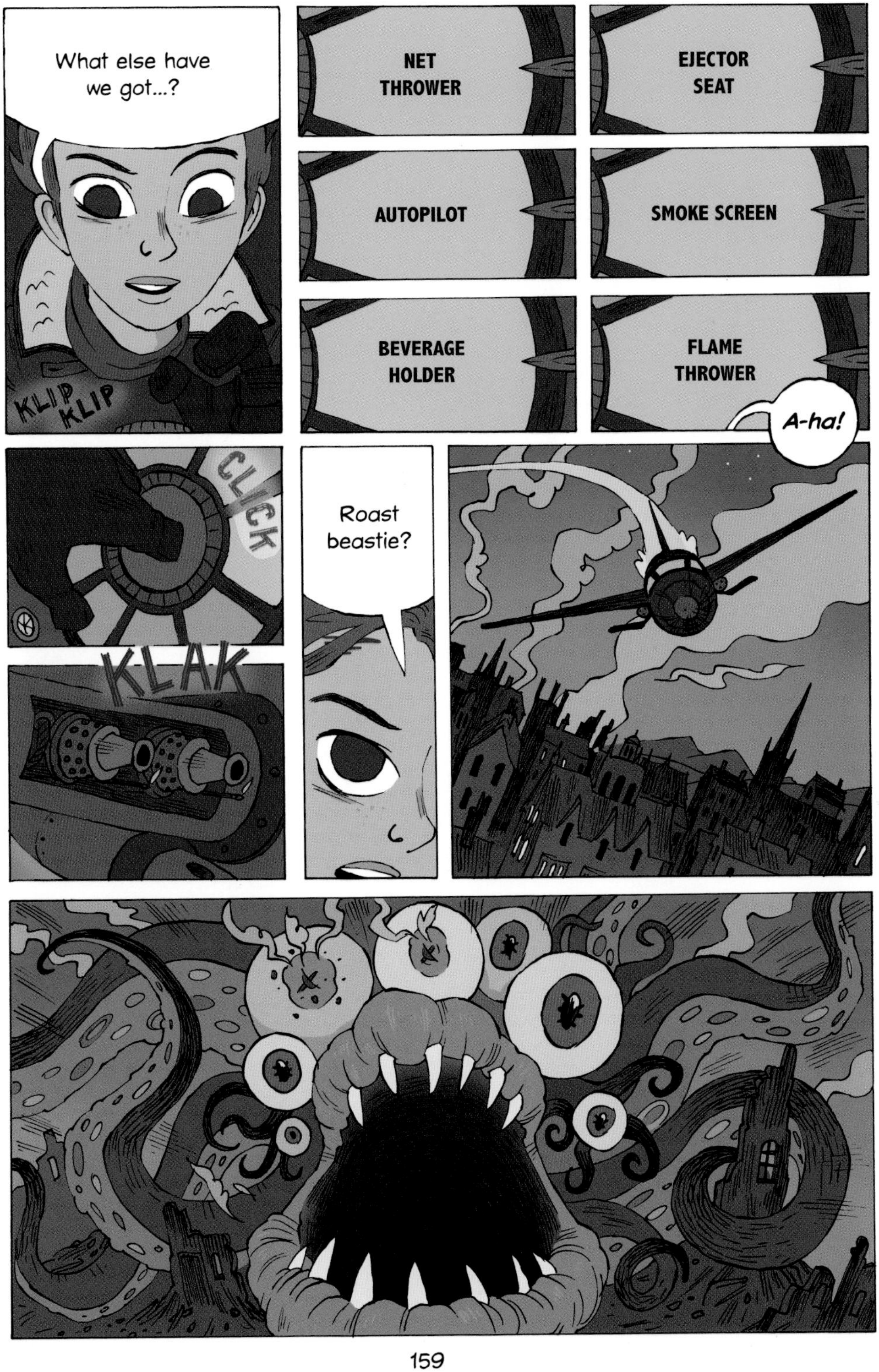
What else have we got...?
KLIP KLIP
NET THROWER
EJECTOR SEAT
AUTOPILOT
SMOKE SCREEN
BEVERAGE HOLDER
FLAME THROWER
A-ha!
CLICK
KLAK
Roast beastie?

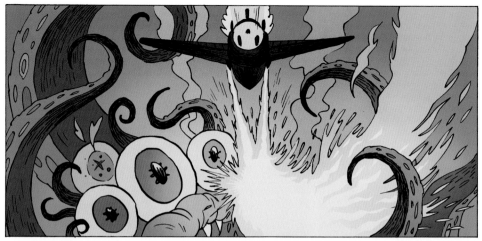

Gaskets! That thing is tough.

And it's nearly reached the palace!

160

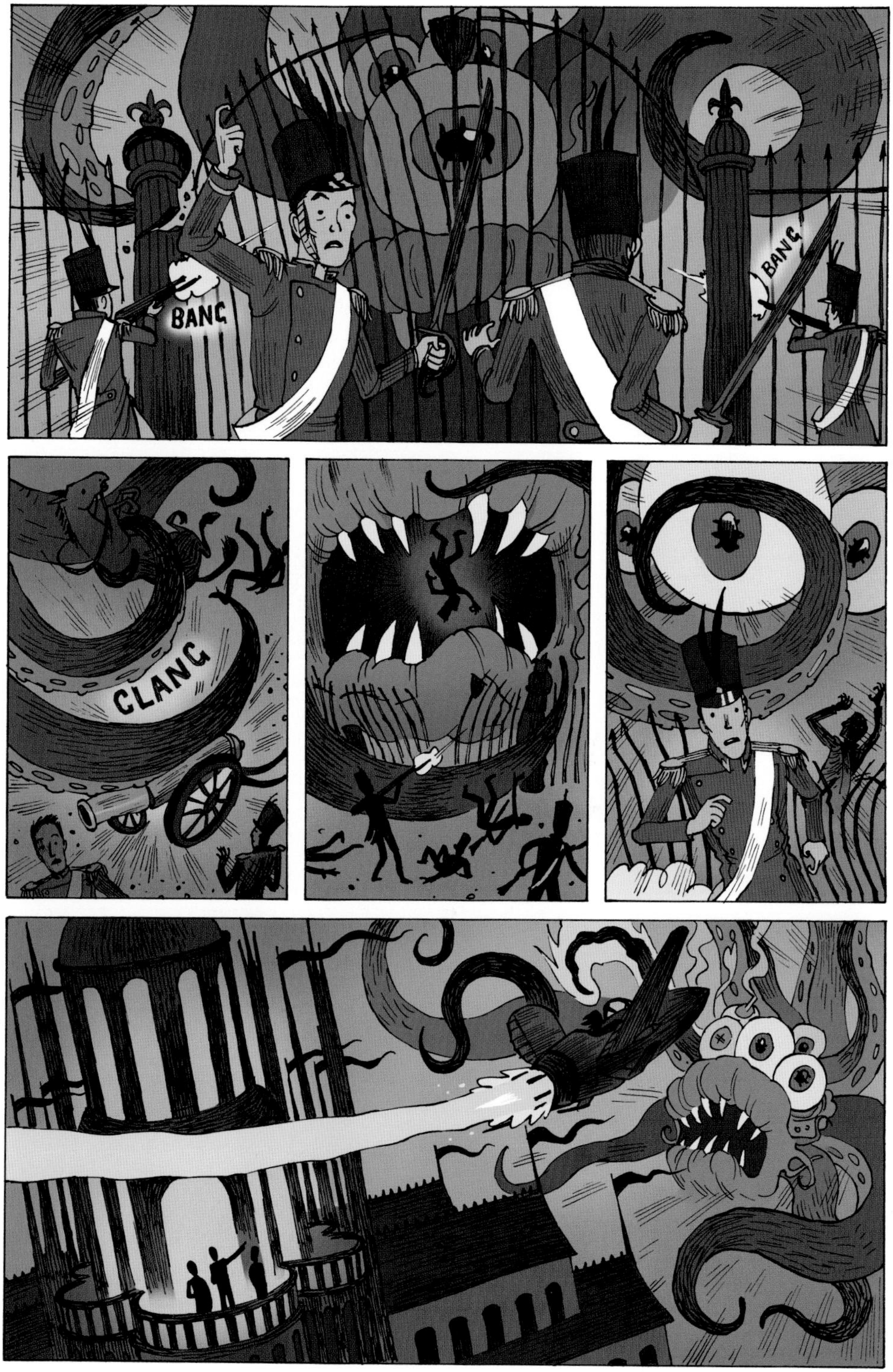
BANG
BANG
CLANG

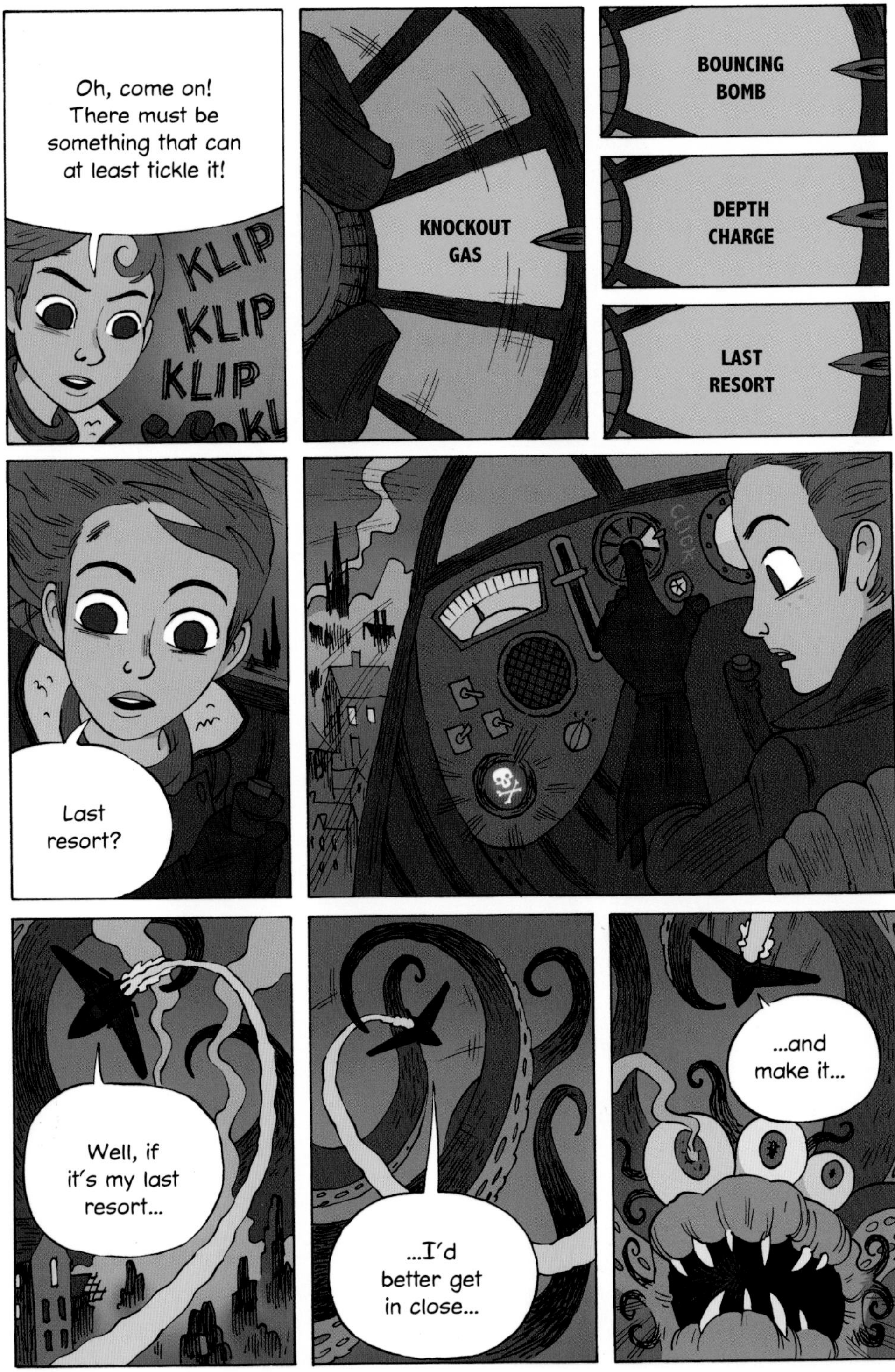
Oh, come on! There must be something that can at least tickle it!
KLIP KLIP KLIP KL
KNOCKOUT GAS
BOUNCING BOMB
DEPTH CHARGE
LAST RESORT
Last resort?
CLICK
Well, if it's my last resort...
...I'd better get in close...
...and make it...

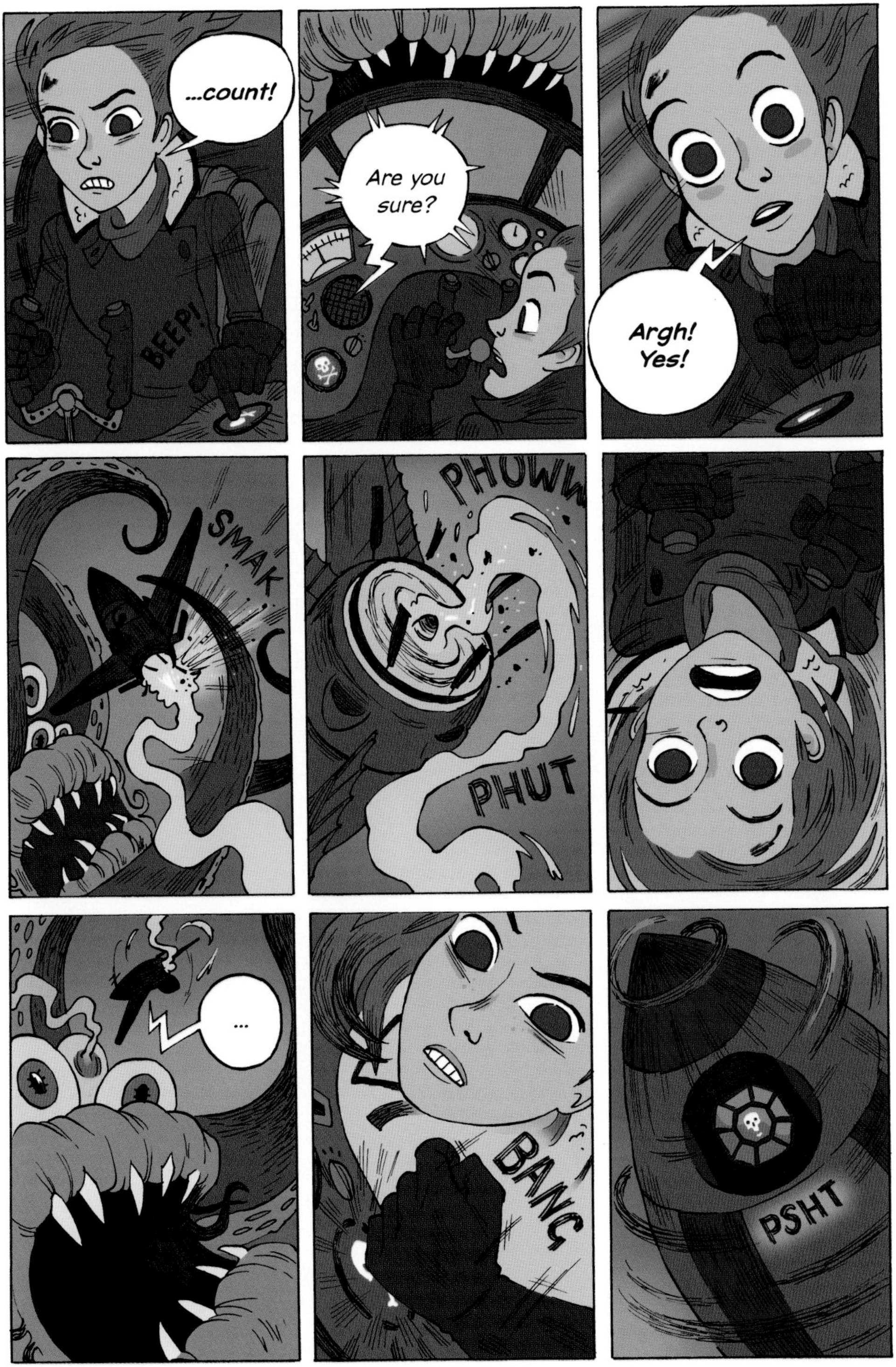
...count!
BEEP!
Are you sure?
Argh! Yes!
SMAK
PHOWW
PHUT
...
BANG
PSHT

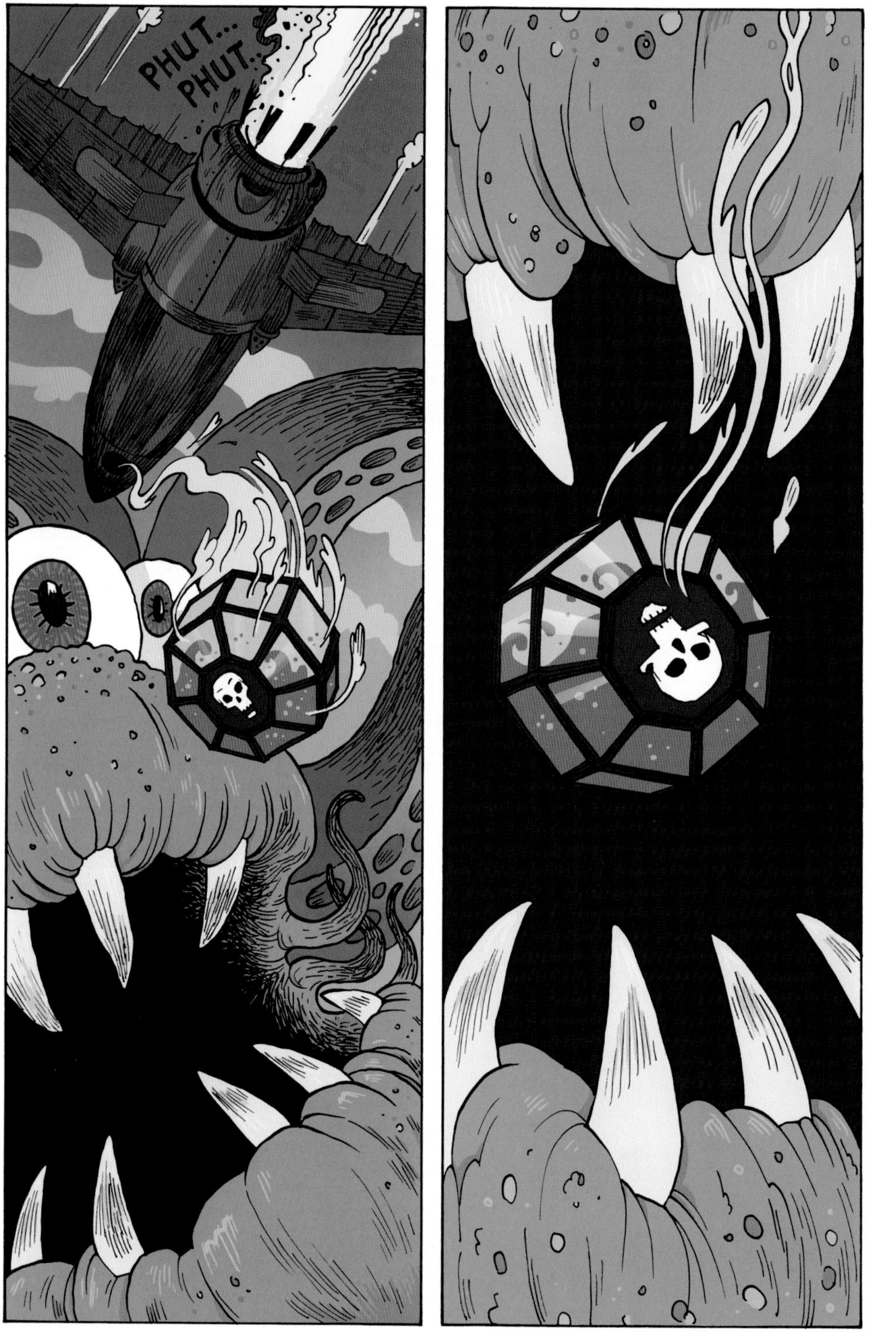
PHUT... PHUT...

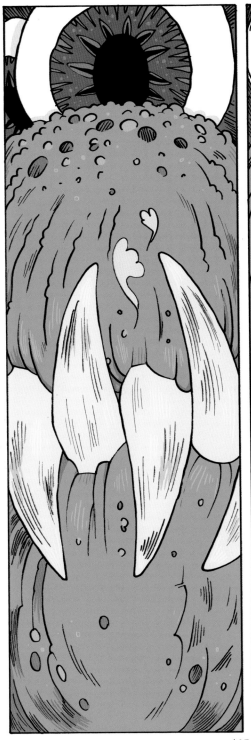
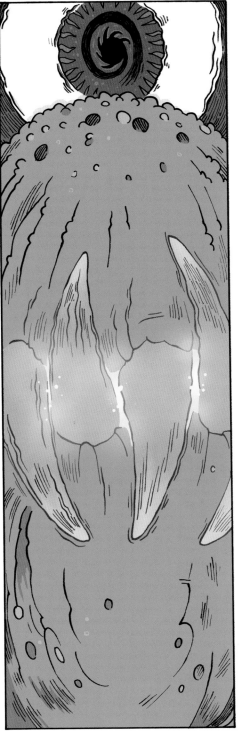

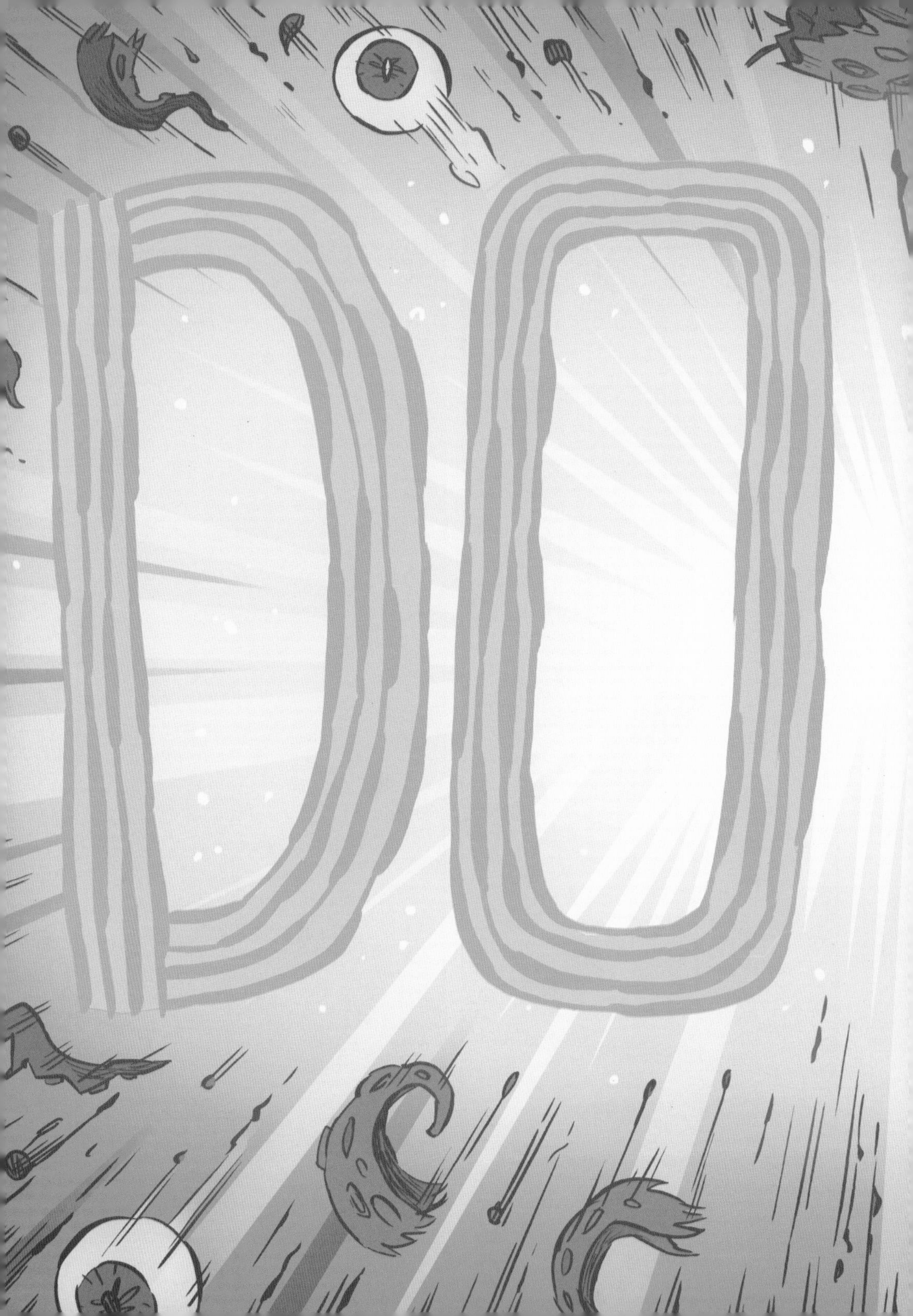
DO

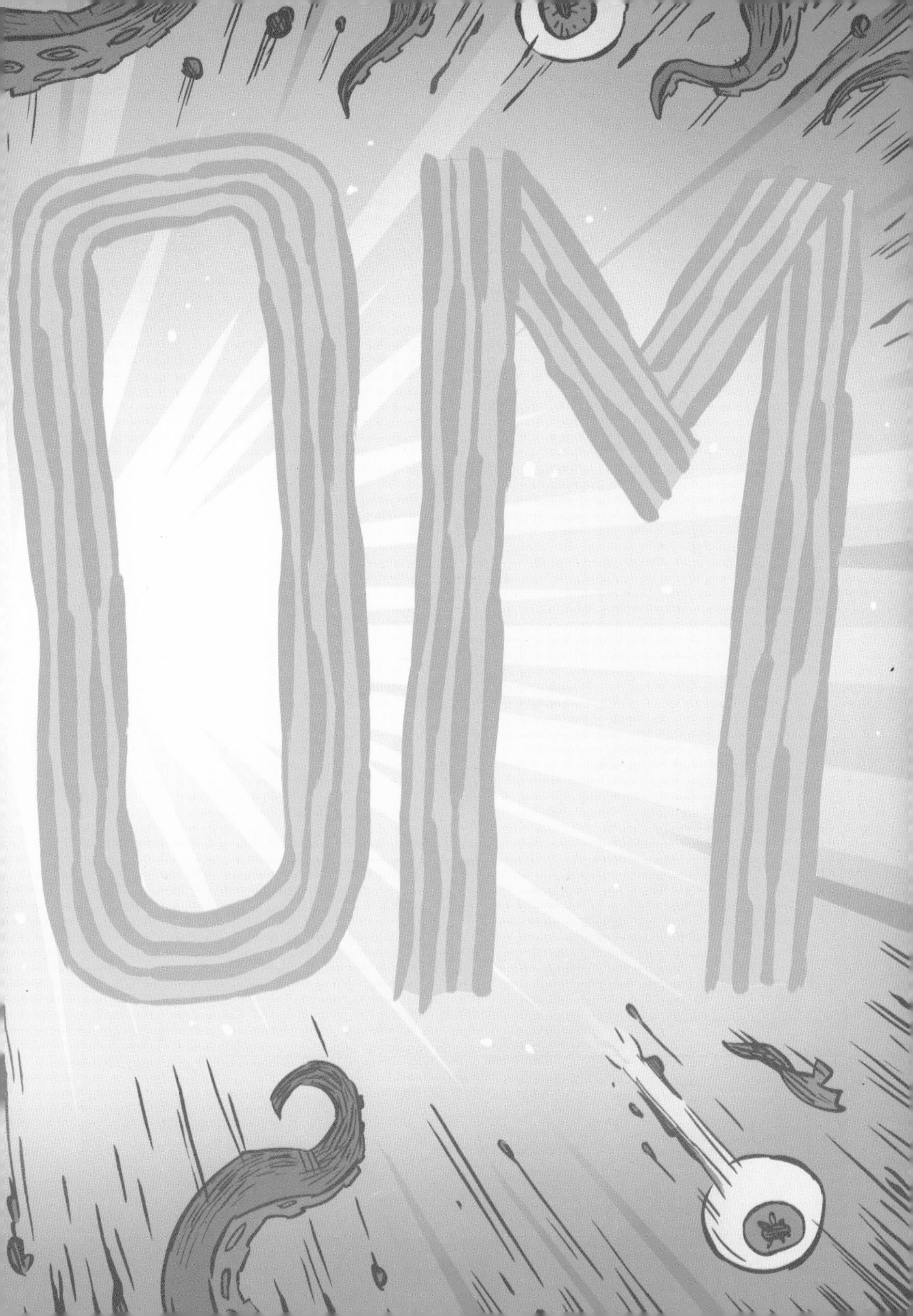
OM

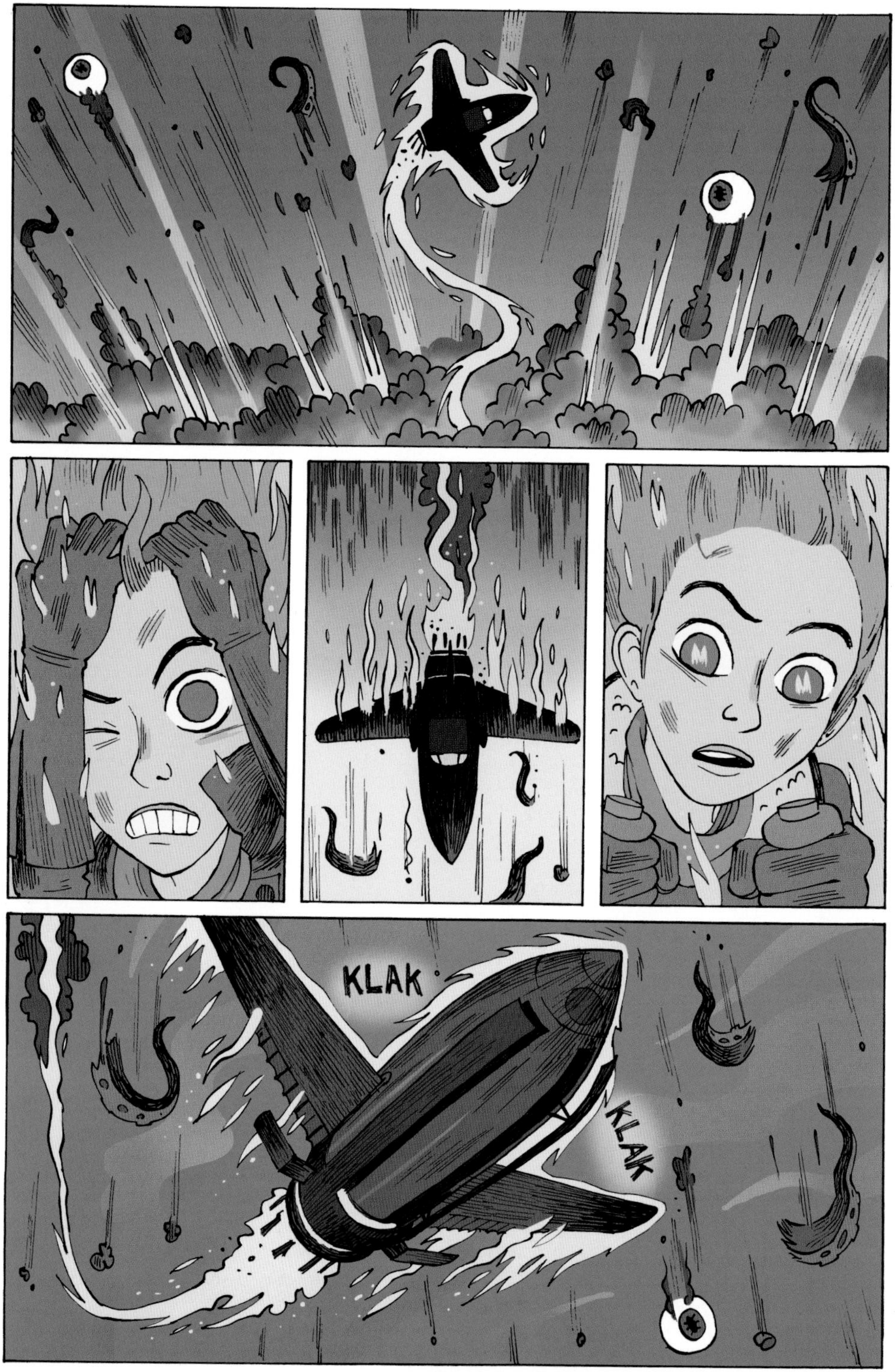
KLAK
KLAK

CRASH

KZZZZZZZZZZZZZZZZZZZZZZZZ

I stink.

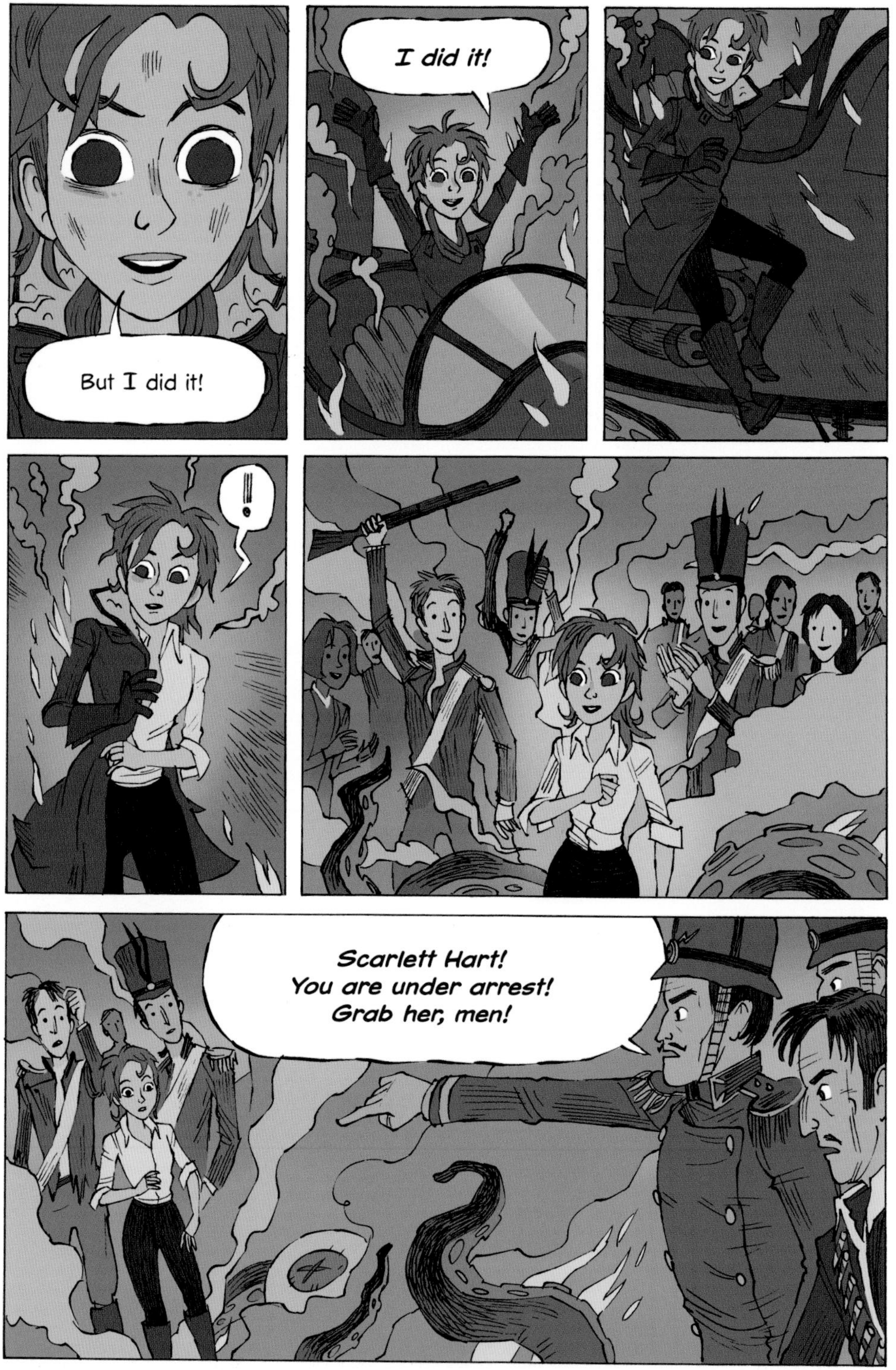
But I did it!
I did it!
!!
Scarlett Hart!
You are under arrest!
Grab her, men!

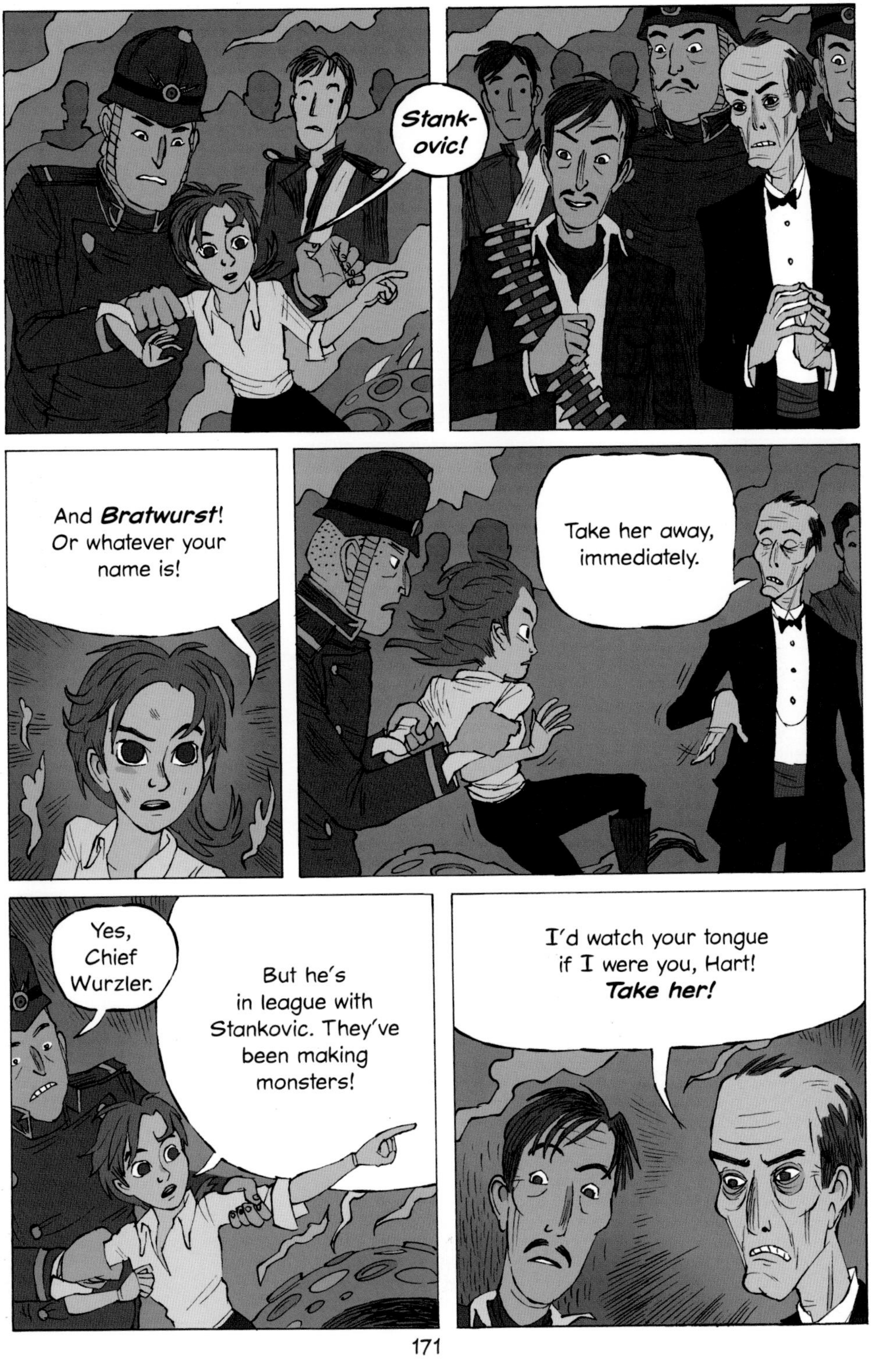
Stank-ovic!
And Bratwurst! Or whatever your name is!
Take her away, immediately.
Yes, Chief Wurzler.
But he's in league with Stankovic. They've been making monsters!
I'd watch your tongue if I were you, Hart! Take her!

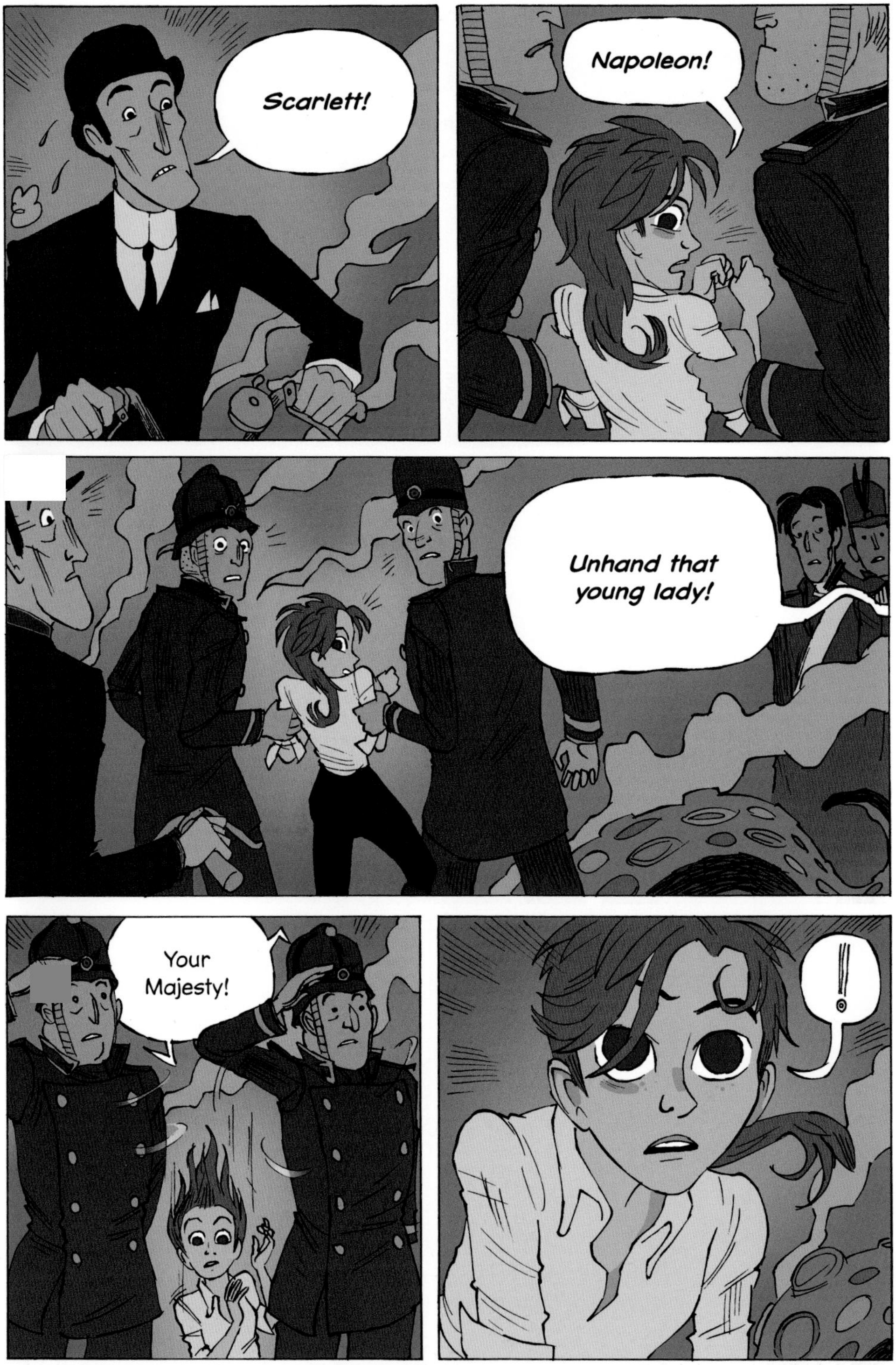
Scarlett!
Napoleon!
Unhand that young lady!
Your Majesty!
!

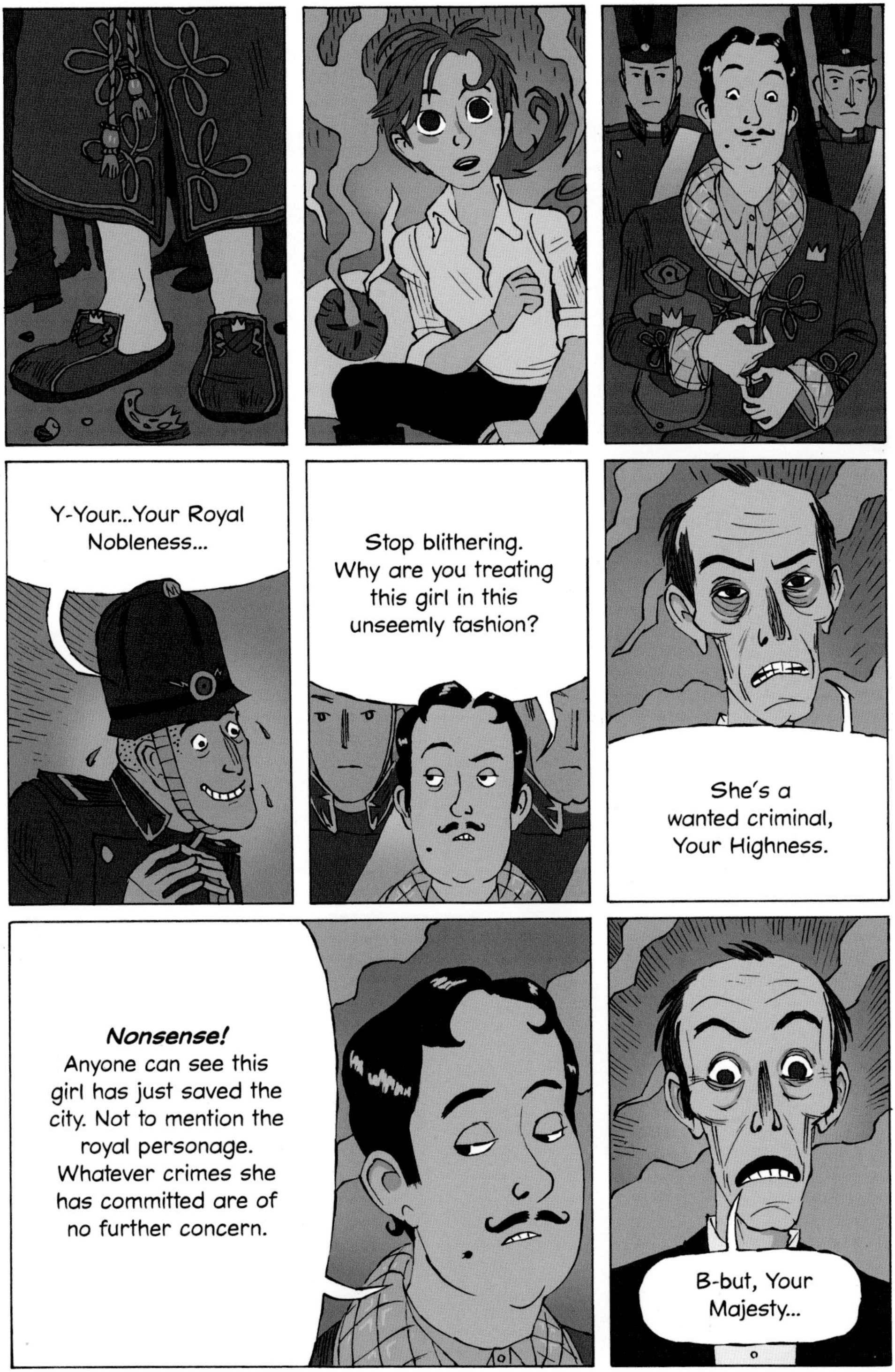
Y-Your...Your Royal Nobleness...
Stop blithering. Why are you treating this girl in this unseemly fashion?
She's a wanted criminal, Your Highness.
Nonsense! Anyone can see this girl has just saved the city. Not to mention the royal personage. Whatever crimes she has committed are of no further concern.
B-but, Your Majesty...

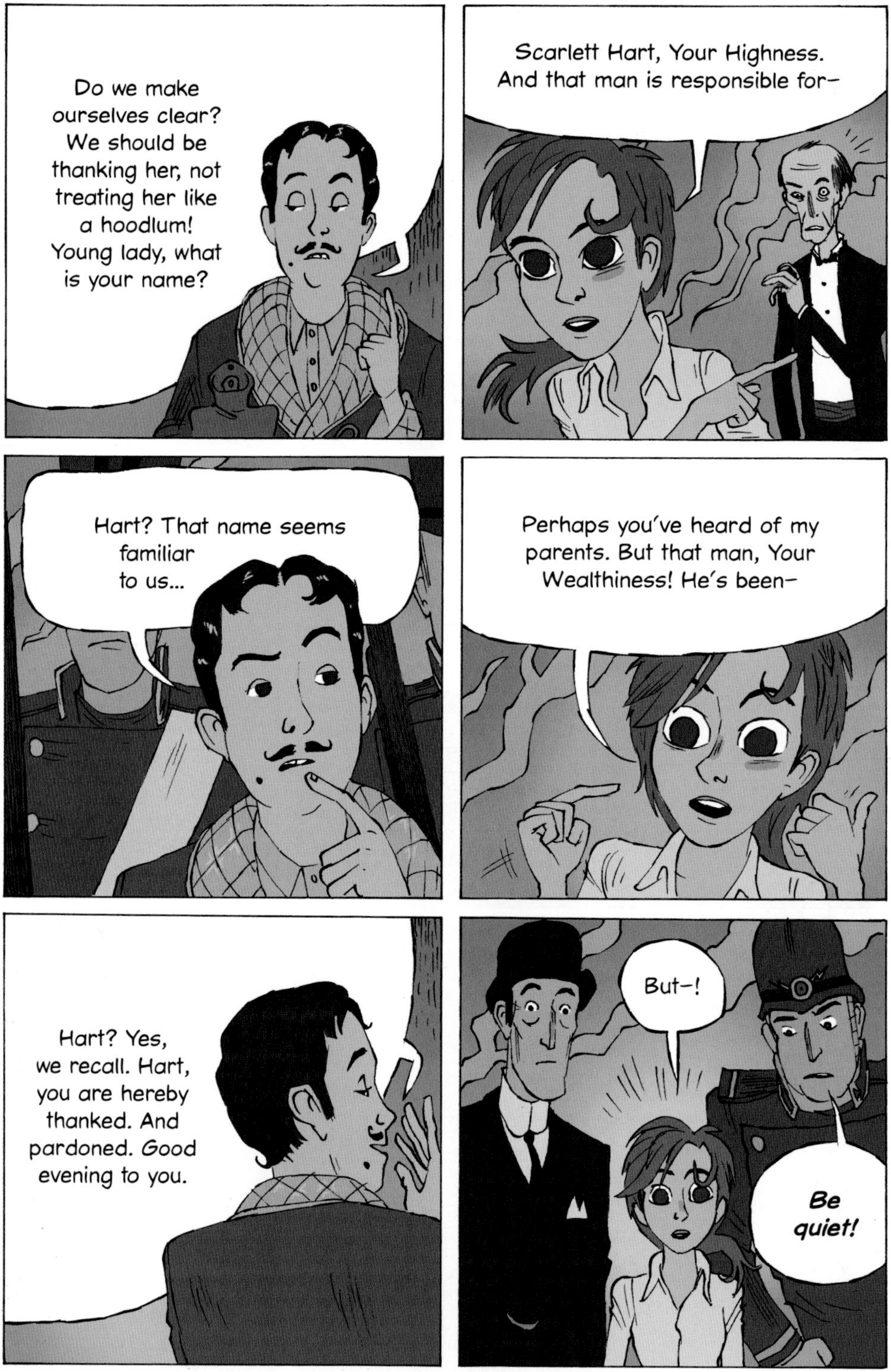
Do we make ourselves clear? We should be thanking her, not treating her like a hoodlum! Young lady, what is your name?
Scarlett Hart, Your Highness. And that man is responsible for–
Hart? That name seems familiar to us...
Perhaps you've heard of my parents. But that man, Your Wealthiness! He's been–
Hart? Yes, we recall. Hart, you are hereby thanked. And pardoned. Good evening to you.
But–!
Be quiet!

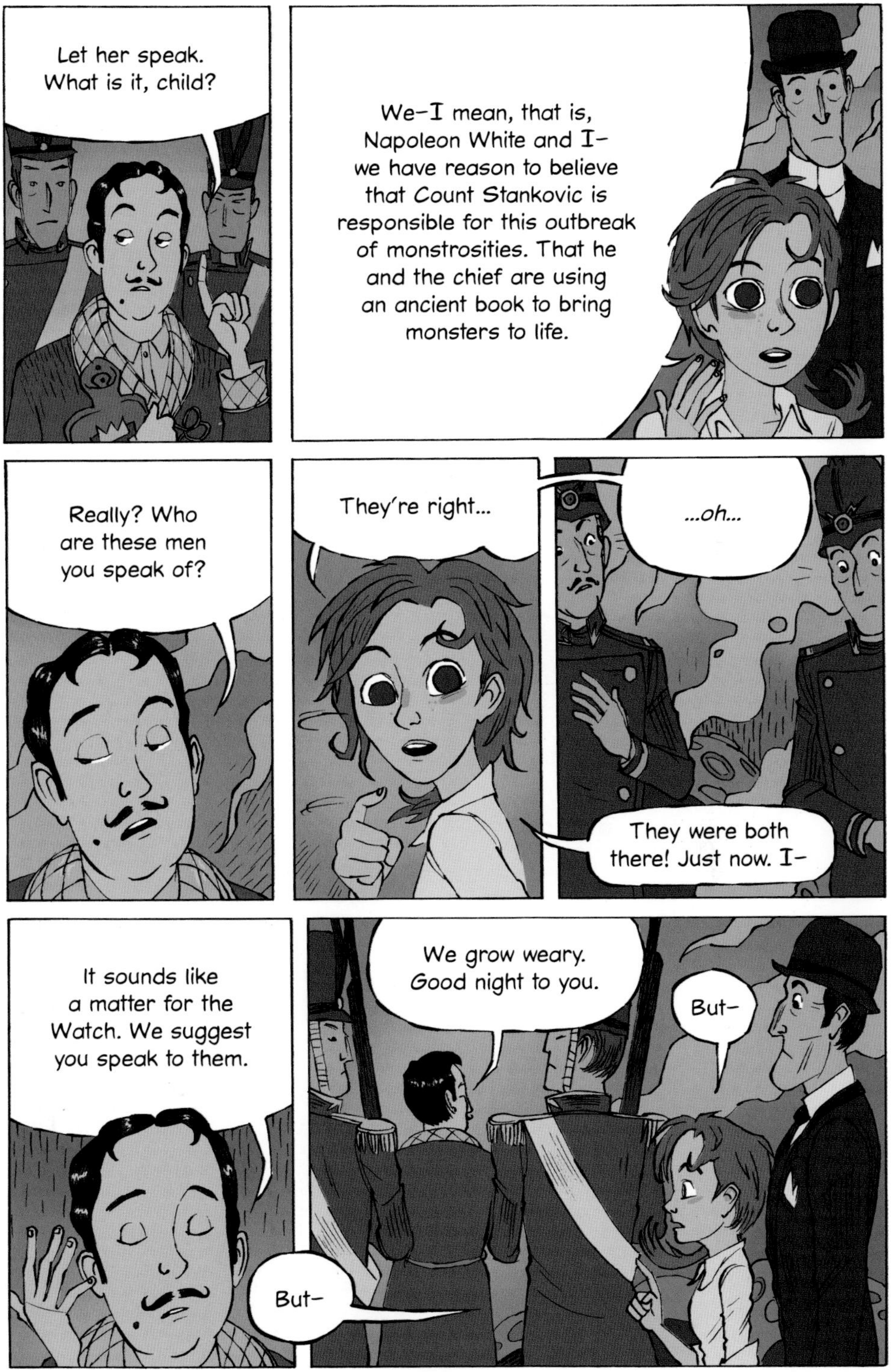
Let her speak. What is it, child?
We–I mean, that is, Napoleon White and I– we have reason to believe that Count Stankovic is responsible for this outbreak of monstrosities. That he and the chief are using an ancient book to bring monsters to life.
Really? Who are these men you speak of?
They're right...
...oh...
They were both there! Just now. I–
It sounds like a matter for the Watch. We suggest you speak to them.
But–
We grow weary. Good night to you.
But–

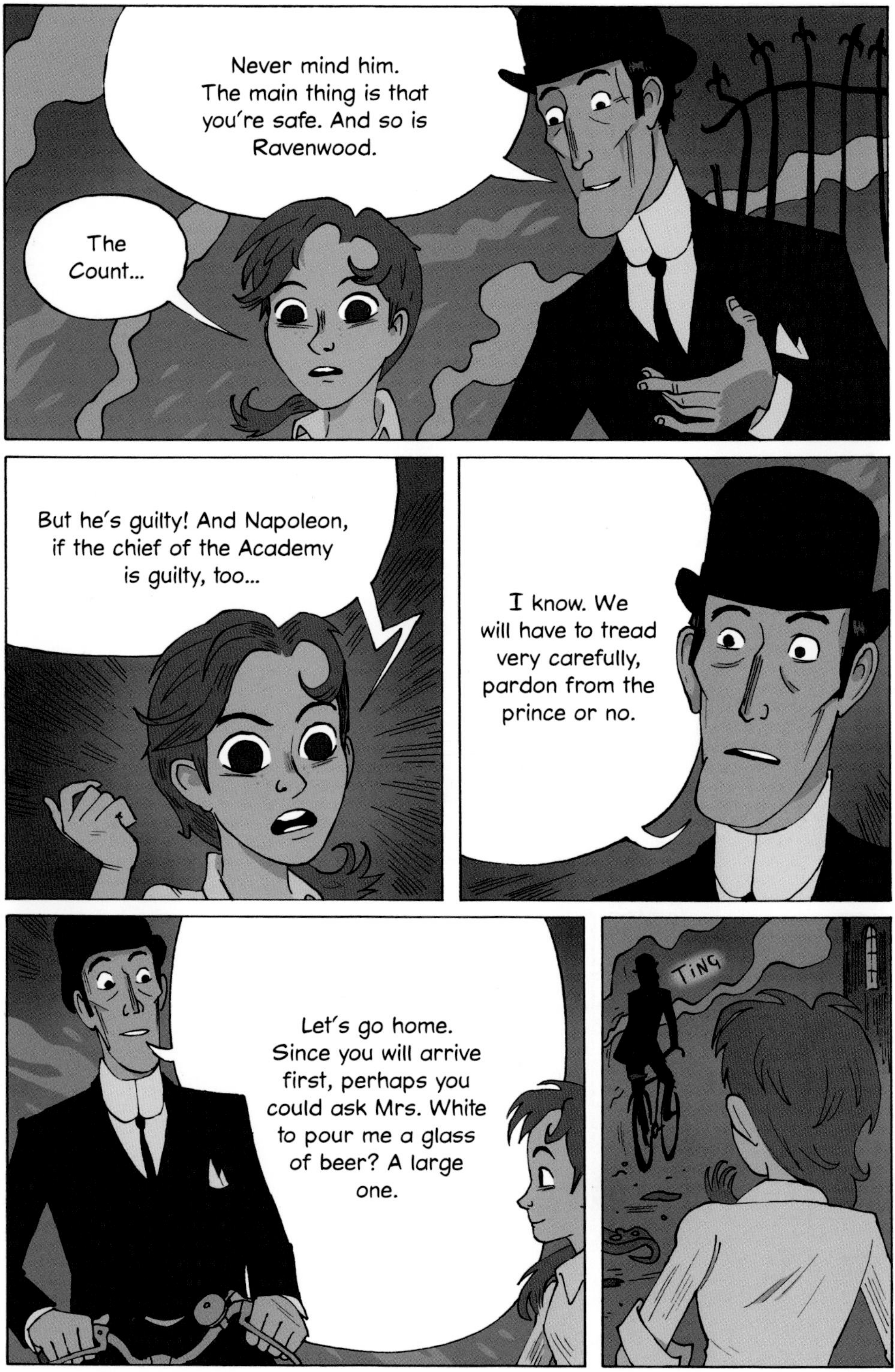
Never mind him. The main thing is that you're safe. And so is Ravenwood.
The Count...
But he's guilty! And Napoleon, if the chief of the Academy is guilty, too...
I know. We will have to tread very carefully, pardon from the prince or no.
Let's go home. Since you will arrive first, perhaps you could ask Mrs. White to pour me a glass of beer? A large one.
TING

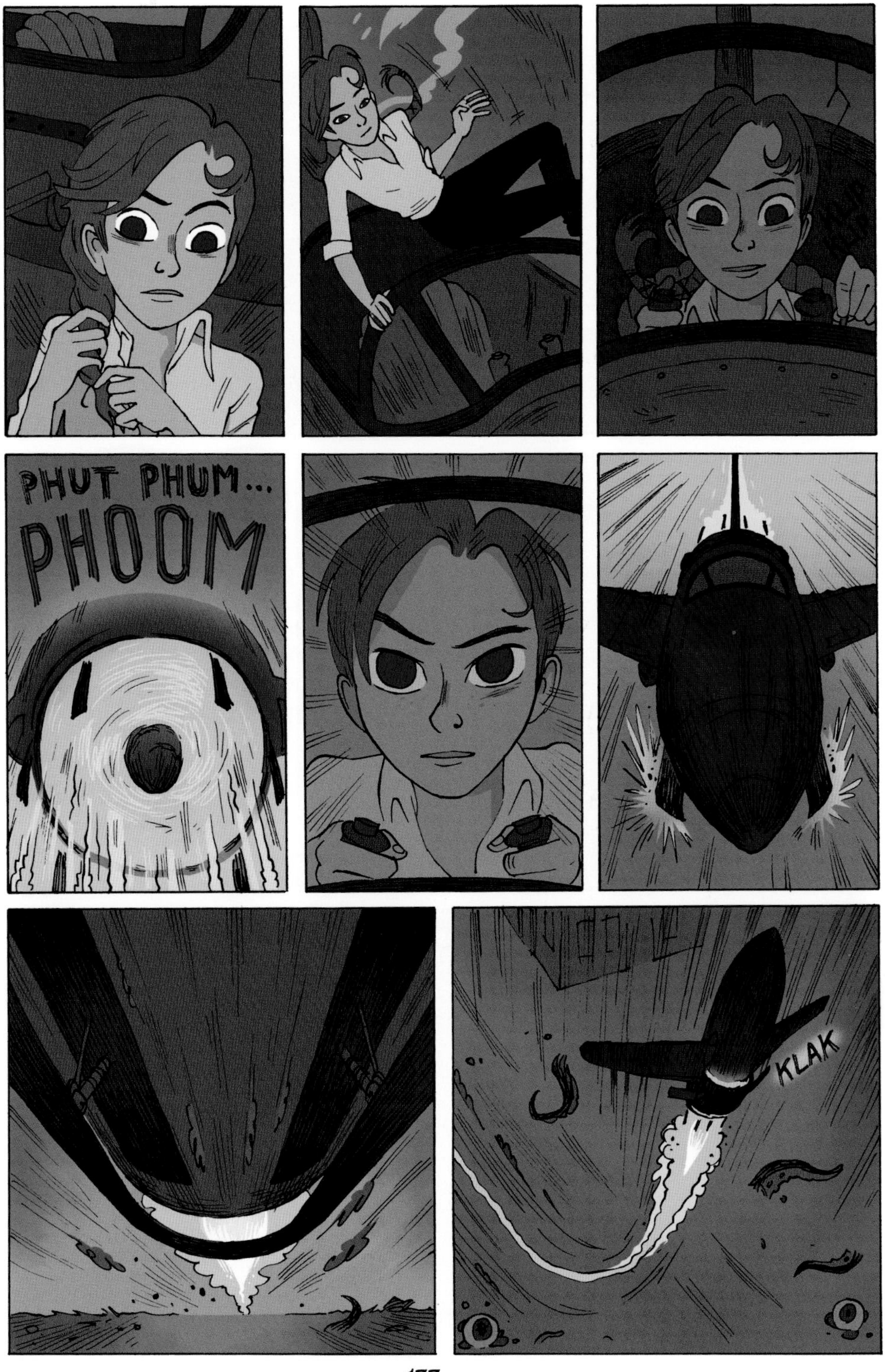
PHUT PHUM...
PHOOM
KLAK

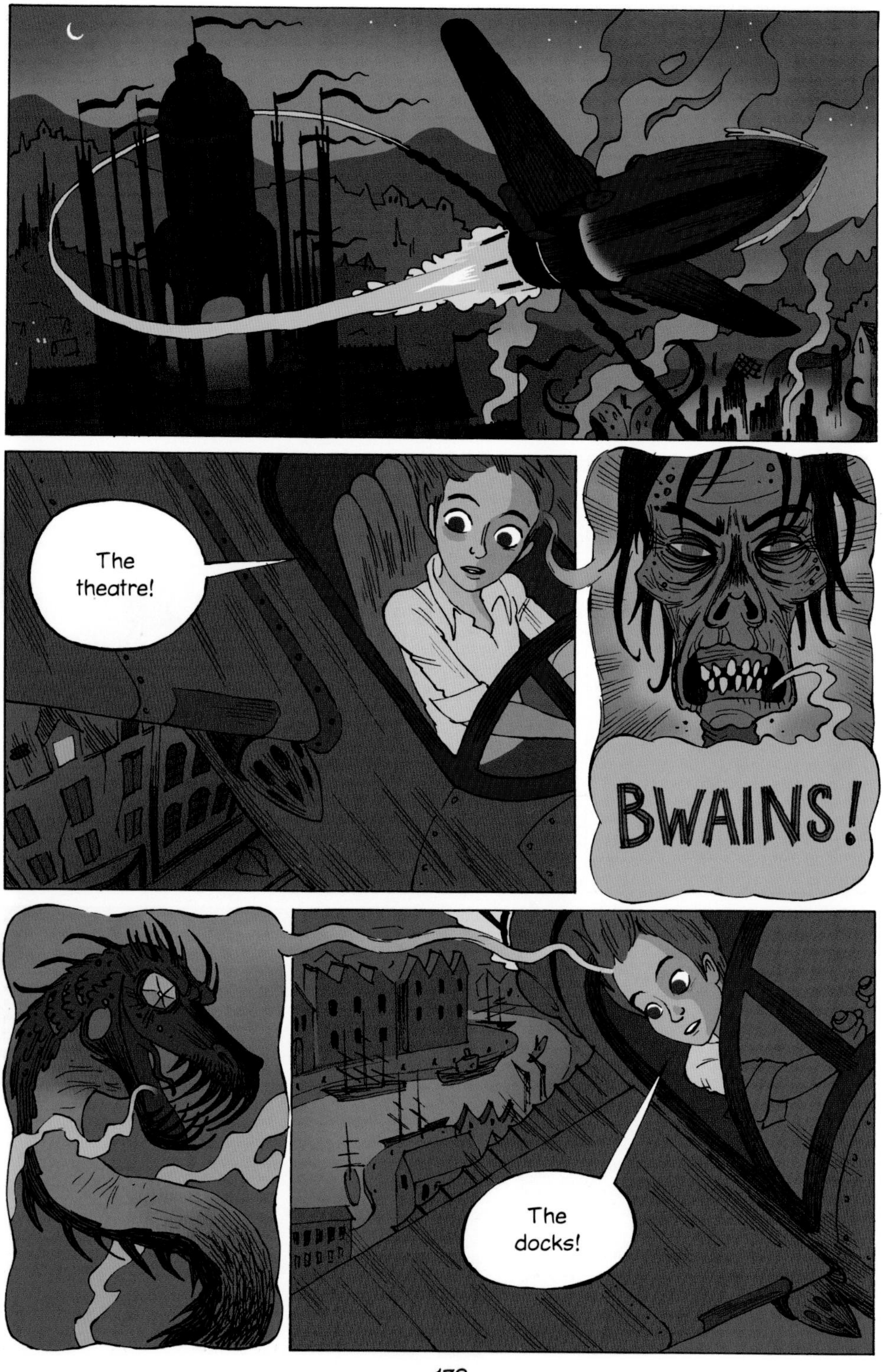
The theatre!
BWAINS!
The docks!

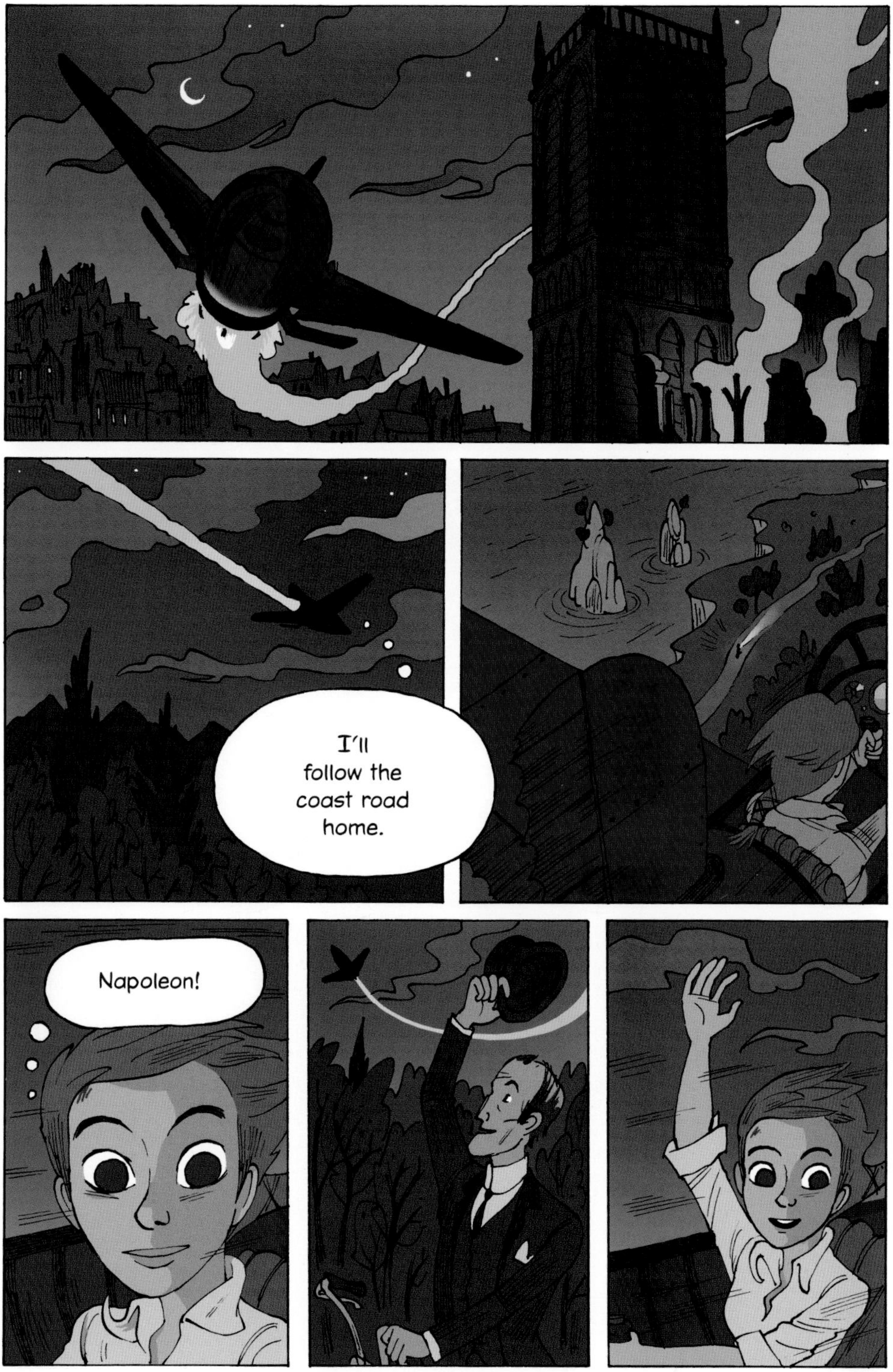
I'll follow the coast road home.
Napoleon!

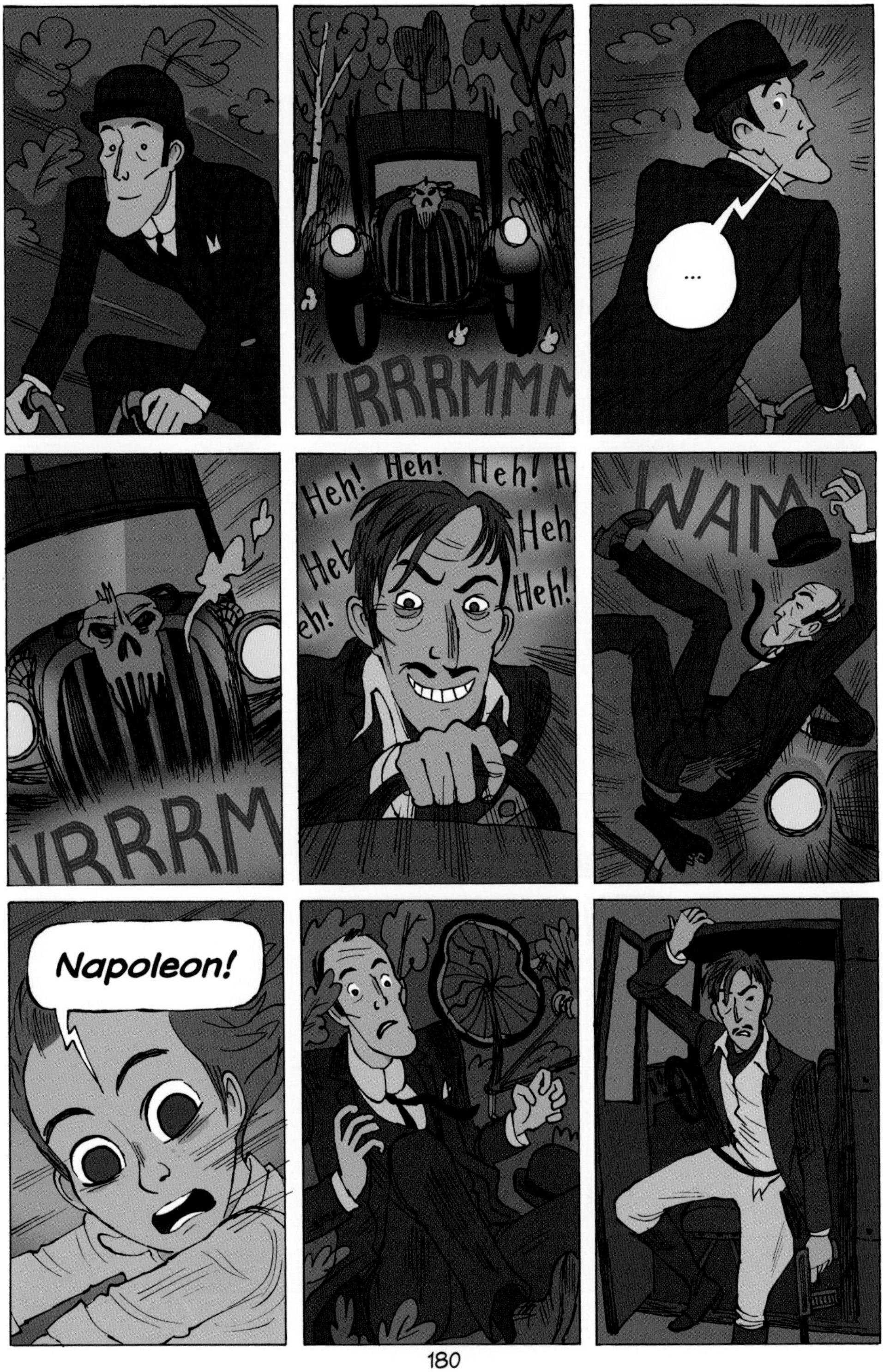
VRRRMMM
...
VRRRM
Heh! Heh! Heh! Heh Heh Heh! Heh! eh!
WAM
Napoleon!

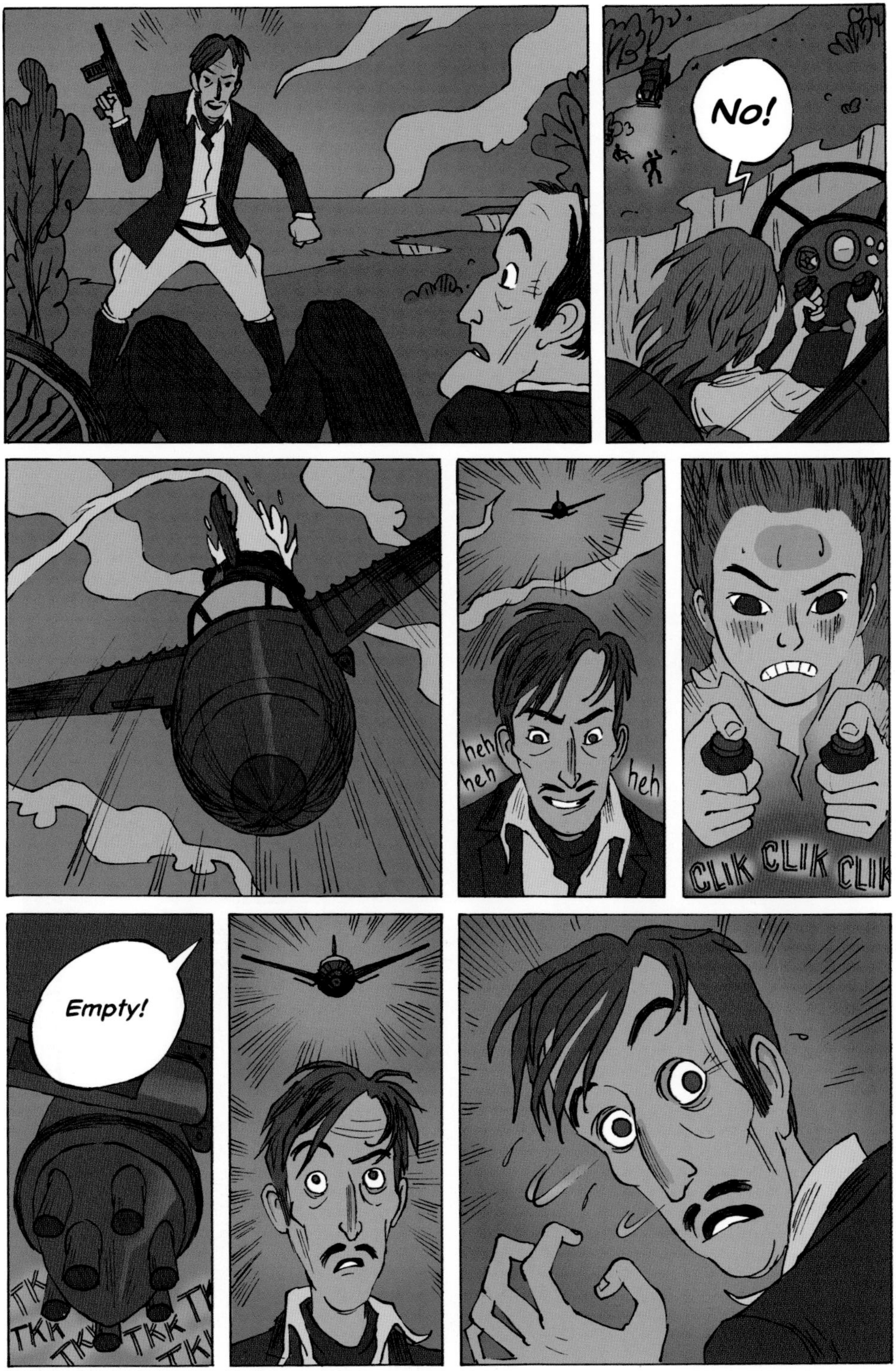
No!
heh
heh
heh
CLIK CLIK CLIK
Empty!
TK TKK TK TKK TK

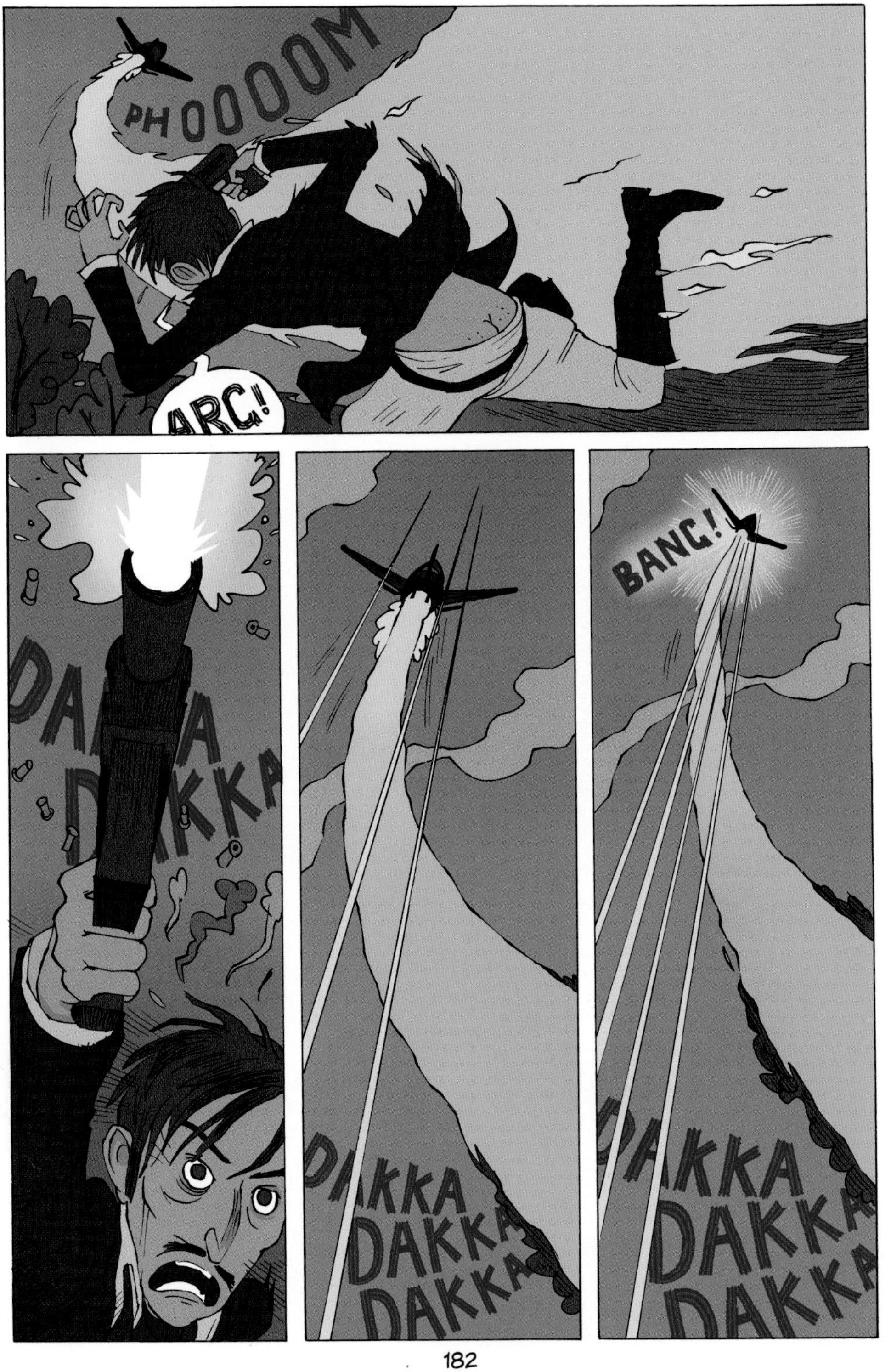
PHOOOOM
ARC!
DAKKA DAKKA
DAKKA DAKKA DAKKA
BANC!
DAKKA DAKKA DAKKA

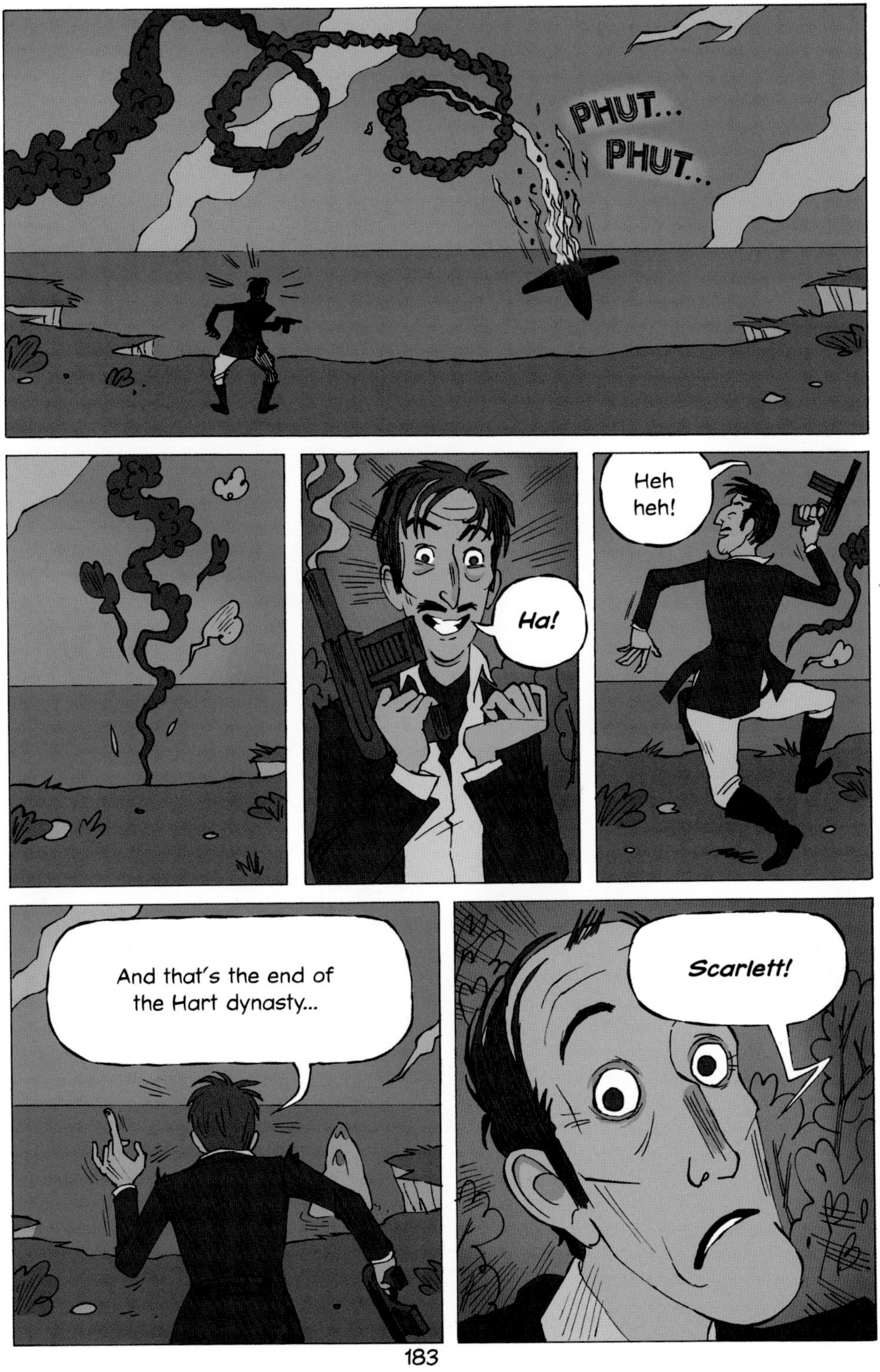
PHUT...
PHUT...
Ha!
Heh heh!
And that's the end of the Hart dynasty...
Scarlett!

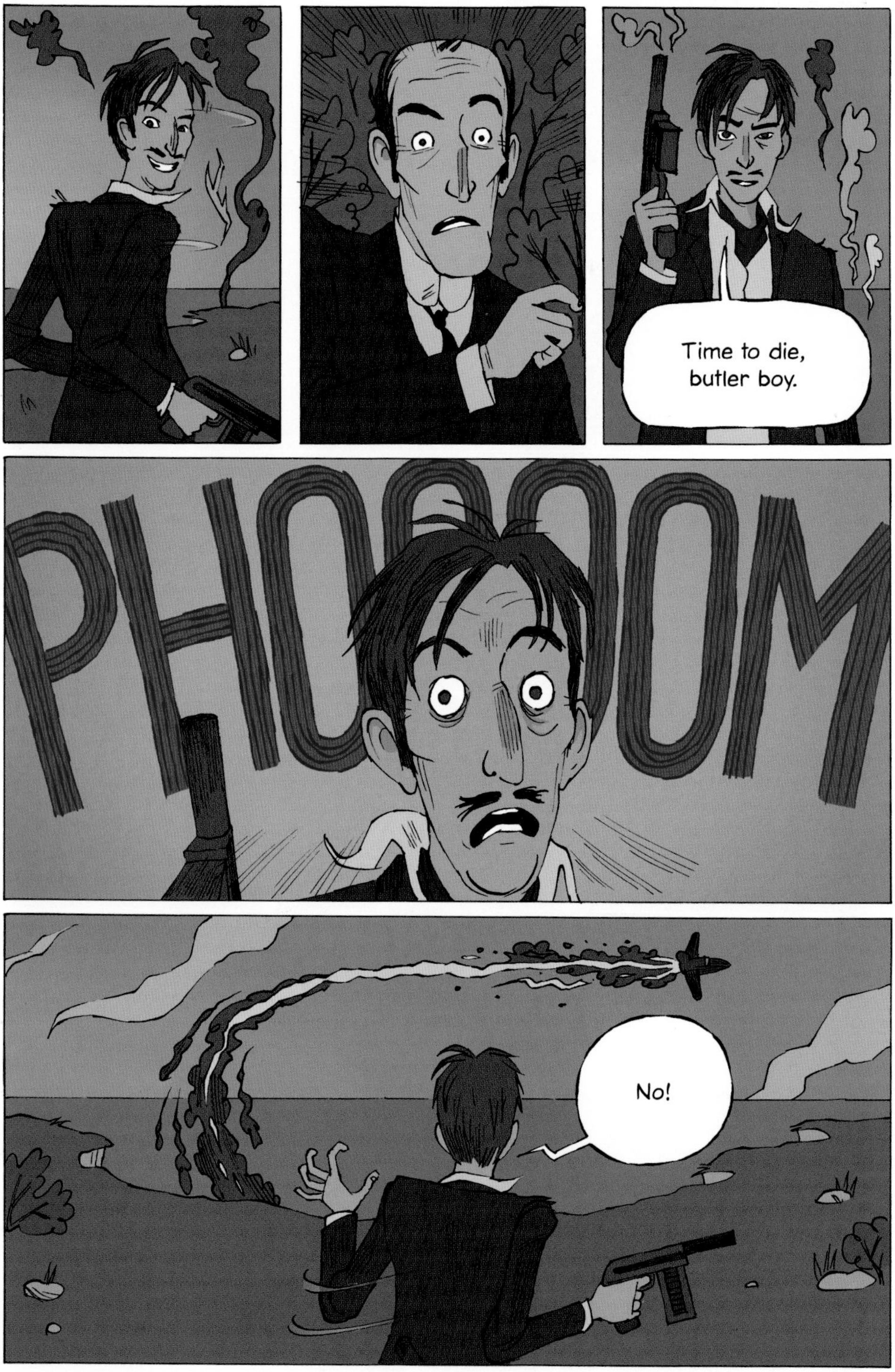
Time to die,
butler boy.
PHOOOOM
No!

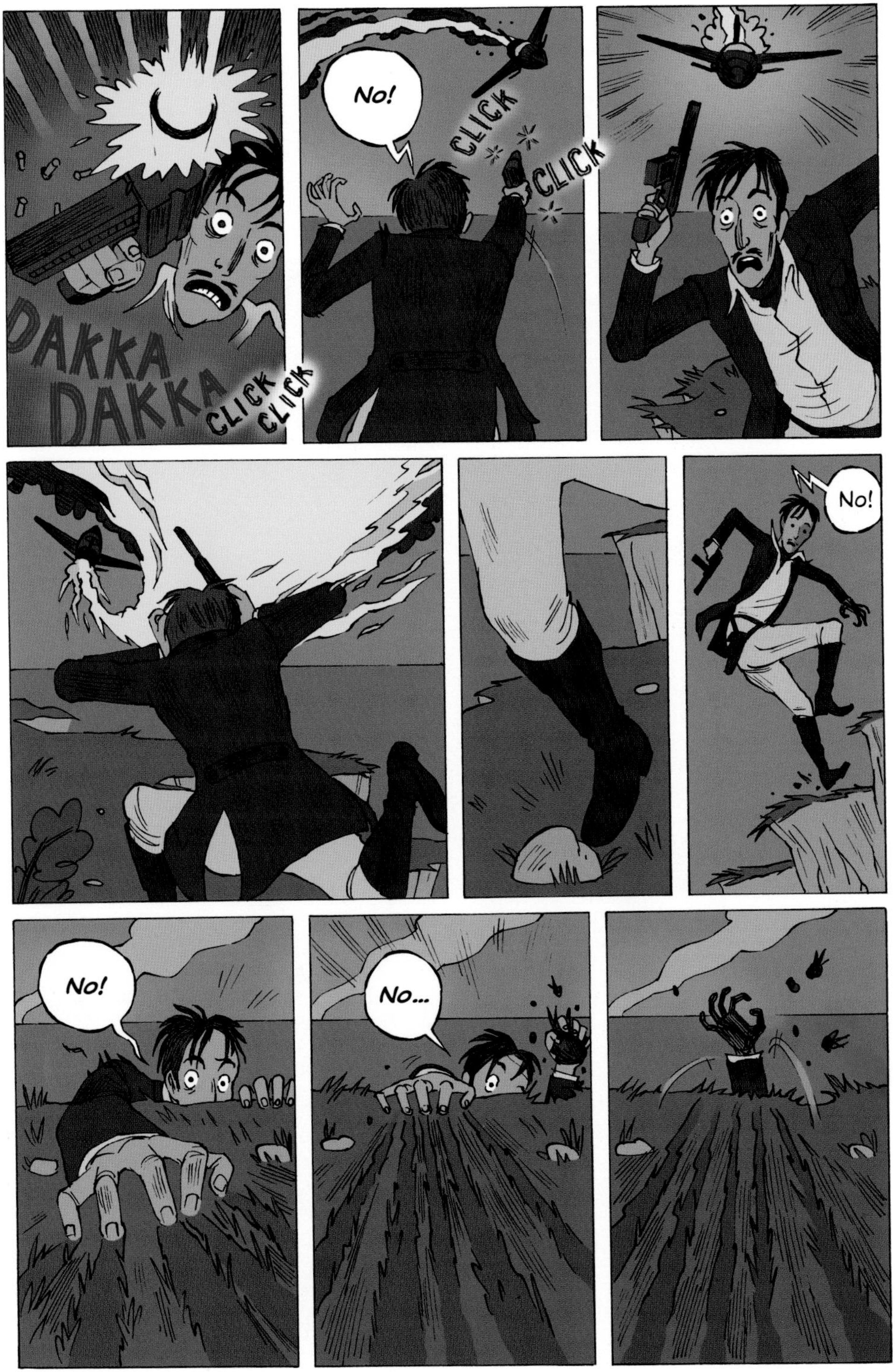
DAKKA
DAKKA
CLICK
CLICK
No!
CLICK
CLICK
No!
No!
No...

PHUT

KKKKKKRRR

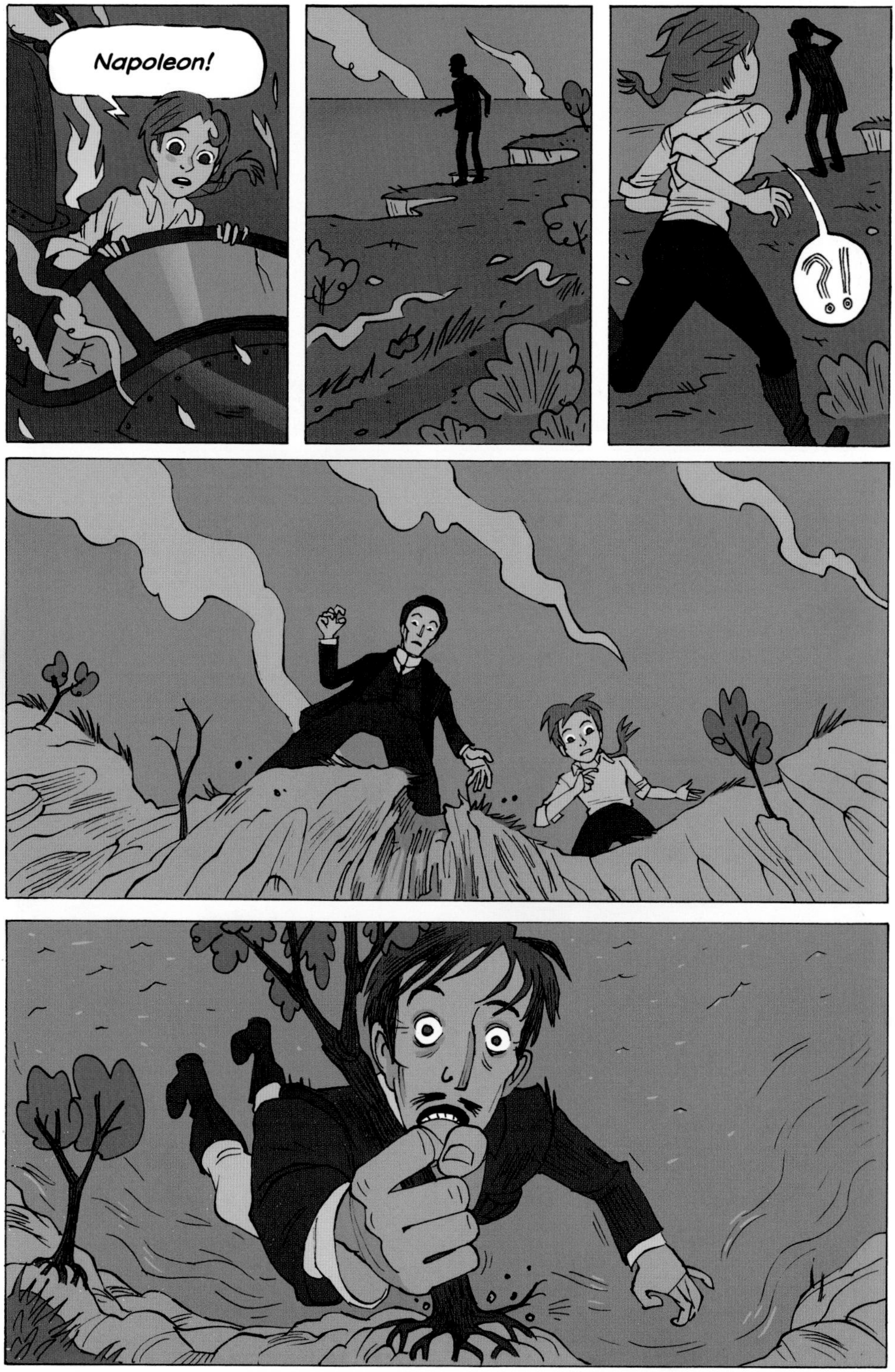
Napoleon!
?!

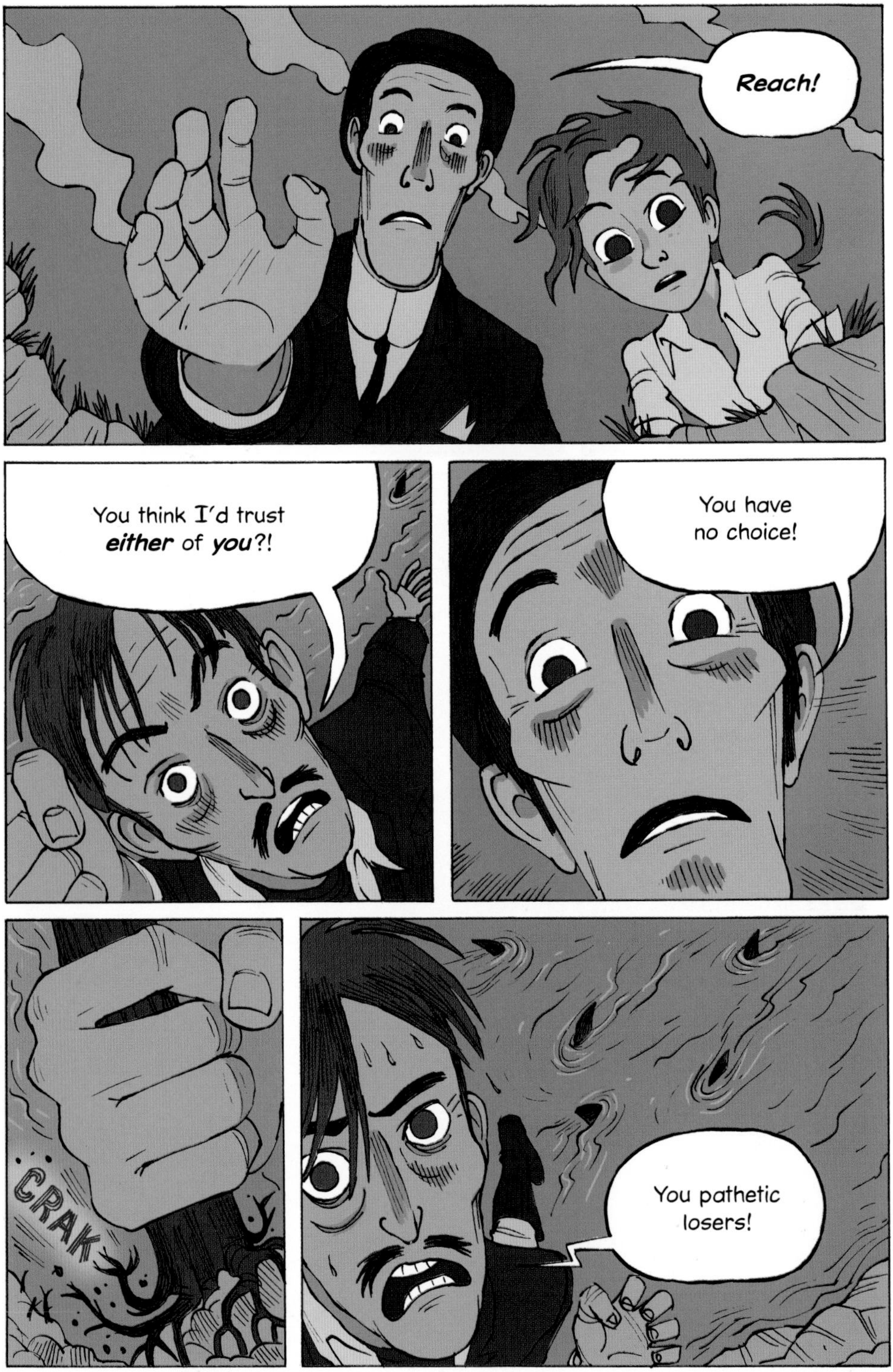
Reach!
You think I'd trust **either** of **you**?!
You have no choice!
CRAK
You pathetic losers!

I strongly suggest you reach for my hand.

Never! I don't need–!

SNAP

?!!

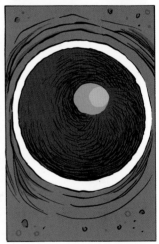

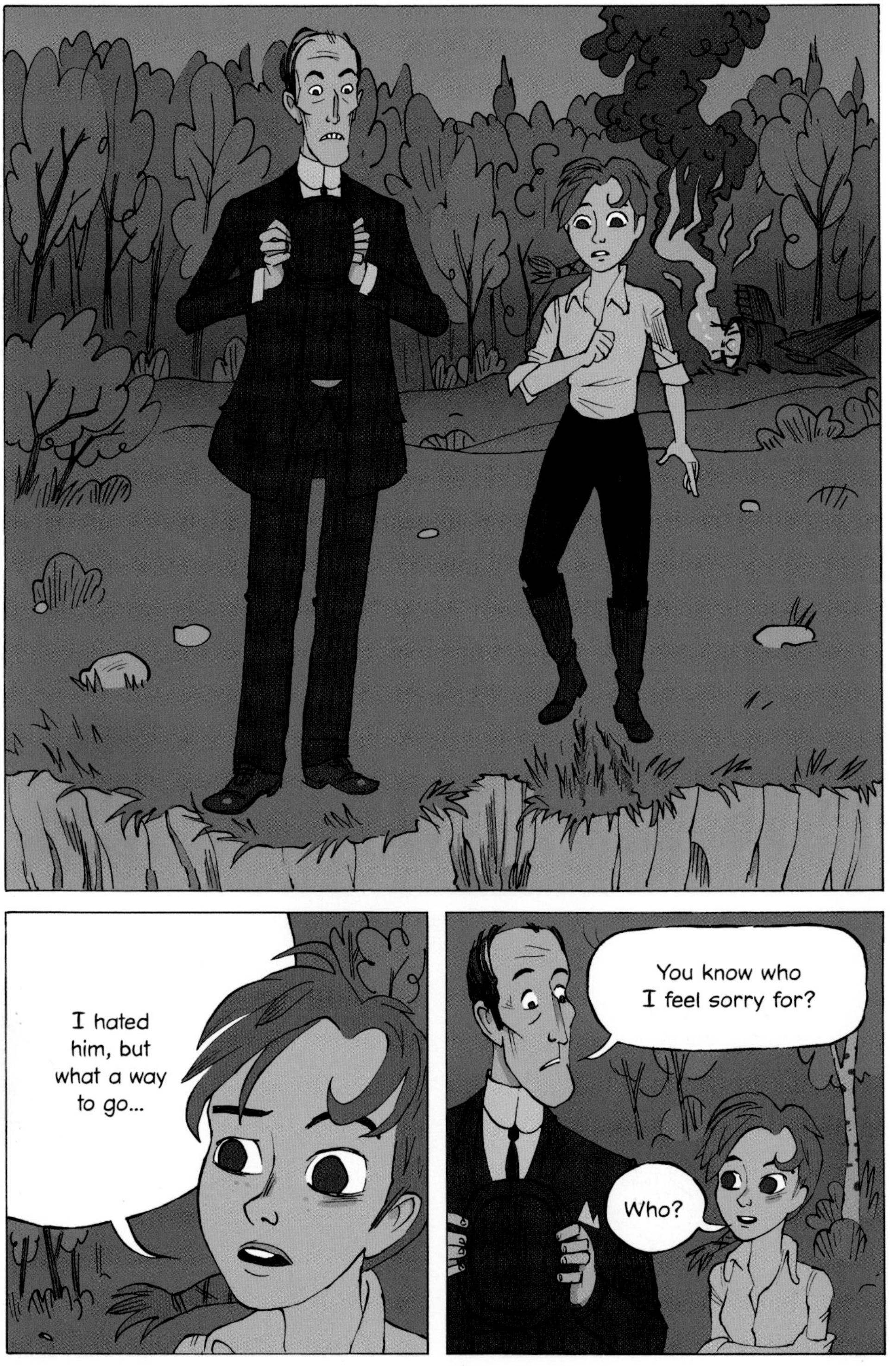
I hated him, but what a way to go...
You know who I feel sorry for?
Who?

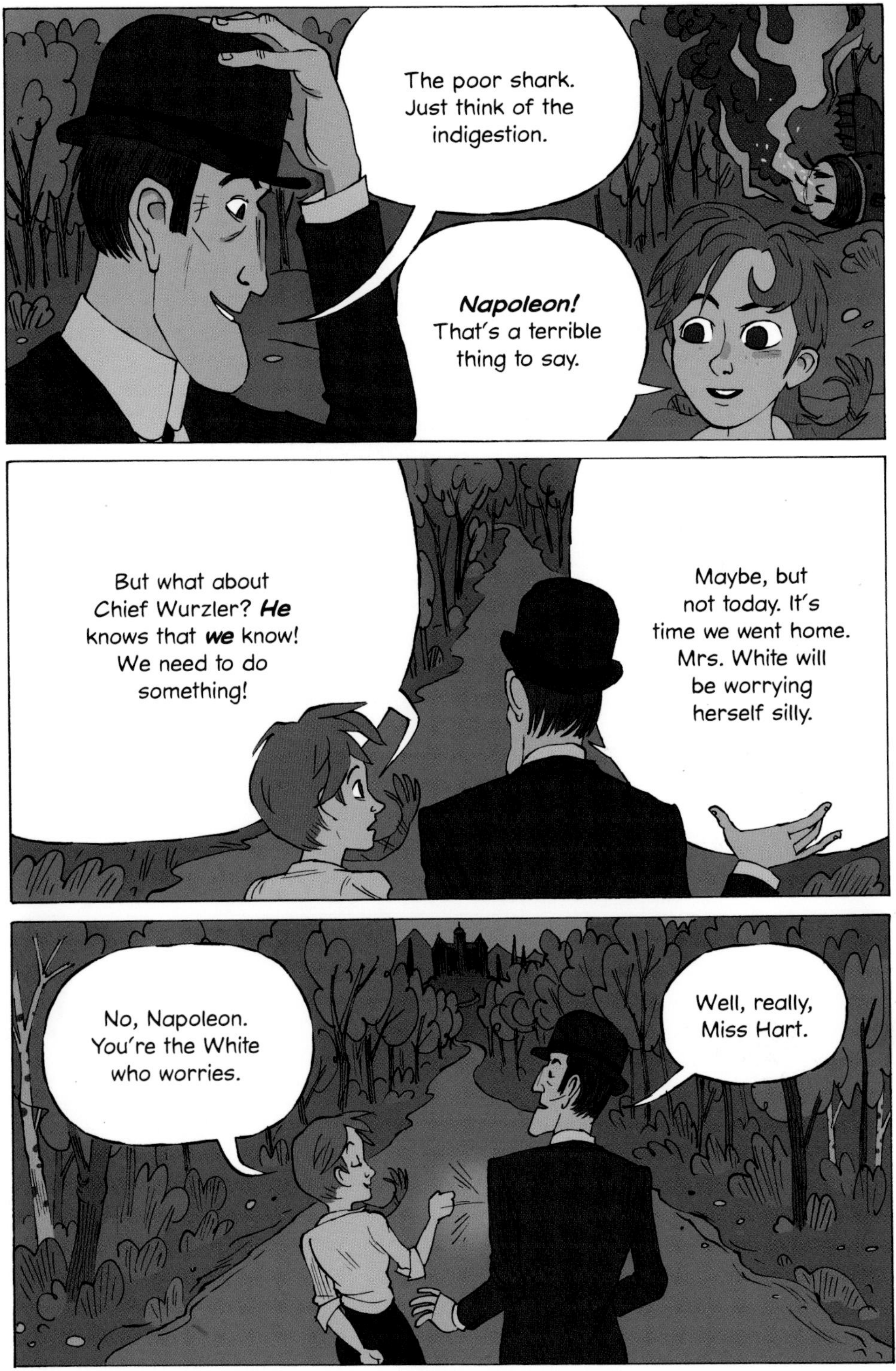
The poor shark. Just think of the indigestion.
Napoleon! That's a terrible thing to say.
But what about Chief Wurzler? ***He*** knows that ***we*** know! We need to do something!
Maybe, but not today. It's time we went home. Mrs. White will be worrying herself silly.
No, Napoleon. You're the White who worries.
Well, really, Miss Hart.

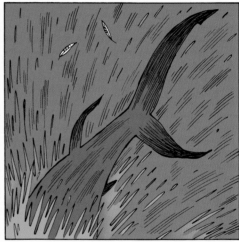

Fin

Heroes

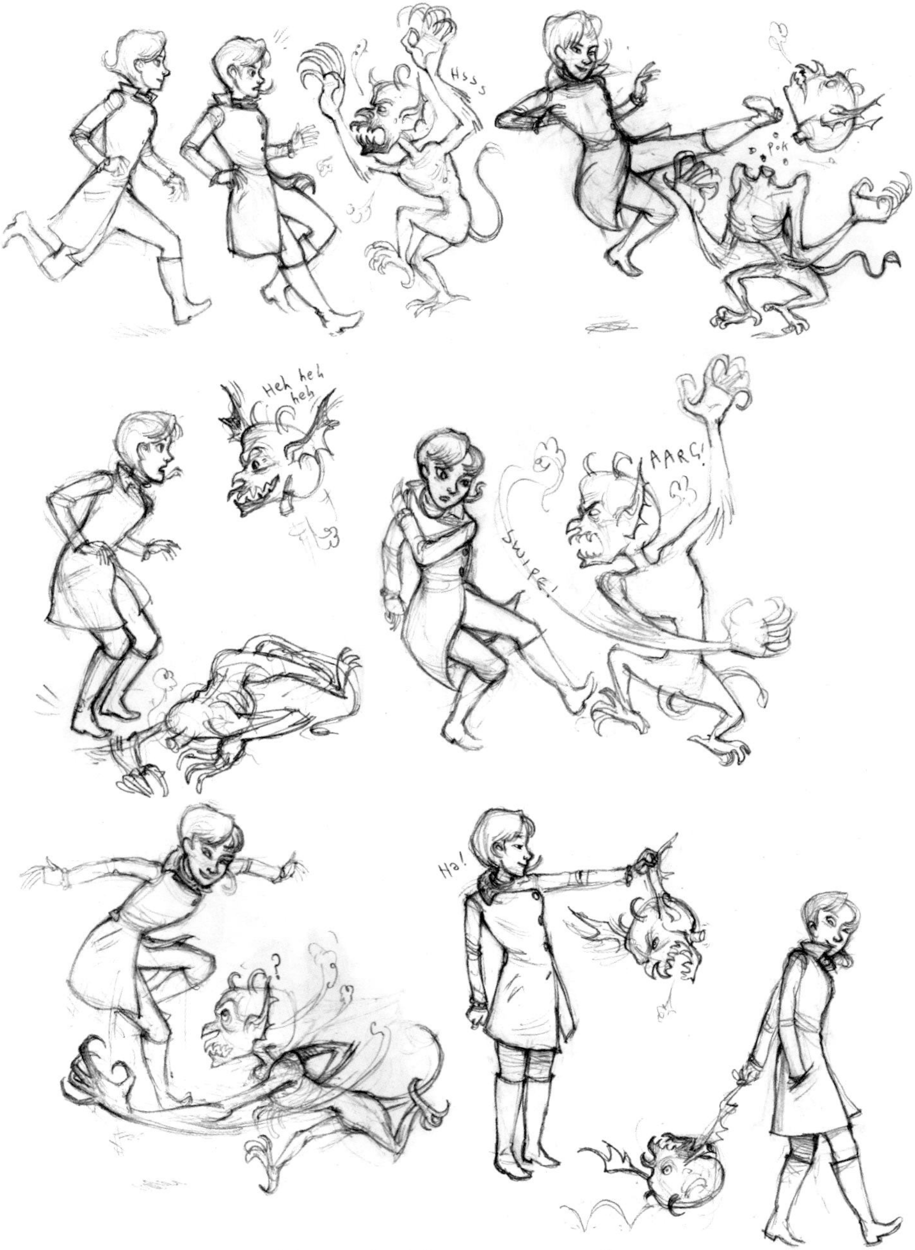
Hsss
Heh heh
heh
AARG!
SWIPE!
Ha!

Scarlett concepts

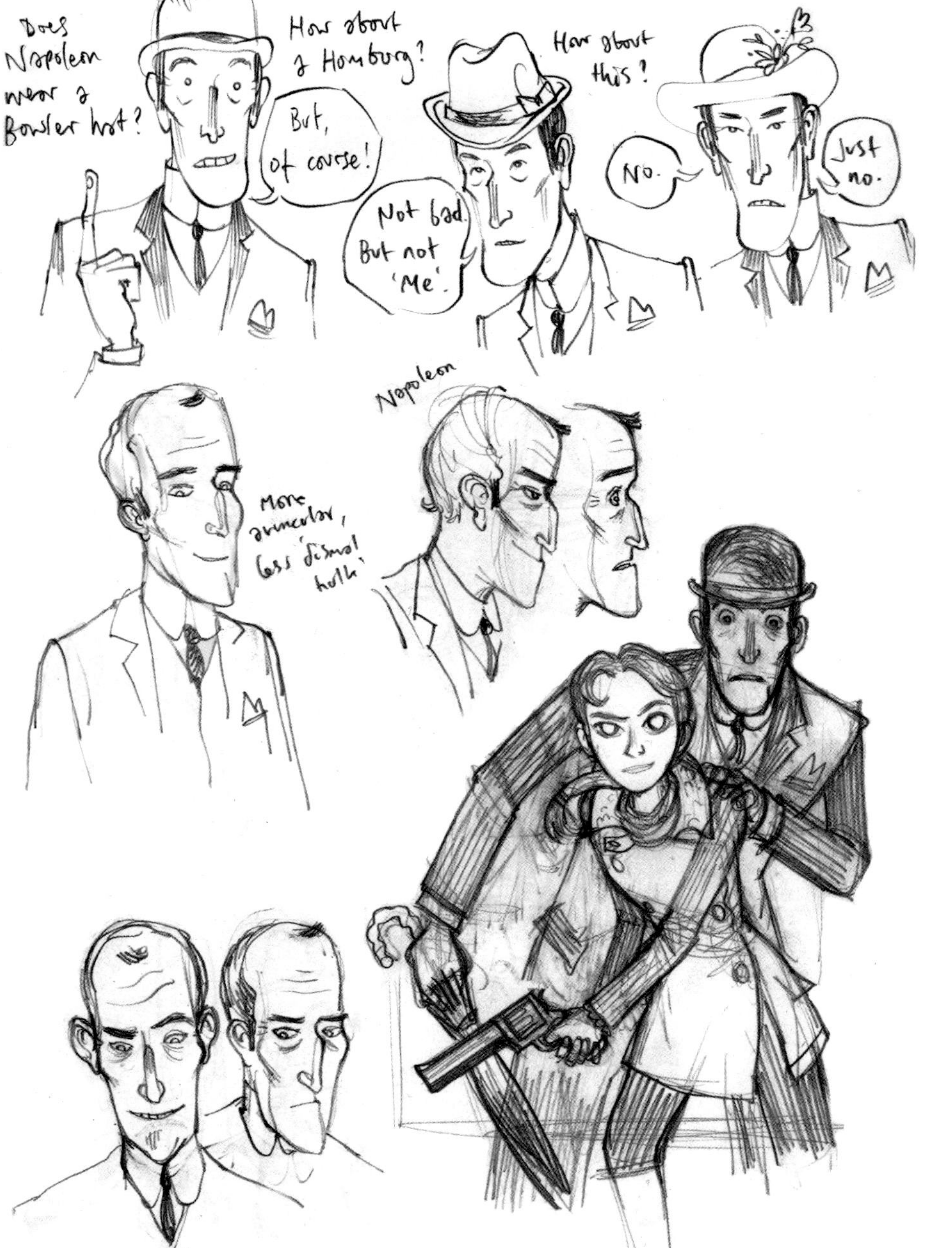
Does Napoleon wear a Bowler hat?
But, of course!
How about a Homburg?
Not bad. But not 'Me'.
How about this?
No.
Just no.
Napoleon
More avuncular, less 'dismal hulk'

Napoleon concepts

Monsters

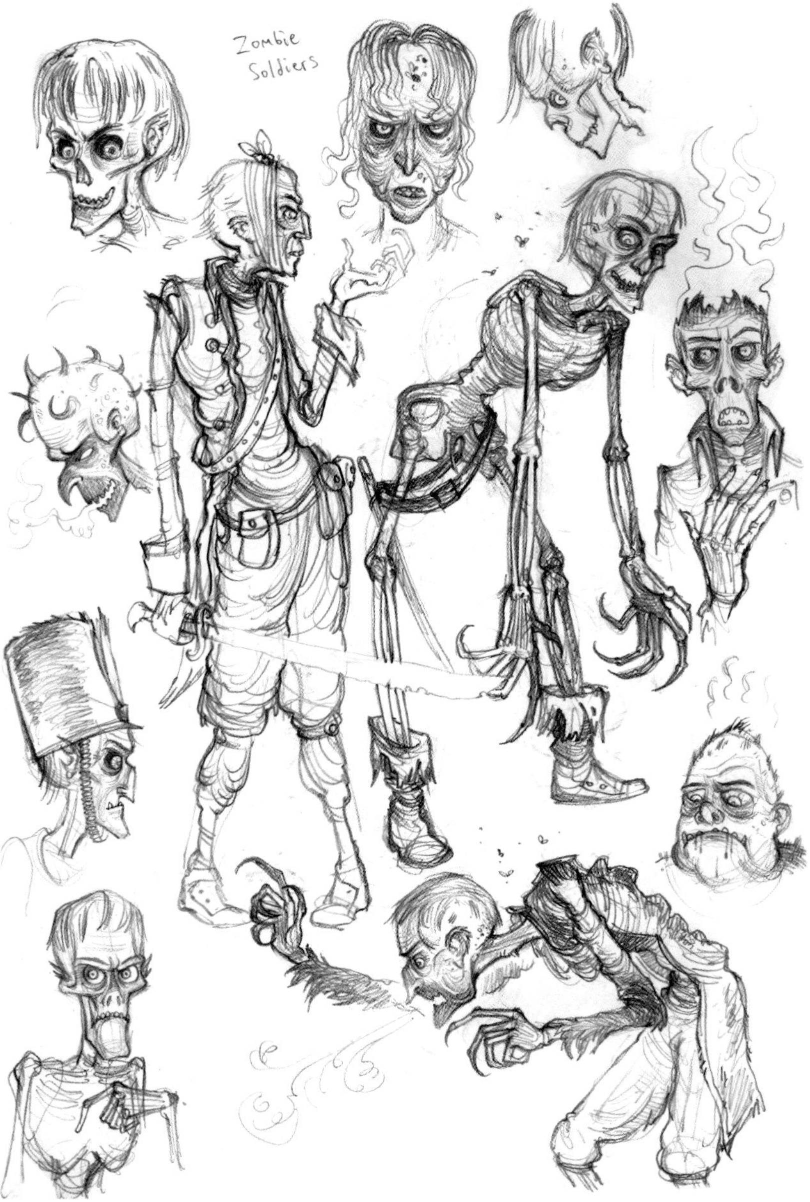
Zombie
Soldiers

Zombie designs

Contraptions

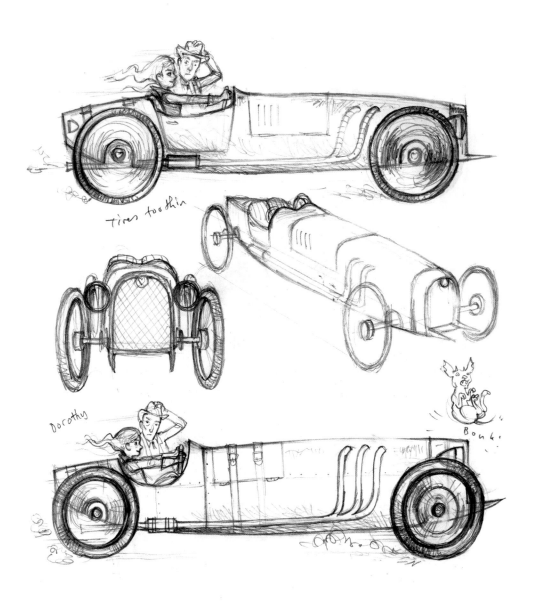

Tires too thin

Dorothy

Bonk

Dorothy concepts and layouts

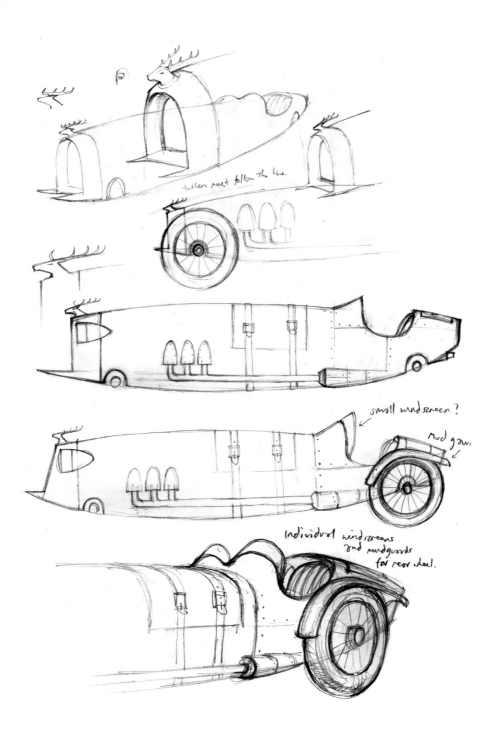

antlers must follow the line

small windscreen?

mud guard

Individual windscreens
and mudguards
for rear wheel.

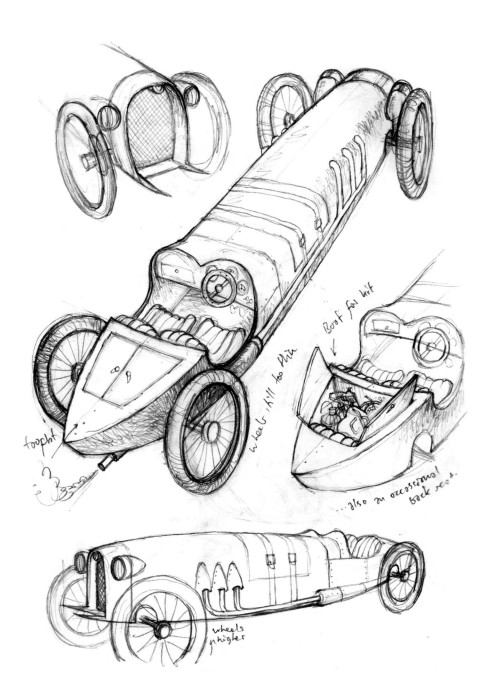

foothit

wheels still too thin

Boot for kit

...also an occassional back seat.

wheels a higher

Villainy

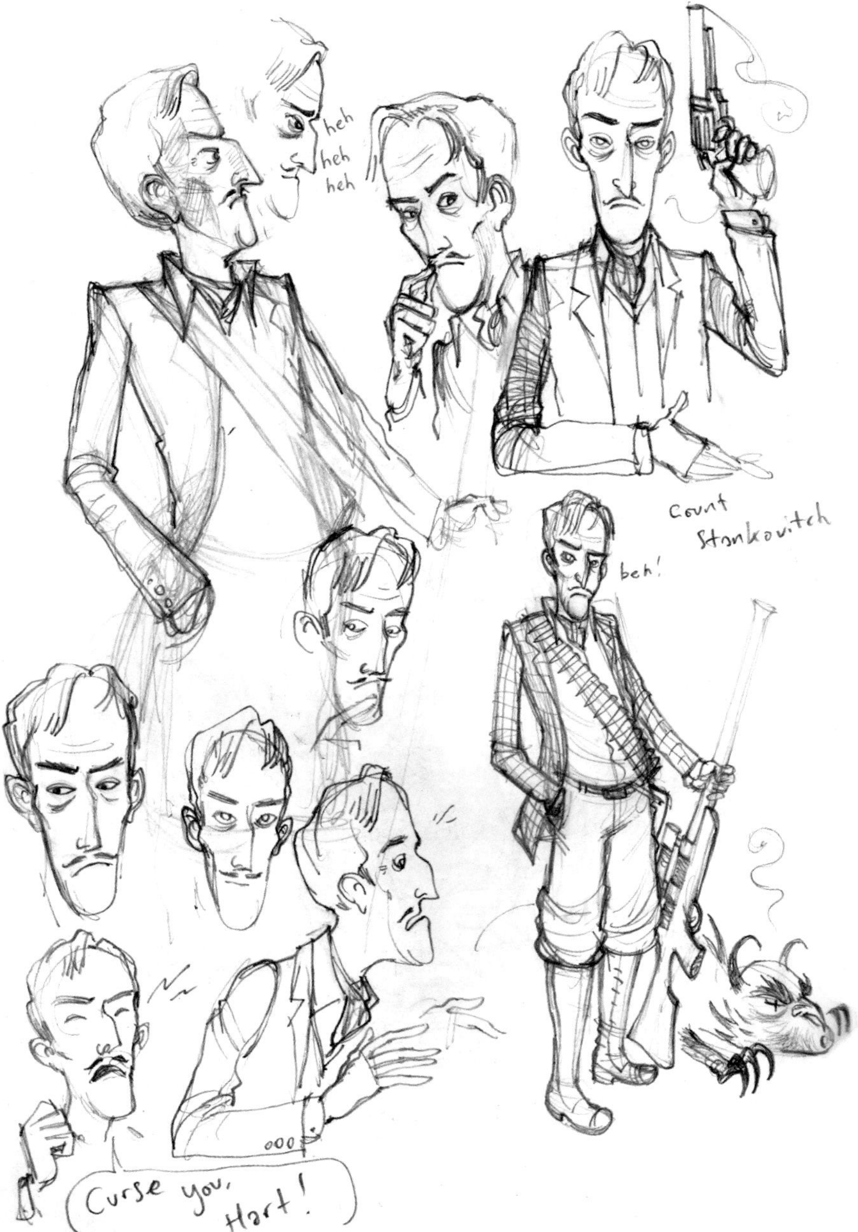
heh
heh
heh
Count Stankovitch
heh!
Curse you, Hart!

Stankovic concepts

First Second

Published by First Second
First Second is an imprint of Roaring Brook Press, a division of
Holtzbrinck Publishing Holdings Limited Partnership
175 Fifth Avenue, New York, NY 10010

Library of Congress Control Number: 2017941166

Hardcover ISBN: 978-1-250-15984-7
Paperback ISBN: 978-1-62672-026-8

Our books may be purchased in bulk for promotional, educational, or business use.
Please contact your local bookseller or the Macmillan Corporate and Premium Sales Department
at (800) 221-7945 ext. 5442 or by e-mail at MacmillanSpecialMarkets@macmillan.com.

First edition, 2018
Book design by Taylor Esposito
Printed in China by 1010 Printing International Limited, North Point, Hong Kong

Hand drawn with Kuretake "Millenium" drawing pens on Daler Rowney
Bristol board, then scanned into Photoshop for coloring.

Hardcover: 10 9 8 7 6 5 4 3 2 1
Paperback: 10 9 8 7 6 5 4 3 2 1